TO RENDER A RAVEN

A HOLLYSTONE MYSTERY
BOOK 3

W. L. HAWKIN

To Render a Raven
Hollystone Mysteries (Book 3)
Copyright © 2018 WL Hawkin
All rights reserved
Published by Blue Haven Press
Tattoo Edition (2020)

Issued in print and electronic format
ISBN 978-0-9950184-6-4 (paperback)
ISBN 978-0-9950184-8-8 (kindle)
ISBN 978-0-9950184-7-1 (epub)
Printed in Canada

All rights reserved. No part of this book may be used or reproduced in any manner whatsoever without written permission, except in the case of brief quotations embodied in critical articles or reviews. This is a work of fiction. Resemblances to persons living or dead are unintended and purely co-incidental.

Published by Blue Haven Press
www.bluehavenpress.com
Author Photo by Tara Lee Hawkin
Edited by Eileen Cook & Wendy Hawkin
Original Art & Cover Design by Yasaman Mohandesi
Yassi Art & Design — www.behance.net/yassi_artdesign

For Grace,
Who taught me to read before I went to school,
bought me my first books from the thrift store,
injected me with armchair wanderlust,
and fed me on ditties and faerie tales.

The Hollystone Mysteries

To Charm a Killer
To Sleep with Stones
To Render a Raven
To Kill a King

Glossary and Pronunciation Guide

I find it frustrating to have to guess at the pronunciation of unique words when I'm reading a book. I especially hate getting one sound ingrained in my brain and then finding out later I've guessed wrong. Or finding a phrase like *Bagh Gleann nam Muc*, I have no idea how to pronounce, and skipping over it. I try hard to let the characters inform you of the correct pronunciation but sometimes that's not enough. What you'll find here is a guide to what I'm hearing in my head as I write. It might not be perfect and certainly doesn't have Gaelic nuances, but it's a start. I'm including it at the beginning of the story so you can refer to it as you read. I hope you find it helpful. There is a glossary of series characters at the end of the story so you can see them in relationship.

Magus Dubh: **Ma**gus with a soft "g" as in magic. Dove
Sidhe: shee. Celtic faeries in Irish folklore
Crann Bethadh: Cran **Ba**-ha. The Tree of Life.
Annwn: **An**-oo-win. The Celtic Underworld
Eliseo: Ell-**ee**-see-oh. Zion shortens it to **Ell**-ee
Slàinte: **slan**-che. A Gaelic cheer meaning "health"
Sorcha: **Sore**-sha
Ballymeanoch: Bali-**men**-ock
Cernunnos: Ker-**new**-nos
Innis Ifrinn: **Inn**-ish **I**-ver-in. The Island Where Sinners Go

THE BIRTHDAY PARTY

AUGUST 1

A trio of ravens huddled in the long shadow of a bristling hemlock at the edge of the dark forest. It was a terror, wasn't it? A terror of ravens? Estrada had read somewhere that the Old English word *ravenstone* meant place of execution. The birds clung to landscapes of death, anticipating a chunk of flesh or an eyeball to gouge. They frequented this forest by Buntzen Lake in British Columbia, but why was this terror here now, staring from blackened eyes? Their muttering reminded him of teenage backtalk—sarcasm punctuated by the odd obscenity. The larger of the three snapped its beak open and shut several times, and Estrada looked for something to fire at it. Why not create a little terror himself? He loved animals but there was something sinister here.

He glanced around the bleached cedar deck to see if anyone else had noticed the birds. Good friends had gathered this afternoon for Lucy's first birthday. Daphne Sky and Dylan McBride, two of the Hollystone witches, were busy preparing food. Michael slouched beside him, and Magus Dubh perched on a mat and sipped from his pint of brown ale. He'd just arrived from Glasgow and was smitten with growlers. No one seemed perturbed by the ravens. Perhaps it was just his imagination. And then the french doors opened, and Estrada turned.

"Lucita," he said, a smile bursting from his heart. Sensara grinned and bounced his baby on her hip. Rising, he crossed the wooden deck, opened his arms and hugged them both—Lucy and Sensara. His family.

Clapping and shouts of "Happy Birthday Lucy!" echoed through the sultry August air. Dressed in a gauzy pink tutu, Lucy was an elfin ballerina. Sensara had tied her straight black hair up in two pigtails and wrapped them with pink ribbons and silk roses.

"Daddy's Lucita," he whispered. "One whole year old today." When he kissed her chubby cheek, his chest rose like a hot air balloon. He tickled her bare toes, and she giggled and squirmed.

"Can I hold her?" he asked, glancing at Sensara. She'd pinned a pink silk rose in her long loose hair and glittered in a golden sun dress. Sensara was a psychic, a healer, a creator of ceremonies, and a skillful witch—the High Priestess of Hollystone Coven. But more importantly, she was the mother of Lucy. Though he was the *sometimes* father, his soul craved more. He could live here with them and they could be an *always* family. Except it would never work, he thought, glancing at Michael, his *oft-times* lover.

"Of course," Sensara said, handing him the squirming pink bundle.

Lifting Lucy above his head, Estrada delighted in her giggles. "Ready to fly?"

"Dada," Lucy replied, scrunching up her nose. Sauntering around the deck, he swung her in the air while she shrieked and glowed like Lugh, the Celtic sun god for whom she'd been named.

Holding her high above his head, Estrada stared into her chestnut eyes. "*Lucita es bonita*, the prettiest girl in the world."

When he held her close, her heart to his, she giggled and jabbered a string of syllables he took to mean something profound.

Daphne came over and fluttered her dark eyelashes against Lucy's cheek. "A butterfly kiss for your birthday, Lulu, and another one from Auntie Raine."

Estrada had never seen a happier child. Living here in this house on Hawk's Claw Lane with Sensara, Daphne, Raine, and their dog, Remy, she was fussed over like a princess.

"A-tee," Lucy said, and giggled. She loved butterfly kisses and gave one back to Daphne, her long dark lashes brushing the woman's tan cheek.

"I love your new hair," said Estrada to Daphne. It was still spiked on top, but she'd bleached the dark tips platinum and shaved the sides, Mohawk-style. Daphne helped Sensara create Hollystone Coven and in the six years he'd known her, Estrada had never seen her keep a hairstyle longer than four months. An earth goddess, she changed with the seasons. Daphne was their rock and his champion, and he loved her for it. "Suits you."

Grinning, Daphne touched the black curls that brushed his shoulder. He'd taken to pulling it back in a ponytail again, but today it was flying free. "*Your* hair's growing like a weed. Been stealing my fertilizer?"

Estrada shook his head. "Never. Not even your organic shit."

"Dada. Bu-fy." Estrada gave Lucy a big butterfly kiss, then swung her high, while the pink veils swept behind her like gossamer wings.

"Enough now. You'll make her sick," Sensara said, holding out her arms to reclaim her child. She was edgy, her tolerance for his friends limited. Not only had he brought his lover, Michael Stryker, but also Magus Dubh, a rather edgy-looking dwarf all tattooed in blue Pictish symbols. Dubh had proclaimed himself Lucy's godfather and flown in from Scotland for the occasion.

"She loves it," Estrada said, reluctantly passing Lucy over.

"Yeah. Well, if she pukes, it's on you." Sensara tried to sound stern but her laughing eyes gave her away. She loved the attention he paid to Lucy. From the time of her birth, he'd spent every possible moment doting on his daughter—not from some sense of responsibility, but because he truly adored her.

"Where'd you get this dress?" Estrada asked, smoothing out the fabric. The bodice and right shoulder were a mass of pink roses, the left shoulder bare. Sensara dressed Lucy like a doll—something he'd never imagined she would do.

"Have you been drinking?" asked Sensara, ignoring his question. Sometimes, she was too damn intuitive. Her gaze shifted to Michael Stryker, who leaned against the swing with the back of his head cradled in his hands. His heavy eyelids riffled as he stared up at the clouds.

Though Michael and Sensara were Estrada's two best friends, they loathed one another. Michael could only tolerate Sensara after smoking several joints—something they'd done together with Dubh in the woods before mounting the back steps. While Sensara detested, not only

Michael's hedonism, but the fact that he and Estrada had shared lovers together over the years. She had high moral standards and blamed Michael for, what she considered, Estrada's lascivious behavior. But Sensara was wrong. Michael was simply a conduit and Estrada did as he pleased. He'd always been bisexual, and polyamory was as natural to him as drinking coffee in the morning.

"Veggies are ready," Dylan said. As they were the only two men in the coven, Estrada and Dylan were good friends who saved each other frequently. Dylan wiped his flushed face with a hanky, then jammed it back in the pocket of his khaki shorts and winked at Estrada. Born with the Celtic gene, he couldn't take the heat or Sensara's tone.

Daphne sauntered over to the barbecue, filled a platter with Dylan's veggie kebabs and started passing them around. She too knew how to shift energy.

Blessed are the peacemakers, thought Estrada, glancing around the deck at his extended family. All the Hollystone witches were here, gathered for Lucy's first birthday and their Lughnasadh ritual, except Sylvia Black, who was spending the summer in Wales, and Daphne's girlfriend Raine Carrera, who was a journalist working under a deadline.

Lucy squirmed until Sensara set her down, then rushed to Dubh and plunked down wide-eyed in front of him on the blanket. Reaching out one tiny finger, she touched the Celtic dragon tattooed on his calf. In the August sunlight, the wee man shimmered like the sea.

"I see you've inherited your father's balls and your mother's intuition." Reaching into the pocket of his leather kilt, Dubh pulled out a small jeweler's box and handed it to the grinning girl. "A gift for a princess on her very first birthday. Go on, precious. Open it."

Lucy's faced scrunched as she tried to pry open the box. After letting out a high-pitched grunt, she pursed her lips and held it out to Estrada.

"What has your godfather brought you all the way from Scotland?" asked Estrada, taking the box from her tiny hand. "Let's see."

When he opened it, Lucy's eyes widened. "Ah?" she said, a sound that meant several things including: tell me what it's called, tell me what you've got, and give it to me.

"It's a charm bracelet with one, two, three, four charms." Estrada pried it out. "It goes on like this," he said, draping it around her wrist and closing the clasp.

Lucy stood and, holding her arm in the air, shook it so the silver charms tinkled and glittered in the sun.

"Thank you, Dubh," Estrada said.

"My pleasure. I am honored to be here for Lucy's first birthday, and doubly honored to join you for your Lughnasadh ceremony." He bowed to Sensara, who returned his gesture with her own bow of Namaste.

Then, turning to Lucy, Dubh said, "Come here, precious. Let Uncle Dubh regale you with the tale wrapped round your wrist."

Lucy stared with grave round eyes, then plunked back down in front of him on the blanket. She might not understand all his words, especially combined with his Glasgow accent, but she was fascinated by him.

Dubh stroked his bushy red beard and winked one of his sky-blue eyes. "Once upon a time there was a princess," he said. "She lived in a wooden fortress beside a thick dark forest. But she wasn't afraid. Do you know why?"

Lucy stared and chewed her bottom lip.

"The bairn was not afraid because benevolent spirits protected her."

"Benevolent?" Sensara turned up one side of her mouth in a grin. She too was charmed by the druid priest.

"Aye, Lady. It's never too early to experience the stellar power of words."

Estrada hoped that some of Dubh's more colorful Glaswegian slang did not slip out in the mix.

"Right outside the princess's window grew an enormous tree called *Crann Bethadh*."

"Ba-ha," breathed Lucy, gazing up at the leafy branches that swayed in the meager breeze.

"Aye. *Crann Bethadh*. The Tree of Life. *Crann Bethadh* was mammoth . . . *so* mammoth, its roots stretched to *Annwn* where it began, while its branches spread far into the Upper World.

Lucy craned her neck to follow his gestures, when he lowered his voice to almost a whisper. "At night, while the princess slept, the gods climbed down and cast protective spells upon her, so she would always be safe. Trees are sacred beings. They protect us, and we must protect them."

Lucy touched the silver charm on her bracelet. "Tee," she said.

"Aye. Trees are your mates."

Dylan turned and winked. "Ach, Lucy. Listen to your Uncle Dubh. He knows about such things."

When Dylan winked again at Estrada, a fond memory of the Celtic Oak King rippled between them, and he envisioned the three of them standing among the stones in Scotland along with Primrose, Sorcha, and the old god, Cernunnos. Their meeting with the gods last summer was something none of them would ever forget.

"Now *this* charm," said Dubh, pointing to a howling wolf, "will also protect you."

"Ah?"

"That's *el lobo*," said Estrada, who was teaching her Spanish.

"Lo-bo," she whispered.

"Your father has a special connection with the canine tribe, so this totem symbolizes your da."

"Dada." She scampered over and climbed up on Estrada's knee.

"Like the wolf, your da is loyal to his pack and defends those he loves. And you, lassie, feature first on that list."

Estrada hugged Lucy and kissed her on the cheek, remembering her arrival, one year ago today. The whole coven had gathered here, and she'd slipped from Sensara's belly into a birthing pool in this very spot. Estrada had caught her in his hands and vowed to never let her go. It was the greatest moment of his life.

"The princess was fortunate to live in the wooden castle with three goddesses—her ma and two aunties who catered to her every need. The crescent moon symbolizes your ma. Like Cerridwen, she is the moon goddess."

"That's this one." Estrada tapped it with his finger. "The moon is Mama."

"Mama, mama."

"Thank you," Sensara said. "That's beautiful. The charms *and* the stories."

Dubh nodded and bowed. Estrada felt relieved Sensara had accepted him into their circle. He was rather eccentric—a dwarf, all tattooed blue, who trafficked in antiquities and practiced Druidry in Scotland. Estrada hadn't told Sensara everything that happened there last year, but he'd said enough to impress her. Magus Dubh, the *Black Priest*, helped free Dylan from prison. And when Estrada was shot, he helped save his life. For those two reasons, she'd invited him to participate in their Lughnasadh ceremony. Now, he hoped she had a third. She was warming to Dubh's charms.

"Suh." Lucy tapped the last charm on the chain. Her sketch books were crammed with yellow globes, bursting rays in all directions.

"Aye." Dubh nodded. "Behold the face of the sun god. This is Lugh's day, and *your* day too."

"Lugh," Estrada said, pointing to the sun.

"Soo-see," she said, referring to herself. Jiggling the charms, she launched off Estrada's knee. Dancing around the deck, she showed everyone her bracelet while chanting the names of her charms. "Soo-see, Dada, Mama, Tee . . . Soo-see, Dada, Mama, Tee."

"Aye. That'll do. She's a brilliant bairn, Estrada. The gods have smiled on you. And you," Dubh said, turning to Sensara. Then, he raised a hand and added ominously, "Be sure she wears it. It's magicked. I added some charms myself."

Sensara cast him a dazzling smile. "I'm honored. Thank you, Dubh."

Having made her way around the circle of guests, Lucy appeared before Michael. "Soo-see, Dada, Mama, Tee," she chanted, shook her arm like a tiny tambourine and danced away.

"Who's Susy," Michael said, and swayed toward Estrada, who swung out his left arm and gathered him in. Michael glanced up, then laid his head against Estrada's shoulder. His fine blond hair tickled his collarbone.

"Are you alright?" Estrada pulled back slightly and frowned. He wanted no scenes today. It was Lucy's day, and everything must be perfect.

"Must be the weed. I have no stamina of late."

None in the past year, thought Estrada. Since his sojourn along the B.C. coast, Michael had changed. Whatever happened out there he kept locked inside—something that was not aiding his recovery. No matter how many times Estrada asked, the answer was always the same. *I don't remember. It's like waking from a nightmare.* But Michael was lying. The truth was unspeakable, and Estrada couldn't imagine something so horrible it couldn't be shared between them. Over the past seven years, the two men had shared everything.

Michael's hand brushed his thigh and Sensara cast Estrada a warning look. She didn't mind the liquor, or even the pot, but she wobbled a fine line of toleration for anything even covertly sexual when it involved Michael Stryker.

"Can I see you alone?" She gestured to the french doors.

After setting Michael to rights, Estrada followed her inside. Sensara's hair shimmered indigo in the sun like a glossy crow's wing. When she turned and grasped his hands, he gasped. It had been a long time since they'd been alone together, and he was both surprised and charmed by this offer of intimacy.

"Michael Stryker," she said. "Are you—"

"Sleeping with him? That's none of your business, Sensara."

She shook her head. "A, I know you are, and B, I don't care." Then, with rolling eyes, she backed up a step and crossed her arms over her chest. "What I want to know is . . . are you still determined to try a healing tonight at the ritual?"

"Oh." Was it *that* obvious? Since they'd returned from Scotland, he'd resurrected his old libertine passions with Michael. It was the only way to get the taste of that Glasgow bitch out of his mouth. But he'd tried to keep his activities far removed from the disapproving mother of his child. Then again, Sensara was a card-carrying psychic. "Yes. Why?"

"Because I doubt I can do anything for him."

"But, you're a healer."

Sensara raised her eyebrows. "I'm not sure it's *me* he needs."

"I've tried to get him to a doctor. He won't go." Michael had never been a big man, now he was a wraith, vanishing before their eyes. "He rarely eats, hardly sleeps." Estrada shrugged. "I don't know what else to do."

"Sit down." Sinking into one of the sofa cushions, Sensara touched the space beside her.

"That bad?" he joked, then joined her.

"When I look at Michael Stryker, I see black. Not shadows, not streaks, just an all-encompassing darkness." She touched his bare arm. "Am I the only one?"

Estrada cocked his head. Darkness? What could that possibly mean? His stomach clenched and he felt suddenly like he might puke.

"You see auras. What do *you* see when you look at him?"

Estrada cleared his throat and took a deep breath to steady himself. "Nothing. I used to see Michael's colors. Now I see nothing."

"Can you see my aura?"

"Sure. Greens, blues, purples around your heart and head . . . a golden glow. You're as lovely as ever. He picked up her hand and kissed it.

Sensara's smile flooded his chest and melted the tension in his gut, so he left his lips pressed against the back of her hand. He hadn't realized how much he'd missed these quiet moments alone. They'd been best friends, lovers, then estranged, and now Lucy's birth bound them in a new, complicated dance.

"How long?"

Estrada held her gaze, couldn't get enough of her. He wanted to lie beside her and whisper like they used to do. "How long?"

"Since you could see his aura?" she asked, drawing him back to the conversation.

"Oh." Estrada paused, trying to remember, and she reclaimed her hand. "Since Scotland. Since I first saw him on the island." He shook his head. "He was badly broken, and so was I."

"But *you* recovered. Thank God."

"Thank Dubh. It if wasn't for him, the Old Hag would've had me." A basalt pillar in the Corryvreckan Whirlpool, nicknamed the Old Hag, had nearly pummeled the life out of him when he'd been tossed overboard to drown.

"You lead a charmed life, Estrada, but Michael Stryker does not. That's why . . . " Sensara paused, catching herself pre-confession, then breathed and sighed. "Michael Stryker is black as soot, and the source of that darkness is deep inside him. It's like a . . . " She bit her bottom lip. "It's like a virus."

"A virus?"

"Yes. It's growing, festering, seeping into his pores and filtering out into his aura."

"Jesus. I thought he was just depressed." Estrada turned away from her, feeling his face flush with heat. How could he have missed something like that? "Are you saying Michael could be infected with something? Like a zombie virus?" Swallowing hard, he felt the bile rise again in his gut.

Sensara snorted. "I don't know about zombies, but whatever this is, it frightens me. It's like nothing I've ever encountered."

Estrada reached out his arm, gathered her in, and held her against his chest. "Sara, I'm sorry. I wouldn't have brought him if I'd known."

"What happened to him out there, Es?"

As Sensara leaned against him, her palms brushing his back, the heat of her hands melted his stiff muscles and brought him back from the edge. Sinking into her embrace, he felt calm again, at home.

"Dylan said Michael was marooned on the coast for days," she continued. "Was shipwrecked in a storm?"

"Yes, a gale."

"There's more to it. I can't see it, but I can feel it."

"Michael can't remember."

Estrada remembered the vision he'd had of Michael when he was in Scotland. The red oak coffin floating in the sea. The coffin etched with the initial *D*. The coffin Michael was locked inside. Should he tell her? Or would it frighten her so much she'd refuse to try and heal him?

Estrada touched her hand. "Sara, you're the best healer I know. I'm sure you can help him."

She shook her head. "He might need someone else. A psychiatrist? Shaman? Exorcist?"

"You think he's possessed?"

Sensara cupped his cheek in her palm. "You're an amazing father, Estrada. Lucy loves you, and I—"

Leaning forward, he stopped her words with a soft kiss. Don't cloud the moment with declarations of love. Closing his eyes, he let it grow. Felt her fingers in his hair. Mouth opening, inviting him in. When at last, their lips parted, her eyes were damp.

"For you, I will try to heal him," she said.

"I hear a *but*."

Her smile was sad. "You're right. I need you to promise me something."

"Anything." Sensara and Michael were his two best friends. He loved and needed them both.

"Promise me that you'll keep Michael away from Lucy. At least until we know what's happening."

"You think this virus thing might be catchy?"

Sensara shrugged. "Whatever it is, it's wicked. Pure evil. Do you want *that* around Lucy?"

Michael trudged down the dusty forest trail behind Estrada. After wiping the sweat from his forehead, he ran his fingers through his limp hair. He'd never been to one of their Wicca rituals. He wanted the healing, wanted to feel better, but somehow, he had to block his mind so Sensara couldn't see what happened out there on that island. He couldn't go on with this . . . this living death. But, Sensara couldn't know the truth.

Michael still didn't believe it himself. This disease that invaded his body left him weak and dizzy, unable to sleep at night or eat without purging. Nights he partied, losing himself in sex and drugs. Days, he curled up on the chaise and bit his nails to the quick, tasted the coppery blood and retched. His hand strayed to the scar on his neck and a black demon arose in his mind—a demon who was the source of this disease. Diego. His scar burned like a brand.

Could Sensara cure the disease without probing his mind? Estrada must never know the results of his folly. He'd hate him for not telling the truth, especially now he was a father. Michael's stupid mistake had imperiled both he and Estrada, yet he dared not tell him now. He'd left it far too long.

The leafy trail opened onto a glade. Daphne spread a blanket on the ground and motioned for Michael to sit. For a moment, he balked. Then he sat. Nothing they did could be worse than what he was already experiencing. The witches did not speak but busied themselves with unpacking. Feeling dizzy, Michael laid on his back and closed his eyes. He wanted to run and hide, but his legs felt like rubber. Perhaps a drink to steady his nerves? Leaning up on one elbow, he pulled a flask of whiskey from his pocket and unscrewed the cap.

Estrada appeared and shook his head. "Not now."

"But—"

"Let Sensara do her work. After we'll go to the club."

Michael handed the flask to Estrada. "Then *you'd* better take it."

"You'll be fine, I promise. Lie down and relax. We're almost ready."

Michael closed his eyes. He must have dozed off because when he opened them again, Sensara stood over him dressed in an ivory gown. She'd caught her ebony hair back with a band etched in stars, and golden suns hung from her ears.

He sat up, curious. Estrada stood behind her swathed in a black hooded robe, his eyelids lined with kohl. Michael had seen him in costume countless nights at the club, but here, he was no magician playing out an act with sleights and tricks and props. Here, he was the High Priest of Hollystone Coven—someone Michael didn't recognize or understand. Someone powerful and intimidating.

They'd formed a circle and lit candles in all directions. Daphne stood on one side, the last rays of the setting sun reflecting in her coral gown. Across from her, Dylan McBride stood wearing a cobalt blue cloak appliquéd in silver Elvish symbols. Dubh was directly in front of him, dressed in a white robe like a classic Merlin. He'd pulled the hood up over his high ponytail. Branches of red berries bulged from his belt.

Michael shivered. Cosplay at the club was one thing, mere theatrics intended to impress the patrons and unleash their fantasies and inhibitions. He dressed up frequently himself in black silk capes and, sometimes, in the Ionian garb of Lord Byron, when the mood struck him. But in the woods like this?

"I don't feel well," he said to Sensara, and climbed to his knees. "Maybe we shouldn't—"

"Sit," she said, holding up a long crystal wand. "We have begun. Our circle is cast, and we are between the worlds." Sensara's tone commanded. Ethereal and grave, the priestess wasn't someone to cross. "We will not harm you, Michael Stryker. We're here to help you. You need only allow it."

Biting his lip, Michael sat back on the blanket and clutched his knees to his chest. When Daphne picked up a skin drum and began a slow steady beat like the throbbing of a heart, it echoed through his veins and his flesh prickled.

"On this First Harvest, we give thanks to the sun god, Lugh. Without the sun, we would not exist. And so, we ask Lugh to join us as we raise the power in this our sacred circle." Slipping inside the drumbeat, Sensara chanted:

"In the rising summer fire,
Grains do ripen, seeds do rise,
Bees rush wildly sucking nectar,
Summer wines unveil our eyes."

The others echoed each of her lines and, despite himself, Michael caught himself chanting the words along with the others.

"Through the clouds, the sun king beckons,
Corn slow roasted over coals,
Ripened peaches dipped in honey,
Fill our bellies, fill our souls."

The drum beat quickened, and the witches stretched and swayed. Then, clapping and singing, they danced around the circle, repeating the incantation.

Seeing Estrada, Michael stood and slipped into the circle behind him. His feet shifted with the dance. Inhaling the scented incense that burned on the brazier, he glanced up at the flickering stars and swayed like a branch in the summer breeze. *Fill our bellies, fill our souls.*

So, this is what Estrada loved. This visceral abandonment. It touched a part of Michael he didn't know existed, something he'd lost years ago. His heartbeat quickened. Lungs expanded. He was panting, running out of breath. Still they leapt and danced, filling the forest with their song.

"Fill our bellies, fill our souls." Chanting the words aloud, Michael realized *his* belly and soul craved something other than food.

At last, Sensara raised her arms to the sky and closed her eyes. "We are filled with your power, Lugh. And honor you with our heart's love."

Tears ran down Michael's cheeks and he sobbed. Estrada clutched him to his chest and held him. Feeling their quickened hearts beating together, Michael was overcome by love. But a searing pain scorched his neck. The scar swelled and throbbed. And, when his lips brushed Estrada's carotid artery, he shuddered. Whatever evil Don Diego implanted with his vampiric kiss was growing inside him. *Vampire.* This was the truth, he dared not utter. In this heightened state, Michael realized he was dying and in his death throes, all he craved was blood. *Estrada's blood.*

Pulling away, he swayed, dizzy with fear.

"Don't be afraid, amigo," Estrada said, as he led Michael to the blanket. "I'll keep you safe. Lie down and let us heal you."

CLUB PEGASUS

Magus Dubh glanced around the room and grinned. "So, this is the famous Club Pegasus." Raising his glass to Estrada, he winked a cool blue eye. "*Slàinte.* To your health, mate." He swallowed the shot of amber fuel and exhaled a flash of flame.

Estrada laughed. "Fire-breathing fey. You must teach me that one."

"Ach, aye. It's a scorcher."

After wending their way through a blistering crowd of masked and bejewelled dancers, Dubh was sucking back the charm of the goth club along with his scotch. Estrada had ensconced them at the manager's table in the balcony, but when the Cocteau Twins caressed the speakers, Dubh stood, nodded, and snaked back through the wavering bodies and down the stairs.

Now, poised on the edge of the dance floor, Dubh felt the music caress him. It had been years since he'd heard "Garlands". His mother's frail falsetto suffused with that of Elizabeth Fraser in his head and when he closed his eyes, Dubh saw her—floating in their cramped Glasgow flat, black fringe bouncing, smudged eyes lolling. He'd often wondered how his fey father found and seduced her. Moira was only sixteen. Was she crossing a ravine one day on the way home from school? Or had he cornered her in an alley? His ma had never talked about it, or about his father. But Dubh liked to think they'd made love in a swathe of bluebells and the bugger'd bought her a curry, at least.

When Dubh's ma sang "Garlands" she seemed to re-connect with her faerie prince; at least, he liked to think so. Hauntingly ethereal, the lament took her places the lad could only imagine. The album peaked with its release, a year before his birth, but *this* was Moira's signature. She'd played it to death when he was young. Dubh still had the battered cover, though the vinyl was a maze of scratches and jags like the scars riveting the inside of Moira's arms. She wasn't quite a junkie; still, she succumbed in the grunge. The virus attacked her liver and left him an orphan at seventeen. He'd pinched a rosary and garlands to lay upon her grave. *Moira Dunbar. Tenement Angel.* His ma had done her best and he loved her for it.

Dubh flinched when a skinny character in fishnets and silk touched his shoulder, then tied a studded mask over his eyes and bowed. "Masquerade Madness," they said, by way of explanation and swaggered off. The floor was heaving in a colorful riot of ball gowns, bustiers, feathered tiaras, top hats, and baubles. Feeling underdressed in his worn leather kilt, Dubh stripped off his black tank and cast it aside. Dancers were beginning to couple and cluster. And when the DJ spun sultry Siouxsie, a redhead etched in black lace, and little else, caught his waving hands in hers and pulled him into the throng. Absorbed by "Arabian Nights" they swayed and sang along.

"What's your name, my lovely?" Dubh asked, as the music faded.

"Death," she said, flashing her dark-rimmed eyes.

"Death? Well, Death becomes you," he said, thinking of his mother. His voice was silenced by a jarring guitar riff, and the woman took the opportunity to vanish into the throng. No wonder, he thought. What an inane cliché. You'll never pick up burds that way, Magus Dubh.

He wandered back toward the staircase, grasping two shooters on his way past the bar.

Back at the manager's table, he set a tequila down in front of Estrada. "I just danced with a charming woman called Death."

Estrada tipped the tequila his way and then downed it. "You were wise to leave her behind, my friend."

Michael leaned back in his chair, head lolling dangerously to one side.

"We should go," said Estrada, glancing gravely at Michael and shaking his head.

Dubh feared the magician had spent too many nights ministering to his lover. Even in the shadows, Estrada's dark eyes were ringed. He was a graver man than Dubh had met a year ago in Glasgow. "Aye. I'll just get the tab."

"No, you won't. You're my daughter's godfather and my guest in this country."

Dubh nodded. *"Taing mhór."* Much obliged. There was no arguing with a man's honor.

On the way home in the cab, Dubh huddled in the back seat beside the two men. There was plenty of room in Michael's flat and they planned to crash there. Dubh leaned down and sniffed his pits. He stunk after two days of travel and couldn't wait to hit the shower and then curl up somewhere for a good long sleep.

As they sped down Granville Street, Michael passed out, thankfully leaning the other way. When his snores resounded in the cramped space, Dubh glanced at Estrada. "Tell me about him," he said quietly, gesturing to Michael.

Estrada sighed. "What can I say? Before I went to Scotland last summer, he was a rock star. Everyone wanted him. Michael believed he was the reincarnation of Lord Byron and swaggered around the club playing vampire—cape, fangs, red contacts."

"He *could* have been Lord Byron, I suppose." Dubh was aware of many lives he'd lived, and Michael not only resembled George Gordon, but seemed to grasp the mad, bad poet intrinsically. "Does he not believe that now?"

Estrada shrugged. "He doesn't dress up anymore. Even for Masquerade Madness, which was his idea."

"It's pure dead brilliant." Dubh fingered the mask in the pocket of his pale green biker jacket. "Obviously, the punters love it. Elaborate costumes. Exotic creations." He thought of Death, bedecked in black lace, and wished she hadn't disappeared.

"Yeah, Michael's a great manager. His grandfather bought him the club when he turned twenty-one. He had a feeling, and he was right. Michael knows what works."

"It's too bad he's caught in the doldrums." Dubh yawned and leaned on his fist. Knackered. It had been two days and nights since he'd slept.

Planes made him anxious and he rarely traveled. "Did Sensara perceive anything useful regarding—"

Estrada shook his head and gestured to the back of the cabbie's head.

When they pulled up to the Stryker house, Estrada stepped out of the cab, leaving Michael slouched against the seat. "Give us a minute," he said to the driver and passed him some cash. Then he gestured for Dubh to follow him. Estrada stood waiting a few feet behind the vehicle, and when Dubh approached, crouched down to rest on one knee beneath the streetlight. A solemn gaze did nothing to mar the magician's beauty. "You should know what you're getting into, Dubh."

"Go on, mate."

"Sensara said, touching Michael's aura was like running her hands through a 'bloody quagmire'. She smelled rotting corpses. It made her gag."

"Good lord," Dubh said. "I remember seeing him at Sorcha's camp. He had broken bones, but that shouldn't have a lasting effect."

Estrada rubbed his chin. "Yeah, well. He was locked in a coffin."

"A coffin?"

"And cast adrift during a storm. I saw it in a vision and never told Sensara. So, please don't mention it." He grimaced with guilt and Dubh felt his pain. Keeping something like that from Sensara must have been hard, even if he did so with good intentions.

Estrada rose and slapped the dust from his jeans, then opened Michael's car door and hoisted him up. After shoving some more cash into the cabbie's hand, he nodded once.

For a moment, they stood silently and watched the cab drive off. Then they turned and streetlights illuminated the Queen Anne mansion with its stone-pillared porch, posh landscaping, and turreted towers. A miniature castle, it had a distinctly gothic feel.

"Is this—?"

"Yep."

"If I had a million dollars . . . "

"With a million you might buy a room. For the whole thing, you'd need several."

Dubh whistled. Michael had myriad problems, but money didn't appear to be one of them.

"Michael lives upstairs in the back tower flat. The house belongs to his grandfather."

Ah, thought Dubh. A man mustn't jump to conclusions.

Together the three men stumbled up the tree-lined drive and turned to follow the brick path around the back of the house. It was an older neighbourhood off West 38th Avenue and well-shrouded with dense greenery. Dubh imagined Michael appreciated the privacy so many trees could provide. The brick path meandered through the park-like backyard and ended at a wooden gate. Ivy climbed the walls. Dubh walked a few strides behind Estrada, who half-steered, half-carried Michael.

"That's strange," Estrada said, pausing. "The sensor lights should have come on by now. There's a key under that loose brick. Can you grab it, Dubh?"

"Aye. Just let me—" Dubh pulled out his phone and turned on the torch app, then gasped. All three men stood staring. Gobsmacked.

A woman's body lay on the wide stone step in front of the oak and stained-glass door. Copper hair. Pale face. A look of terror tainting her wide brown eyes. Red lips freshly painted. A white satin slip edged in lace. A red rose between her breasts.

"*What the fuck?*" Estrada said.

"Mate, this is murder. Call the polis," Dubh said, slipping into his Glasgow slang.

"Murder," echoed Michael, falling to his knees. Crouching on the stone step beside the body, he covered his face and sobbed. "Oh, Ruby. I'm *so* sorry."

Sorry? thought Dubh. Sorry for what? He glanced around nervously and scratched his beard. Was the killer still close? Watching them from behind the cedars? Through the tall trees, Dubh could see lights blazing in the upstairs rooms of the house next door. Someone shouted on the far side of the cedar hedge and dogs began barking up and down the street.

"Don't touch her," Estrada said. "Where the fuck is Nigel? Ruby would never be here without him." Pulling out his phone, he called, and then waited. "Fuck. It's gone to message."

"You know her?" Dubh asked.

Estrada bit his bottom lip and nodded. "Her name is Ruby Carvello."

"Who is she?" Dubh glanced at Michael. There had to be a connection.

"Nigel's girlfriend." Crouching beside Michael, Estrada wrapped an arm around his shoulder. "I'm sorry, amigo."

Dubh shook his head in confusion. "Nigel?"

"Nigel Stryker is Michael's grandfather. Ruby's been his mistress for twenty years." Pausing, Estrada glanced down at the beautiful dead woman beside him. "Sometimes, when his wife goes abroad, Nigel and Ruby stay in the attic in Michael's flat."

Dubh stared up at the turreted tower with its gray stonework strewn in ivy. If Ruby was posed on Michael's doorstep, there was a chance Nigel was upstairs—if he hadn't been abducted or worse. A rich businessman who owned Club Pegasus, he likely had a slew of enemies.

Michael glanced up wide-eyed at the tower window, his face a fresco of shadows and sorrow. He was obviously thinking the same thing.

"You two stay here," Estrada said. "I'm going to find Nigel."

"No mate. Don't go in there. If the polis come . . . or you touch something."

"Well, *fuck*. I can't just stand here. Nigel could be injured or . . . " Estrada shook his head. Couldn't finish his sentence.

"Aye, but trust me. Call the polis."

"No!" Estrada said emphatically. "No cops."

Dubh's fey senses were overwhelmed by the smell and taste of blood, yet he could see no wounds, no ligature marks, no bruises, no pooling blood. Perhaps, the poor woman had been asphyxiated. Crouching down, Dubh tilted her head gently to the left and then to the right. No bruising, but two bloody puncture marks marred the right side of her neck. Someone was fucking with Michael. Someone familiar with his vampire fetish.

"Look at this," Dubh whispered.

"*Jesus,*" breathed Estrada, rubbing his hands over his face.

"What is it?" asked Michael. And then he saw the marks on Ruby's neck. Gasping, he stared up at Estrada and ran his hands through his hair. Dubh still held the torch and in the harsh light, Michael's face blanched even paler. "Victor," he breathed.

"Victor Carvello? You think *he* had something to do with this?" Estrada said.

But Michael didn't answer. His hands stayed in his hair. His red-rimmed eyes stared straight ahead. When Estrada reached down and touched his shoulder, Michael didn't move, didn't soften. His body was as rigid as a manikin.

"It's okay, man. Don't worry about Carvello." Estrada grasped Michael's right arm and moved it down to his lap, but his other hand stayed caught in his hair. "Michael?" Leaning forward, Estrada stared into his eyes. Michael's unblinking pupils did not return his gaze. Estrada waved his hand in front of Michael's face. No reaction. Finally, he grasped Michael's left arm and moved it to his lap. "What the fuck is *this* now?"

"Catatonia," Dubh said. "I've seen it before, mate."

"What?" asked Estrada, squinting in confusion.

"He's catatonic. Better call the paramedics."

"No. No cops and no paramedics. He's breathing fine." Estrada snorted, then leaned down and padded Michael's pockets. He pulled out car keys and handed them to Dubh. "His car is out back in the lane. A red BMW convertible." Scooping Michael up in his arms, he started down the back path. "Just watch him and wait for me in the car."

"What are you going to do?" asked Dubh, struggling to keep up.

"First, I'm going to find Nigel. And then, I'm going to find out what's happening next door."

The shouting had grown louder and Dubh could see the flash of a red revolving light through the trees.

"It's the polis, man."

"Yeah, and before they find us, I need to find him. Let's move."

Estrada stepped gingerly over Ruby's body, leaned down, and pried the key from under the brick. Closing the stained-glass door quietly behind him, he retrieved the flashlight and a pair of black leather gloves from the cedar chest.

As he scrambled up the wooden steps, he pulled them on. If anyone was in the flat, they'd hear him coming, but there was no time for stealth. The cops would check for prints and his would be everywhere in Michael's flat—except in the attic. That space was reserved for Nigel, and there'd be a hodgepodge of prints. Ruby wasn't the only woman he entertained in that room.

Glancing around Michael's flat, Estrada noticed nothing was disturbed. Turning the antique brass knob that led to the tower, he took a deep breath, then opened the old oak door. Another flight of stairs. And then, a sanctuary from another time.

Estrada saw the antique bed first—empty, crumpled sheets, but no blood. Then he saw the pale bare foot jutting out beyond it. *Nigel.* Unconscious. Bloody. Bruised. Leaning over Nigel's face, he listened. Heard a ragged inhale. Felt a warm exhale against his cheek. Exhaled himself.

"Nigel. Something's really fucked up here man, but I'll figure it out. Help's coming and you're going to be fine."

Estrada descended the stairs and closed the door behind him. Thank God, Michael was old school and kept a landline. Once he called 911, Estrada knew the police would trace the call and come to investigate. He picked up the receiver and punched in the numbers. He heard the voice of the emergency operator, then set it down on the table and left the line open. The police would be here in no time. He kept the gloves on as he scrambled back down the stairs. And, just to make things simple, he left the door ajar.

Ruby stared up at him.

"I'll find the motherfucker who did this, and I'll kill him."

As he stepped over Ruby's body, Estrada heard a baby crying. He followed the voices around the side of the Stryker house and hid, listening and watching, in the cedar hedge.

Joe Barnes stood on the lawn between the two houses with his baby thrown over his shoulder like a sack of potatoes. One squad car. Two uniforms. Joe appeared to be arguing with them. Glancing from cop to cop, he sighed heavily. "I'm telling you—my wife is gone. She's not in the house. She didn't go for a walk. She didn't leave us. She's been abducted."

"Just take us through it one more time," said a young blond officer.

"Like I said, a noise woke me. I looked for Nora. The window was wide open in Zachary's room and Nora was gone. The bastard left a red rose on the windowsill for fuck sake."

Estrada stiffened and swallowed hard. *A rose?* Had the same man who murdered Ruby abducted Nora Barnes? Perhaps Nora had seen Ruby's murderer from Zachary's window and could identify him. But if he was a killer, why *take* her? Why not kill her? Unless... Estrada glanced around the shadowy yard. Had the bastard tossed her body in the bushes?

Time to go. Any minute now the cops would descend with search teams and sniffer dogs. If Michael was still catatonic when he got back to the car, it was a short drive up Granville to West 12th and Vancouver General Hospital. Once Michael was safe, he'd have a chance to think.

THE TERROR OF RAVENS

From its perch on a flagpole overlooking the False Creek Yacht Club, a monstrous raven surveyed the sky above the harbor. After ruffling the long shaggy feathers below its beak, it let out a terrifying croak and flew like an arrow straight down.

Landing on the deck of *La Sangria*, a fifty-foot power yacht, it emitted a low gurgling croak and transformed into a man. Wild sooty hair stood out from his head in dreads. Zion rubbed his dark eyes and squinted into the streetlights. His vision was much sharper in his raven guise. Zion was surly and hungry and tired of waiting. Drinking the woman's blood had only whet his appetite. He could drain the entire fucking Coast Guard fleet.

When his sight adjusted, he noticed Leopold Blosch leaning in the doorway. He'd pulled on a pair of blue jeans and a simple white T-shirt. As pale as Zion was dark, Leopold's straight silver hair slid across one shadowed cheek bone and hung halfway down his back. His bottle-green eyes were edged in red. He was pretty in a sunken-cheeked sort of way and reminded Zion of the man Christophe brought to Le Chateau last year—the man they were messing with now. Michael Stryker. The man the vampires called Mandragora. Stryker was a wannabe vampire who managed a goth club in Vancouver. Zion had tasted him then and had a jones for him still. Blood could do that to you.

"Why you staring at me like that, Chef? You got an itch needs scratchin'?" Zion considered Leopold Blosch to be his underling since he'd sired him, and he didn't much like his attitude.

"You didn't have to break *both* his legs," Leopold said. The chef was obviously in one of his sulky moods. When he got snotty, Zion had to curb an urge to kick his pretty head in—like he'd done to Nigel Stryker.

"What do you care?" Zion stretched his naked limbs, then cleared his throat and spit over the railing.

"It was unnecessary. We had the woman."

"A man with one leg can walk. A man with no legs ain't walkin' nowhere."

Leopold scoffed and flung his head so that his pretty platinum hair hit the doorframe.

"You still too human, Chef. When you age a little, you'll understand that immortality is boring without sport." Zion scratched his dreadlocks with long curvy nails. "Wind's picking up."

"Eliseo is late," Leopold said, stating the obvious.

Zion wasn't concerned. Eli wouldn't risk fucking up and offending Father. "How's your friend, Chef?" he asked, gesturing to the cabin with his chin.

"She's still unconscious."

Zion curled his lips and sniffed. Her scent, wafting through the cracks, aroused him.

"Stay away from her," Leopold growled. It was a pale threat the chef could never back up. "Don Diego said he wants her alive and unharmed."

"A taste wouldn't hurt. We could share her, Chef."

Leopold grimaced. "I'm not hungry."

"Starving yourself won't change anything." Laughing, Zion rubbed his belly. "You can't die. You already dead."

"Shut up."

"Ruby Carvello was a little salty and a little sweet. Just the way I like my women," Zion teased.

Leopold Blosch walked across the deck, hung over the railing, and retched.

Zion sniggered. "You'll be a puker till you use those fangs the way they was intended."

"Shut up."

His disgust only spurred Zion on. "Don't fret, Chef. You laid the lady out as pretty as a picture. Those roses were a nice touch. Make them think."

Hearing the soft beat of raven's wings, they both glanced up.

"Finally. Leopold wiped his mouth with the back of his hand.

"Looks like Eli got the prize," Zion said, scowling. "Father's favorite never fucks up."

Estrada was curled up on a vinyl couch in the waiting room at Vancouver General Hospital. He and Dubh had been there for hours, had seen the paramedics arrive with Nigel, and watched nervously as the cops followed them in. Estrada had left the scene of a murder and he didn't want that little secret to slip out. But when he saw Nigel, he went to the counter and informed the nurse he was there. When Nigel regained consciousness, Estrada wanted him to know he wasn't alone. And he needed to know what the fuck happened.

Magus Dubh emitted calm even breaths and the occasional snore from an adjacent two-seater. Estrada closed his eyes and tried to sleep, but though exhausted, he couldn't calm his racing mind.

Catatonic. Estrada knew Michael had been descending into his own personal hell this past year, but how had it come to this? Was it the shock of finding Ruby murdered or something else? When he closed his eyes, Estrada pictured those two bloody marks on her neck. Whoever killed Ruby intended it to look like a vampire attack. What were Michael's first words when he saw Ruby lying there, so pale and punctured, a red rose at her breast? *I'm so sorry, Ruby.*

Fuck. Estrada grasped his belly to ease the pain in his gut. *Michael knows who killed her.*

"Sandolino Estrada?" The voice was male and jarred him from his reverie.

Opening his eyes, Estrada looked up and brushed his messy black hair back from his face. The young doctor was bald by choice and looked like he'd been on shift about twenty-four hours too long. A name tag dangled over pale blue scrubs. Dr. Charles Chin.

Estrada nodded.

"Mr. Stryker asked to see you."

"Michael?" Standing too quickly, Estrada wavered and grasped the back of the couch to steady himself.

The doctor shook his head. "Nigel."

"Oh. We brought Michael in. He's Nigel's grandson." He glanced at Dubh who'd sat up and was rubbing his eyes.

"Are you family?"

Estrada thought a moment. "I'm Michael's partner. So . . . yeah." He'd never referred to himself in that context before, but hospitals were notorious for delineating what information could be shared.

The doctor shook his head. "I'm sorry. There's been no change."

As they walked down the hall together, Estrada's boots clicked against the polished tile.

"Has Michael been diagnosed with any kind of mental illness in the past?" the doctor asked.

"No, but . . . " Many times, Estrada had considered that Michael was bipolar, but there was no official diagnosis. Michael flatly refused to see a doctor. This might be his chance to get the help he needed.

Dr. Chin waited.

"Michael suffered trauma last summer." He told the doctor the bare bones of what had happened. There was no need to mention the coffin floating in the sea. "He's been different since then. Depressed." Estrada bit his bottom lip.

The doctor nodded, as if that would suffice. "We're treating him now. I'll let you know when you can see him."

Two uniformed officers stood in the hallway outside Nigel's room— a pretty, freckled girl scout and a hard-mouthed Korean cop. She nodded once as her eyes met Estrada's. Why were the police here? Were they protecting Nigel and Michael from another attack? Or, were his friends suspect?

Calm down, Estrada told himself. Of course, the cops are here. Ruby Carvello was murdered. There will be police and questions, inquiries, investigations, and scrutiny.

"In here." Dr. Chin pointed to a curtained space inside a small room. "We'll be moving Mr. Stryker to a private room shortly."

"How bad is he?" If they were moving him, that meant they were keeping him, and hospitals didn't keep anyone unless it was necessary.

"Complete fracture in the left tibia. The right tibia will require surgery to realign the bones. But, he's stable."

"Jesus."

"His bones will heal. Our concern is head trauma."

"Head trauma? You mean, someone put the boots to him?"

Dr. Chin nodded. "We'll keep him immobilized and monitor his concussion." He checked his watch. "You have about ten minutes before we prep him for surgery. He wanted to see you before he went in."

"Thank you," Estrada said.

With a nod, Dr. Chin slipped off down the hall.

Estrada walked into the room and pushed back the pale curtain. Nigel was cranked up in bed. He looked ashen. Both his legs were wrapped. His arm was hooked up to an I.V. His eyes looked dazed and bloodshot.

"Sandolino." Nigel always called him by his first name. In a way, Estrada liked it. Being called Sandolino helped him remember what it was like to be someone's son. His own father used to call him that in the time before he disappeared.

"Hey. How're you feeling?" Estrada asked, gently touching Nigel's shoulder. It was a stupid question.

"Ruby. They murdered my Ruby." Nigel's eyes filled with tears.

"They? Did you recognize them, sir?"

Nigel shook his head and bit his bottom lip but had no words.

"Nigel?"

"Stark naked."

"Naked? Who was naked? The killers?" Adrenaline surged through Estrada's body. There were only two reasons for killers to attack naked—to engage in sex and to protect their clothes. He bared his teeth and broke out in a sweat. If they'd raped Ruby, he'd kill them.

"I thought the bastards were going to . . . " Nigel closed his eyes for several seconds as Estrada quietly seethed. And then, he revived. "The police . . . They don't know if . . . "

"I'm sorry, Nigel. I know how much you loved her." Leaning over, Estrada clutched Nigel's hand. "I'm going to get these bastards. But I need your help. What can you tell me about them?"

Nigel blinked slowly as he tried to remember. "Tall, thin, pale, long blond hair, almost white."

"That's good," Estrada said. Long platinum hair was a solid detail.

"He reminded me of Michael." Nigel chewed his lip. "The nurse said you brought him in. He can't speak?"

"He'll be alright, sir."

Nigel sniffed, and then his eyelids riffled.

"What about the other one?"

"Black. Dreadlocks." He touched his cheekbone. "Black teardrop tats."

"That should make him easy to identify."

"Son-of-a-bitch broke both my legs."

"Did they say anything? Mention a name?" It was a long shot, but sometimes criminals were too stupid or cocky to care.

Nigel screwed up his face, as if sifting through the memory caused him pain, and then it flew out in a rush of words. "When I woke up, the blond was standing over me. He grabbed me by the throat. Flung me into the wall." Nigel touched his throat, feeling for bruising. "He was strong. Too strong. He lifted Ruby with one hand. When she screamed, he let her go. Then that black bastard grabbed her by the neck and squeezed until she passed out. I couldn't help her. Couldn't get to her."

"I'm sorry, Nigel." At least, she was unconscious. That was one small mercy.

"He dropped her and kicked me, side sweep, broke my leg. When I fell, he broke the other one."

"Do you have any idea why these guys would come after you and Ruby?"

Tears dripped from the corners of Nigel's eyes and he dragged his fist across them.

Estrada didn't want to think about what happened to Ruby, and he sure as hell didn't want to make Nigel think about it, but he had to know everything. It was the only way to find her killers. He tried again. "Did the police tell you anything?"

Nigel nodded and cast his eyes down. "Something about a rose. But I don't—"

The nurse appeared behind Estrada. "It's time."

"Yeah. Look Nigel, I'm here for you and Michael. Whatever you need, I'll be right outside."

But the nurse had cranked up the drugs and Nigel was already drifting off.

When Estrada returned to the waiting room, Dubh was sitting on the couch with two large coffees in paper cups and a bag of food.

"Where'd you get that?" Estrada asked. The mingling aromas of salsa, eggs, sausage, and coffee made his stomach growl. In all the chaos, he'd forgotten about food.

"Cafeteria. I hope you like breakfast burritos," Dubh said. "I brought you two."

"Thanks man. What time is it?"

"Just before six."

Estrada ripped off the paper and swallowed both burritos in a few bites, then washed them down with black coffee. "Not bad," he said, after wiping his mouth with one of the paper napkins. "Listen, Dubh. I'm sorry your visit has turned into a nightmare." Estrada pulled a set of keys from his jacket pocket. "You don't have to stay here. Grab a cab and go back to my place. Sleep. Shower."

"I'll go when you go."

"I can't leave. Nigel's just gone into surgery and Michael . . . I don't know how long—"

"I have a mate with schizophrenia who suffered with catatonic spells," Dubh said.

"That's how you knew."

"Aye. The doctor gave him drugs. Benzos."

"Did it help?"

Dubh nodded. "Some. But, he's an addict now."

"Michael doesn't need anything else to be addicted to." For the past year, he'd lived on nothing but booze, drugs, and sex.

"There might be another way. I've been thinking—"

Estrada's phone rang. "It's Sensara. Why's she calling now?"

"Sara?"

"Estrada. Thank God you picked up. This is Daphne. You have to come back to the house."

"Why? What happened?" His heart pounded so hard it hurt his chest.

"Just come."

"Tell me, Daphne." He heard her breathe in the phone, waited, and then couldn't wait. "Daphne!"

"It's Lucy. She's gone."

"Gone?" The burritos he'd just wolfed down surged back up into his throat. The sour acid burned, and he coughed and swallowed to quash it down. Hunching over, he clutched the phone with trembling fingers.

"She's been kidnapped."

"Kidnapped?" For a second everything went black and he felt like he was going to pass out, then the image of a red rose appeared. He gasped to stifle a scream. No, it couldn't be. Not his Lucy.

"Just come. Please."

"But—"

Daphne hung up.

"What's happened?" Dubh asked.

Estrada stared at the phone. Couldn't speak. Couldn't breathe. His chest tingled and his hand rose reflexively to calm his thundering heart. It felt like it might explode.

"Look at me, mate. I think you're having an anxiety attack."

Estrada turned his head slowly toward Dubh, who took one of the napkins and dabbed at his mouth. "You've bit your lip, mate. Take a few deep breaths and tell me what's going on. What did Daphne say?"

"It's Lucy. She's been kidnapped."

"Kidnapped?"

"Jesus. This is fucked up. Who the hell would kidnap a baby?"

Dubh shook his head. "Some motherfucker who wants to get you while you're down."

Estrada's mind was spinning. "Me?"

"Ach, aye."

"*Fuck*. I can't think. Let's just go."

Estrada drove Michael's BMW as far as his Commercial Drive flat, and then drove his Harley out to Buntzen Lake with Dubh on the back. He needed to feel his fists on the throttle. He opened her up as they hit the freeway and the cool fierceness of the wind fired his senses. He knew the calm *normalcy* of the past year was just a mirage and his world was imploding. He could taste it—a kind of bitter acid that coated his dry mouth.

At the summit of the hill above Buntzen Lake, the ashes of a million blackened trees sullied the usually fresh mountain air. Forest fires. One more thing he couldn't control. Estrada pressed the throttle . . . wanted to punch something. And then they were there, and he knew for everyone's sake, he could not.

Dubh slipped off the back of the bike and coughed as he wrenched off his helmet. "Is that wood smoke? I didn't notice that yesterday."

"Wind's changed direction." Estrada's lip trembled. "Every summer more forests burn down."

Taking a step back, Dubh touched his hand to his heart and his jaw fell.

At noon, the air rippled with heat and the blue-gray haze of tragedy. The house on Hawk's Claw Lane—a house Estrada had come to love—looked surreal with a police cruiser and a forensic investigation van parked in the driveway. The forest fires engulfing them were tragic, but all he could think about was Lucy. Seeing police vehicles made her abduction real.

Estrada banged on the door and then opened it with his key—one of the benefits of being a father. A wiggly, wagging black Labrador retriever jumped him. He bent forward to steady the beast, as Sensara slid down the stairs in a thin black T-shirt dress. Her hair was caught back, her feet bare.

She grasped his shoulders and stared, her brown irises flaring wet like molten rock.

"You alright, Sara?"

She shook her head, then buried her face in his chest and clung to him.

Estrada wrapped his arms around her, held her, and waited. He didn't want to inflict anymore pain but there were things he needed to know. "Tell me," he said at last. "How did—"

"Stolen from her crib."

"Someone broke in?" He ground his teeth. Every muscle taut. He wanted to punch a wall or a face. But couldn't. Sara needed him to step up. Be the man. Find their child.

"I left her window open. It was so hot." Stepping back, she grasped her temples as tears dripped down her cheeks. "We should have bought a fucking air conditioner. I just fucking hate air conditioners. And now the smoke—"

"This is not your fault, Sara. Whoever took Lucy didn't come in her window. No one could scale that wall. It's too high."

He clenched his fists until his fingernails bit into his palms. The tension taunting the back of his neck spiraled into his scalp. His head ached. He wanted to get drunk. To fuck. To do anything but stand here and talk about his child's abduction.

"But the doors were all locked," Sensara said.

Estrada could see the tight muscles in her neck jumping under her skin. He laid his clammy hands against her neck and shoulders and squeezed until she squealed from the pressure.

"Sorry," he said, shaking his head. "I'm just trying to—"

"I know. I know." She touched his cheek and stared into his eyes. "And I know how hard this is for you."

"We'll find her Sara, but I need to know everything." Estrada glanced down as the black lab settled against his ankles. "What about Remy? Didn't he bark?"

She shook her head. "No one heard him."

"That's weird." Remy loved everyone but barked ballistically whenever a stranger came near the house. Maybe the kidnapper brought steak, he thought. But, how could anyone get into Lucy's bedroom without going upstairs? "What about that tree? Could he have climbed it and swung over?"

"*Crann Bethadh*? That's impossible." Dubh had been standing silently behind them, watching and listening.

"You're sure she didn't just climb out of her crib and hide?" asked Estrada. "She's agile, and you know how she likes to play *teek*." Peek-a-boo was one of her favorite games, a baby version of hide and seek. "Did you look—"

"Of course, I fucking looked," she yelled and stamped her foot. "We all did. I just . . . I can't feel her." Sensara's confession elicited more sobbing. "Not here. Not anywhere."

Estrada gathered her in as she collapsed in his arms. "That doesn't mean . . . " He caught himself before the word *dead* tumbled out. "You're just in shock."

A professional psychic, Sensara was often called on by police to help with criminal investigations. She'd found several missing kids. But, could she find her own? Or was she too close, too emotional?

"The bracelet," Dubh said. "Was she wearing it?"

Sensara buried her face in Estrada's shoulder and wouldn't look at Dubh.

Daphne appeared beside Sensara and rubbed her bare arm. "We thought she might roll on it and hurt herself when she was asleep," she said, then bit her lip to hold back tears. Raine wandered in from the kitchen and slung a protective arm around Daphne. These three were as formidable as Macbeth's witches when riled.

"You took it off?" Dubh was indignant and not about to let it go.

Sensara stepped back, breaking Estrada's embrace. "Well, it sat on her dresser all night and it didn't keep the monster from creeping in and stealing her, did it?"

"It was magicked to protect *the wearer*. Not to keep some demon from entering the premises. I told you—"

Estrada raised his hand. "Stop talking about monsters and demons."

"Sorry, mate," Dubh said. "We need to sit down and figure this out."

Daphne and Raine locked arms with Sensara and led her into the livingroom and the men followed in their wake.

"I'll put the kettle on," Daphne said, after the women deposited Sensara on the couch.

"Who has time for tea?" Estrada couldn't sit still, was bouncing on the balls of his feet, smacking his fist into his palm.

"What else can we do? The police are upstairs taking the place apart," Sensara said.

"What aren't you telling me, Sara?" Estrada's skin had been prickling since he walked in, and his feelings of trepidation weren't coming from the energies in the house, but from the women. They were hiding something. "Did the kidnapper call or leave a note or something?"

Sensara glanced at Raine and bit her trembling lip as Daphne reappeared.

"What is it? And don't fuck with me."

"We found a rose," Daphne said.

Estrada's eyes widened. "Where?"

"In her crib."

"*Fuck!*" Estrada turned and slammed his fist into the wall. Then leaning over, he clutched his bruised and bleeding knuckles. "*Fuck.*"

"What?" Sensara sprung to her feet. "What do you know?"

"It was red, wasn't it? A red fucking rose."

Sitting back, Daphne nodded.

Collapsing on the floor, Estrada caught his head in his hands. Though his mind was spinning, he couldn't find words. The thought of Ruby's murderers taking his baby was just too much. And then he remembered Nigel's description of the bastard who'd broken both his legs and a pain cut through his gut.

"We've had an eventful evening ourselves," Dubh said. "Someone is playing a cruel game."

"Explain," Daphne said.

"When we arrived back at the Stryker home last night, we discovered a murdered woman on the steps in front of Michael's door," Dubh said.

"Murdered?" Sensara took a quick breath. "Who? Someone you knew?"

Estrada stared down at the floor. "Ruby Carvello. Nigel Stryker's mistress."

Sensara stared at him confused. Of course, she wasn't privy to this side of his life. It was the stuff he kept hidden.

"Nigel is Michael's grandfather. He raised him and Ruby . . . Well, she's like a mother to Michael."

"A mother murdered on Michael's steps," Sensara said. "I knew that fucking—"

"The point is," Dubh said, interrupting her. "The woman was posed with a red rose across her heart."

Estrada climbed to his knees and caught Sensara's moist hands in his, but she pulled away and crossed her arms over her chest. Sitting back on the floor, he took a deep breath.

"Then, we discovered the woman next door was missing," Dubh said. "She was taken from her child's room on the upper floor. The same as—"

"Oh my God," Daphne said.

"A red rose was left on the windowsill," concluded Dubh.

Sensara's eyes widened. "They're connected?"

"Yes. By three red roses." Estrada's mind raced with all the things a red rose could represent. *Passion? Love? Sacrifice?*

"But how?" Daphne asked.

"Michael Stryker," Sensara said, rising like a whirling cobra.

"We don't know that," Estrada said defensively.

"*His* doorstep. *His* neighbours. And he was here yesterday with Lucy. Where is he now?"

Estrada shot her a scathing look. She had no right to blame this all on Michael. He was as much a victim in this debacle as anyone else. And yet, he knew she was right about one thing—Michael was the common denominator in all this chaos.

"He's in hospital," Dubh said.

"Why?"

"Michael's ill, and the shock of finding Ruby tipped him over the edge. He's being treated for catatonia," Dubh said.

"What?" asked Daphne.

"Michael is catatonic," explained Estrada. "He can't move or speak. He's . . . stuck."

"So, you're saying, our one connection is comatose?" Sensara's indignant question reverberated around the room.

"Michael would never do anything to harm Lucy," Estrada said.

"But that thing inside him. That . . . that . . . *virus*." Sensara jumped up. "I told you to keep him away from her."

"Virus?" Daphne stood. "What virus?" She looked from one to the other. "What are you two talking about?"

"Get a grip, hens," Dubh said. "There's far too much accumulated power in this room to be hurling shite. You're liable to start the fucking house on fire."

Daphne cocked her head.

"Ach aye. I've seen it happen."

Sensara stomped into the kitchen trailed by Daphne and Raine.

"What virus?" Estrada heard Daphne whisper.

"Perhaps a cuppa to settle things down?" Dubh yelled.

By the time they returned with a tea tray, Sensara had calmed down.

Estrada waited until everyone had poured and sipped before he spoke. "There's something else."

"Of course there is." Twirling the silver pendant at her neck, Sensara cast him a glance. It was a crescent moon in Celtic knots set with a rainbow moonstone. When she was anxious, as she was now, the stone cast an eerie red glow. Estrada had given it to her after their first Beltane ceremony and was relieved to see she still wore it despite everything that had happened to them over the past two years.

Daphne laid her hand on Sensara's shoulder. "Let him tell us what he knows."

Estrada took a deep breath. "I talked to Nigel this morning. He's *also* in the hospital. But he saw the men who attacked him and can identify them. So, the police have a description of these bastards, and so do I."

"Does Nigel know them?" Daphne asked.

"No, but he described them. One was black, and the other, white."

"That's nothing." Daphne's partner, Raine Carreto, was a journalist for an alternative newspaper in Vancouver, and spent copious hours reading police reports and racing around the city. "Any distinguishing marks? Scars? Tattoos?"

Estrada shrugged. "Dreads, and a black teardrop tattooed below each eye."

"Like Little Wayne?" Raine pursed her lips. "A tat like that's not too common. It could be gang-related."

The bastard was either stupid or arrogant to show his face, thought Estrada.

"When I checked Lucy at two o'clock, she was sleeping in her crib," Daphne said. "When did you find . . . ?"

"We left the club just after two."

"So, these two men murdered one woman and abducted another woman in the city, sometime before two. And then, came all the way out here to kidnap Lucy?" Raine shook her head. "That drive takes close to an hour. It doesn't make sense."

"Michael Stryker," Sensara said. "I know it. The man's evil."

"He's sick," Estrada said.

"I'll kill him. I'll spin a spell that'll turn him inside-fucking-out."

"Excuse me, Ms. Narato?" It was a police officer, one of the women from the forensics unit.

Sensara's cheeks flushed.

"We're finished upstairs for now, but we'd like to speak with you again before we go."

"Yes, of course," Sensara said, awkwardly.

"Are you the child's father?" she asked, appraising Estrada.

"Yes."

"Good. We'd like to speak with you too. And we'll need your fingerprints so we can eliminate your prints from those we found upstairs. We can do it here like we did for the others, or you can come down to the station. It will also help if you would be willing to give us a DNA swab."

Estrada's jaw dropped.

"No rush," she said, backing out of the room. "Just let us know when you're ready."

No rush? My daughter's been fucking kidnapped. Giving his fingerprints and DNA to the cops was the last thing he wanted to do, but for Lucy he'd give his life.

"Yeah, I'll be right there."

Sensara whirled and walked from the room with Daphne and Raine trailing close behind.

Dubh gestured to the french doors. "I have a suggestion, Estrada. It's something I've been ruminating on all night and now I think it's imperative."

"What is it?"

"Let's talk outside before the police get a hold of you. I think I know a way to save your mate from being turned *inside-fucking-out* by a very angry and powerful witch."

"Soul retrieval," Dubh said, in a tone just above a whisper. Then stared and waited.

Estrada squinted in the sunlight. "Like a shaman might do?"

The two men had wandered to the back of the yard away from the chaos, to a place where grass edged forest in a dark, jagged line.

"Aye."

"Sensara said Michael might need a shaman."

"Well, I concur. If you could meet your mate in the Underworld, perhaps you could ascertain the truth."

"Me?" Estrada didn't know anything about being a shaman.

"Who else, mate?" Dubh spied a hefty branch bereft of bark, picked it up, and ran his hands over the rough bleached surface.

"You think Michael's lying?" Estrada kicked around in the loose debris with the toe of his boot and wondered what Dubh could see in the slightly curved cedar.

"Or hiding something. Not because he's evil. He's protecting himself, or possibly you."

Estrada slouched to the ground and leaned back against the soft mottled skin of the old cedar. He was exhausted but knew there'd be no sleeping—not until he found Lucy. And until he'd sorted Michael, he had no idea where to begin looking. "I've never done anything like soul retrieval. I wouldn't know where to begin."

"I do, and I can guide you." Dubh hunkered down cross-legged on a large flat rock. Pulling a penknife from the pocket of his leather kilt, he began picking away at the wood.

Estrada watched with interest. "You're a shaman, Magus Dubh?" Primrose had once said, Dubh had powers and didn't always use them for good. His father was Sidhe, which made the wee man half-faerie.

"Aye, and so are you, mate. I know you've traveled in the faerie realm and I've felt your power. Last summer, I watched you conjure the old Celtic gods."

Estrada remembered the shock and pleasure he'd felt at meeting the Oak King and Cernunnos by the Ballymeanoch Stones in Scotland. Dubh spoke the truth. Estrada *had* journeyed in other realms, and once his spirit had shifted into the body of a raven. In meditation, he could still conjure that sense of flying, wings outstretched and buoyed by the winds. Anything was possible.

"Druids call the Underworld *Annwn*, but you can call it anything you fancy. If your Michael's anywhere, that's where he'll be." Slivers of cedar sailed through the air as Dubh whittled away.

"An-oo-win," Estrada said, slowly pronouncing every syllable. "Is this *Annwn* a mythical place or . . . " He shrugged, then interlaced his fingers atop his head in a vague effort to control his spinning mind. Too much had happened tonight. Lucy kidnapped. Michael catatonic. Nigel, in hospital with broken legs and a concussion. Nora Barnes missing. And Ruby Carvello dead—with puncture wounds in her neck. If you drew it on a police wall, the arrows all pointed to Michael.

"There are countless levels of consciousness beyond this linear time and space. A shaman leaves this ordinary state and enters an altered state. I know you've done it before. It's the place where magic happens."

Estrada didn't remember his time with Primrose in Faerie, but knew he'd been there. His body had lain for days in her cottage in Ireland, while they played in the other realm. And he'd seen her again that day in Taynish when he'd gone searching for the Oak King's gift. Was he in an altered state that day too? It seemed, Dubh's transfusion of faerie blood had saved his life and opened portals.

"How would I . . . ?" He shook his tight shoulders, relieved to be thinking of something positive he could do. The aimless waiting made him feel impotent.

"I can lead you into a trance and talk you through it," Dubh said rather casually. "You'll need a crystal to catch Michael's soul. Sometimes a soul can be fragmented. His could be whole or in shards."

"Shards? Michael's soul could be in shards?"

Dubh looked up from his work. "Ach aye. Life has a way of busting us asunder and leaving us fractured." As he said this, he flipped a hefty chunk of wood into the air.

The scent of the splintered cedar conjured memories of sweats. Estrada leaned back into the mother tree and took a deep breath.

"And Michael must want to return. You can't force him."

"He's afraid. That's why he's keeping secrets."

Dubh stopped carving and glanced up, his blue eyes bright and wizened. "Secrets you must crack for the sake of your bairn."

"Yes," Estrada said, grasping his jaw to soothe the clenched muscles. "So, I need a crystal. What else?" For Lucy, he'd do whatever it took. Kill or be killed.

"A drum?"

"Daphne has a drum. She'll help us." Though Daphne was Sensara's best friend, she'd always been Estrada's champion, and he knew he could count on her for anything.

"Brilliant. Then I can accompany you," Dubh said.

"What about Sensara?"

"I think you must keep Sensara and Michael in separate corners. At least for now. She can't abide your liaison with him."

"You noticed." Estrada grimaced. He'd felt the tension, of course, but never voiced it. If they could all live together with Lucy, life would be perfect. Estrada and Michael enjoyed a liberal lifestyle that allowed for sexual freedom, and there was no jealousy between the two men. They'd often shared partners over the years. So, Michael accepted Estrada's devotion to his new family. But Sensara. She believed in monogamy and would never agree to share him. That's what tore them apart before.

"We'll need privacy," Dubh said, bringing Estrada back to the task at hand.

"Let's use the glade where we celebrated Lughnasadh. I'll talk to Daphne about crystals and drums."

"Aye, sure. That'll do."

"And we need to do it now. I don't know how Sara will get through the night knowing that Lucy is out there alone with—"

"We'll get these fucks," growled Dubh.

Estrada leaned up on his elbows to see what Dubh was carving in the cedar. "Is that a killer whale?"

"Aye. I saw a small pod once off the Isle of Mull. I was just a wean, but I never forgot them. This one's for your bairn when she comes home."

Estrada smiled. Magus Dubh had a magician's touch, a shaman's power, and a counselor's charm. For a moment they sat quiet in the calm of the darkling trees. Then Estrada's thoughts drifted back to Michael and what they were about to do. "What about Michael? Doesn't *he* have to be with us on this journey?"

Dubh thought, then shook his head. "Nah. If your mate's willing to return, you'll catch his soul in the crystal, and as long as it remains safe, he will be too."

"And, what about us? If something happens there? If we get killed?"

Dubh scratched his beard. "I don't know, mate. It's never come up before. But I suppose if we died in the Underworld we might get caught up like Michael."

Estrada broke out in goose bumps when he remembered his death sleep in Ireland. Who would rescue Lucy if he slid into a coma?

As if reading his thoughts, Dubh sniffed and wrinkled his lips. "Best not to test that theory."

UNDERWORLD

Nora Barnes awoke with a raging headache. Opening her eyes, she found herself prostrate atop a large bed that seemed to be shifting from side to side. Perhaps that explained the nausea.

Leaning up on her elbows, she glanced around. The bed took up much of the space in the small triangular room. Cupboards were built into wood-paneled walls. It took several seconds before she realized she was in a stateroom in the bow of a boat. Closed portholes and hatches along the ceiling cast dappled light across the ocher quilt beneath her. She listened for the voices of her captors. Nothing. Just the sound of water lapping against the hull.

Hazy memories played through her mind. Zachary had woken her with his crying. Joe was face-up and snoring beside her. That man could sleep through an earthquake. She had glanced at the clock and noted it was not quite two.

When she'd opened the door to Zachary's room, the first thing she saw was an immense raven perched on the railing of his crib. "Get out! Get out!" she shouted, with flailing arms. Still, it clung to the rail until she grasped a pillow and hurled it. Then, rather than leaving, the bloody thing alighted on the ledge of the open window. Turning to Zachary, she ran her hands over his small firm body. What was it doing to him? Was he hurt?

Then, she heard a whooshing sound behind her, a shattering exhalation. When she turned, a man's hand clenched her neck. Squeezing tighter and tighter, he lifted her off the ground. She couldn't scream. Couldn't breathe. He stared into her eyes and grinned. He was going to kill them both. This . . . this . . . *demon raven*.

But he *had* stopped. He must have. Because she wasn't dead. The realization did nothing to quell her anxiety. Nora clutched her head to stop its pounding and the man's face reappeared in her mind. She would never forget it, or the sinister grin he wore as he strangled her. She'd met killers through her legal work and knew this was a man who enjoyed killing. Black dreadlocks framed his face like a hood, a black teardrop tattooed on the dark skin beneath each of his blood-red eyes. And the smell. She'd found a dead rat once in an alley—

Nora retched and caught the vomit in her palm, then stumbled through an open doorway into a bathroom. After rinsing her hands in the sink, she fell to her knees in front of the toilet and emptied the rest of her churning gut. She gulped some water to slake her thirst, then staggered back to the bed. How would anyone ever find her? And Zachary? What had that monster done with her baby? A sharp pain like the stab of a knife cut through her chest. Gasping, she curled up and rocked herself through the tears.

Then she heard it. The wail of a child. Milk shot from her breasts and two wet patches appeared on her white cotton nightgown. "Zachary!" Was *he* here too? Locked in another room? The cry came from the other side of the door. And then it opened.

A young man stood in the doorway holding a bundle in his arms.

"Zachary!"

"I trust you are well, *Señora*," he said, with a thick Spanish accent.

The hairs on Nora's arms stood straight up with a shiver. This was a different man. A boy, really. Much younger, almost a child himself—pale-skinned and raven-haired.

"Give him to me," she said, and leaping from the bed, she charged across the room.

"Of course, *Señora*." The boy handed her the bundle of blankets.

"Zachary." Nora clutched the warm bundle to her chest. Her breasts ached with his crying. He needed feeding and she needed to nurse. "Get out," she commanded.

The boy nodded and turned, then retrieved a bag from outside, set it on the floor, and shut the door.

But Zachary's cry sounded strange. If there was one thing a mother knew, it was the cry of her own child. Perhaps, it was just shock. Nora prayed that was all. If they had injured him in any way, she would kill them. Laying him on the bed, she pulled back the covers.

She gasped. It was a girl! A girl several months older than Zachary. Dressed in a white onesie etched in yellow butterflies, she was dark-haired and beautiful but—

"This is *not* my child," Nora yelled. Turning, she ran to the door and jiggled the handle. Locked. She banged on it, furious. "Where is he? Where's my baby?" Were there others? Had they kidnapped other mothers and babies and somehow mixed them up. "You've made a mistake!"

The child rolled off the bed and fell on the carpeted floor with a gentle thud. She laid quietly for a second, and then her face contorted, and she began to wail.

"Oh my God." Scooping the poor thing up in her arms, Nora bounced her gently against her chest. Immediately, her milk let down.

The child stopped crying, grasped her breast with a tiny hand and lowered her head. She was hungry, poor wee thing, and wanted to nurse.

"Alright. Alright. This may help us both."

When Nora lay down on the bed and unbuttoned her nightgown, the child immediately clamped down on her nipple and suckled. The release of oxytocin calmed the distraught woman.

"There now. Don't be afraid, sweetheart. I'm here, and we'll figure this out together."

"You chose well, Chef." Zion smirked.

Leopold glanced at him, then cast off the bowline. He felt heartsick. He was a criminal. There was no denying it. He'd stood by and watched Zion break a man's legs, kick him in the head, and then murder a woman. He'd waited while Zion nearly choked the life out of Nora Barnes—a woman he respected and admired—then, he'd helped carry her here, and watched the bastard lock her up in the stateroom. The only thing he'd objected to was Zion's desire to drink her blood. He was as guilty as these other two fiends.

"Señora Barnes is already nursing the child," Eliseo said. "El Padrino will be pleased."

Pleased enough to set me free? thought Leopold. That was the deal. *Help me with this one thing, Leopold Blosch, and I will give you your freedom.*

Eliseo shifted, and the boat moved slowly forward.

Leopold stood stiffly and ground his fingernails into his palms. It took everything he had not to jump off the side and make a run for it while his two co-conspirators were busy undocking and clearing the harbor. But they would come after him. And they were older and stronger, could shift from raven to vampire in a second. They'd bind him, and deliver him to Diego, and he'd never be free. Leopold had seen others at Le Chateau de Vampire. Others, who'd been made sons against their will. Others, who'd not been given the opportunity to barter for their freedom.

"How did you know the woman would care for the child?" Eliseo asked.

"I know her," Leopold muttered. Joe and Nora Barnes were regulars at Ecos, Leopold's vegetarian bistro in Vancouver. They hadn't come as often since Zachary had been born, but before that, they frequented Ecos three or four times a month. They were both lawyers, and big tippers, though Nora did mostly pro-bono work on the Downtown Eastside. She saved women from violent pimps and got them into treatment programs. Leopold had nothing but respect for her. "Nora will cooperate and then they can both go home."

Zion laughed, a deep belly laugh that sent shivers running up Leopold's arms. "You as fresh as your food, Leopold Blosch."

"What do you mean?"

"Don't tease him, Zion." Eliseo cast the tattooed man a look that silenced his sniggers.

Zion swaggered over to the bar, popped the cork from a bottle of red wine and stretched out on the white leather sofa to guzzle.

"Ignore that scrap of offal. Zion worked as a slave in the California mines until El Padrino rescued him and made him one of us. He wants everyone to suffer as he has."

"When was that?"

"After the Gold Rush. Eighteen fifty."

Leopold tried to comprehend. He didn't want to become like Zion. Once the man was a slave to gold, now he was a slave to blood. What would it be like to live with this bloodlust for a century and a half? Surely, that would turn any man into a monster.

"And you? Were *you* with him then?" Zion had said that Eliseo was the original Salvador. He'd been with Don Diego since the beginning and looked identical to the son the vampire had lost at sea—the son he couldn't live without and began to clone. How many young men had Diego turned into Salvadors in his quest to replicate his drowned son? How many fought it like he did?

Eliseo nodded. "I was nothing until El Padrino sired me. An orphaned beggar living on the streets of Lima."

And now you're a thief and a killer, Leopold thought. "When? How long?" he asked.

"Why does it matter?"

"Zion keeps telling me I'm young and I'll change. But, you're not like him, Eliseo. I need to know there's a chance I won't become like *him*."

"For two hundred and twenty years I have traveled with El Padrino." This was almost too much to comprehend. Though old, Eliseo had somehow kept an innocence despite centuries of hunting humans for food.

"Tell me what will happen to Nora and the child."

Eliseo pushed down on the throttle and continued to stare out the window as the boat lurched forward. "Don't trouble yourself. El Padrino will see to them."

Zion appeared beside him. "Oh yes, Chef. He'll see to them." He tipped the bottle and took a long swig, then wiped his mouth with the back of his hand. "Just like he saw to us . . . and you."

―※―

Late afternoon shadows stalked across the glade as Estrada and Dubh settled down upon the earth. They laid side by side as they had a year before at the Glasgow Royal Infirmary—the night Estrada offered his blood to save the wee man's life. Dubh had been gutted by an assailant and was dying because the hospital couldn't find a blood match. The man had cut Estrada with the same knife he used to cut Dubh, so the magician carried some of Dubh's fey blood in his veins.

The bond they forged that night had never disappeared. The two men shared memories and, at times, each other's thoughts. Estrada hoped this would help them now as they traveled through a realm he'd never experienced.

Daphne and Raine were seated at either end of the consecrated circle on a north-south axis. Holding their frame drums, they pounded out a double pulse like the pumping of a heart. As Estrada breathed deeply, he felt himself sinking deeper into the earth with each beat.

When the drumming stopped abruptly, Estrada flinched and opened his eyes.

Sensara stood above him in the glade, eyes flashing, hair wild, chest heaving from the run. "Did you think I wouldn't know? Lucy is *my* daughter. I'm coming. Wherever the hell you're going."

Estrada and Dubh sat up and glanced at each other.

"Sara—" Estrada began.

"Do no harm. I know that and I won't. But I've got to know the truth." She stood rigid as a staff, one small muscle in her jaw pulsing.

"If *you're* there Michael will be frightened." Estrada feared Sensara's wrath though he'd never admit it aloud. "He might refuse—"

"I must agree," Dubh said. "We cannot enter the Underworld with rampant emotions—especially anger. Our only mission is to find Michael Stryker and bring him back."

Sensara took a deep breath in and exhaled what would have been fire had she been a dragon, and not a witch.

"Please Sara. Stay and be part of the circle but let Dubh and I do this alone."

"Why don't you sit in the east and play the rattle?" asked Daphne.

Listen to her, thought Estrada. Please. Daphne is always the voice of reason.

The women exchanged glances. Sensara held her ground and they all breathed in the silence. "Where is it?" she asked, at last.

Estrada leaned back on one elbow as the tension drained from his muscles.

"Here." Daphne reached into her bag and pulled out a dried gourd packed with seeds. "We'll be stronger together."

"Fine." Standing at the edge of the circle closest to Estrada, Sensara leaned down and whispered. "You should have told me. I'm her *mother*."

"And *I'm* her father. You know how much I love her. Trust me. I promise, I will find her and bring her home. But first, I must help Michael. It's the only way we'll know what's going on. Will you let me?"

Holding her hand over her heart, Sensara took a deep breath. "I broke the space," she said to everyone. "I apologise."

Estrada watched her walk around the outside of the glade murmuring prayers of protection.

When Sensara returned, she sat on the ground in the east quadrant and glanced first at Daphne, and then at Raine. "The circle is cast. We are between the worlds," she said.

Sensara was the High Priestess of Hollystone Coven. She could do things Estrada had never seen anyone do. He must trust her, and she must trust him. They had no choice.

When Estrada laid back against the earth and closed his eyes, he sensed the energy had shifted. Sensara's power mingled with the others' and amplified it. Dubh's arm rested beside his, so close he could feel its heat. The drums and rattle created a rhythmic pulse that signaled the beginning. He took a deep breath and as he sighed it out, felt his body sink into the spongy moss.

"We travel to the Underworld to search for the soul of Michael Stryker and return it to his body," Dubh said. "We travel with respect for the creator and all creation. And we seek to do no harm."

Estrada could feel the amethyst crystal throb against his upturned palm. It was alive, the quartz vibrant with energy. Daphne said amethyst was a stone that aided addiction and recovery. In Michael's current state, it could be nothing but beneficial.

Muscle and bone melt into the spongy moss as Estrada slips into a trance. He knows he must leave his body lying like a heap of clay on the earth, so his spirit can journey into the Underworld. He is not afraid. Abandoning the physical world, his liberated soul soars as light and unfettered as dust.

Dubh is still speaking with his Scottish lilt, but his voice has faded to a whisper. Soothing and reassuring, Estrada clings to it.

"We stand in the center of an oak glade. The oak is the druid tree, portal to other worlds. The trees here are ancient. For thousands of years they've stood in this place. Their roots reach into the center of the earth. Their branches stretch into blue cloudless climes. Their breath mingles with our own and welcomes us. Their green leaves rustle in the wind. We acknowledge them with quiet reverence and greeting."

When Dubh pauses, Estrada hears crackling leaves. Scuttling rodents. The piercing cry of an eagle overhead. Twittering songbirds in the undergrowth. Even the creeping of insects and the soft beat of butterfly wings whisper through his mind.

"The glade expands to reveal a rocky stream. You hear the dance of water over stone, smell the scent of dampened earth and fecund moss. Built across the stream is an ancient stone bridge. Curving like a crescent moon above the water, its sides are swathed in verdant mosses."

Estrada opens his spirit eyes to a pastoral scene as something from a Wordsworth poem appears before him.

"Walk to the bridge," directs Dubh. "Touch its cool smooth surface with your palm."

Estrada glances down at his feet. They're bare and carve imprints in the mossy carpet.

"Beside the bridge, you find a coarse linen sack. Stuff your worries in the sack. Whatever concerns you, whatever is troubling you, must dissipate before you cross into the Underworld. Be quick. There's no need to name each one or dwell on them."

Estrada grasps the sack and stretches its mouth wide with both hands.

"Hastily now, draw everything negative from your mind. Toss it over the side of the bridge and release it to the spirits of the stream."

Estrada leans toward the sack, cups his hands around his mouth, and blows into it. Fear and anger fly from him. He's surprised by the weight of it. After drawing the string tightly, he knots it so nothing can escape, then hurls it skyward and watches it soar. The sack arcs and descends, then splashes into the stream and sinks. As the water swirls in darkened eddies, Estrada feels buoyant as if floating in the sea.

"Follow the path across the bridge. At the edge of the glade, one tree beckons. It is most ancient and wise."

Crann Bethadh, thinks Estrada, remembering Lucy's charm, and her sweet voice. *Ba-ha.* Lucy is the best thing that's ever happened to him. His child. His progeny. *Daddy's Lucita.* Bound by blood and soul. His heart swells with such love, he forgets everything but her. Her straight black pigtails wrapped in pink ribbons. The glow of her chubby cheeks.

Dubh's voice draws him back, and Estrada struggles to let the memory go. "Walk to the tree and place your hand against its fine old bark. When you push against the side of the tree, a crack appears and a door opens—a door large enough for you to pass through."

The tree throbs against his palm, its crevassed bark a panoply of time. Inside it's dark, but as his eyes adjust, Estrada can see a spiral staircase leading both up and down. It's like Yeats' gyre, he thinks, and the words of the poem play through his mind. *"Turning and turning in the widening gyre, the falcon cannot hear the falconer. Things fall apart. The center cannot hold."* But hold it must. His daughter and his lover—two of the people Estrada loves most in the world—have been wrenched from him. He can't rest until he brings them both safely home.

"Walk down," Dubh says.

Estrada obeys. Each footfall is a descent into darkness, and then a torch flares in the smooth golden wood of the tree. Light. A sign of hope and promise. Inspired, he quickens his pace, skipping down the spiral stairs, sinking deeper into the tree where the rich wood scent fills his senses. At last, he comes to a circular door. Shoves it open and steps out.

"Michael? Where are you, Michael?"

Estrada runs barefoot across the cold damp sand until he meets a river. It's not very wide, he decides. Perhaps half a mile. Above, the sky is a violet haze studded with stars, the full orb of the moon reflecting in the dark water. In the distance, he sees the river cascading from a snow-capped mountain. Swirling over jagged rocks, it forms a natural barrier across the land. But here, the water is still.

Tiny ripples erupt, created by the lips of fish. A sudden splash here, a metallic flash there, reveals the presence of life beneath. But what life lives in the Underworld? Lovecraft's Dagon? Or worse? Dare he try to swim across? There's no bridge.

On the distant shore, Estrada sees the ashen smoke of a campfire uprising in the hills.

Michael?

Estrada knows this is where he must go.

"I am here for Michael Stryker," he says aloud. "Let me pass."

He waits, hoping by some miracle the waters will part as they did for the Israelites. But he's no Moses. And so, he wanders downstream wondering how deep this river is, how fast and deadly the current. Every few minutes, he glances up at the stream of smoke, convinced Michael is there, curled into its warmth.

He decides to swim across and walks toward a sandy bank where he can wade in. But his feet feel suddenly weighted. Trudging of their own accord, they catch the rippling edge, but won't let him venture any deeper. Is this a sign? Some form of protection?

At last, he arrives at the edge of a precipice where the land ends abruptly. Beside him, the river surges over the cliff, thundering into a huge gully over one hundred feet below. As Estrada stares into the swirling darkness, the spray from the waterfall moistens his skin. A ripple through his gut draws him back, and he stands stiffly, not knowing which way to turn. His feet have dragged him here, and yet, there's still no way to cross the water.

Where's Dubh? He remembers Dubh said they would journey together, but Estrada hasn't heard his voice since entering this realm.

When the bird appears on the horizon, Estrada thinks it's a common raven like those he saw in the trees on the day of Lucy's birthday party.

Corvus Corax. But as the creature draws nearer, he realizes it's six times the size of any raven he's ever seen. It's as if he's dropped a million years through time. A pterosaur in this primeval landscape, it flies toward him. He sucks in a quick breath and steps back.

Massive wings rise and fall with muscular force. Talons poised beneath a fan of inky tail-feathers. It's coming straight at him. His heart is pounding, adrenalin spiking. Etched in moonlight, the creature glows iridescent, its thick hooked beak clamped tight in focused flight. Ducking behind a boulder, Estrada crouches and prays it will pass.

It crosses overhead and circles out over the river, flying in the direction from which he's come. When Estrada exhales, he realizes he's been holding his breath. Relief spreads through his tense muscles as he squats and leans back against the boulder. And then, behind him—a throaty cackle, a whoosh of hurricane wings, and the creature is on him. Meaty thighs stretch and talons skim his forehead, slash and burn.

Blood dripping in his eyes, Estrada leaps off the cliff. Through the air, arms flailing, and then in the final second, he wraps his forearms around his shins, takes a deep breath and breaks the surface like a cannon ball. The force of it shoots him straight to the bottom where his feet collide with pebbled ground. Knees still bent; he uses the power of the impact to springboard up through the frigid water. Arms wrenching, he holds his breath and fights his way to the surface. Bursts through, gasping and treading water as he searches for the creature. It's nowhere he can see. The current from the waterfall carries him downstream and into the center of the pool.

Find Michael. I must find Michael. If strange creatures pepper this landscape, Michael could be in danger.

He swims to the far side, in the direction of the smoke, the place from which the bird first appeared. When he crawls out at last and collapses on the sandy beach, his heart is beating like a bellows, pumping blood from the slash across his forehead. It drizzles down his eye, his cheek, and into his mouth. Copper and salt. He tugs off his T-shirt and rips it into strips. Kneeling over the water, he washes out the wound, and then ties the bandage tightly around his head.

The forest here is a thick mass of shrubbery, so Estrada lopes along the riverbank until he comes to the waterfall. The moonlight creates a rainbow haze in the spray. Which way?

Confounded, he sits on a boulder, takes a breath, and waits for inspiration.

A howl startles him and he turns. A massive wolf stands at the edge of the forest. The size of a pony, it's pure white with streaks of gray and black around its muzzle and shoulders. It stretches its neck and howls again, the high-pitched cry reverberating in the enclosed gully.

Is it friend or foe? Estrada picks up a sharp rock and stands poised to fight.

The wolf stares with eyes glowing black as obsidian.

Estrada returns the stare and feels nothing but kinship. *Trust your allies*.

"Are you here to help me?" Estrada asks. Opening his hand, he lets the rock fall.

The wolf turns and disappears into a dark rift in the forest wall and Estrada follows. A thin, but well-worn game trail meanders around boulders and through switchbacks up into the hills. The farther he gets from the river, the stronger the scent of wood smoke becomes. Now, his gut quivers and he's certain Michael is there.

Estrada is panting and sweating by the time he encounters the shallow stream. It's so warm his hair's drying in the smoky breeze. His mouth is parched and he can barely swallow. Kneeling, he cups the spring water in his hands and drinks. On the far shore he spies imprints of the wolf's enormous paws in the sand. Wading into the water, he crosses and examines the tracks. They're bigger than his outstretched hand and sink several inches in the sand. As he follows the flash of white through the trees, he hopes he's right about this wolf. This could be a trap.

Estrada hears Michael before he sees him. He's fighting with someone and crying. Estrada draws closer, hides in the bushes and watches, though his heart aches for his friend.

Michael is leaning against the ruin of a stone hearth where the remains of a fire smolder. A pale naked man grasps his right shoulder and holds him firm. Estrada sees terror in Michael's face—green eyes wide, jaws clamped tight.

Damp black hair streams down the man's back. His fingers are leathered like gloves. Estrada sizes him up as if he were a UFC opponent. His back and shoulder muscles are well-defined, his calves bulging. The man is short, but uncommonly strong. Wiry. Welterweight.

Estrada is taller and heavier, a streetfighter. He can best this bastard. He takes a breath, flexes his muscles, and feels the blood surge. He's about to lunge when—

"Did you love him?" the man asks. With his free hand, he gestures like a conductor.

Michael turns away, gags and spits.

Who? Estrada wonders. Who are they talking about? He doesn't know why he's waiting to hear Michael's answer. He feels like a voyeur yet is hesitant to interrupt this intimate moment. Perhaps the truth lies in this conversation. And Lucy's life hinges on the truth.

"No," Michael says at last.

"I knew," the man says. "I knew you didn't love him." This confession elicits rage. As he squeezes Michael's bicep, his fingers sprout claws. Like black crescent moons, they encircle Michael's thin arm. The skin splits and blood drips down.

The sharp crack of splintered bone is like a spur in Estrada's own arm. Pushing back the bushes with both hands, he leaps into the glade.

The man turns with a half-grin and flashes Estrada a glance from the corner of his eye. "At last," he says. "I've been waiting." His pecs are as developed as his biceps, his cock stiff. Running the claws of his free hand beneath his nose, he sniffs, and then licks. "Ah, I could not wash it off. The taste of your blood excites me too much, Estrada." Rolling the r, he emphasizes his Spanish accent.

Estrada's stomach clenches as his mouth fills with saliva. He gathers it up and spits at the man's feet. How is *his* blood on this man's claw? He touches his forehead where the bird cut him, and flinches. Is this the flying creature?

The man grins seductively, then tastes the blood again and licks his lips. "We shall have a fine time together."

"Not in your life."

"No. In my death . . . and yours."

Magus Dubh appears suddenly beside Estrada. He's holding a wooden staff in his right hand. Without a word, Dubh hurls it. In midair, the staff transforms into a gold and brown boa constrictor and coils itself around the man's neck.

Grasping the snake behind the head, the man stretches it with both hands and sinks his teeth into its scaly flesh. He shakes his head like a terrier and rips the beating heart from the reptile. His teeth are razor-edged. When he spits it out, the snake shivers and goes limp. The man unwraps it from his neck and hurls its corpse back at Dubh. As it hits the ground the snake changes back into a staff, though a piece is missing. The man draws back his lips in a snarl and Estrada sees fangs amidst the blood.

He remembers the marks on Ruby's neck and shudders. "Fuck me. Is he—"

"Aye," Dubh says. "He's Vampire."

"A snake? So cliché. Surely you can do better than that, pagan priest."

Dubh picks up the staff and nods, then recites an incantation in Gaelic and the staff bursts into flame. "Wheesht!" Dubh shouts and hurls the flaming torch at the vampire's head.

When the fire meets his flesh, the vampire bursts into flame. Screaming, he dives into the stream. When he emerges, his skin is blistered, his cock flaccid.

What would have happened had there been no water? Is he combustible?

Enraged, the vampire backhands Michael and sends him careening across the glade.

"Leave him alone," Estrada says, and leaps. His bare foot connects with the creature's femur and he hears it crack.

Taken by surprise, the vampire falls on his ass, then glances up, and laughs.

A knife hand strike across the neck to smash the vagus nerve, and a torrent of raging punches fly from Estrada's fists. *Michael. Lucy. Ruby. Nigel. Nora.*

The vampire is on his knees, his mouth level with Estrada's crotch. His flesh is pulp, his smile lurid.

"You can't charm me, you motherfucker." Estrada growls, and raises his fist to strike again.

Lifting a corner of his lip, the vampire snarls.

"Estrada!"

Hearing his name, Estrada casts a glance at Dubh.

"You can't kill him like that."

The vampire cackles and blood splatters over Estrada's belly.

"Decapitate." Hissing, Dubh tosses him the staff.

As it touches his hand, it turns into a silver dagger. Estrada grasps the vampire's hair in his left hand and brings the blade down against the pale neck. He will saw the fucking head off, if that's what it takes.

But in that moment, the vampire shifts into its avian form and slips from his grasp. Perching on the ground, it stares at him through mesmerizing eyes, and suddenly Estrada can't move. A feathered comb juts straight out from the top of its head like an arrow. Though it has ravenish aspects, it's different. Enormous. Its feathered wings like indigo leather.

Estrada glances down at the scaly talons to break the creature's stare, then rocks backward as the curved beak opens to reveal a curling black tongue.

The creature hisses, and jagged toothy projections along the roof of its enormous mouth emit a stench of death. Raising both wings high, it pushes off with muscular legs, then uses the winged force of the downstroke to launch itself into the air.

Estrada's legs crumple from the adrenalin rush and he falls on his ass. "Jesus, Dubh, what the fuck was that?"

"Ask your mate." Dubh gestures to Michael, who slouches against a fallen log holding his broken bleeding arm.

Estrada crawls across the grass, slides down beside Michael, and hugs him to his chest. He listens to him whimper like a kicked puppy for a moment, and then gets antsy.

"Tell me about this fucking vampire. Why does he want to kill us?" He keeps his voice low and one arm tight around Michael's shoulder. He doesn't want to frighten him—still needs him to want to come home.

"I . . . I'm sorry." Michael shakes his head. "It's all my fault."

"Why?"

"He's angry." Michael raises his head. His puppy eyes are bursting with regret. "When you left last year, I took a lover. I was mad, and I missed you." He touches Estrada's cheek. "You always leave me."

So, this is my fucking fault? thinks Estrada, then swallows his words before he can say them aloud. "I'm with you, now." Leaning in, he kisses Michael. It's gentle and affectionate—a brush of tongue, a soft curving of lip over lip—and quite unlike most of their kisses.

Michael melts against him, his quickened breaths becoming audible.

"Trust me," Estrada says. "Tell me what happened. We can't have secrets between us."

Michael blinks slowly. "Christophe," he whispers, then pressing a fist to his lips, he mutters through it. "Christophe kidnapped me."

"Kidnapped?"

"I wanted to go home but Christophe wouldn't turn around. He took me to this place in the islands. He said it was the ultimate gift." Michael scoffs. "But he planned to give me to—"

"The vampire."

Michael nods. "I ran. Stole a boat." He bites his lip. "Christophe followed me."

Estrada doesn't care about some ex-lover. They've shared a host of lovers over the years and none of them mattered. Why should this one be any different?

"Does Christophe have Lucy?"

"No. He . . . No."

"Then . . . " Estrada's mind is reeling. He's afraid to ask but knows he must. "Does the vampire have Lucy?"

Michael tightens his lips as tears swamp his tired eyes. He nods.

Estrada gasps, crosses his arms across his chest and hangs on, feeling as if he's been speared by a steel rod. Squeezing his eyelids tight, he prays this is all a bad dream.

"I'm sorry, man. I didn't—"

"But why? Why take *Lucy*? What does he want with her?"

"Revenge."

Estrada's eyes widen, and he stares at Michael as the bolts click into place.

"He's the one who locked you in the coffin and tossed you in the sea," Estrada says, remembering his vision. The calligraphic *D* etched into the heart of the rose. Like the rose on Ruby's chest, in Nora's house, in Lucy's crib. "Holy fuck, man. What's his name?"

"Diego," Michael whispers. "Don Diego."

For a moment, words will not come. And then, a racket of cawing crows descends, breaking the spell. Estrada jumps up, bracing himself, searching for a weapon.

Across the glade, Magus Dubh raises one hand and shakes his head. The message is clear though his lips don't move. *No danger. They're just crows.* Like a bull terrier, Dubh is standing guard.

Estrada kneels in front of Michael. "Why didn't you tell me this last year when you came to Scotland? Or when we came home?"

"I couldn't." Michael's face tightens and tears seep from his eyes.

"Why? We've always shared everything." Estrada knows this is the crux of it. The secret too horrible to speak.

"Christophe was obsessed with me. When he thought I'd been lost in the storm, he gave up. He drowned."

Now the overheard conversation makes sense.

"Diego loved Christophe like a son, and so, he will avenge his death."

"By killing you."

"No. Not me." He touches Estrada's cheek. "Diego wants *you*. He wants to turn you into a vampire."

"But he doesn't even know me."

Michael covers his face with his hands. "Diego wants to take the only thing I love." He stares up into Estrada's burning eyes. "He wants you."

Feeling suddenly weak, Estrada slips down from his knees onto one hip and clasps Michael's hands in his. The two men have never talked of love, though now Michael has said it, Estrada knows it's always been there. This yearning beyond sex. This constant desire to touch, to talk, to be together at all costs.

"But how would Diego know a thing like that? We've never—"

"I told him," confesses Michael.

You told him but didn't tell me?

"Diego was killing me, and he said I'd never loved anyone but myself, and I . . . I said that wasn't true. I said I did love someone and I . . . I made a stupid mistake. I said your name."

Estrada catches Michael's face in his palms and draws their foreheads together. "You were scared so you told the truth. Faced with death what else can a man do?"

"Let him kill me."

"No." Estrada shakes his head. "Don't say that." His heart is breaking along with Michael's and he can't stand it. Not a man to easily share his feelings, Estrada fiddles with his hair and glances across the glade at Dubh, who sees his discomfort and ambles over to join them.

"So, why take Lucy?" Dubh asks, hunkering down beside Estrada.

"Diego is a father. His son died over two hundred years ago and, since then, he's been trying to replicate him by creating more sons. He calls them his Salvadors. His saviors."

A blade scrapes across Estrada's heart and he curls forward, pressing his arms against his chest. "Vampires. My baby is with vampires." Saying the words aloud stops his breath.

Michael bites his lip and nods. "He knows you'll come for her."

Estrada is afraid to ask the question but knows he must. "Will Diego hurt her?"

"I don't think so. At least—"

"At least?"

"Not *before* you arrive." Michael shrugs.

"Fuck man. What have you done?"

"I'm sorry." Squeezing his bloodshot eyes tightly closed, Michael turns away.

"We'll fight him together and we'll bring Lucy home."

Dubh stands and begins to pace, twirling the staff in the air like a baton. "Aye, lads. We know more about this fucker now than we did before."

Estrada has never seen anything like it—a snake, a torch, and a silver dagger. Then again, he's never traveled in the Underworld with a fey druid before.

"Is that why you—?"

"I wanted to know if we could kill the prick," Dubh says.

"And?"

"Ach, aye. He'll succumb. It won't be easy, but it can be done."

"Then, it's time we went home." Estrada looks at Michael and pulls the amethyst crystal from the pocket of his jeans.

Michael shivers. "I can't go back there. He killed Ruby and—"

"This fucker's got Lucy. Remember? And you're the only one who's been to his lair." Estrada touches Michael's cheek and runs his fingers across his lover's lips to reassure him. "We'll go there and rescue Lucy and destroy him together," he growls. "I need you, man. I need you beside me."

Michael trembles at his touch. "But how? How do we go back?"

Estrada looks at Dubh for direction. He's never brought a soul back from the Underworld.

"I think it's best if you lay down and close your eyes," says Dubh to Michael. "Think of a pleasant time when you and Estrada were alone together."

Michael smiles in his memory.

Dubh looks at Estrada. "Have you ever given anyone mouth to mouth resuscitation?"

"No, but I know how it's done."

"Well, instead of blowing air into Michael's mouth, you're going to suck his soul into your body, and then blow it into the crystal."

"Shotgun. The way we share smoke." The color is returning to Michael's cheeks.

"Aye. That'll do."

It's so quiet in the glade, Estrada can hear Michael's heart pounding in his chest. And then he realizes it's not his heart. It's the drums. The sound is coming from the earth and the sky, reverberating through plant cells, air molecules, and grains of sand. It's as if Nature has come vibrantly alive.

Estrada kneels on the ground beside Michael and closes his eyes. The amethyst crystal throbs in his right hand. He touches Michael's forehead and takes three deep breaths. On the fourth, he touches his lips to Michael's and inhales deeply. When he can take in no more, he holds the crystal to his mouth and slowly exhales. Opening his eyes, he watches a fine vapor sink into the amethyst, turning the purple shards silver. When Estrada looks down again, Michael has vanished.

"Is he—?"

"Aye."

Estrada stands and shoves the crystal deep into the pocket of his jeans. "He'll like traveling in my pocket," he says, needing some levity. "Will he remember?" Dubh shrugs and Estrada lets it go. "I hope we don't run into Diego again," he says. He's exhausted and can't imagine being trapped forever in the Underworld.

"I believe the vampire was a manifestation of Michael's mind."

"You mean, he's not real?"

"He's real enough," Dubh says.

Estrada considers this and touches his bloody forehead. A violent manifestation that took its pound of flesh. The slash stings and blood has matted in his hair.

"How do we get back?" asks Estrada.

"In the boat," says Dubh.

"Boat?"

"Aye, the currach I used to paddle here."

Estrada cocks his head. He doesn't understand.

"The skin boat. You ran right by it."

"What kind of skin?" asks Estrada.

"Ach, don't ask questions you don't want the answer to."

PETER FUCKING PAN

Back in the glade, Sensara greeted Estrada with a barrage of questions he couldn't answer. How could he tell her their child had been abducted by a shapeshifting vampire named Don Diego? Or that this creature locked Michael in a coffin and tossed him in the sea. *Or* that Diego intended to turn *him* into a vampire to avenge the death of a young man he considered his son? If Sensara knew the extent of it she'd be terrified, and she might take that terror out on Michael.

"We found him," was all Estrada said. "Tomorrow, if Michael is stable, I'll know more."

When Estrada touched his forehead, the hair on his arms shivered straight up. There was no wound and his flesh felt warm to the touch, but cold seared his brain as if an icicle lodged beneath his skin. If Diego had this effect on a man in the Underworld, what had he done to Michael in the material world? *Had* Diego infected him with a virus as Sensara believed?

Vampire myths evolved from humanity's fear of disease and decay. But what if the legends were true? What if a real vampire virus existed that could be transmitted like AIDS or rabies, blood to blood? Was Michael a vampire? No. He couldn't be. If he was, he'd be attacking people and drinking blood, not lying comatose in a hospital bed. It made no sense.

Daphne saw the panicked look in Estrada's eyes and invited him and Dubh back to the house for supper. Then, she convinced them to stay the night. Neither of them had slept in two days. Without food and sleep they couldn't do anyone any good. She cooked up a huge pot of cheesy pasta and broccoli, and they huddled around the table in strained silence, sipping wine, and dragging their forks across their plates.

A police detective arrived and asked if they'd heard anything. They were nearing the eighteen-hour mark, and it was odd there had been no communication from the kidnapper. The detective was convinced Lucy had been taken for either ransom or revenge. Why else would someone steal an infant from her crib? Whoever took her knew the house and had fooled the dog. It must be someone they were acquainted with. Was there anyone who might do such a thing? Anyone acting oddly? Another man who believed himself to be Lucy's father? Sensara laughed, and then cried.

Then the detective questioned Estrada. Just over a year and a half ago, another girl had been abducted from this very house. That was an odd coincidence. Could the two crimes be linked? Estrada reminded him that both of the men involved in Maggie Taylor's abduction had died in Ireland. Later, he remembered they'd never found Grace's body or evidence of his death. Maggie's mother still owned the house on Hawk's Claw Lane, and Remington Steele, the black lab, though he seemed thoroughly happy with his three foster mothers.

The dog was curled up now on the couch beside Dubh and both were fast asleep. Tomorrow morning, on his way to the hospital, Estrada would drop Dubh off at his flat on Commercial Drive. The poor man had been wearing the same faded brown leather kilt and ripe T-shirt since he got off the plane from Glasgow. Dubh had spotted a metaphysical bookshop on The Drive and wanted to research vampires. "None of us have tangled with these fuckers before," he'd said. "A little lore might just save our arses."

Estrada showered, and sat out on the back deck in his black trunks. The night air was cool against his skin, the waning moon patched with scattered cloud in a darkling sky. The wind had shifted and was now blowing the smoke eastward into the valley. He took a few deep breaths and tried to relax. Something was bothering him, besides the obvious, and he didn't know what it was. Though his eyes were bagged, his brain wouldn't shut down.

Another journey was coming. That was a given. Michael had been discovered by kayakers on an island far up the strait. Don Diego's lair had to be somewhere nearby. What had Michael called it? Le Chateau de Vampire? *The Castle of Vampires?* Surely, that was where this mad creature had taken Lucy. Estrada was counting on Michael to remember where it was and lead him there. That was the message in the roses. Diego may have murdered Ruby Carvello just to fuck with Michael, but what about Nora Barnes? What had become of her?

By one a.m. Estrada was so disheartened he crawled into Sensara's bed. He just needed to hold her. That was all. It was the first time he'd lain beside her since they'd conceived Lucy, and he missed her. The scent of her. The feel of her skin. He remembered their last night together in vivid detail. She'd seduced him in the hallway outside Michael's flat, was too desperate to care about condoms. Loved him when they went in and hated him when they came out. But, in that intimate moment, they'd created Lucy, and that was the best thing they'd ever done.

Cuddling close behind her, Estrada held Sensara's lithe body in the crook of his arm and didn't move even when it went numb. She'd cried herself to sleep and he dared not wake her, though hours passed in a turbulent tangle of thoughts meditation couldn't touch.

His sweet Lucita was the joy of his life. He prayed to the gods to keep her safe. If Diego was using her as a pawn, he wouldn't harm her; at least, until he got what he wanted. Moreover, if Diego understood what it was like to love and lose a child, he might just let her go. If he cared enough to avenge his son's death, he must have retained some spark of humanity. Despite the myth, this vampire appeared to possess a soul.

This is what Estrada told himself. This is what he must believe. Still his tears wet the pillow as he crushed it against his face to silence his grief. He visualized Lucy cradled in his arms and wrapped her in pink clouds of love and protective spells. *Lucita es bonita. My beautiful Lucita, I know who has taken you, and I'm coming for you.*

For a while, he dozed and dreamed. And then he flinched—not knowing why. Opening his eyes, he stared at the amethyst crystal on the bedside table. A faint pulsing glow emanated from it and Estrada reached out and touched the throbbing stone. Michael's spirit slumbered within. *He loves me and I love him. What if one or the other of us hadn't returned from the Underworld? What if Michael died never hearing those words? In the morning, I'll tell him. I'll put everything* right and we'll go and rescue Lucy. This thought gave Estrada some comfort and again he dozed.

When he awoke, morning was breaking and light edged the blinds in pale gray streaks. Sensara's back was wedged against his chest, her small bare feet tangled with his. He brushed his lips across her shoulder tenderly and sighed. Once his best friend, then his lover, now the mother of his child, an intimate bond connected them like a spider's thread. He needed to make love, to bury himself deep in her charms.

When she turned, and pressed against him, he stroked her hair. Then, catching her face in his palm, he kissed her, gently at first, and then with great need. As her soft mouth opened to accept him, he growled. In a world gone mad, love was the only way through.

When Estrada peered into Nigel's hospital room late the next morning, he was surprised to see a stranger there—a stranger wearing white leather loafers that matched his trousers and button-down shirt. The shoes were obvious because the man was leaning back in a chair with his feet propped up on the bed just a breath short of Nigel's cast—pretentious and vaguely threatening. The distinctive oils of Prada cologne eclipsed the scent of bleached hospital linens. When the man turned, Estrada saw his own face reflected in his mirrored aviator shades.

"Victor Carvello," he said, with a quick nod and disingenuous grin, then waited for Estrada to identify himself.

Estrada did not. Nor did he accept the proffered hand.

So, this was Victor Carvello—a man so terrifying, Michael had slipped into a catatonic state to avoid an encounter with him. Nigel and Victor had been friends many years ago, but some rift had left them estranged. Estrada had never met the man, who was something of an unspoken legend in the Stryker home. Even Ruby rarely saw her father.

Estrada glanced at Nigel, who slept soundly. "How long has he been out of surgery?"

Carvello shrugged. "I just arrived. Red eye from Vegas." Obviously, the man knew about his daughter's murder.

Estrada stared at Nigel, while Carvello stared at him, until the silence grew unbearable.

"I'm just waiting to see Michael," he said. "The nurse is with him."

"Better do it soon. I hear they're moving him to the psych ward. Too bad. I always liked that kid."

"Psych ward?"

Nigel stirred and opened his eyes. "Sandolino . . . " His voice was raspy, his gaze unfocused. He'd had surgery on his leg first thing that morning and was still recovering.

Estrada moved to the side of the bed. "Hey, how are you feeling, sir?"

"I've been better."

"I'll second that," Carvello said.

Nigel turned at the sound of Carvello's voice. "Victor. You're here."

"Well, I had to come, didn't I? Had to see the man who got my little girl killed." As Carvello kicked his feet off the bed and stood, Nigel blanched.

"Nigel is not to blame for Ruby's death." Moving closer, Estrada slipped off his black leather jacket to expose his tattooed arms and slung it over a vacant chair. All he knew about Carvello was that he was rich, connected, and feared. Was the man packing a gun?

"Don't get excited, Magicman. I'll take my revenge out on the killer, not the prick who's been fucking my only child for twenty years." Carvello smirked, took off his sunglasses, and stashed them in his pocket.

Estrada clenched his fists and glanced at Nigel, who shook his head. He didn't want trouble and could tolerate Carvello's crude scorn if that's what it took to appease him. Out of respect for the man he considered his father, Estrada could keep his cool—at least for the moment.

Both men were in their early sixties but Carvello looked about forty-four. Tanned and lean, with no inappropriate wrinkles and no gray hairs, he obviously employed cosmeticians, stylists, and surgeons along with his thugs. His amber eyes rimmed upwards like cat's eyes and were slightly crossed. It was his only flaw. Estrada's skin prickled. He knew Nigel could take care of himself but in his current condition, he feared leaving him alone with Carvello. As soon as he could, he'd call Club Pegasus and get a couple of the sentinels down here. Just in case.

"Nigel needs his rest," Estrada said, "and I—"

"*You* need to see your boyfriend before they lock him up and throw away the key."

"What?" asked Nigel, trying to pull himself up.

"They're probably just taking Michael for observation and a psych assessment," explained Estrada. "But, you're right. I do need to see him before they move him." He glared at Carvello until those cat's eyes flickered.

"I should be going too." Carvello was, at least, perceptive. Opening his wallet, he took out two business cards. "If anything happens, you call me first," he said, handing one to Estrada and flipping the other on Nigel's bedside table. "First. You got that?" He walked out the door, then popped his head back in. "If you don't, you'll wish you had."

Estrada paced up and down the polished hallway outside Michael's hospital room. He glanced at the time on his phone. 12:17 p.m. What was the nurse doing in there? Time was ticking by. He needed Michael to help him rescue Lucy. He needed Michael to keep him sane. Michael was his anchor and his refuge. He'd always been there. Free and open and supportive of whatever it was he needed. Now, Estrada realized just how much he'd taken him for granted. It wasn't until he'd heard Michael's confession in the Underworld, he'd even understood the complexity of their relationship. *Diego wants to take the only thing I love. You.*

Estrada had never thought about it before, but he spent much of his time performing on the road, so was always coming and going. *You always leave me*, Michael had said. And it was true. While Estrada was traveling, Michael was mired in Vancouver managing the club. Sure, he complained from time to time, but Estrada never listened. After all, they weren't a couple, just a couple of guys.

Now Estrada realized, the only time Michael had been away from Vancouver was to come and rescue *him*. And he'd done that twice in the past two years. First, he'd flown to Ireland when Estrada lay in a coma. Then he'd come to Scotland six months later when Estrada was lost in the Inner Hebrides. Michael was injured and traumatized after his experience on the coast, but still he'd come. Both times, Estrada had been riding the edge of death. But *that* was the extent of Michael's travel—except for his cruise up the coast with this Christophe character, who was now the cause of all their problems. Estrada couldn't blame Michael for wanting his own adventure.

Finally, the nurse walked out and padded down the hallway in her white runners, and Estrada hastened to Michael's side. He smelled vaguely of soap and mint and Estrada assumed the nurse had just sponged him down and cleaned his mouth. After moving Michael gently to the side of the bed, he brushed the hair back from his face. It was then he noticed the pink oval scar on Michael's neck. Of course, he'd seen it before and mentioned it. Michael had said he'd injured himself while running through the bush on the island. When he appeared in Scotland, his right arm and left hand were both in casts, his neck bandaged. After what he'd witnessed in the Underworld, Estrada now wondered what really happened out there on that island. Glancing at the scar, a chill ran through his body. It looked nothing like the fang marks on Ruby's neck; still, Estrada remembered the snake and the staff. Could this scar be a souvenir from Diego?

Michael's eyes moved beneath his lids. He was dreaming and it was time he awoke. Estrada kissed his forehead, and then, with moist hands, he pulled the crystal from his pocket and silently offered a prayer. If this didn't work, he didn't know what he'd do. Positioning the crystal at the crown chakra, just above Michael's head, Estrada whispered, "Come back, amigo. I need you." Closing his eyes, he took several focusing breaths, conjuring the beat of the frame drums and the rattling gourd in the tree-brushed glade. Then, after one deep breath and with all the energy he could muster, he blew gently and evenly on the crystal.

When Estrada opened his eyes, the crystal was glowing like a Himalayan salt lamp. He repeated the breath while imagining Michael's spirit floating like a fine mist into his body. A quick gasp, and then he stared in awe. Like a trail of dust motes in sunshine, Michael's soul settled into its earthly home. Except for Lucy's birth last summer, it was the most incredible thing he'd ever seen.

A few seconds later, Michael's eyelids riffled, and trembling, Estrada touched his cheek. "Hey amigo. You're home." Sliding into the bed, Estrada pulled him close and massaged his thin back and shoulders. Michael moaned. When he turned and lifted one corner of his lip in a soft grin, Estrada caught the back of his head and drew their mouths together in a sweet kiss. Sliding onto his back, Michael caught Estrada's face between his hands and the kiss deepened.

Rising on his elbow, Estrada moved over Michael's frail body and settled against him. "I thought I'd lost you," he whispered as their foreheads touched. "If you ever do that again, I'll fucking kill you. Don't you know how much I need you?"

"I can tell," said Michael, cheekily. "You could cut a diamond with *that*." His eyes were sunken and blue-bagged, but his pupils flickered for the first time in months. "But where are we?" Michael glanced around.

"VGH. But we're alone . . . enough. And you, my friend, are naked under this gown." After almost losing his lover, he needed to feel his flesh and forget everything else.

Michael growled when Estrada's hand strayed beneath the sheets. Covering Michael's lips with his own, Estrada closed his eyes and breathed into the warm, familiar mouth. Surely, this was love—this aching to crawl inside another man's skin and feel nothing but the pleasure his touch inspired. Estrada heard the chink of his zipper, felt Michael's hand offering freedom and release. Michael's lips gnashed against his neck, as flesh to flesh, their friction rose like fire.

Estrada too, felt this need to devour. To pierce and to possess. *I love you*, he thought, then whispered with ragged breath, "I need you, man. I need you now."

"Could you possibly wait until he's released?"

They both looked up panting into the tight-lipped face of a nurse.

"You're lying on the call bell," she said. "I'll just go and fetch the doctor, shall I?"

"Granddad?" Michael's voice was faint, almost a whisper. He stood beside his grandfather's hospital bed and stared at an old man. This was the first time Michael had seen his grandfather since the attacks and he seemed to have aged overnight. Nigel's eyes were sunken. His lips dry and chapped. His skin sallow against the pale blue sheets. Bits of adhesive and needle marks marred the backs of his hands near the bulging veins. He was still recovering from surgery and the doctor wanted to monitor his head injury, but in a day or two, he could go home.

Beatrice—Michael had called his grandmother Beatrice since he hit his teen years—was on her way back from London. "The old battle axe" was a term Nigel frequently applied to his wife, and he wore the scars to back up his claim. How they'd stayed together all this time was a mystery to Michael. Perhaps, Beatrice was coming home to finally end it. How else could she react? Ruby Carvello had been murdered on their doorstep after spending the night in bed with her husband.

"Granddad," Michael said again, a little louder. Still, his voice wavered. Truthfully, he didn't want to awaken his grandfather. Nigel hadn't only done battle with a monster; he'd lost the love of his life. And, it was all Michael's fault. Once Nigel awoke, the noose hanging around Michael's neck would tighten. He'd see the pain in his grandfather's eyes and know he put it there.

Michael glanced nervously at Estrada, who stood at the end of the bed. "Tell Nigel what happened," Estrada had said. "He has friends with yachts. He can help us save Lucy." But how do you tell your grandfather his girlfriend was murdered by a vampire because of something you did? Would Nigel even believe him? Or would he think he was crazy?

"Help me," Michael mouthed.

Estrada was suddenly beside him, his familiar scent a balm. Exhaling, Michael touched his lover's cheek and kissed him lightly on the lips. He'd need to be more careful. His kisses had left marks on Estrada's neck. He'd almost drawn blood.

TO RENDER A RAVEN 71

"Nigel," said Estrada, and laying his hand on the man's shoulder, gave him a little nudge.

Nigel's eyelids fluttered, and then his blue eyes opened and he blinked several times.

"Hey. There you are," Estrada said.

"We're sorry to wake you, Granddad, but we need your help."

Hearing his voice, the old man focused on Michael's face. He moved his lips and tried to swallow, cleared his throat, and grimaced.

"Give him a minute." Estrada crossed to the other side of the bed, poured a glass of water from the pitcher on the bedside table, and held the straw to Nigel's mouth. "Take a sip, sir. Throat hurts like a bitch, doesn't it?"

Nigel sipped and nodded. "Thank you, Sandolino." His voice was raspy, his throat still bruised by surgical tubes.

Nigel was the only person who called Estrada by his first name, which Michael thought was funny. Even funnier was how Estrada called his grandfather "sir" like he was some professor in a prep school. But they both seemed comfortable with it.

"How are you, Granddad?" Michael asked, grasping his warm dry hand.

"I'll survive. But you two . . . " He shook his head. "What's wrong? It's about Ruby, isn't it?"

Michael took a deep breath and sighed. "Yes, and about the people who killed her."

"Do you know who did it?"

"We have some leads," Estrada said.

"These *people*. They also abducted Estrada's daughter."

"Lucy? Lucy's been abducted?" Nigel's eyes widened as he digested this new information. "But, she's just a baby."

"Yes. They took her last night," Michael said.

"My God. Did they contact you?"

"In a way," Estrada said. "They left red roses. One with Ruby, one in Lucy's crib, and another on Nora Barnes' windowsill."

"Nora Barnes?"

She's likely fodder, thought Michael. Christophe had said, *that* was the only use Diego had for women. "She's missing too," he said. "We don't know why."

"She must have seen them. Zachary's window faces Michael's doorway and that's where they left the rose."

"But roses? Why leaves roses?" Nigel shook his head.

All they were doing was making the poor man more confused. They had to tell him. Everything. As much as he hated to admit it, Michael had entangled Nigel in this tragedy, and it was up to him to fess up and make it right.

Michael perched on the side of Nigel's bed. "Granddad," he began. "Do you remember last summer when I boated up the coast with Christophe?"

Nigel cocked his head and squinted in confusion. "Christophe?"

"He was a guy I was seeing last summer."

"When you were shipwrecked?"

"Yes. Well, Christophe took me to . . . " Michael paused, leaned back, and ran his fingers through his limp hair. How was he going to explain?

"Fuck this. We're wasting time." Estrada caught himself wringing his hands and crossed his arms over his chest. "They're vampires, sir. Vampires killed Ruby and took Lucy."

"Vampires?" Nigel snorted. "I know you boys are into some weird shit, and I've seen my own share of weird shit, but vampires? There's no such thing."

"Did the police tell you about Ruby?" asked Estrada. "About the wounds."

Michael reached into his pocket and extracted a silver flask. He unscrewed the cap and downed half the contents. The whiskey burned his throat. He inhaled the fumes and rubbed his nose. Fumbled in his pocket. Needed a cigarette. Found his silver cigarette case and then realized he couldn't light up. Scowling, he pulled out an e-cigarette he kept for emergencies. It was nothing like the real thing, but it was, at least, something.

"Puncture wounds. Yes, in her neck, but that was just a stunt," Nigel said. "Someone playing games."

"It wasn't a stunt," Estrada said solemnly. "You must believe us, sir. We need your help."

Nigel covered his face with his hands. "My God, are you saying that's how she died?"

"Yes," Estrada said. "I didn't want to believe it either, at first. But I believe it now. Vampires are real and this one's got my baby."

No one spoke as the horror of his statement sunk in.

"But why? Why would . . . ?" His words trailed off as Nigel struggled to understand.

"It's a message. He wants Estrada." There was no point hedging now he'd confessed to Estrada. It would all come out.

Nigel stared at Estrada and swallowed. "He?"

"Diego." Estrada crumpled in the plastic chair and leaned back with his hands behind his head. He looked wasted. "He knows I won't stop until I find Lucy."

"He's a father too, you see." After priming his e-cigarette, Michael took a long slow haul of the tobacco-flavored juice and held the vapor in his mouth, waiting anxiously to feel the hit.

Nigel squinted and cocked his head. "How?" The notion of vampires siring children seemed too much to comprehend.

Michael inhaled the vapor, turned his head away from his grandfather and blew the smoke out in a stream. "Diego considered Christophe as a son, and the night of the storm, he drowned."

"Your friend drowned? Why didn't you say something?" Reaching out, Nigel touched Michael's hand.

He shrugged. "It's a long story. But Diego blames me for Christophe's death and this is his revenge."

"Tell me about this Diego."

Michael felt the nicotine hit the back of his throat. Relaxing, he took another long draw on the e-cigarette and wished it was a joint. "He's a Spanish nobleman. He's old."

"How old?"

"Centuries. Christophe said, Diego sailed with Quadra in the late seventeen-hundreds. He took me to a palace he built in the islands. He wanted Diego to make me—"

"Good God," Nigel said, cutting him off. "Tell me this is a hoax. I feel like I'm in a Stephen King movie."

Michael glanced at Estrada. "I made him watch *Salem's Lot*."

Estrada raised one corner of his mouth in a soft grin. "Everything Michael is saying is true, sir."

"I'd never lie to you, Granddad." Michael grasped Nigel's warm, dry hand. "Diego wants to hurt *me* by hurting the people I love. You, Ruby, Estrada."

Nigel glanced at Estrada. "By taking your daughter."

"By turning me into a vampire."

"So . . . " Nigel rubbed his temples. "These men who attacked us were vampires?"

"Yes, sir."

"He calls them his sons." Michael rolled his eyes.

"That's how they got into the attic."

Michael could see his grandfather's mind spinning as he relived the incident. Standing, he tried to think of something funny to say to relieve the tension in his chest. "Yes, Granddad. They can fly, like in *The Lost Boys*. Do you remember? We watched that one too."

"That's how they got Lucy too," Estrada said. "They flew in through her open window."

"Don't they need to be invited in?" asked Nigel.

Estrada shrugged his shoulders and glanced at Michael.

"In some of the fiction," said Michael, who'd been a fan all his life. "But these vampires are real and we know very little about them."

"They're strong," Nigel said. "The bastard picked up Ruby with one hand."

Michael felt sick at his stomach. He needed to end this ragged conversation that was just making him feel guiltier and get the fuck out of this hospital. "The thing is, Granddad, we need a boat."

"A boat." Nigel furled his brows. "I have friends with yachts, but it's midsummer. They're all out on the water."

"Someone must be around," Estrada said. "And they'll have to come with us. We need someone with experience, someone who knows the boat and can navigate the coast. A man we can trust."

TO RENDER A RAVEN　　　75

Michael unscrewed his silver flask and took another long belt of whiskey. "I can skipper a yacht," he said, feeling braver by the gulp.

Estrada shot him a confused glance.

"I learned when I was a kid." He'd never told Estrada about his summer working as crew aboard *The Deception*. Everyone who boarded Victor Carvello's yacht signed a confidentiality contract under threat of death. Michael had seen gruesome photos of three people who breached it that summer. Their decapitated bodies washed up some weeks later in Sonora and were attributed to a Mexican drug cartel. The images still haunted his dreams.

"I can make some calls, but I'll need my black book." When Nigel's face fell forward the wrinkles multiplied. "Poor Ruby. She must have been terrified."

"It would have been quick," Michael said, knowing it likely had not. Vampires reveled in the blood, its taste, and its effect on their libido. Like deep, red, aged wine, it bred a hunger only release could satisfy. His cravings told him this and more.

Estrada stood and stretched. It seemed he too was restless. "We have another problem. Michael can't remember where Diego's lair actually is."

"I know it's on an island, but I don't remember names." Taking the e-cigarette from his pocket, he took another long haul. As he held the juice in his mouth, he realized that Christophe had never mentioned places.

"Landmarks?"

Michael stood and paced around the room trying to remember. He inhaled the juice and exhaled another billowing cloud of smoke. He'd been angry the day they arrived at the palace. He'd wanted to go home the second day out, but Christophe kept teasing him with this *ultimate gift*. He'd felt like a prisoner and now realized he was. It wasn't until Christophe announced they'd be there in a couple of hours that Michael had gone up on deck to look around.

"It was north of Quadra Island." That was one place Christophe *had* mentioned when he told the vampire's story. "And it was busy. Cruise ships, freighters, fishing boats—"

"Shipping lane," murmured Nigel. "Johnstone Strait."

"We turned into a maze of tree-studded islands that all looked the same. Except, I remember there were ruins . . . native villages."

"Good," Estrada said. "Where were you when the kayakers found you?"

Michael shrugged. "They radioed for a helicopter."

"Coast Guard," muttered Nigel. He was still talking though his eyelids were drooping. "They told me. In my journal. I wrote it down."

Michael leaned over and touched his grandfather's shoulder. He loved him as much as any boy could ever love a father. "We should go and let you rest, Granddad."

"We should go and get his black book and journal," Estrada said. "I want to be out on the Salish Sea tomorrow. No more fucking around. The longer this vampire has my baby, the more chance he'll hurt her."

Michael was in the bathroom taking one last piss when he heard a voice. *Victor Carvello.* A cold shiver ran through his body. Estrada warned him that Carvello had arrived from Vegas, but hearing that voice nearly paralyzed him again. Grasping his flask, he tipped it to his lips. Damn. The bloody thing was nearly empty. Fumbling, he extracted his e-cigarette and took another hit. The buzz of nicotine calmed his shakes and brought everything back.

Michael hadn't seen the man since the summer they'd sailed around the Baja aboard *The Deception*. That was the summer Carvello introduced him to sex. He was twelve. At the time, Michael thought the attention and all the expensive gifts were cool. But now he realized, Carvello was just a rich, connected pedophile who'd pimped him out to wealthy clients—mobsters with a penchant for young boys. He'd never told Nigel or Estrada. If either one of them knew, they'd kill Carvello. Literally. And if they tried and failed, Carvello would come after them all. Michael had seen firsthand what Carvello could do. He took another puff, then opened the door a crack, and listened.

"What fuckery is this? I told you to call me if anything fucking happened," Carvello said.

"Nothing happened." Nigel was suddenly fully awake.

"*Something* fucking happened. It's a good job the nurses here know how to take orders."

"What do you mean?" Estrada, who'd been standing near Nigel's bed, positioned himself just outside the bathroom door.

Michael could touch him from where he stood. Inhaling his lover's scent, Michael started to salivate. His yearning to taste Estrada's blood was getting harder and harder to control.

"What do I mean?" Carvello glared at Estrada. "I mean that *Michael* has awoken from his tragic fucking stupor."

"Oh," said Estrada. "We thought you wanted us to call you if we had more information about Ruby's killers."

"So, do you?"

This could go no further. The one thing Michael did not want was Victor Carvello involved in his business. He was terrified of Carvello—still dreamed of bloated headless corpses—so the less the bastard knew, the better. He had to stop this. Opening the door, he stepped out.

"Well, well. Peter fucking Pan."

"Mr. Carvello."

The man had not aged. Dressed in slim white jeans, white button-down shirt, and an ivory vest, Carvello looked like he'd just stepped out of a Valentino ad.

"Call me Victor, please." He walked across the room and embraced Michael, who stood stiffly, wishing he could rip the bastard's bloody throat out. "Or Uncle Vic," Carvello whispered, his stubble grazing Michael's cheek.

Michael stuck the e-cig in his mouth and vaped. Then to calm his quaking guts, he pulled out his silver flask and finished off the whiskey.

"So. What do you know, fellas? Who are these bastards? And don't fucking lie to me. I have a sixth sense about these things."

"I saw them," Nigel said.

"Granddad," Michael said anxiously. He didn't want Carvello involved in any of this. The less he knew the better.

"Really," Victor said. "Do tell."

"One of them had dreadlocks and black teardrops tattooed on his cheeks."

"What? Did you fuck with some gang? Rip somebody off?"

"Granddad!" Once Carvello sunk in his teeth, they'd never get rid of him.

"The fuckers murdered my daughter and broke both your legs, Stryker. Obviously, you pissed *somebody* off."

"You should go." Estrada turned to face Carvello. "Now."

Michael saw Estrada's biceps flex, saw him glance down at the knife he always carried in his right boot. And in that moment, Michael wanted him more than he ever had before.

"Hey, calm down, magicman. The Strykers and Carvellos go way back. I only came by to offer my services." Opening his ivory vest, Carvello flashed a pearl-handled revolver, the barrel of which was concealed in an inside pocket.

"If we need your services, we'll be in touch." Estrada picked up Carvello's business card from Nigel's bedside table. "But right now, Nigel needs to rest."

Carvello bit his bottom lip and stared at Estrada. "Someone is going to pay for murdering my Ruby."

"Someone will."

Carvello sniffed and pivoted on one of his white loafers. "I'll catch *you* later," he said, as he slipped by Michael. Then, stopping, he turned, and patted his cheek. "Still as soft as Peter fucking Pan."

Deep within Michael's gut an ember of rage ignited. Someone is going to pay alright. Someone is going to make *you* pay.

MAD, BAD & DANGEROUS

Before sunrise, Leopold flew to Granville Island market in his raven guise. Mornings had always been his favorite time to shop, which he did personally for Ecos, his vegetarian bistro. The market wasn't yet open to the public, but fresh produce was being unloaded from trucks. He perched on a railing, absorbing the atmosphere, and remembering his former life.

Some vampire lore claimed a man's soul vanished at his transformation, but Leopold's soul was still very much intact, his memories raw and distinct. Attachment causes suffering, the Buddha taught, and Leopold understood this in one insightful flash. No bodhi tree for him. Enlightenment arrived via two fangs in the carotid when Diego deceived him, drugged him, and sucked the life out of him.

He'd come to Le Chateau that night with his financial advisor and three other clients who'd drunk themselves into a stupor on the yacht. Lorne Wiseman had convinced them that visiting this incredible venue in the islands would change their lives. It did. Leopold was the only one Diego chose to keep. The others he fed to the minions. Later, their pale empty bodies were weighted and cast into the sea, and Wiseman's yacht went into the boathouse for a makeover.

When someone left the door ajar, Leopold flew inside the market. Lights exploded as vendors arrived to prepare their shops for morning buyers. Landing behind a wall of crates, he morphed into his manly form. Each change came quicker, though the pain of cellular transformation was no less severe. He stood and stretched, rubbed his sore muscles, then grasped a bag and began to steal.

One thing vampire lore got right was speed. Leopold was quick and agile, a blur to human eyes. And they wouldn't miss the heady bulbs of garlic—one thing the lore got wrong—or snow-white leeks, the crisp green celery, burgundy carrots, or perfect red tomatoes. He smelled their leaves and moaned. Then, he pocketed pink Himalayan salt, forbidden rice, handfuls of fresh basil and cilantro, and lentils as bright as sea anemones. A bouquet of fresh cut flowers caught his eye, and he shoved it into the bag last.

When a raven flew out the door carrying the swinging bag in his talons, two men stared up with stunned looks on their faces and laughed.

Back on the yacht, Leopold found pots in the unused galley and cooked. This had been his life. This searching for the freshest ingredients, this cooking to perfection. It was the least he could do for Nora, the woman he'd betrayed to barter his freedom. The scent of bubbling soup upset his stomach. What an irony, he thought. A strict vegetarian, now the only thing sustaining me is blood.

He ladled the steaming soup into a bowl, set it on a tray with the vase of flowers and two spoons—surely the child was old enough to eat—and walked to her cabin door. He knocked quietly and stared at his hands. They were a creamy white flecked with gray, the color of sour milk, the nails pale blue. I'm a freak, he thought. A dead freak. Despite this, Nora Barnes would recognize him. They were more than acquaintances. They were friends.

Why Leopold? she'll ask. *Why did you steal me away from my husband and child?*

To save myself, he'll answer guiltily. *To save myself from eternal hell, I bargained with your life. I'm sorry, Nora. Please forgive me.*

Leopold knocked again. It must be done—this confession and contrition.

Hearing no murmur of invitation, he touched the key that stood in the lock. When he realized it was turned in the open position, a wave of panic struck him. He set the tray on the floor and flung open the door.

Zion was stretched across Nora on the bed, his long muscular arms clutching the mattress like a vulture, his face buried in her hair.

"No!" Leopold screamed.

Zion turned and leered, his mouth tainted with her blood. And Leopold launched himself at the surprised vampire. Hooking his elbow around his neck, he wrenched it with all his strength. The two vampires tumbled to the floor and Leopold began to punch, rage leaping like an angry lion.

Then, hands grasped his arms, tore Leopold backwards, and flung him through the air. He hit the wall and glared at Eliseo, who had broken up the fight.

The child whimpered in her cot, and then began to howl. Nora stared straight ahead and didn't respond.

Eliseo stood over Zion with his hands on his hips. "The woman was not to be harmed. Nor the child."

Zion turned up his scarlet lips and swiped a fist across his face.

"If she's dead—"

"It was just a taste, Eli. Seeing her in that flimsy nightgown. I got hungry and—"

"No more. You will not touch her again." Eliseo walked across the room, took Leopold's hand and pulled him up. "You're good to her. El Padrino will be pleased."

Leopold felt hot tears sting his eyes and drip from the corners of his lids. How could he have sacrificed her to these demons? Nora would never forgive him now.

"I'm amazed," Eliseo said, touching his wet cheek. "A vampire who cries real tears. Close and purify the wounds, Leopold Blosch, and do not grieve. The woman will not remember."

Leopold continued to stare at Zion as ragged thoughts ripped through his mind.

Eliseo scooped up the tray and balanced it on the palm of his hand like a circus performer. "Tend to her, my friend, and feed her your wonderful soup."

Though Eliseo played the clown, Leopold didn't smile. He didn't care if Diego was pleased or not. All he wanted to do now was kill the vampires. Kill them all.

Estrada was stretched out on the burgundy leather couch in Michael's flat. Though he disliked police, he had to admit, they'd been remarkably efficient. Nigel's attic haven was still sealed off with crime scene tape, but after forensics had finished their work, they'd been allowed back into the house early that evening.

The wrought-iron ceiling fan cast its faint breeze over Estrada's bare skin. At nine p.m. the temperature was eighty-four degrees, rather unusual on the coast. He adjusted the patterned shawl beneath him and sipped his cinnamon dolce latte. The rich fabric felt luxurious and prevented his skin from sticking to the leather. Leave it to Michael to find a shawl woven in wine and gold silk from the pattern in an ancient Persian rug. *Byron would have loved it,* Michael always said.

After a strenuous end to their brief hospital foreplay, Michael had gone to soak in the clawfoot tub. He'd given and taken surprisingly well for a man who'd been catatonic that morning. Perhaps it was the *I love you* Estrada whispered amongst those first luxurious kisses. The old Michael seemed to have returned. How long had fragments of his splintered soul been trapped in the Underworld? Since his initial encounter with the vampire or longer?

Leaning back on the couch, Estrada leafed through Nigel's journal looking for references to Michael's shipwreck and the Coast Guard. He'd found a stack of journals, including this one, in a locked freezer off the kitchen. Picking locks was another of his magician's skills. Nigel didn't follow a yearly schedule, but merely started a new notebook when the last one was full.

Most of what he saw, he couldn't comprehend. The man wrote using capital letters, short phrases, initials, symbols, and numbers. Obviously, there was more here than anecdotes about the Vancouver weather.

In Scotland, Estrada was told that the Stryker family were criminals, big enough to warrant international attention. *We know they're dirty,* the detective had said, ironically. Whatever the code meant, Estrada didn't want to know. He'd rather continue to think of Nigel as the father he'd lost, rather than The Godfather.

Entries for last June started a third of the way through, and his mind raced back to the events of last year.

Summer Solstice was June 20th. That was the day, Dylan fell asleep beside the Ballymeanoch Standing Stones in Kilmartin Glen, then ended up charged with murder and locked in a Scottish prison. That was also the day, Estrada had offended Michael and they'd parted miserably. A few days later, when Estrada had flown to Scotland to find the real killer and get Dylan out of prison, he and Michael had remained estranged. *You're always leaving me*, Michael had said in the Underworld, and it was true.

Using his finger as a guide, Estrada followed slowly through June's coded maze of letters and numbers into July.

Finally, on Friday July 11th, something: WHERE'S M? LEFT TUESDAY.

Tuesday? Estrada counted backwards. Tuesday was July 8—two weeks after he flew to Scotland. That must have been the day Michael left for the island with Christophe. Estrada remembered apologizing to Michael by email and getting that one response. *I've found someone who will do anything I want.* Now, he knew that someone was Christophe. Estrada cleared his throat and read on.

Saturday July 12: M NOT PICKING UP. Nigel had obviously started calling Michael when he didn't return for work on Friday. Then.

Sunday July 13: S CALLED FROM SCOTLAND. MICHAEL! GALE? COFFIN? CCG S&R 1-800-567-5111.

S stood for Sandolino. Sunday was the day Estrada saw a vision of the red coffin floating in the storm . . . the calligraphic *D* encircled by the rose. He'd called from Tarbert and told Nigel to call the Canadian Coast Guard. CCG. Estrada wondered what story Nigel had invented for Search and Rescue. He flipped through three more pages. At last he found it.

Thursday July 17: MICHAEL! CG CHOPPER HARDWICKE ISLAND to VGH. CALL S.

Nigel *had* called and shared the news, and then Estrada nearly drowned at sea himself. The next time he saw Michael was July 24th, when he appeared on the island of Jura in Scotland, a broken man. Michael had been out on the coast for nine days. For how many of them was he shipwrecked alone?

Estrada took out his phone and searched up Hardwicke Island. He stared at the map. It was located where Johnstone Strait funneled into

Discovery Passage. If Michael had been traveling south in the yacht when the storm hit, Nigel was right. He must have come down Johnstone Strait from somewhere up near Telegraph Cove, near the northeastern tip of Vancouver Island. Michael said they'd turned into a maze of islands. That could be—

His thoughts were interrupted by the doorbell. Michael was still soaking, so Estrada stashed the journal under the sofa cushion. He might be reading Nigel's private thoughts, but he couldn't risk anyone else finding it. He found his jeans lying in a heap of discarded clothing. After tugging them on, he slipped down the wooden stairs and opened the door.

Victor Carvello stood there with his hands in his pockets and an *I-come-in-peace* grin on his well-honed face.

"Before you say anything," Carvello began, "you should know that Nigel told me what fuckery you're up to." He used his hands like a maestro when he talked, fingers flying in rhythmic syncopation to his tone and words. Occasionally, he punctuated it with a shoulder pat or chest stab. "He may be wasted, but if what Nigel says is true, I can be of considerable fucking aid in this situation."

Estrada leaned against the doorframe and chewed his lip.

A hand grasped his shoulder. "Listen magicman. *You* need a boat so you can rescue your baby girl from this *whatever-the-fuck* and *I* need recompense." Carvello sniffed. "Father to father. *Capisce?*" He snapped his fingers with his free hand and winked. "I have a yacht at my disposal and it's being prepped as we speak. We leave at dawn."

"We?"

"Yeah. We. I am aggrieved at my daughter's misfortunate death. But a real man doesn't cry. He burns the bastard's balls off." Carvello produced a silver Zippo from his pocket and flicked it into flame to illustrate his alliterative phrase.

Carvello was melodramatic, but manageable, and things were manifesting. Estrada now knew where Michael had been shipwrecked *and* he had a boat. He was two hurdles closer to finding his baby.

"Come in and lock the door behind you." Estrada climbed three steps and turned. "But if you fuck with Michael, I'll fuck with you in ways you can't even imagine."

"Don't worry about it. The Strykers and Carvellos are practically family. There's nothing we can't sort out, *synergistically*."

Michael appeared on the landing dressed in slouchy black leggings and a hooded black silk shirt with tails Estrada had never seen before. Something was different about him. Something indefinable. It was a look, but also an energy. With his wet hair combed back from his face, his cheekbones looked sculpted in shadow. He raised a lip in a menacing sneer and exposed a fake fang. This was a Michael he'd not seen in over a year. This was Mandragora. Had the threat of Victor Carvello somehow galvanized him?

The fang didn't faze Carvello. "Ready to hunt pirates, Pan?" he asked, and punched Michael in the shoulder.

Estrada didn't think Michael could get any paler, but his flesh faded to a chalky mauve, as Carvello swaggered past him into the flat.

"The trip will do you good, kid," said Carvello, over his shoulder. "You need some sun on that *chiffon* skin."

"Trip?" Michael asked

"Affirmative. We're going yachting like we used to, eh kid?"

"Why did you let him in?" Michael whispered.

"He has a yacht," Estrada said.

"I can't go on a yacht with him."

"You have to. Diego has Lucy, and you're the only one who's been to his place in the islands."

Carvello leaned out the door. "Relax, kid. I just ordered pizza. You look half-fucking-starved."

Michael glared at Estrada. "Can I see you in the bedroom?"

"Don't fight now, boys." Carvello swaggered around the living room, admiring the Persian carpets, the cognac chaise, the nudes on the walls, and then, "Ah, nice wine bar," he said, and the sound of a popping cork eclipsed the second of silence.

Perching at his vanity table in the bedroom, Michael outlined his eyelids in black, then, for the first time in over a year, he popped in his red contacts. Sitting back, he appraised himself in the myriad lights encircling the mirror.

"Have you ever seen a decapitated body that's been floating in the ocean for days?" he said.

Estrada shook his head and continued to stare at his lover.

"Well, I have. Three of them. And you know who cut off their heads?"

Estrada gestured with a thumb to the other room. "I'm not afraid of him."

"Well, you should be. Carvello's a killer. Jesus Estrada, he's top of the fucking mob."

"Perhaps, he'll be a match for Diego then."

Michael rolled his eyes. "I'll go on the yacht, for you and Lucy. And I appreciate what you did for me today. I really do. But I can't stay here for his pizza party." Michael stood, and slipped his feet into a pair of black leather ankle boots.

"Where are you going?"

"Out. Don't wait up."

When Michael grasped him, and pulled him in, Estrada felt the edge of the fang caress his carotid artery. An icy pain struck his forehead and, for a moment, his heart skipped a beat.

<hr />

Caliber and his crew—the sanguinarians Michael Stryker partied with a year ago in West Vancouver—had been discovered in full blood-letting mode by his mother when she arrived home unexpectedly from a business trip. Caliber—so named because of the diameter of his invading fang—and his entire nest, had been promptly evicted. They'd now taken up residence in a rather shoddy East Vancouver basement. Michael gleaned all this information in two phone calls. On the third, Caliber extended an invitation to their new digs, along with directions. To the sanguinarians he was not Michael Stryker, but Mandragora, an eccentric celebrity, "mad, bad, and dangerous to know."

Michael now sat in Crimson, his red convertible, trying to muster up the courage to shove open the grungy door and invade Caliber's circus. He needed to feed. The desire to drink human blood had been building slowly over the past year, but since he'd awoken this morning beside Estrada in the hospital bed, it had multiplied exponentially. The sexual festivities back in his flat had only increased his need. In close quarters on a yacht, he'd never be able to contain it. The only solution was to drink his fill now and hope it would satiate his desire. The anticipation of tasting blood again made him hard.

Michael pulled up the handle to open the car door and then halted. A thin, bedraggled creature had emerged from Caliber's lair. He wandered toward the car dodging garbage in the alley, then glanced up.

A grin of recognition appeared on his face. "Mandragora?"

Michael pulled back his lips in a thin smile. "Christian, is that you?"

"Yeah, man. I heard you were coming by. We haven't seen you in months."

"I just discovered your whereabouts. I was about to knock, but I'm in no hurry. Do you need a ride somewhere?"

"Sure," Christian said. "I always loved this car—2001 BMW Roadster convertible, right? It's a classic."

"You got it, man. Her name's Crimson." Michael leaned forward as a rush of adrenaline shot up his legs from his toes. "Jump in."

When Michael parked in the shadowy end of a blind alley and raised the top on the red convertible, Christian glanced at him in confusion. It was, after all, a warm sultry night with no hint of rain.

Michael pushed the lever on his seat and leaned back, bracing his hands behind his head. "I've got plenty of cash," he said, casting his gaze down.

"Oh," Christian said, with sudden understanding. "Fifty?"

"Double that if you're good."

Christian flashed a mouthful of yellow teeth and in.

Michael's right arm came down and caught Christian in a headlock. His left hand held the razor.

Christian, who was used to blending bloodletting and sex, didn't fight, just winked his consent. Michael knew for a hundred, he'd play "sip and suck" with the legendary Mandragora. It would up his reputation amongst the others in the nest. Michael was actually doing him a favor and he wouldn't hurt the kid. All he needed was a fix.

But when Michael accidentally nicked Christian's carotid artery and the coppery blood shot out, he lost control. Catching it with the edge of his fang, he spread it wide. Christian stiffened and fought as Michael sucked and swallowed. Surprised by his own strength, Michael felt lusty shivers coursing through his body. The blood and the act of taking it galvanized him, and he reveled in his ability to dominate.

And then the kid went limp. Dropping the depleted body back in the passenger seat, he slumped. Couldn't swallow past the lump in his throat. So much blood. So fast. *I'm sorry, man. I didn't mean to hurt you.*

Michael's phone pinged to signal a text. Pulling it from his pocket, he glanced down and saw Estrada's name.

AT MY PLACE WITH DUBH. MEET TOMORROW 7AM MOSQUITO CREEK. TELL SECURITY BERTH 27. BE COOL AND LET'S DO THIS, AMIGO

I did this for you, compadre, but you can never know.

After checking for witnesses, Michael got out and opened the passenger door. He carried Christian's body into a shadowy corner and laid him down. Then, he pulled the kid's phone out of his pocket, called 911, and whispered, "Help me. St. James Church." Maybe there was a chance. Maybe. After wiping down the phone, he left it on the ground beside the kid's limp fingers.

Back in Crimson, he pulled out of the shadows and into the street. When his belly heaved, he pulled over, cracked open the door, and puked. Blood puddled onto the dirty pavement—an ocean of blood.

Michael wiped his mouth and leaned his forehead on the steering wheel until he heard police sirens.

Fuck. I'm no better than Carvello. Christian was just a kid.

RAGNARÖK

Estrada surveyed the posh aft deck of the *Ragnarök* where he, Dylan, and Dubh waited to get underway. "How did you get your hands on a boat like this?" he asked Carvello. He wasn't surprised—just fishing. The more he knew about the man, the better.

"Technically, it's a yacht," crooned Carvello. Sipping his coffee, he leaned back on the tan vinyl couch and crossed his legs. His skin glistened in the sun and a citrusy scent wafted on the morning breeze.

Moisturize and protect your George Clooney glow, Estrada thought, running a hand over his stubbled cheeks. He'd neglected to shave and felt suddenly shabby in his skinny jeans and pale gray T-shirt. Carvello glittered in white again—white trousers, white polo shirt trimmed in cobalt blue, plus he'd added a white ball cap to the ensemble. Estrada wondered if he'd acquired an entire yachting wardrobe, or if this was his usual summer attire.

"Let's just say, young Bjorn didn't score the winning goal the last time he frequented my establishment."

Ah, gambling debts. Carvello owned a hotel on the strip in Las Vegas. Could the owner of this yacht be a Canuck? Carvello had a penchant for bestowing monikers. Bjorn was almost certainly not his real name, but it was possible the yacht belonged to a Vancouver hockey player.

"What's the sticker on a craft like this?" Dubh perched at the far end of the couch and stroked his beard. In the morning sunlight, it burnished red and gold. Faerie genes. Or perhaps Viking. He'd doffed his leather kilt for another, just as weathered, in green canvas. A leather-sheathed knife hung from his belt.

Carvello's hands rose like a cogent politician. "Hmmmm . . . one and a half?"

"Million?" Dylan rocked back in his chair.

When Estrada arrived at the security gate that morning at 6:45 a.m., he'd been surprised to see Dylan standing there clutching his duffle bag. No doubt his fighting kilt was stashed inside. Estrada had informed Dylan they were going after Lucy's kidnappers as a courtesy, but also given him an out. Dylan hated the sea, even before that bastard in the Scottish Hebrides bound him to an anchor and tossed him overboard last summer. "It's Lucy," was all Dylan had said, when the two men bumped fists at the gate.

Carvello nodded. "U.S. of course. She's sixty feet, but a few years old, so you gotta factor in depreciation. Still, the baby can fly."

Baby, Estrada thought. They'd been fucking around for three nights now while his baby was with vampires. Where the fuck was Michael?

"If Peter Pan doesn't show," Carvello said, as if reading his mind, "which one of you charming fucks wants to help me skipper?"

"He'll *be* here." Estrada narrowed his eyes. "And his name is Michael." He pulled out his cell phone. "He's only forty-five minutes late and we can't leave without him. Michael is the only one who's seen Diego's lair."

Carvello glanced at him with something bordering feeling. Perhaps, losing his only daughter had instilled some empathy.

"Ever been to sea, Tyrion?" Carvello said to Dubh.

Magus Dubh rolled his eyes and glared at the lame reference to Tyrion Lannister from *Game of Thrones*. Estrada heard the word *knob* though Dubh's lips never moved. Sometimes, the two men connected on the strangest things.

"Hey, Tyrion's a tough little bugger and up to his eyeballs in whores," Carvello said, with a wink.

"Aye, that may be. But *my* name is Magus Dubh."

An uncomfortable silence ensued, and then— "What do you know about the sea, Magus Dubh?"

"I was born on an island, so I suppose it's in my blood."

That's not all that's in your blood, Estrada thought.

TO RENDER A RAVEN

"Come up to the helm and I'll show you how to drive a yacht, in case Peter—"

"He'll *be* here," Estrada growled.

"Well, I need more coffee," Carvello said, putting down his empty cup. "Where are those girls?"

Sexist too, thought Estrada. He'd called Sensara late last night and brought her up to speed with the rescue plan. Naturally, she was there waiting at the berth with Daphne when he arrived. Raine would have come along too, he suspected, if she hadn't had a story due the next afternoon. When they boarded the yacht, Daphne had scoped out the galley with glee, and then brewed coffee before disappearing below deck with Sensara to claim the VIP suite. She loved to cook and would, no doubt, ensure they were well fed. But, if Carvello pulled any of his sexist bullshit on either of the women, he might end up overboard.

Glancing through the glass doors, Estrada saw the women's shadows in the galley. They were sifting through the groceries Carvello had delivered. Estrada felt oddly relieved the women had decided to share a bedroom. Sensara glanced at him with a longing look when the question of sleeping arrangements came up, but he didn't react. He liked what had been simmering between them since Lucy's birth. Hopefully, one night in her bed hadn't set them back two years. When he had the chance, he'd remind her how much he loved and cared for her. But he wanted to continue exploring this newfound love for Michael, who was acting stranger by the minute. Unfortunately, seven souls on a yacht didn't leave much room for privacy.

Estrada's cell phone pinged. *Michael.* He'd finally responded to his flurry of texts. "Michael's at the gate. I'm going to get him."

"And so it begins," Carvello muttered.

Estrada found Sensara lying out on a sleeping mat on the bow early that afternoon. She looked like she'd been born yachting in her white tank and capris, had tied a turquoise scarf around her hair and pulled it down over her eyes to shut out the world. Her small tanned feet were bare, the toenails painted peach. He'd been watching her for some time through the tinted glass, while he dozed on the couch. Meditating in the corpse position, she was likely hoping for visions. Still, he couldn't resist snatching a moment alone with her. The sun shone from an azure sky flecked in wispy clouds. If they weren't on their way to confront a murderous vampire, life would be perfect.

They'd raced up the coast as far as Sechelt, then turned west and crossed the Strait of Georgia south of Lasqueti Island. Dubh was now at the helm beside Carvello, and they were cruising along the east coast of Vancouver Island. Daphne and Dylan were in the galley making lunch and Michael was downstairs sleeping—nothing unusual for him. He'd always been a creature of the night and had arrived that morning looking bedraggled, with nothing but the clothes he'd worn out the night before. His behavior was a cause for concern but, for the moment, Estrada had other things on his mind.

He laid on his side, propped his head up on his arm, and stared at Sensara.

Her glossed coral lips spread into a smile. "Hello, Storyman."

His heart sighed. She hadn't called him that since their affair almost two years ago. He thought she'd never call him that again.

"I tried for stealth. How did you—?"

"Nothing preternatural. I know your scent."

"Really. What do I smell like?"

"Musky cinnamon coffee."

"Ugh, like the guy at the cafe that didn't change his shirt after a workout?"

"Much better than that," she said, and pushed the scarf from her eyes. Her face was blotched with weeping.

"I'm sorry you're so sad, Sara."

"You're as sad as I am. You're just better at keeping it together."

I have to, he thought. If I let everything I was feeling run rampant, my heart would explode. Estrada ran a finger down her cheek where the tears had dried. "We'll find her and get her back. I promise."

"I just can't imagine what she's going through all alone with those *things*." The disdain in her tone made his skin crawl.

"I know you're the one with psychic gifts," he said, "but I feel in my gut that Lucy is alright, that she's being cared for."

Sensara touched his stubbly cheek. "You're not just saying that to make me feel better?"

"No. It's the one thing keeping me sane. When I close my eyes, I see her swaddled in blankets. She's calm and fed and sleeping. I just keep sending her love and wrapping her in pink clouds of protection."

"I like that," she said. "Let's do it together."

Estrada kissed her on the lips, a sweet affectionate *I love you* kiss, and then laid down beside her on his back and closed his eyes. When their fingers entwined, he felt their power merge.

"We're strong together, Sara."

"We are."

Moments passed as their breathing merged into one unified breath.

"Oh," she said, at last.

"Can you see her?"

"Yes. She's still in her favorite onesie, the one with the yellow butterflies. She's beautiful, the most beautiful baby ever born."

"She's us," Estrada said, squeezing her hand. "The very best parts of us."

"You're right, Es. She's *not* alone. Someone is lying beside her—a woman in a white cotton gown. They're sleeping on a bed in a room just like the one Daphne and I are in."

"Lucy's on a boat?" His brain scrambled to keep up with what she was saying.

"I think so. It's triangular and there are portholes along the ceiling. I feel like it's close."

Estrada sat up and stared at all the boats surrounding them in the strait. Any one of them could be concealing his baby. "You found her," he said, and scooping Sensara up in his arms, he held her to his chest. His tears came then and mingled with her own. "God, I love you, woman."

Sensara opened her eyes wide and stared into his. "Really?"

"Yes. I always have and I always will."

She touched his cheek and slid her fingers through his hair. "Remember how good it used to be?"

Estrada sighed. Two years ago, they'd been best friends. They'd laughed and played and cast their healing spells. And then the coven had charmed a killer and changed everything.

"We'll get it back, Sara. I promise you. And we'll get *her* back."

Michael slouched on the foredeck with his elbows wrapped around his knees. It was two a.m., and everyone was asleep, including Estrada. The night was his, and he savored it.

Carvello and Dubh had anchored the yacht in a bay just off the tip of Quadra Island. Quadra, Michael recalled, had several names, and was the Spaniard who'd introduced Diego to the Inside Passage in the late 1700s. When Christophe mentioned passing this island, they'd been sailing three or four days. The power of *Ragnarök* was fifty times that of the sailboat—unless the cloying Frenchman had told the crew to take their time. That was a possibility. Nothing Christophe had ever said or done could be trusted now. The whole charade had been orchestrated to feed him to the vampire, one way or another. The only thing he knew for certain was that Quadra Island meant they were halfway to hell.

Michael unscrewed the cap from his second bottle of red and took a long haul. He could taste oak tannins, the hint of chocolate, tobacco, fig—all the myriad flavors vintners use to describe a wine's bouquet. These were individual tastes he'd never noticed before. He guzzled more, then pulled another cigarette from the silver case in his leather bag and lit it with a flick of his monogrammed lighter. He ran his thumb across the engraving. *Mandragora*. Inhaling the tobacco, he felt revived. Somehow, in all this insanity, he'd found himself again.

Leastwise, he'd found Mandragora.

The indigo sky was studded with stars, while the waning moon's reflection shivered across the leathered sea like a flickering candle. His night vision was clearer, his hearing sharper too. He reveled in his heightened senses. Water lapped the keel, reminding him of long-lost lines from his beloved Byron. "The waves lie still and gleaming, and the lulled winds seem dreaming."

Beyond that were other sounds. Phantom splashes. The haunting cry of a raven. The harried hooting of an island owl. Nocturnal predators like himself.

Shadows of pine-studded rocks clutched and held him like Gaia. In this darkness, only she knew his secret—the canines that grew longer and sharper each night. Michael touched them with his tongue, nicked the flesh and tasted copper. Soon he'd no longer need a blade. Soon, he could no longer kiss Estrada without fear of cutting him. And, if he cut him, then oh, he would taste him. Sensation rushed up his inner thighs and found its mark. Vampire had its perks.

Running his tongue along his lips, Michael's thoughts strayed to the dreadlocked vampire at Le Chateau. How he had thrilled to *that* kiss. The memory sent another lusty shiver through his loins. Would others feel the pleasure he'd felt when he drank from them? Could he learn to control his hunger like he controlled his release? If so, he could drink from Estrada without fear. Love him and delight him, take him to a place they'd never known before.

A cacophony of shrill high-pitched whistles exploded off the starboard bow. Michael lurched right, upsetting the wine bottle. Then reaching out with extraordinary speed, he grasped it before it fell. A riot of rapid clicks and then a whoosh. Something was out there.

He sauntered to the bow rail and stared at the sea. The water roiled with life. Then a killer whale leapt clear of the water, breached, and dived. Water soaked his skin, and Michael laughed.

"What's happening?"

Estrada was suddenly behind him, his fingers curled around his shoulder.

"Whales!" Though Michael had grown up in Vancouver, he'd never seen them in the wild. Not close like this. Their ferocity electrified and delighted him.

"Don't fall in," Estrada said, grasping him tighter.

"They're everywhere. Look." Standing at the edge of the bow, the salty wind caught and tugged at their hair and Michael felt more alive than he'd felt in years.

"Must be hunting."

"Hunting, yes." Hunting had its own allure. Michael had discovered that last night after his first disastrous kill. Whispering through the inky Vancouver streets and alleys like a phantom, he'd courted many potential victims. The city breathed them in and spewed them out like orca's breath.

"Come back from the railing, amigo. I'm afraid you're going to fall in."

Estrada stood behind him. The seductive scent of a day spent in sea and sunlight wafting from his pores, while all around night's shadows thrust them closer together. Thighs brushed the back of Michael's legs. Hands grasped his arms. Breath caressed the soft flesh behind his ear. And, the glistening black and white whales cut the space between sea and sky with their phantom splashes.

"It's perfect," Michael said.

"What?"

"This moment. It will never be more perfect than this ever again."

Estrada's arms locked around Michael's chest and held his brooding heart.

"They're leaving now," Estrada said, at last.

"Yes, there's only that one moment, and then it's gone."

"Come to bed," growled Estrada. "We'll make other moments."

"Not like that one." Sex had lost its luster in the glow of marauding orcas.

"You're poetic tonight, amigo."

"I've always been. You've just forgotten." Michael glanced up at the night sky. In the shambles of sickness, we almost lost me, he thought. Like a black dwarf, my light languished. But now.

Estrada's lips brushed his neck. "Your skin's cold. Come to bed."

"Let's lie here on the deck. I want to feel you behind me while the stars 'wander darkling in the eternal space.'"

Estrada laughed. "I'll get some blankets, my Lord Byron. Don't fall in. Those orcas may still be close."

"No," Michael murmured. "They've gone . . . like the moment."

EVERYTHING'S GOTTA EAT

Leaning back against the leather seat, Eliseo twirled his dark curls between his thumb and finger. "Leopold Blosch is starving himself. You must take him hunting, Zion."

Zion sniffed and rubbed his nose. "Hunting? Why me?" He was perfectly content to pilot *La Sangria* from the flybridge. The night was cool and dark, and the waning moon cast shadows across the water. They were cruising slowly through the strait, just south of Broughton Archipelago, waiting for the heroes to catch up. The *Ragnarök* was perhaps a day behind. Cruising long days without stopping, the humans only rested at night and when the northwest winds blew fierce in the late afternoon. He'd flown over several times to observe their progress; in fact, he'd just returned from spying on the one he'd tasted and still craved. Michael Stryker.

"You know why," Eliseo said.

"You don't trust me with the cargo, eh Eli?"

"*You* are his sire, Zion. So, *you* must take Leopold Blosch and instruct him in his first kill."

"But the chef refuses to drink blood. He's an *abstainer*," Zion said, with disdain. "How can I force him?"

"Do you remember *your* first kill?"

"It makes me hard to think of it."

"Tell me."

"McClintock." Zion caught the hard C on his tongue, then spat. "I ripped his throat out and painted myself in his blood. I needed no instruction."

"So, you must find Leopold *his* McClintock."

"How? The chef loves everyone, even the animals." When they'd offered him the blood of a deer, he'd turned his head in disgust.

"Father told me he wants Leopold Blosch to fully turn, so he will stop wanting to leave Le Chateau. He must kill for love or hate."

"Well, that ain't gonna happen, Eli. The chef doesn't hate a soul. And, he's got no family. He only loves animals."

Eliseo pursed his lips in thought. "Well, if Leopold loves animals, who must he hate?"

"The folks who kill 'em?"

"Exactly. There is wildlife in these islands, Zion. Poachers come stalking trophies. Black bear, grizzly, deer. Follow your nose. Let Leopold see the carcasses of the ones he loves alongside their slayers."

"That's clever, Eli. I see why Father favors you."

"Zion, if you can make Leopold Blosch accept vampire, El Padrino will favor you."

"Where is the chef?"

"In the saloon, drinking wine to ease his hunger."

Zion stood and stretched, then glanced at the digital clock on the console. 2:32. Still hours before dawn. He might just enjoy this.

Eliseo took over the controls. "I will anchor in Boat Bay and see you there."

Zion waved a hand as he slipped downstairs into the saloon.

"Chef. You sober enough to fly? Eli wants us out on surveillance."

"I thought you just came back."

"I did. But, he's a slave driver, this one. Wants us to explore the islands."

"For what?"

"What else?"

"I'm not hungry."

"I'll tell you something, Chef. Starving yourself will only make you weak."

Leopold shrugged, then rolled his eyes.

"You think you're the only man who ever suffered?" Zion scraped his fist across his nose. "When my mother and I were caught by slavers in Africa, I was eight years old. The man who took us, sold us to a bastard named McClintock, who owned a gold mine in California. McClintock raped my mother whenever he felt the urge and worked us like mules underground. I was like you then, Chef. Sad and angry and scared. I refused to eat and wanted only to die."

"I'm sorry," Leopold said.

"I should have killed the motherfucker; instead, I grew weak. When McClintock used my mother up, he broke her neck and I could do nothing to stop him." Zion touched the black teardrops below his eyes and ran his fingers down his cheeks. "These are hers."

"What happened to McClintock?"

"Diego." Zion's lip curled into a grin. "Father made me strong. Gave me freedom. I owe him for that."

"I don't owe him for anything," Leopold said.

"Maybe not. But if you want to help the woman and child, you must be strong. Everything's gotta eat."

Leopold put down his wine glass, then stood and stretched. "I'll fly, but I won't eat," he said, and shifted into his raven form. That, at least, was coming easier.

Broughton Archipelago was a provincial park and patrolled by rangers, so Zion flew east toward Knight Inlet and the mainland, close to the treetops, senses alert. The earth below was a dense swathe of evergreen cut with rock, the odd lake, pond, or marshland. Along one such lake, Zion smelled smoke, and then blood. He lit into a tree and waited for the chef, who followed close behind.

A black-tailed deer was strung up by its back legs from a pole. Its throat was cut. Its belly splayed and emptied of entrails. Not far from the camp, a black bear had also picked up the scent and was on the move.

Zion heard a whooshing sound and glanced at Leopold. He'd shifted back into human form and hunched naked in the crooked branches of the hemlock tree. Tears glistened in his eyes.

"Why did you bring me here?" Leopold whined.

Zion shifted and stood in the tree, his arm wrapped around a branch.

"Does it make you mad to see the deer butchered like that?"

"Mad, sad, sick. Deer are the gentlest of creatures."

Zion sniffed. "Young female too. Perhaps she left a fawn nearby. We could look for it."

"How could someone do that?"

"Everything's gotta eat, Chef. And up here, you eat what's walkin' by your window. Carrots don't sprout outta rocks."

But the chef had stopped listening. Shifting back into his raven form, he dived toward the pole from which hung the deer. Landing on the earth, he shifted back.

Zion followed, impressed by how quickly Leopold had learned to transform from human to raven. Most of Diego's new sons took months to shift like that. The chef had mastered it in a couple of weeks.

"I'm going to bury her. There must be a shovel here somewhere."

"Bad idea, Chef. There's a black bear who wants to claim this carcass. Might just as well let her have it. Bear's gotta eat too."

But the chef had opened the shed door and was rummaging inside. Reappearing with a hatchet in one hand and a shovel in the other, Leopold stalked to the pole. Reaching up, he hacked through the rope that held the deer. The carcass fell with a loud wallop, head and shoulder crashing into the earth—a hundred pounds of dead meat.

A shot blasted from the cabin window and would have hit the chef in the gut had he not jumped clear.

Zion raced to the cabin before the crazy old hunter could get off another round. Kicking down the door, he faced an old woman in a flannel nightgown. Scraggly gray hair. Puckered face. She trembled as she pointed the rifle at his head.

The chef sprung from behind like a cougar, tore the rifle from her hands, and knocked the old woman to the plank floor. He didn't know his own strength. She hit her head on the woodstove and stopped moving. With two fingers, Leopold felt the artery in her wrinkled neck.

Zion stood back on his heels, feeling a sense of pride. The chef was poised to make his first kill.

And then they heard the breathing. Fast, frightened, pulse-pounding, terror breaths. The two vampires stared at each other, and then they saw the old man. Cowering in his bed, he'd pulled the blanket up around his chin.

Zion smelled piss. He gestured to the trembling old man. "You want?"

"Did *you* shoot the deer?" Leopold asked.

The man couldn't speak. He shook his head randomly yes, and then no, trying for the answer that might save his life.

"How could you?"

"Take him," Zion said. "You saw what he did to the deer. Ripped out its guts and hung it in a tree."

The old woman revived and started wailing like a banshee.

"Shut the fuck up." Zion took two giant strides toward her. "Take him, Chef. Do it now."

The chef held his hands over his face and took a deep breath. "No. They're just an old couple trying to survive. I hate what they do, but I won't murder them."

With one long hand, Zion scooped up the old woman from the floor and tore into her throat. The screaming sank into a gurgle and then she was gone. He dumped her body on the floor and leapt up on the bed. The old man barely struggled. They were as scrawny as two old roosters and Zion's mouth tasted like he'd sucked an old dirty penny. He glanced around the cabin and found a bottle of whiskey on one of the dusty shelves. Uncorking it with his teeth, he took a mouthful, swished it around in his mouth, and spit it out. Then he guzzled some more.

Leopold scooped the old woman up off the floor. "I'm sorry," he said, though she was nothing but a carcass now. Like the deer. Her blood stuck to his silvery hair and drizzled down his chest. He carried her to the bed and laid her down beside the old man, then covered them both with a quilt.

Zion polished off the whiskey as he watched. Fucking Chef and his morals. Why did Father have to choose a son with a conscience?

When they walked out of the cabin, the deer was gone. Bear musk permeated the air and the shrubs were beaten down where she'd been dragged off.

"Damn." Leopold kicked the ground. "She deserved a burial." Picking up the shovel, he hurled it through the cabin window.

"Everything's gotta eat, Chef. Even you. You'll see."

Magus Dubh sat out on the aft deck alone nursing an ale. It was well past two in the morning, and he couldn't sleep. This coast reminded him of home; at least, his childhood summer home—the Isle of Mull in the Inner Hebrides. For eight weeks, each year, his mother blew him a kiss at the bus station in Glasgow, and sent him off to his Aunt Jackie, so she could party without fear of the SWS swooping down and apprehending her boy. Ah, Moira. At least, she'd sent him somewhere blessed. Aunt Jackie cooked and fed him and let him roam free. Moira loved to hear the stories he brought home, and he did his best to thrill her with his adventures. The summer he was ten, he'd found a goat's skull on the beach and imagined all kinds of hellish rituals. Bleached and polished, it sat beside his bed for years. His mother had named it Nick.

Dubh fingered the fragile talisman he kept in his pocket, then pulled it out and held it in his palm. A small circular salmon bone, it glowed in the darkness. He'd caught the fish himself one summer in Ireland's River Boyne, where legend says Finn MacCool tasted the Salmon of Knowledge and became the wisest man in all of Ireland.

Closing his eyes, Dubh sent out a quick appeal to the gods. *Send us knowledge that we may know justice.* For as they pushed on, he knew justice drew ever closer.

After bucking the fast-moving current in Discovery Passage for several hours, the westerlies kicked up along with a flood tide. Carvello found refuge for the *Ragnarök* in Rocky Bay Marine Park. Several other boaters had the same idea, and the blue bay was dotted with white sails and power yachts. They were close to Chatham Point—the juncture between Discovery Passage and Johnstone Strait—which meant, if all went well, they'd be in the area Michael was shipwrecked tomorrow.

Dubh wondered how they'd know it when they found it. Michael—who was their only witness—had taken to *hiding* below deck by day. There was no other word for it. The man had changed. Dubh felt it the moment he boarded the *Ragnarök*. What he didn't know was why or how. He assumed it had something to do with Victor Carvello, who continued to tease him with his *Peter fucking Pan* shite. There was history there. That's why Dubh spent days seated beside the obnoxious mobster and watched his every move. Estrada was far too wrapped up in placating his two lovers to see what transpired at the helm and below deck.

Just tonight, Dubh had followed Carvello downstairs, while Estrada had a nightcap with Sensara in the saloon. The one thing about being small was you could scuttle in and out of places without being noticed. On his way past Michael's room, Carvello had pushed open the door and stuck his head in. "Feel like some company, kid?" he'd said. The next sound Dubh heard was a boot bouncing off the door. Carvello just laughed. "I'll be in the Captain's Quarters in case you change your mind. King-sized bed. Just like the old days."

Carvello was a predator. Of what intensity, Dubh was not yet sure, but he *would* find out.

After tucking the blanket around his cold bare feet, Dubh laid back and closed his eyes. He was just nodding off when he felt a strange energy and blinked.

Michael Stryker, naked as a bairn, opened the gate and slipped out. There was nothing behind the aft deck, but four steps on either side leading down to a compartment that housed the tender. Beyond that was sea.

The splash was subtle. Dubh sat up and peered over the edge of the couch. Michael was swimming easily through the cold, placid water. Dubh could just see his head. Below the surface, his arms pulled in a smooth strong breaststroke. He covered the fifty yards in no time, then climbed up onto the rocks and disappeared. Several kayakers had set up tents along the shoreline of the park.

What was Michael up to? Thievery? Or did he just need time alone? Perhaps, Carvello was having more impact than he realized.

A loud incessant horn blasted Estrada out of bed. He glanced across to Michael's side and found it empty. That was unusual. It looked like it hadn't been slept in at all.

Estrada reached across and flicked on his phone. 6:00

The neurotic horn blasted again, and then again. Every thirty seconds, another blast sent a surge of adrenaline through his veins. Growling, Estrada crawled out of bed and pulled on his jeans and a hoodie.

Venturing into the saloon, he glanced out the windows, but could see nothing but a gray wall. The boat was completely shrouded by fog.

"What the hell?"

"We're fogged in, magicman. You got some trick up your sleeve to fix this fuckery?" Carvello sprawled in a leopard print robe on the couch in the saloon. With his slightly crossed, upturned eyes, the man had all the makings of a snow leopard.

The horn blasted again, and Estrada clenched his fists.

"That's the lighthouse keeper at Chatham Point warning us to stay put," Carvello said.

"Don't get comfortable. We can't waste a whole day stuck in this bay."

"Well, we can't go out in the strait." Carvello threw up his hands. "It's too dangerous in this soup."

"If it's that dangerous, no one else will be out there." Of all the things that could have stopped them from saving Lucy, fog was the one thing Estrada hadn't anticipated. Men, you could fight. Even vampires. But nature was a harsh adversary. "You must have radar on your million-dollar yacht. Find a way to keep us moving."

"You don't get it. Johnstone Strait is a major shipping lane. Every fucking freighter, cruise ship, yacht, and tugboat from Alaska to California uses it, and most won't pull over and wait out—"

"Find a way. We're going."

"Hell, no. We're not!"

Exasperated, Estrada turned away from Carvello's fuming and spied Michael. Seated on the beige couch beside Dubh out on the aft deck, he was wrapped in a blanket. His wet hair was slicked back from his face, his flesh like chalk, his lips lilac. He was still wearing his red contacts and he'd lined his eyes in kohl.

"What the fuck, Michael? Where have you been?"

"I went for a swim. I've been lying around so much."

"A swim? I thought you hated—"

"Pools. I hate pools. Chlorine and piss." Michael shivered. "But the sea is different. Alive. I feel like a new man."

You *look* like a new man, thought Estrada. Leastways, a different man. "So, you went swimming in the fog?"

"It was clear then. It's shallow here, and the water's warm. You should try it."

"No thanks. We won't be staying long enough." The continual blast of the foghorn was driving Estrada insane.

"We can't venture out in this," said Dubh, who'd been sitting quietly listening to their banter.

"We can and we will. I won't sit here all day and listen to that."

"Come downstairs." Michael stood, clutching the blanket around his waist, then touched Estrada's cheek with a cool palm. "I'll distract you."

Estrada scowled.

When Michael passed Sensara at the top of the stairs, she shot him an acid glance.

"Let's coffee-up and get out of here," Estrada said.

Dubh slid into his canvas kilt and pulled a sweater from his bag. "If we get hit by a freighter, we'll never find Lucy."

"I know it's risky, but we can't waste another *fucking* day," he said, and pounded his fist against his chest.

Dubh leaned back and cast him a curious glance.

Sensara appeared at his side. "Estrada's right. Every day is another day Lucy is alone with those vampires."

Estrada took a deep breath to calm his racing heart. "I'll take responsibility."

"I'll make the coffee," Daphne said.

Dylan cranked up the bow anchor while Estrada listened to Dubh argue with Carvello. He trusted him to get his point across.

"Listen. I'm responsible for this fucking craft, not him," Carvello said. "If we go out there and get hit—"

"We won't," Dubh said. "We'll go easy and use our horn and we'll be fine."

Carvello acquiesced when he realized the anchor was back in the boat. He didn't have a choice. They'd started to drift.

As they edged out, Estrada held tightly to Sensara. He didn't like to second guess himself, but between the eerie mist enveloping them and the blasting foghorn, he could barely breathe.

"We need some extra eyes on the bow," Carvello said. "Why don't you two lovebirds fly out there and keep watch."

"Bad idea," Dylan said. "If we hit something, you *will* fly—right off the bow."

"We'll be fine," Sensara said. "Come on, Estrada. Bring your coffee. I'll get some blankets."

"Well, if you're going. I'm coming too." Dylan stood.

"And me," Daphne said. "It takes a coven, right? We can cast protection spells."

So, the four of them sat out on the sunpad sipping coffee. The light at Chatham Point flickered through the fog as they passed, but no buildings were visible. No trees. No rocks. No shoreline. Just a hazy beam of light and the relentless blast of the foghorn. Carvello kept it slow. Estrada knew he was playing the map on his console like a video game. He even had a joystick. The problem was, there were other craft out here too, trying the same maneuver. For the first time, Estrada could feel how unnerved the man was, and it scared the hell out of him. He gritted his teeth. Carvello was an experienced skipper. He probably should have listened.

Still, the farther they progressed, the more Estrada relaxed. They'd finally escaped that infernal lighthouse foghorn. Now, there was nothing but engine, waves hitting the keel, and fog all around. Every few minutes, Dubh blasted their horn to alert other craft to their presence. Estrada glanced at the helm but could see nothing through the tinted window.

"How long has it been?" asked Sensara.

Estrada checked his phone. "It's half past eight."

"Over two hours. Will it stay like this all day?"

"Doubtful," Dylan said. "It should dissipate by noon."

"Is it normal to see fog this thick in the summer?" asked Daphne.

"There aren't degrees of fog. When the temperature rises and the warm wind blows over the cool water, it creates a cloud on the ground."

"Science brain." Estrada punched him in the arm.

"Not really. I've just done lots of field work with other science brains."

A sudden deep blast riveted through Estrada's gut. Jerking, he spilled his coffee all over his jeans. It was so intense, he felt like he had his ear to the amp at a rock concert with the bass player stuck on one note. A second later, the cruise ship appeared off their starboard bow less than a stone's throw away, lights flashing, bass horn blasting. Glancing up at the massive black keel, the four of them clung to each other and the railings as the yacht rocked from side to side.

"We're going to tip!" yelled Sensara.

"Get inside," Estrada said. Clinging to the railing, the women inched toward the doorway.

And then the wave struck. The yacht tilted to port and then flipped back to starboard, so low in the sea that water poured over the deck. Dylan hollered once and was gone. The cruise ship was still passing, the horn still blasting, the water still churning, and Dylan had slid into the abyss between them.

"Man overboard!" Daphne shouted.

"Cut the engine!" Estrada yelled through the tinted glass and made a slashing gesture across his neck.

The motor stopped and Carvello appeared clinging to the doorway.

"Where is he? Did you see?"

Estrada edged over to the bow and stared into the sea. Dylan was somewhere in that roiling mess between their boat and the cruise ship.

"Grab the life buoy and if you see him, throw it close enough that he can grab it," Carvello said. "He'll be behind us. I'll go to the stern."

"Dylan!" Estrada yelled over the blasting horns. "Damn it! Dylan!"

And then, Estrada did what his gut said he must. He tossed the life buoy overboard and dove into the sea. It wasn't a thought, just an impulse.

Underwater, the sea churned with a different intensity. Estrada could see shapes and colors, muted grays and darker hues. But what he needed to see was white—white khakis and a white sweater. In this seething mass of gray, surely, he could find white.

He'd been down two minutes when his lungs burned. He fought his way up and realized he'd swum past the stern. The cruise ship had bulled by them and left them in its wake. They hadn't even seen them. Treading water, Estrada caught his breath and glanced at the yacht. Carvello was yelling and pointing past him. Estrada turned and dove again, swam in that direction, and almost hit Dylan before he saw him.

Half-floating on his back, Dylan gasped.

"I got you man," Estrada said.

Dylan relaxed in his arms. "O-k-k-kay," he stuttered, but his skin was as white as his sweater. His eyes wide and round.

Carvello flung the buoy and Estrada swam for it, pulling Dylan along with him. Once he caught it, he shoved it over Dylan's head and clung to the side. Carvello pulled and they began to move.

Daphne and Carvello wrenched Dylan up on the aft deck and Sensara wrapped him in blankets. Estrada followed.

"Are you going to pull me out of every ocean in the world?" Dylan whispered through chattering teeth.

"It's only been the two so far," Estrada said, remembering their near-death experience in Scotland a year ago.

"It's my fucking *karma*."

"No. This was my fault. I'm sorry." Estrada looked at Carvello. "You were right, man."

"Hey, you saved the kid's life, magicman." The hands flung up again. "You did good."

The fog had dissipated and Dubh was alone at the helm when a message came over the marine radio later that afternoon.

PAN PAN. PAN PAN. PAN PAN.
ALL STATIONS. ALL STATIONS. ALL STATIONS.
This is
VICTORIA COAST GUARD RADIO

VICTORIA COAST GUARD RADIO
VICTORIA COAST GUARD RADIO

Kayaker missing as of 06.00 hours August 5. Last seen camping at Rocky Bay Marine Park near Chatham Point Light Station. Alert if located.

VICTORIA COAST GUARD RADIO OVER

Dubh sat back in his chair and tugged at his beard. Michael Stryker had disappeared just after two a.m. and not returned until six, when the foghorn began its blasts. *Four hours.* Dubh pretended to wake up when Michael sat beside him. "How can you sleep through this?" Michael had asked. Dubh shrugged. "I grew up in Glasgow. I can sleep through a gangland shooting."

When Estrada appeared, Michael had acted as if nothing was askew. In all the confusion, the fog, and Dylan falling overboard, Dubh hadn't given it another thought. But now, the hairs on his arms stood on end.

What was Michael doing on the beach for four hours? And, why did he lie to Estrada? Was he to blame for the missing kayaker?

THE CURSE & THE COVEN

At sunset, when Carvello anchored the *Ragnarök* in a still bay off Hardwicke Island, Estrada opened another bottle of wine. This may have been their toughest day yet. Dylan, still sullen after falling overboard and nearly drowning, had retired to his cabin. Lord knows what demons he'd met in the sea. Carvello was so pissed he'd been forced to travel in fog, he'd also gone below. And Dubh, always the constant, sat out on the aft deck, broody and silent. He was mulling, but mulling what? The only person who seemed anywhere close to normal was Daphne. As usual, she'd prepared supper for them all, then cleaned up and retired to her room.

Michael had not appeared since his nocturnal swim. Estrada had remained upstairs all day to restore equilibrium among the others. Not that his efforts had accomplished much. He had no idea what was happening with Michael, who, while spending copious hours alone in the stateroom, seemed to have transformed back into his old self—the eccentric goth club manager who reveled in spiking his patrons' shots with erotigens and orchestrating orgies. Returning his soul from the Underworld had somehow melded his fractured personality and resurrected Mandragora, his alter ego—a libertine Lord Byron, quite impossible to contain. And this Mandragora was sick, just how sick he did not know.

Estrada shivered and glanced out the tinted window. Sensara had been meditating out on the bow for the last hour and was now stretching before bed. As they drew closer to Diego's lair, her moods grew more intense. Her aching breasts were a continual reminder that her baby had been stolen by a vampire because of something Michael had done. Estrada understood her infinite pain and wished only to ease it. At the bar, he grabbed two glasses and a bottle of wine. Shiraz. Her favorite.

When Sensara accepted the wine she smiled, and Estrada kissed her cheek. Her long dark hair smelled of rain and sea and pine sap.

"Rough day, eh? You okay?" He sat down beside her on the thick sunpad and felt the cool night embrace him.

She gulped some wine and set the near-empty glass on the table. "Yeah. I just . . . I worry for her and I miss her. It was her and me, you know, twenty-four-seven, and now . . . " She leaned her head on his shoulder. Couldn't say Lucy's name out loud.

"I know."

"No. You *don't* know." She backhanded him across the chest. "If you did, you wouldn't have jumped into the ocean."

Estrada glanced with curious eyes, had not expected anger.

"You could have drowned."

He shrugged. "But, I didn't."

"But you could have. And, if something happens to *you*, we'll never find *her*."

"Shit, Sara. I'm sorry." He hadn't thought that far. He'd just reacted. Dylan overboard. Save him. "If I could spin a charm and turn this whole thing around, you know I would."

"I just . . . I can't lose you too."

"You haven't lost *her* and you won't lose *me*. Never. I'm in this for the long haul."

Sensara tilted her head and stared at him with furrowed brows, and he realized, she didn't trust him.

Sitting his glass beside hers, he took a quick breath, then caught her chin in his hand and kissed her. Lips imploring, breathing her in. They hadn't touched like this since the night Lucy disappeared. And right now, it was all he wanted. Sex helped him cope when he was fretting, and sex with Sensara—and Michael for that matter—provided something more. The comfort of familiarity. For a moment, he could lose himself and forget the unbearable grief eating away at his insides.

"How? As Lucy's father, or . . . "

"As whatever you want." The offer surprised him as much as it did her. He kissed her again and in the heat of it, Sensara fell on top of him, winding her fingers through his hair, her breath quickening with kisses that grew ever deeper. Sliding her hands up his torso, she tugged his shirt over his head and smiled.

He returned the smile as his hands slipped beneath the soft lycra to find warm flesh.

Gasping, she pulled off her tank to free her engorged breasts and kissed him in an agony of need.

With two strong arms, he lifted her sideways, slipped off her capris and tossed them aside. Her skin was sweet and damp and salty on his lips.

Her soft cries mingled with his own, as unzipping his jeans, she played him.

"Sara . . ."

"Make love to me."

"I haven't got—"

"I don't care."

"Last time you got pregnant."

"Please," she said, and covered his mouth with hers.

That was all he needed.

Gasping, she danced a rhythm he'd never felt before, her every fiber melding with his flesh. The wave grew. He tried to slow it, to control it, but her legs clung and crushed and there was nothing but her and—

"My God," he cried, falling on his back. "That was—"

"Damn. Am I too late?"

Michael. Estrada turned at the sound of his voice. He sat on a corner of the sunpad only inches away, chest bare, his black pants slung down around his hips, and quite obviously aroused. How long had he been there watching? His red contacts flashed.

Curling his lip, Michael grinned. "Round two?" he said, then sprawled beside Estrada and threw an arm across his bare chest.

Estrada felt his hard heat against his thigh.

"You're a pig," Sensara said, drawing back. Grabbing her clothes, she pulled them on.

"Oh, don't be like that, priestess. Estrada and I share everything. You must know that."

"Stop it, Michael," Estrada said, his voice ripe with warning. Fists clenching and unclenching. The alcoholic stench was suffocating. "What have you been drinking?" It was something beyond wine. Sitting up, Estrada grabbed his jeans.

Sensara stood and stamped her foot, then stretched both hands to the sky and took a deep breath. Lowering them, she pointed both palms directly at Michael. "Michael Stryker. You cause nothing but pain." The energy shot from her palms like bolts of electricity. Static cut the silence and Estrada smelled the acrid stench of burning metal. "And so, I cast this curse. From this moment forward may your karma accelerate and strike you three-fold."

"Sara!" Lurching forward, Estrada caught her hands in his, the energy burning like the jolt of an electric fence. "No. You can't—"

Clutching his heart, Michael gasped as if he'd been stabbed. "Oh my God. I'm cursed . . . cursed by the Wiccan Priestess. Oh, woe is me." Laughing, he fell back on the sunpad.

"Take it back," Estrada pleaded. "Take it back now."

Sensara shook her head and stared with glassy eyes at Michael writhing on the deck.

"Look, he's just drunk and winding you up."

"He's evil. Evil and cruel and our baby's out there with monsters and you could have died and Dylan—"

"Sara, please."

Daphne and Dubh were suddenly there on the deck beside them. She threw her arms around Sensara and held her. "You've got to unwind it, Sensara. It's baneful. Karmic Law. You know that. It will come back on you three-fold. And you don't want that. Not because of this jerk. We'll help you."

"She's right," Dubh said. "It will take all of us to reverse it. Call a coven."

Michael stopped laughing and sat shaking his head. "You people are fucking feeble."

The raven came from nowhere. With a wingspan the size of Sensara's outstretched arms, it flew past Michael's head with a sudden loud whoosh, circled and tilted with talons outstretched. Sliding sideways, Michael shrieked and clutched his neck.

For a moment, Estrada thought Michael was acting again, and then he saw the blood drizzling between his fingers. He thought of the pterodactyl that cut his forehead in the Underworld—the pterodactyl that was Diego—and for a moment he couldn't move or speak.

"Fucking thing scratched me."

The raven settled on the roof, screeched, and stared.

"Fuck, Sensara!" Michael screamed.

"That wasn't me."

"Of course it was fucking you."

Two other ravens appeared off the port bow and flew in low circles around their heads, taunting, and teasing. Screaming, the girls ducked. Wings whooshing, the huge black birds harassed them, then landed on the ledge. Their eerie high-pitched cries cut the night.

"Get inside and close all the doors," Estrada yelled.

Sensara grabbed Daphne's arm and they rushed to the doorway.

Reaching down, Estrada grasped Michael's hand and hauled him upright. He was trembling.

"I'm gonna hurl—" Michael held his gut, then retched and spewed a mess of liquor and bile.

Estrada gagged from the stench but caught and held Michael by the hips while the ravens flew in heckling orbits around their heads. Squawking in near-human tongues, he heard the word *curse* repeated over and over. When at last, Michael stopped vomiting, he dragged him to the door.

"They're leaving," Dubh said.

"For now." Estrada thought again of Diego and the pterosaur that attacked him in the Underworld, the slash of those talons across his forehead. Did Diego employ ravens in his nest? Could these ravens be the same three that huddled in the trees at Lucy's birthday party? The terror? Were they being followed? Or had the ravens been summoned by Sensara's curse?

Carvello stood by the helm wrapped in his leopard robe. "What the fuck was that?" he asked, hands in the air.

"A mistake," Estrada said. "One, we will rectify as soon as I get Michael to bed."

"Someone's got to clean up that puke."

"Someone will. Please, just find me a first-aid kit, then go below. This may take some time."

~~~

The edge of Hardwicke Island was a jumble of evergreens and bleached driftwood, scarred by rock. After thirty minutes of cruising in the tender, Estrada was beginning to think they'd never find a place to disembark. It was a small inflatable and the five of them were crammed in like herring. He'd left Michael back on the yacht. After the raven attack, he'd passed out and bed seemed the safest place for him. Carvello was there too, in case the ravens returned. Finally, Estrada spied something promising. They'd been blessed with a clear night and against the dense forest wall, the waning half-moon illuminated a sandy spit. Ghostly and vacant, the land emitted a beckoning glow.

Estrada motioned to Dylan, who turned the tender in a wave of white spray and sped them into shore. When the motor died, his ears rang with the silence.

Dubh hopped out first, since he'd been sitting on Estrada's knee. Climbing free of the tender, Estrada breathed in the still night, while his body swayed with the sense of the sea. He felt the peculiar sensation of land beneath his feet, as he offered his hand to each of the others. A starry panoply flickered over the open water of Johnstone Strait. The beauty of the wild places. If they weren't convening to banish Sensara's hasty curse, it might have been romantic.

The sandy beach was strewn with boulders, rocks, shells, and haphazard driftwood logs deposited by the tide. A kayaker's haven. And, in the midst of it, they discovered a charred rock-ringed circle. As they unpacked, Dylan collected dry tinder and built a tidy fire in the pit. Daphne dragged a flattened slab of driftwood beside it to serve as an altar, and the witches began collecting. An oyster shell brimming with sea water. A globular grandfather stone honed by time and sea. Branches of sweet cedar cut with the carved boline Estrada carried in his jacket pocket. A honeyed candle oiled with the frankincense Daphne carried in hers. Always, an homage to the elements.

"I brought this," Sensara said, and opened her hand to reveal the charmed bracelet, Dubh had given Lucy for her birthday. "I thought we could use it."

Dubh nodded. "Aye, Lady. We'll spell it forth."

"And this," she said, pulling a small framed photograph of Lucy from her bag.

"Ah, Lucita." Estrada took the photo from her hand, kissed it, and held it to his heart.

"We'll find her," Daphne said. "I feel positive tonight."

"Me too," Estrada said, though his heart ached. "And since we're unraveling Michael's curse, I brought this." He pulled a long lock of fair hair from the pocket of his jean jacket.

Sensara raised her eyebrows with automatic disapproval.

"We need *something* of Michael on the altar."

"I know."

"Also, I found *this* on the deck." Estrada held up an iridescent raven feather almost twice the size of his outstretched hand. "I think we should use it."

"Aye," Dylan said. "Those birds need binding or banishing."

"I'm sure they're the same ravens I saw the afternoon of Lucy's birthday party."

"What?" Sensara's eyes widened. "Why didn't you tell me?"

"I didn't think much of it until I saw them again tonight. There were three ravens in the trees right before you brought Lucy outside."

Sensara shivered. "What are they? Messengers or . . . "

Estrada shrugged. "I honestly don't know. But they're following us."

"And fucking with us," Dubh said. "If they'd all come at us with beaks and talons—"

"Hitchcock," Estrada muttered.

"Are we ready?" Standing rigid, Daphne pulled her deer-skin hand drum from its hide case along with a beater. The ravens terrified her. Estrada had never seen that before.

"Yes," Sensara said. "Shall we begin?"

"I wonder . . . " Dubh said. "The invocation . . . "

"The god and goddess," Sensara said.

"Aye, but who?"

"The Morrigan?"

"Aye, sure. The Morrigan is a warrior goddess associated with the dead and birds of prey. But I wonder . . . We already know a fight awaits us at the dragon's lair. What we really need is some powerful magic to render these ravens."

"Who do you have in mind?" Estrada asked.

"Cerridwen. You, my Lady, are much like our ancient Welsh goddess. She is a mother, a shapeshifter, and a powerful witch."

"We know her," Sensara said. "To invoke Cerridwen is to invoke the Great Mother herself."

"Aye, but the choice is yours, Lady," he said, bowing to Sensara.

"As our child is in danger, the Great Mother seems fitting."

"And may I . . . "

Sensara cocked her head and eyed him curiously.

"May I invoke her?" Dubh asked.

"If you have a special connection to the goddess, then yes, please do, for all our sakes. And what of the god?"

"Cernunnos," Estrada said. "He's as old as time and I feel a personal connection with him."

"Aye," Dylan said. "If the horned god would honor us with another visit, that would be brilliant."

"We met Cernunnos in Scotland," Estrada explained.

Dylan and Dubh nodded.

"Met?" Daphne said.

Estrada smiled. "In the flesh. Cernunnos is a hunter and we need one in our midst. We still don't know exactly where this place is."

"Anyone else?" Sensara said.

"Let's keep it simple." Estrada doffed his jacket. "And let me call on Cernunnos."

"Of course." Sensara began to strip off her clothing and the others followed. "Glad I packed my wand," she said, twirling the crystal between her fingers. "Did anyone bring a compass?"

"I did." Daphne was already holding it in her hand. "North is that way. Over the water," she said, pointing.

"Aye, right beneath Polaris," Dubh said.

"I didn't know you were a stargazer," Dylan said.

"Oh aye. The Big Dipper shines over our island too. You must have seen it in Kilmartin Glen?"

"Many times. And over the harbor at Tarbert too."

"I learned the tricks of the stars on Mull, when I was a boy. A Scot has no need for a compass."

"Alright. Let's take our places." Sensara was growing impatient. "Estrada, can you hold North? And Magus, South?"

They all walked to their quadrants.

"Right. I'll begin." Walking sunwise, Sensara cast a large circle with her wand, while chanting the invocation.

"I conjure this circle as sacred space
I conjure containment within this place
Thrice do I conjure the Sacred Divine
Powerful goodness and mystery mine
From East to West and from South to North,
I cast this circle and call Magic forth."

Standing in the center beside the altar, Sensara said, "Our circle is cast. We are between the worlds." Then she glanced at Daphne, who stood with her back to the black pine-studded forest.

Turning, Daphne raised her right hand and drew a large invoking pentagram. "I call upon the powers of the East, the sun and stars, birds and blossoms, breath and breeze, and all that glows in the freshened air."

From his position in the South, Dubh raised his right palm in salute. "Let there be peace in the South. I ask that all good and positive forces lend their fire to this coven by joining us here tonight."

Smiling, Sensara turned to Dylan. Raising both arms wide above his head, he gazed out over the strait. "I invoke the powers of the West, of the sea, of the rain, of the blessed unconscious."

Estrada was last. Standing facing the North, he used his boline to carve a pentacle in the night sky and enclosed it within a circle. As he etched, white light flew from his blade like the sparks from a knife-grinder's stone. "Ancient Spirits of the North, join us this divine night. Fecund earth and glacial mountains, trees and stones, and forest creatures, I invite you into our circle. Grace us with your power and strength and bless us in our endeavor."

Standing in the center beside the fire and the altar, Sensara touched her wand to the sky and then to the earth. "Centered between the Upperworld and the Underworld, I call upon the ancestral spirits to join us in this sacred space. We invoke only positive entities into this liminal landscape between the threads of earth, sea, and sky."

"All hail, Cernunnos. Lord of Fertility and Spirit of the Hunt."

"Hail Cernunnos," came the echo.

"We invoke the goddess Cerridwen, who wanted only to bless her child with peace. We ask the Great Goddess to bestow blessings and power upon us and aid us in our quest to find and free our stolen bairn, Lucy. That she may find peace once again and be reunited with her mother and father and all those who love and cherish her."

"All hail, Cerridwen," Sensara said.

"Hail Cerridwen," came the echo.

They paused then, engulfed by the eerie silence of the island night. Leaves fluttering in the sea breeze seemed to stop mid-turn, while the fire dulled its crackling, and even the waves whispered. All grew witched with waiting and wanting.

When Sensara joined them in the circle, the witches grasped each other's hands and stretching their arms wide, began to breathe as one. The priestess's voice, emerging from somewhere deep within her soul, uttered the incantation. Slow and quiet at first, and then raising in pitch, tempo, and energy as the others joined the chant.

"In the stillness of this night, we call the goddess, come to light

In the stillness of this night, we call the god to aid our fight
In the stillness of this night, God and Goddess, lend us sight
In the stillness of this night, God and Goddess, make it right
Come to light, aid our fight, lend us sight, make it right."

When Estrada stamped his foot with the four-beat rhythm, the others picked it up and they danced sunwise around the circle.

"In the stillness of this night, God and Goddess make it right.
Come to light, aid our fight, lend us sight, make it right."

As the energy rose, Estrada felt himself lifted from the ground. The only thing keeping him from taking flight were the hands anchoring him firmly on either side—Sensara on his right and Daphne on his left. But their voltage drove through him like the spark of flint on steel.

When Estrada glanced across the circle toward Dubh, he was startled by an image emerging from the spiraling sparks of the fire. He blinked. Still, it remained. An elongated male form, it shimmered in the flames. Was he hallucinating? Sometimes, the ritual energy could turn one's spirit eyes real. He looked around the circle. No one else appeared to have noticed. Driven by the dance, they were building the energy to a frenzied peak.

Breath ragged, Estrada continued to stamp out the beat as his vision sprouted a full rack of antlers, eighteen points, and above the bridge of the long nose, he recognized those coppery kohl-crested eyes. *Cernunnos.* Like Dubh, his chest was tattooed in Celtic spirals. The golden serpentine torque he wore coiled around his neck glinted in the firelight. Estrada's heartbeat quickened. He'd called and the horned god had come.

At the crescendo in their chant, Sensara called a halt, and they all stood reveling in the power.

Casting himself upwards from the fire, the horned god leapt to the earth on muscular legs, the clatter of his cloven hooves echoing between their breaths.

"Shaman. You summon me again," he said, his voice dripping brandy.

"Yes. Thank you for coming *again*. I need you. *We* need you."

"What's happening?" Sensara asked.

"Cernunnos is here. Can't you see him?"

"They cannot," Cernunnos said.

"I can see you," Dubh said.

"You are of the Sidhe. Both in blood and memory."

"Aye, Lord." Dubh bowed. "You honor us with your presence."

"I come for the shaman. We are bound."

"Bound?" Estrada wasn't sure he liked being bound to the horned god.

"*Sow-r-ka*," Cernunnos said, drawing out the vowels, trilling the *r* and hardening the *c* to make Sorcha's name sound both exotic and potent. His brown eyes grew wide and feverish, even as his purply lips curled down. Cernunnos stroked his beard and sighed so deeply, Estrada thought it could only be love he felt for the red-haired woman they'd both met in Scotland. "We laid together three days and nights, and so, I owe you more than I have given."

Estrada stood speechless, pondering, yet another impossibility. He remembered the deal they'd struck last summer. Cernunnos was to come for Sorcha the following Beltane—May first—three months ago. But, *three* days and nights? Had Cernunnos stayed at Sorcha's camp in Kilmartin Glen? Estrada had been so involved with Lucy, he'd completely forgotten about the Irish archaeologist and her offer to *merge* with the horned god. She'd agreed to the tryst to help free Dylan from prison, but also because she was a little crazy. Sorcha wanted to experience the god of the ancient people whose bones and shards she brushed from the earth.

"How *is* Sorcha?" Estrada said, at last.

"Sorcha? Is he talking about Sorcha?" Eyebrows furled, Dylan stared at Estrada. "What's he saying?"

Sorcha had been Dylan's lover for a brief time last summer. She'd helped Estrada get him released from prison and was also the reason he'd ended up there.

Cernunnos shook his head. "She has not yet returned."

"I don't understand," Estrada said, shaking his head. "Returned from where?"

"It is of no consequence," the horned god said. "I am here to repay a debt. What is it you desire of me, shaman?"

Now, Estrada *was* concerned. Had Sorcha gone somewhere with Cernunnos? If so, why had he returned without her? Hopefully, not because Estrada had summoned him.

"If Sorcha is in danger, you must go to her."

"Sorcha's in danger?" Dylan stood stiffly with his hands on his hips. He stared into the fire, trying to see this creature who spoke of the woman he still loved with a fierce and futile passion.

Estrada ignored Dylan's question. The longer they kept the horned god engaged in conversation, the longer Lucy was left alone with the vampires.

The god stretched to his full height and shook his antlers. "What is your request, shaman?"

"A vampire stole our child," Estrada said.

"Diego." Cernunnos scratched his feathery beard with long fingernails.

"You know Diego?"

"I had hoped the vampire would exact his revenge on the human."

"The human? You mean Michael?"

"Yes. Man for man. That is justice. That is our way."

This notion left Estrada momentarily speechless.

"But you say he took a child?"

"My child . . . Our child," Estrada said, gesturing to Sensara. "And we need your help to find her and bring her home."

"So, Michael Stryker still lives?" The horned god sounded surprised, as if he expected otherwise.

"Yes, but he's not well, not himself."

"I did what I could, but I cannot interfere in what is fated," the god said. The fire popped and crackled as a gust of wind caught the burning logs and sent a spray of sparks and smoke spiraling northward.

Estrada coughed and moved out of the way. "Are you saying Michael is destined to die?"

"As is every human." He swaggered a few paces, cocking his head this way and that.

"Riddles. Can you never just give a straight answer?" Estrada felt his jaw clench. Took a breath and rubbed the back of his neck to release the tension. The lives of his daughter and lover were at stake. He needed real, honest solutions. Not palaver.

Cernunnos glanced at Lucy's photograph and nodded with understanding. "She bears your beauty, shaman." He smiled sadly. "It was wrong of Diego to steal her, so I will help you find her."

Dubh picked up the silver bracelet and held it out to the god. "Please, if you can, tell us how she fares."

Cernunnos held the charm between his palms, then closed his eyes. "The child is well fostered," he said, at last. "She eats and sleeps. Is blessed. Is loved."

"Thank you." Estrada clutched Sensara's hand. "He says Lucy is being well cared for. She's blessed and loved."

"Loved?" Choking up, Sensara touched her heart.

"And what of the goddess Cerridwen?" Dubh asked.

"The goddess is everywhere," Cernunnos said. "Do you not see and feel her?"

"Will she help us?"

"The goddess thrives in the essence of your priestess and her sister. How are they called?"

"Sensara is our high priestess, and this is Daphne."

"What's he saying?" Daphne asked.

"Tell him we want to see him," Sensara said.

Estrada glanced at Cernunnos. He wasn't sure he wanted them to see the god. The last woman who saw him was Sorcha, and what had become of her?

But Cernunnos stamped his hoof, snorted, and swaggered toward Sensara.

"He's coming," Estrada said, shuffling closer to the priestess.

Cernunnos sashayed around Sensara who stood rigid holding her wand across her chest in a defensive stance. Now fully visible, Estrada marveled at his tattooed torso, the perfection of his muscled back and buttocks, and the serpentine torque encircling his neck in twisted gold. The god's beauty was staggering.

"Don't fret, shaman. One day we shall know each other intimately. It is our destiny."

Estrada cleared his throat and glanced at Dubh.

"You can't escape destiny, mate." Dubh giggled.

When Cernunnos ran his mulberry lips along Sensara's neck and shoulder, she shivered though she couldn't see him. "She's powerful and imbued with your scent, shaman."

"I heard that," Sensara said, thrilled she could engage in the conversation.

"Sensara and I are—"

Cernunnos raised his hand. "I understand."

He sashayed over to Daphne and ran his hands over her head and shoulders. "This woman is powerful too. Like her Greek namesake, she is unknown to man and loves her sisters of the earth."

"I can hear him too," Daphne said. "How does he know these things?"

Estrada shrugged. "He's a god."

"I give you all the gift of sight," Cernunnos said.

Sensara and Daphne both gasped when the god was suddenly revealed. Dylan, who'd seen Cernunnos before, merely nodded and grinned. Cernunnos pranced around the circle on cloven hooves reveling in the awe he'd created among the witches.

"How will you help us find Lucy?" Estrada asked.

Cernunnos fixed his gaze on Estrada. "I will blaze a trail to the child. Trust me and follow it."

"What about Michael's curse?" Dubh asked.

"Curse?"

In the shock of seeing Cernunnos again, Estrada had almost forgotten. "Sensara cast a curse on Michael. She was angry, she—"

"I cannot remove a curse cast in anger by a witch. Your priestess holds the power to do that herself. But know it will dissipate only if she truly wishes it."

"And the ravens?" Dubh asked.

"They are not ravens, though they may be dispatched as ravens."

"Not ravens," Estrada said. "What are they?"

"Diego's progeny."

Dubh gasped. "Vampires? The ravens are vampires?"

"Shifters, like Diego," Estrada said, remembering the giant bird he'd seen in the Underworld. "Somehow, he's given his progeny the power to transform into ravens."

"Ach, aye. That's how they travel unseen."

"And how they got into Lucy's room," Sensara said.

"And Michael's flat," said Estrada, with sudden understanding. "And Nora Barnes' home."

"What a perfect disguise," Daphne said. "The raven is a trickster and being native to this land, no one would even notice them."

Sensara went pale. "They attacked us. Came right to the yacht."

Estrada remembered their frantic cries and Michael's dread. Did he know? Picking up the raven feather, he held it in the candle flame. "Fire be your weakness and your destruction," he said. The feather flared and cast a menacing glow over the glade. When it reached the end, he flicked it in the fire, and a small explosion of sparks flew up. "So mote it be."

Cernunnos was suddenly standing before him. Estrada stared up into sultry eyes, as warm hands clasped his shoulders. "To vanquish Diego, you must unleash your power, shaman." His voice was a whisper of wild honey. "Accept whatever is offered on this journey. Do not hold back."

"What do you mean? What will be offered?" Estrada cleared his throat and swallowed uneasily. He was dealing with vampires.

When Cernunnos blinked his kohl-edged eyes, his thick mulberry lips relaxed into a crooked grin. An overture was being made. *Accept whatever is offered.*

"Do not be afraid, shaman. Trust your instincts and know that I am with you."

The hands caressing Estrada's shoulders slid up his neck and clasped his jaw. And, when those mulberry lips curled around his own, Estrada's body ignited with a passion he could not contain. Closing his eyes, he opened his soul. Every molecule vibrated with an energy he'd never felt before. Hands grasped his back and pulled him close. Estrada's fingers climbed the long, braided hair and stroked the pointed tips of boney antlers, as he surrendered to the horned god. One kiss—and in that one kiss, a spiraling galaxy of exploding stars.

And then, Estrada crashed to the sand and the horned god was gone. His body felt like stone, yet his mind raced. How many nights had he played the god and got it wrong? He'd thought of Cernunnos as a fertility god. With his stone-tipped spear, he killed animals to feed his people, and with his fleshy spear he impregnated the goddess to ensure the continuation of the tribe. But it wasn't that simple. The horned god was sexual, but there was more to him than that. Cernunnos was the ultimate lover with a heart as vast as the milky way.

"He loves you," Dubh whispered.

Estrada glanced around the circle. "Did they all see?"

Dubh shook his head. "The others turned away, but I couldn't. I've worshipped the horned god too many years. I couldn't take my eyes off him, or you."

Estrada shrugged, then stood and dusted himself off. Sensara stood across the circle with her gaze cast down. He went and held her. "I'm sorry, Sara. I didn't know that was going to happen and I couldn't—"

"There is no need. We are between the worlds."

"You mean, whatever happens in Vegas . . . "

Smiling, she took his hand. "I'm ready to unravel the curse, High Priest. Will you help me?"

"Of course," Estrada said.

Still holding his hand, Sensara walked with him to the altar. Picking up Michael's lock of hair, she held it in her other hand and spoke her incantation.

"In anger, did I lay a curse. I ask that it now be reversed. Let no harm come to him from me. But only good. So mote it be."

She held the hair over the candle flame, as he'd done with the raven feather, and then flicked it into the fire. It flared and stunk and they both drew back.

"So mote it be." Estrada kissed her hand and walked back to his space in the northern quadrant.

"Our requests have been heard and answered in this sacred circle," Sensara said, as she took the cedar branches from the altar and cast them in the fire. "And, we have much to consider. We will take what we have learned this night and journey on." Picking up the oyster shell, she dipped her fingers in the seawater and extinguished the candle, then poured the rest of the water into the sand and turned over the shell. "We thank the gods and goddesses for their blessings. Merry meet, and merry part, and merry meet again."

Holding her wand, Sensara walked widdershins around the circle unraveling with grace the sacred space she had cast.

"Merry meet, and merry part, and merry meet again," they echoed.

She understands, Estrada thought. She'd accepted his intimate kiss with Cernunnos without jealousy. And in acceptance was hope. If she understood that love was as boundless as the universe. If she understood his need for freedom . . .

Afterwards, they sat quietly watching the fire from the silence of their fractured circle and passed around a bottle of red wine. When he licked his lips, all Estrada could taste was mulberry. *Know that I am with you.* How long would the god's essence stay with him? *He loves you,* Dubh had said. And he was right. Estrada felt a love like none he'd ever felt before. A heart-rendering love. The love of a god.

FORGIVE

Leopold splashed water on his face and stared into the bathroom mirror. He hadn't shaved in days and his long blond hair, matted by sea wind, hung in sticky, bloody knots. Eyes, though still green, flickered red-rimmed and monstrous. He was becoming like *them*.

He ran his fingers through his hair, clawing at the knots, reveling in the pain. For a moment, he had wanted to kill the old couple and feed on their blood. He was starving, and it had taken all the willpower he could muster to resist, for he knew once he crossed that line, there was no turning back. Worse still, he'd forsaken Nora Barnes. Too frightened to reveal himself, he'd left her imprisoned with the child for days, alone and vulnerable. Could she forgive him? Would she? Perhaps, if *she* could forgive him, then he could forgive himself.

Slipping through the saloon, he heard their voices. Zion and Eliseo were still on the flybridge, caught up in reliving the story of their attack on Michael Stryker. Hovering in the shadows, Leopold watched and listened.

"He's turning," Zion said, as he licked Stryker's blood from his fingers. "I can taste it."

"El Padrino said he would."

"I didn't know a man could turn from just a bite." Zion grinned. "I drank from him the night Christophe brought him to Le Chateau. He must be another one of mine."

Eliseo shook his head. "No. A bite from one of us would not cause the change. The human must drink our blood at the point of death for that to occur."

Zion's face fell in disappointment.

"El Padrino ripped the flesh from Stryker's neck when he found him on the island. It is Father's venom you taste. It flows through Michael Stryker's veins."

Zion grunted his displeasure.

Leopold had noticed that Zion had developed a profound interest in this Michael Stryker. If Diego turned Stryker, he would own him, just like he owned them all. This is what had Zion in a sulk.

"How long before Stryker changes?"

"I don't know. But we must keep a closer watch on him, I think." Eliseo paused and scratched his hair with his long nails the way a raven might groom with his beak. After so many years as a bird he was becoming as birdlike as he was human. "Where is Leopold?" he asked, at last.

"Crying in his soup?"

"Leopold Blosch has a backbone made of eggshell." Eliseo coughed and cleared his throat. "I will let him pout for now."

Zion shrugged and glanced at his fingers, looking for a spot he might have missed. "Stryker's blood makes me hungry."

"We're close to Telegraph Cove and it's not yet midnight. Take the night to hunt. I will stay and watch our weak brother."

Weak? thought Leopold. Father's favorite was a con and a pretender. He felt offended by Eliseo's casual remarks. A man who builds a million-dollar restaurant business from nothing is not weak. He'd show Eliseo his backbone was made of steel, not eggshell. But not in a way the boy would be expecting.

With Zion gone, Eliseo would sit alone under the stars and strum his guitar, and Leopold could take his time with Nora. For he realized now that *she* was his salvation. If Leopold was ever to redeem himself, Nora must understand and forgive.

Leaving the two vampires, he slipped downstairs to his room. It was the smallest cabin, with just a single bed, but a case of toiletries had been left by a previous occupant in a corner of the closet. He grabbed it, stripped, and stretched in the shower. Steam rose in clouds as the water drizzled through his hair. He shampooed away the grease and blood, scrubbed his skin with a nailbrush and body wash, then towel-dried, and applied lotion. After prying a pair of nail scissors from the case, he cut his beard and shaved. Finally, he brushed his teeth and applied lip balm. It felt good to be smooth and moist again.

Leopold appraised himself in the mirror. Platinum hair fell like a winter waterfall to well below his shoulders. He looked pretty. Almost human. Except for the eyes, and the razored canines hiding beneath his thick glossy lips.

I will let him pout, Eliseo had said. Hah. A brooding man doesn't look like this. Now, he wouldn't frighten Nora. He climbed into clean white jeans and pulled a long-sleeved white T-shirt over his head. Then, he took a few deep breaths and covered his eyes with shades.

The old Leopold still existed; at least, on the outside.

Stopping by the galley, he sliced the remaining tomatoes, drizzled olive oil and balsamic vinegar over them, chopped herbs, and ground some salt. He ripped off a hunk of bread and set it all on a tray. Since his soup ran out, they'd been feeding her from cans like a dog. They knew nothing.

Leopold took a breath, knocked on her door and counted to twenty. If she wasn't decent, that would give her time. He knocked again, then unlocked and opened the door.

Of course, she's asleep, he thought, seeing her lying on the bed. It must be almost one. In just a month, he'd forgotten what it was like to be human and grow tired with the darkness. But the sudden tensing of her body told him he was wrong. She wasn't asleep. Only pretending. He smelled the sweet musky scent of fear, as sickly as lilies.

"Nora," he whispered. "Nora, it's me." Reaching out, he turned on the soft bathroom light rather than flood the room with a harsh glow.

Nora turned over slowly and rubbed her eyes. "How do you know my name?"

Had they never used her name? Never talked to her except to bark orders?

"It's me. Leopold Blosch."

"Leopold?" She spoke as if she didn't recognize the name.

"From Ecos, the bistro."

"Leopold?" she said again, this time knowing the name, but questioning why he stood before her now, in this place of terror and suffering.

Leopold admired her beauty in the dim light of the room. Nora wasn't much older than he was, perhaps in her early thirties. He couldn't see her eyes, but remembered they were the color of coffee beans. Her short nut-brown hair framed a square jaw that revealed character. When she chewed her plump lips, he saw they were dry and cracked. His fingers touched his own moist lips and he wanted to scream. How thoughtless he'd become. They'd ripped the poor woman from her home in the middle of the night. Given her nothing of comfort but the child. How callous. He would bring her his toiletry kit as soon as he could.

"Please don't be afraid, Nora. I need to talk to you." He felt suddenly feverish and wished he'd drunk more wine. His throat was tight, his tongue thick. Could he find the right words and say what must be said?

"Did they kidnap you too?" Nora asked, brightly. And then her face fell. "Or, are you . . . ?" She clutched her neck. Her voice faded and the scent of fear flooded the small room.

"I won't hurt you. And I won't let them hurt you. I promise."

"You're *with* them?" Drawing back against the headboard, she pulled up her knees to shield her chest. The child whimpered in its cot.

"Please, let me explain." He moved toward her, holding out the plate with its glistening tomato salad. "Soon, you can go home. You *and* the child. I brought you food. It's fresh." He smiled.

"Why? Why am I here? Why did you take me from Zachary and Joe?"

"Diego needed someone to nurse the child until . . ."

"Until what?" Nora shook her head.

Leopold realized then, he couldn't finish his thought. He couldn't even finish this ragged conversation. What was he thinking? How could he ever explain?

"I'm sorry," he said.

"I thought you were my friend." Her shoulders slumped and her fingers touched her mouth.

"I *am* your friend. You and Joe."

"Then why? Why would you—"

"Diego imprisoned me, Nora. But he said, if I found him a woman to nurse the child, he'd let me go free." His feverish eyes darted from her condemning face to the food he carried in his hand. The bread had fallen into the wet tomatoes and gone soggy. Herbs slithered in their oil.

"Diego?"

"He's a man . . . a man intent on revenge. But you mustn't worry. Diego promised you wouldn't be harmed. Not you or the child. It won't be long now. The child's father is following us. Once Diego has *him*, he'll set us free." Leopold realized he was babbling but couldn't stop himself. "Please forgive me, Nora. I couldn't stay in that prison."

"So, you traded *my life* for your freedom?"

"Not your *life*, Nora."

"Yes, Leopold. My life. You ripped me from Zachary and Joe and gave me to these men."

"They're not . . . " Leopold sat the plate on the floor and slumped beside it.

"They're not what?"

"In another day or two we'll reach the island. I promise you won't be harmed."

What else could he say? To tell her they were vampires would only spike her terror. To tell her *he* was a vampire would vanquish all hope. There was nothing left to say, except, "One day I hope you can forgive me, Nora."

Michael awoke from another nightmare starring Carvello. Sweating and shaking, he shifted in the bed trying to remember when he'd last taken his Ativan. Sometimes, he felt as light as a cloud but other times, like now, he was a block of stone. Tombstone. Stoned. He had to piss but was too tired to stand.

An image played in his mind. Carvello standing on a deck, backdropped by the Pacific. He always wore white and black and that ridiculous captain's hat, except when he wasn't wearing anything at all.

Other faces appeared in his dreams. Faces Michael had tried to forget. Leering, drunken men with hairy chins and gaping mouths reeking of booze. For years, he'd convinced himself his time aboard the *Deception* was a "coming of age". From boy to man in eight short weeks. The summer of lust. They'd lavished gifts on him. He still had an emerald ring the size of his pinkie nail stashed in a marble box.

But the last few days, the nightmares revealed something else. What Carvello did was wrong. What the others did was wrong. It was *all* wrong. Those two months had changed him. What if it had never happened? What if he'd stayed home and played video games with his friends that summer? Who would he be? Anything would be better than who he was.

It was quiet and the boat's rhythmic rocking calmed his anxiety, until a pain crept through his gut. He checked his phone. 2:00. Day or night? The boat was anchored somewhere in the strait. Where was Estrada? He hadn't seen him in hours. He vaguely recalled watching Estrada make love to Sensara. Or was that a dream too?

His mouth felt so dry he could barely swallow. His tongue was swollen. He felt in his pocket for the small brown plastic bottle of Ativan, pulled it out, popped it open, and dumped the little treasures on his palm. The label said there were thirty. He counted ten. How many days? He popped one in his mouth and chewed. And then there were nine. Sawdust and bitterness. Perhaps, he should just take them all and be done with it. No one would care.

Pain snaked through his lower back. He really had to piss. He looked around for something to piss in, and then sighed. You're not an invalid, asshole. Stop feeling sorry for yourself and go to the toilet. Lay off the booze and drink some water.

 Bouncing off the walls, he stumbled to the head, let it go, then leaned on the sink and stared at the monster in the mirror. He stuck his head under the tap and used his hand to splash water over his head. When he straightened up, he felt woozy. The water dripped, stinging, into his blue-rimmed eyes. Why did he look so sleep-deprived when all he'd done for days was sleep?

Diego's crimson scar throbbed as if it had a pulse of its own. He tilted his head the other way. A scarlet slash edged in dried blood ran across his neck from shoulder to chin. What happened? He scratched his scalp with his long nails and gathered up his hair, then tilted his head back. It looked deep and raw. Infected. He couldn't remember. Another blackout?

He shoved open the shower door and turned on the hot tap. Stepping inside, he stood with his hands upraised and let the steamy stream wash over him. When it hit the scratch, he flinched, then opened his mouth and drank the scalding water. Piping hot. He could turn the tap the other way, but no, he deserved this. He couldn't remember what he'd done, but he knew it was bad. When had he ever done anything good? Even Estrada had deserted him. He turned his head and let the boiling water burn Diego's scar. Bracing his body against the sides of the stall, he counted to five, then slid into a heap.

Finally, he pushed against the shower door and crawled out onto the floor. He would never be pure. His pale skin was painted in bright red swathes. Standing, he wrapped a towel around his hips and turned off the tap. He found his leggings on the floor and pulled them on, then popped the pill bottle into a side pocket and stumbled into the hallway. Where was Estrada?

He opened each door and looked inside. Every room was empty. The beds made as if no one had even slept in them. Was he still dreaming?

One step at a time, he climbed the stairs. Through the windows of the deserted lounge he saw only black. Where were they? Even Dubh was not sleeping on the aft deck as usual. Had they gone ashore? He stared at the booze, then opened the bar fridge and grabbed a ginger ale. His throat stung but the putrid taste changed. He took another mouthful, popped the pills from his pocket and swallowed one, and then another. And then there were seven.

He hated being alone at night when everyone else was out on the prowl. Where had they gone? To the island? Stretching out on the white leather couch, he closed his eyes. He was almost asleep when he felt something on his bare chest. Like the brush of a cat's paw, it tickled.

Michael flinched and opened his eyes. Carvello knelt beside him. Adrenalin coursed through Michael's veins. Fuck. Is this another nightmare?

"You haven't changed," Carvello said.

"Yes, I have," Michael said defensively. "I'm a man now."

Carvello shook his head and his lopsided grin widened. "Nah. You're still Peter fucking Pan."

"Actually, I could rip your throat out." Michael grinned back at Carvello and the edge of his upper lip tingled against his fang.

"But you won't." Leaning over, Carvello shoved his lips in Michael's face.

The stench of Prada made his stomach flip. "Get away from me," he yelled, shoving Carvello with such force the man reeled backwards. Michael stood, muscles flinching. "I hate you, you pervert. You had no right."

Recovering, Carvello stood his ground and sent Michael an incredulous stare. Then his lip curled with understanding. "You never said no, kid."

"I was twelve," Michael said, surprised by the small boy voice seeping through his lips. Tears burned his eyes.

"Come on. I didn't hurt you." Carvello turned to the bar and poured two glasses of wine. He gulped from one and held out the other.

Michael waved it away. "You *did* hurt me. I remember." Snot trickled from his nose. Sniveling, he swiped at it with his fist.

Carvello guzzled the rest of his wine and then downed the other.

"Relax kid," Carvello said.

These were words from Michael's nightmares.

"Have some wine. Remember the good times, the nights it was just us two."

"I don't want to remember." Michael realized suddenly he'd been fighting to forget these memories his whole life.

Carvello shrugged. "You could have said no, kid."

"I WAS TWELVE," Michael screamed, each word driven by anger. He remembered the men, their breath stinking with smoke and booze, the nails, the teeth. "I was twelve on a fucking boat in the middle of the fucking ocean and you sold me to fucking monsters."

Carvello shrugged.

"It was wrong. Say it was wrong."

"Would that make you feel better?"

Michael straightened and wiped the tears from his cheeks. Nothing could ever bring back his innocence. Not a confession. Not a conviction.

"I was good to you, kid."

Michael sat back down on the couch, touched his fingers to his lips and felt the razored canines. He sighed. "You used to massage my back with olive oil."

"That's right, kid. I have the touch." Carvello leaned over and ran a finger down Michael's shoulder. "Should I get the oil?"

"Where are the others?"

"Gone off to the island to do some of their weird shit."

"Get the oil." Turning on his side, Michael watched Carvello stalk across the room in his white robe splashed with black roses. What other lambs had the leopard slaughtered? Rich, connected, with an army of thugs at his back, the man thought he could take whatever he wanted.

Michael touched his tooth and his thumb stung like a paper cut. He stared at the blood, licked it, and smiled.

Carvello swaggered over to the stereo, turned on the soundtrack to *Dirty Dancing* and skipped down to Eric Carmen's cut of "Hungry Eyes". After cranking up the volume, he danced his way back. Surround sound flooded the room.

"You're so pale," Carvello said, when he returned clutching the brown bottle of olive oil. "You need to spend some time on deck."

"I hate the sun."

"You used to love it."

Flipping onto his belly, Michael tried to relax as Carvello rubbed his back with the oil. It smelled rich and fruity and reminded him how much he loved dirty martinis.

When Carvello's hands wandered too low, Michael flipped onto his back.

Carvello, who'd been balancing on the edge of the leather sofa, teetered and almost fell.

"Trade me places."

"You sure kid?"

"Never more sure."

When Carvello stood and slipped off his robe, Michael stood and stared. Victor Carvello was an old man—an old man whose time had come. Michael's heart pounded. Even through the music, he could hear the blood rushing through his veins, and then he realized, it was not *his* blood he could hear. It was Carvello's.

Tilting his head, Michael stared into those wide brown hungry eyes. Carvello licked his lips. He thought he was about to devour his prey.

Then Michael took a step forward, grasped Carvello's face with both hands, and sunk his teeth into the lip. Ignoring Carvello's muffled screams and struggles to free himself, Michael continued to hold him firmly by the jaw, bite, and swallow. Closing his eyes, he swooned.

Then, an intense pain in Michael's groin took his breath away and he released his jaws.

"You bit me, you little fuck!"

The next thing Michael knew, Estrada was holding him. They were all around and Carvello was still yelling. The music stopped.

"He *fucking* bit me!" Carvello held his face. Blood streamed from his mouth, down his chin.

"Cover yourself." Sensara threw Carvello his robe.

"Walk with me," Estrada whispered in Michael's ear, and they stumbled down the stairs together.

Michael's balls throbbed. He was going to hurl again. When he wiped his mouth, he saw Carvello's blood staining his hand. But, through all the pain, Michael smiled. He was no longer prey and soon the predator would be no more.

LEVI'S COMING

The night was as clear and still as ice, and just as bitterly cold. Quite opposite to the torrid day. Magus Dubh curled into a ball on the aft deck, tucked blankets around his body, and envisioned fire spiraling up his spinal cord and down his limbs. It worked for a while. He fell back asleep, stretched out, and awakened with one dangling frozen foot. Grasping it, he rubbed it briskly to bring back the blood. Fuck it.

He crept inside and made himself a hot chocolate. No one stirred and Dubh reveled in the silence. Perched at the helm with his fingers wrapped around the mug, he stared out the window. The half-moon carved a path across the rippling waters and cast the forested islands into relief. In another hour, there would be enough light to hoist the anchor and continue their journey up the coast. But, in this moment, he breathed in the peace. Dubh may have grown up near the Barras of Glasgow, but the blood of his fey father craved the wild places and the intense peace of the witching time.

A light blinked amidst the black trees on Hardwicke Island. A kayaker must be up with his torch and draining his willie. It flickered and was gone. And then it flared again—like a geyser straight up from the ground. Were the fuckers lighting fireworks? With such a high risk of forest fire, he hoped not. The coven had broken the campfire ban to build their ritual fire, but he insured it was dead out by pouring seawater over it. After experiencing the smoke of the massive forest fires, Dubh was diligent.

He slipped down from the seat and walked out on the aft deck for a better look. There it was again. A spritz of fire. But he heard no bang, no sound at all—just water lapping against the hull. And then it blazed up several feet and continued to blaze.

Spunkie.

The word hadn't crossed his mind in years. There was an old codger on the Isle of Mull who used to tell tales of the Spunkie—strange fires that burned seemingly out of nowhere. The English called them Will o' the Wisp. Sometimes, the flames appeared over a bog and lured travelers to their death; other times, they tricked a sea captain and caused a wreck.

You'll not trick *this* sea captain, Dubh thought.

And then it blazed again. The flames were now as tall as a two-story house and almost as wide. Leaning his chin on the railing, Dubh stared at the fire in alarm. And then, a giant stag crossed before it, and the hair on the wee man's arms stood on end. Stepping back, he rubbed his eyes. Was he seeing things? Or . . . *Cernunnos?* He said he'd blaze a trail. Had he meant that literally?

The stag strutted back and forth before the blaze, antlers backlit by the fire.

Look after him. The god's thought seeped into Dubh's mind. Cernunnos was honorable and would aid Estrada as he promised.

"You love him," Dubh said aloud. "I know. We all do."

As if he'd heard—which no doubt he had—the stag shook his antlered head and raised his muzzle to the wind. His tall neck was thick and well-muscled.

"I see you, Lord. And don't fret. I've got his back."

Warmed by the thought of the god's protection, Dubh wrapped himself in one of Daphne's afghans and curled up on the white couch inside. The next sound he heard was a voice on the marine radio.

"Did you hear about the kayaker from Rock Bay? Over."

The lighthouse keepers were talking. Dubh had found their channel earlier quite by accident.

"No. Did they find him? Over."

"Affirmative. Over."

"Condition? Over."

"Alive but confused. Minor injuries. He walked out of the bush and stumbled into someone's tent about an hour ago. Out."

Dubh glanced at his watch. Six a.m. The man might be alive, but that didn't mean Michael Stryker hadn't been involved in his disappearance. After catching Michael sucking blood from Carvello's face last night, Dubh knew no one was safe around the man. If indeed, he still was a man.

———

Estrada leaned against the galley counter and sipped a second cup of Daphne's delicious after-dinner coffee. The setting sun blazed a scarlet trail over the water. Surrounded by bilious gray clouds, the sky threatened rain but for the moment, it was spectacular. Dubh and Dylan were at the helm, looking for a good place to anchor for the night. Carvello had not emerged from his captain's quarters all day. Michael was sleeping. And Sensara and Daphne were doing yoga on the bow. The yacht purred, and Estrada breathed in the peace of the moment.

It had been another long day of cruising through pine-studded islands with little to do but think. But they were almost there. The Broughton Archipelago was close. So close, Estrada could feel it. He felt warmed from the inside, but not from the brew. Cernunnos had given him hope. Lucy was *blessed and loved*. Those were the most wonderful words he'd ever heard in his life. He now knew in his heart that his baby was safe and cared for, and he would find her and bring her home. One layer of anxiety had dissipated and he could breathe more easily. Unfortunately, Michael's behavior last night had created another.

As soon as Estrada had tucked Michael into bed, he'd collapsed. "I took some pills," he'd confessed. "You'll sleep it off, amigo. You always do." Michael's breathing was slow, his heart barely beating. Benzos, thought Estrada, recalling his conversation with Dubh in the hospital. Michael did not need another addiction, but from what Estrada had observed, that was exactly what was happening—the drowsiness, the lethargy, the erratic mood shifts, the irritability. Unless. Unless it was more than benzos.

How much had the virus contributed to Michael's attack on Carvello? A thought had been distressing Estrada all day. A thought he dreaded to acknowledge. Michael might be becoming one of *them*. How that could happen, Estrada didn't know, but from what he'd seen through Carvello's stiff and bloody fingers, Michael had bitten a piece of flesh right out of the man's lip and cheek. And he appeared to be swallowing the blood.

The image reappeared in his mind and he fought to push it back. No. It can't be true. Michael can't be a vampire. Dashing to the bar, he poured himself three fingers of whiskey and chugged it down. He needed a diversion—would do anything but get caught up in the fear of what could be. Everything he'd ever read on manifestation, told him not to dwell on negativity. To think the worst will make it real. Live in the moment. When the buzz hit his brain, he felt lightened (enlightened?) certainly light-headed, and leaned against the bar. He hadn't been drunk in a while and the idea was appealing. Unscrewing the bottle, he poured himself another splash of Wiser's. Estrada had the glass against his lips and the first trickle on his tongue when Daphne burst through the door and squealed and he spilled it down his shirt.

"What the hell?" he shouted and pulled off his soggy T-shirt. Dumping it in the bar sink, he rinsed his hands.

"Come here," she said, then rushed back out onto the bow.

"What's going on?" Estrada asked, following her out.

"Dolphins!" Leaping and careening, the pods surrounded them, while the sea quivered with their passing. "See the dark dorsal fin on top and the white underneath? They're Pacific white-sided dolphins."

"They're so close," Sensara said, taking her cell phone from her pocket.

"Cut the engine, Dubh," yelled Estrada. "Dylan, come here. You've got to see this."

Sensara leaned over the bow rail and grinned as she filmed. "This is incredible. A good omen."

The dolphins had approached from behind and were traveling in the same direction, flanking the yacht and swimming beside them. A hundred or more, all sizes, young and old, leaping and diving.

"Really?" Estrada asked. "A good omen?"

"Dolphins are nothing but good."

"Yeah? You really think it's a sign?"

Smiling, Sensara touched his shoulder. "Yes. Dolphins are protective, healing, joyful. They're magic. They've even saved people who were shipwrecked."

"They're likely chasing herring or sardines right now," Daphne said. "They hunt in packs, like wolves, to chase and trap schools of fish."

"How do you know these things?" asked Estrada, messing up Daphne's hair.

She laughed. "Raine wrote an article last year. You can see how easily the poor things can be trapped in gill nets."

"Are they endangered?" Estrada asked.

"They're not *en*dangered but they're always *in* danger. Tuna and dolphins are close companions, so wherever there's commercial fishing, they get caught up in the nets. The fishers are supposed to release them, but laws aren't enforced and thousands of dolphins get injured and die."

"That's so sad," Sensara said.

"Forget sad." Grasping her hands and Daphne's, he spun them in a circle. "Dolphins are joyful. Remember?"

The women laughed and for a moment all was good.

As Dubh turned on the engine and the yacht began to move forward, Estrada scanned the waters. The dolphins had moved ahead of them.

"Speaking of shipwrecked . . . " Daphne pointed into a bay not far to their right. "That guy looks like he's in trouble." A man was kneeling in a small boat and waving something white. They could barely see him in the gathering dusk.

"Aye," Dylan said. "We better stop."

He went inside and pointed him out to Dubh, who slowed the engine, and turned the yacht in that direction.

As they pulled closer, the man waved them off and gestured around him. "Rocks," he yelled, and shook his head.

Dylan went to set an anchor when Dubh cut the engine. "I'll have to take the tender," he said, as he walked by Estrada.

"I'll come with you," Estrada replied, and wandered down to the stern.

When Dylan released the inflatable, the two men climbed in. Estrada sat watching as Dylan turned, and fired up the small outboard motor in just a couple of strokes.

Estrada felt suddenly inadequate. He might be a magician, but Dylan knew how things worked in the real world—what tools to use and how to use them. There were things Estrada had never cared to know, like how an engine worked or how to change a tire. Now he realized, knowing these things made a difference. You could help people. Save lives. Be independent. Dylan wasn't dependent on anyone. The two men Estrada had depended on—the two who were supposed to be piloting the yacht—were both hunkered down below deck and neither was dependable. Without Dylan and Dubh, they'd be screwed.

Dylan squeezed the throttle and they whooshed across the waves toward the man. He appeared to be in his early thirties. As they drew closer, Estrada recognized the breaching orca on his Canucks cap. He'd taken off his T-shirt to use as a flag, so a bare chest showed beneath his weatherproof jacket. His pale blue jeans looked damp and uncomfortable. Seated at the back of the small open boat, he clung to the tip of a large rock protruding from the sea. *Lund* was printed in white across the red paint. It looked like it had seen better days. Estrada was surprised to see the man out here in a dodgy boat by himself and was immediately suspicious. A backpack, plastic tackle box, net, and fishing rod lay by his feet. But there were no oars and no lifejacket. Estrada might not know much, but he knew better than to go boating without those two essentials.

"Thanks for stopping," the man said, as they pulled alongside his craft. "I broke my prop on the rocks."

Dylan appraised the propeller which the man had pulled up out of the water. "She's busted alright."

The man rubbed his pale hands together. "I've been clutching this rock for the last hour, afraid of drifting or sinking."

"No oars?" Dylan said.

When he shrugged, Estrada saw the faint red blush in his aura grow stronger. "I left in a mad dash. Everyone was talking about an amazing dolphin superpod."

"We just saw them." Estrada grew excited again. "Did you?"

"Just from a distance."

Dylan eyed the man warily.

"The rule is to always leave the craft ready for the next guy," the man explained. "So, I assumed there'd be jackets and oars in the boat."

"Did ye, aye? Well, you know what happens when you assume," Dylan said, half-grinning.

"Where you headed?" Estrada asked.

"A lodge up in the Broughton islands. Not far."

Broughton. Estrada felt a rush of adrenaline careen through his whiskey-laden limbs. "We're going that way. Right Dylan?"

"Aye, we can give you a tow."

"Thanks. I owe you one."

Dylan moved the inflatable closer. "Estrada. Grab the rope tied to his bow. Slip it between those cleats and tie if off. Make sure it doesn't tangle in our prop when we move."

Estrada hoped this wasn't another mistake. He thought of the fog. Making a mistake out here could get you killed, or worse yet, get your friends killed. *Trust your instincts*, Cernunnos had said. He turned back and glanced at the man as they cruised slowly back to the *Ragnarök*. The man smiled and gave him a thumbs-up. How could helping one man in trouble be a mistake? Especially a man who was going the very place you needed to go.

Daphne and Sensara were out on the back deck filming a small pod of orcas when they pulled up in the tender. Estrada and Dylan helped the man out of his dodgy boat and tied it to their stern.

"That's Robson Bight," the man said, gesturing across the water. "It's an orca reserve. You'll get some great video here."

"Fantastic," Daphne said.

Estrada could see Sensara sizing the man up. Trying to pierce the veneer of his friendly façade to find his hidden secrets. He sighed with relief when she held out a hand and introduced herself.

"Name's Levi," the man said. "I appreciate you stopping to help."

"It's the law," Dylan said. "You do have a boating license?"

"Yeah, of course. But not everybody obeys the law. Especially out here. A couple of yahoos went by earlier and looked the other way. Didn't want to spoil their party."

Dylan nodded. "Hockey fan?"

"Gotta love the Canucks." Levi took off his ball cap and ran his fingers through his dark brown hair, then put it back on and pulled it low over his eyes. They were cedar green but looked bloodshot. Like maybe he'd been partying himself.

When they moved into the saloon, Estrada went straight to the bar fridge and opened a few beers. It had been a long day and after last night's freak show, he could use some comic relief.

"Ladies, can I interest either of you in a nightcap?"

Daphne shook her head. "No thanks. I need an early night."

"Me too," said Sensara. "We'll leave you to it."

By midnight, Levi and Estrada were pissed, and stretched out on the sunpad under a slight flurry of stars. Dubh was in the saloon examining navigational maps, and everyone else had gone to bed.

Sometimes, you meet a stranger and feel like you've known him forever. That was the way it was with Levi. He's a godsend, Estrada thought, chuckling to himself. With his dark hair flung back from his strong cheekbones, and shirtless with his blue jeans slung low on his hips, Levi reminded him of Cernunnos. Estrada had forgotten how much he liked to banter with strangers. Especially sexy strangers.

"Seriously? You're a bartender at Forbidden?" A converted warehouse, Forbidden had been retrofitted into an eighties goth bar by an eccentric entrepreneur plugged into the Vancouver music scene. You never knew who'd be rocking the stage. Estrada had partied there several times.

When Levi smiled, his face lit up and for a moment, the darkness of the past few days vanished.

"You must make a shitload of tips," Estrada said.

"I do alright," laughed Levi. "Make a pretty drink, get a pretty tip."

"Have a pretty face, get a pretty tip." Levi was striking—a young Heath Ledger—and Estrada could never resist flirting with beauty.

Leaning up on his elbow, Levi ran a hand through his hair. When it fell back across his fine brow, the corner of his mouth lifted into a soft lopsided smile.

"Seriously, man. If you ever feel like defecting, come by Pegasus. Forbidden is our competitor and I can set you up. You could get creative, stir up some witch's brews, name your own concoctions."

"What do you do there? Wait. Don't tell me. You're the manager."

"Nope. Michael Stryker is the manager. I'm the magician."

"Really? Like Criss Angel? Stunts? Illusions? That kind of thing?"

"Yeah. Hypnosis, escapes, sleights, near-death experiences . . . all wrapped in a gothic cloak. Our crowd is big on cosplay and the medieval scene."

Levi grinned. "Sounds like fun. Got any tricks up your sleeve?"

"Always." Estrada put his hand in the pocket of his leather jacket, then pulled it out and launched a fireball into the air.

"Shit man!" Levi jumped backwards and hit the window. The fireball flew over the gunnel and sizzled in the water.

"Don't panic, man. It's just a trick."

"But, how did you—?"

"I can't tell you that. But, if you want to see some *real* magic, stick around."

"When are you going back to town?" Levi asked.

Laying back on the mat, Estrada crossed his hands behind his head. "Not sure."

"You been out here long?"

"We left Vancouver on Tuesday." Estrada closed his eyes. It felt like the first time he'd relaxed in days. Was it Levi? Or the possibilities he presented? Escape from the chaos and constant sadness created by the abduction of his child. "To tell you the truth, I don't even know what day it is."

"This is a gorgeous yacht. Not having a good time?"

"It's fucked up, man." Estrada was suddenly nervous that Michael or Carvello would appear and spoil his dalliance.

"Yeah? How so?"

Estrada sniffed. "You wouldn't believe me if I told you."

"Try me."

Estrada sat up and uncapped another couple of beers. He offered one to Levi, then downed most of the other. Rolling onto his side, he glanced at Levi. In the shifting darkness, he caught the man's profile as he ran the cool rim of the beer bottle along his lower lip. "Let's just say, I'm enjoying getting drunk with you."

"Ah, cabin fever."

"Something like that."

"Well, it's been my pleasure to get drunk with you. I wish I *could* stick around."

"Why can't you?"

"Well, you see, *that* is Cracroft Point." Levi pointed to the dark spit of land beside them.

"So?"

"It's a marker. Blackney Pass is right around the corner and leads into the islands of Broughton Archipelago. That's where I'm staying."

Broughton Archipelago. Estrada was suddenly sober. *Lucy.* They were so close. Adrenalin surged through his body and he clenched his fists to contain it.

"You ever hear of a party palace hidden away in those islands?" Estrada asked.

"Yeah. I've heard rumors. Drugs. Sex. S&M. Whatever you want. Lots of rich Americans frequent it. They call it Le Chateau."

"The Castle."

"Yeah. Some of the guys I work with threatened to crash it, but none of them have the balls. The place is a fortress."

"Really. You know where it is?"

Levi nodded. "I could find it. But, it's invitation only. You're not thinking of going there?"

Estrada shrugged. Cernunnos said he'd carve a path. And now, lying beside him, drinking beer, was a man who knew about Diego's place.

Levi shook his head. "Not with these girls, man. They'll get eaten alive."

Estrada stood suddenly, took Levi's hand and pulled him up. His flesh was cool, and rather than let go of the stranger's hand, he held it, and placed his other hand on Levi's shoulder. "I need your help, man."

"Considering you rescued me earlier, how can I say no?"

"First, we need to tell Dubh." Estrada glanced into the saloon and then back into Levi's green eyes. "Then, I'll explain everything."

―――≷―――

Magus Dubh was perched on the white chaise and mulling. Dylan had gone to bed, but he wasn't tired enough for sleep. Not yet. He had too much on his mind.

Neither Michael Stryker nor Victor Carvello had emerged from below deck all day. And when villains are silent there is much to fear. From what Dubh had heard of Carvello, he wasn't the kind of man to let things go and was most likely plotting revenge. Dubh didn't condone what Michael had done, but the bastard deserved Michael's wrath, and if it came down to saving one or the other, Dubh knew who he'd champion. Even if he was a vampire.

Surely Estrada suspected that Michael was turning. Dubh hadn't shared his suspicions yet. The man had enough to worry about, and the kayaker had been found. Still. After what they interrupted last night, Dubh was now certain. Michael was verging on vampire, which meant he craved blood. Perhaps Diego's venom intensified as they drew closer.

Michael hadn't just bit Carvello as payback for some past trauma. He was delirious with his blood. Dubh could feel darkness growing inside him—the same darkness Sensara had felt—the reeking copper bog. What would happen if he turned on *them*? Was his love for Estrada strong enough to overcome Diego's influence? In thrall to the vampire, Michael might not have a choice. It was time he sat down with Estrada and had a heart-to-heart.

Another Spunkie. Each time the flare appeared, Dubh's skin broke out in goosebumps. That was the way of deep magic. Verity. Divine guidance. They were getting close. And yet—

Dubh shook his head to extinguish his dark thoughts. He must remain positive. They had Cernunnos on their side. They had magic. They had love. They were heroes and heroes always win.

He smiled at the scene playing out before him. In the chaos of juggling his lovers, Estrada appeared to be courting another. The two men had drunk a dozen beers while lounging on the bow. Levi, he knew, meant *joined*, and that is what he saw unfolding before him. An extraordinary joining. Ordained by the gods?

And then, Estrada stood and pulled Levi to his feet. When he stared back at him through the dark glass, Dubh held his breath.

"We're almost there," Estrada said, as he walked through the door into the saloon. Though he'd drunk several beers, he was suddenly sober. His heartbeat quickened. "Levi knows about Diego's lair."

"I haven't heard it called that, but I've heard of a party palace in the Broughtons called Le Chateau," Levi said.

"Did ye, aye?" Dubh was suspicious.

"He can show us where it is," Estrada said, detecting the edge of sarcasm in Dubh's response.

The wee man spread the navigational map out on the coffee table. "Alright big man. We're here," Dubh said, drawing an X with his pencil at the southwestern tip of West Cracroft Island. "Show us Le Chateau."

Levi sat down beside Dubh and picked up the pencil. "Right. Boat Bay Conservancy—that's where we are now. Once we circle around this point, we're in Blackney Pass." He drew a faint line. "It runs between Hanson and Harbledown Islands into Blackfish Sound. Cross it at slack tide tomorrow morning, and you'll reach your island by tomorrow afternoon."

A shot of adrenalin raced through Estrada's body. Lucy. Tomorrow afternoon.

"If you thread your way through the islands at the south edge of the marine park—"

"Hang on. If *we* thread our way. Where will *you* be?" Estrada wasn't ready for Levi to disappear. His gut was telling him the man was an asset and must be there when they confronted Diego.

"The lodge where I work is in the park, so I was hoping you could drop me there on the way by. Tomorrow's Saturday and they're expecting a float plane full of guests, so . . . " Squinting, he ran his fingernails through his hair. "Sorry, but I have to work."

Estrada sniffed and rubbed his nose. "Go on."

"Anyway," Levi said awkwardly, "the park ends here." He drew a large arc. "Village Island is just to the east. There are ruins there—a pole and the remnants of an old school. It's Indigenous land and there'll likely be tourists—mostly kayakers. Broughton Archipelago Marine Park is a haven for sea kayakers because of all the secluded passages."

"So, avoid." Dubh had been avoiding blissed-out kayakers all the way along the coast.

"If you follow around Village Island into Knight Inlet, you'll find the island you're searching for right about here." Levi penciled in an X and drew a circle around it. "It's not on this map or *any* map I've ever seen." He shrugged. "I don't know why."

"You've been there?" Dubh asked.

Levi shook his head. "It's invitation only. As I told Estrada, some of the guys at the lodge talked about crashing it. The proprietor offers some rather unique experiences."

"What's the island like for mooring?" Dubh asked.

"There are docking facilities."

All three men turned at the sound of Michael's voice. Estrada flushed with surprise. Michael hung like a serpent in the doorway. He'd thrown on a black silk shirt over his leggings, but it fell open to reveal his pale chest. He clutched his silver cigarette case and lighter, had obviously arisen to quell a nicotine fix.

"A path leads up to the palace," Michael continued. "I suppose, that's what you'd call it. It's not your traditional Arthurian castle—it's more Alhambra—though Diego has a torture chamber that would impress the Tudor kings."

"So, the stories are true. You've seen it." When Levi leaned forward, his hair fell in his face and he glanced warily at Estrada.

"Don't worry man. Torture's not our thing," Estrada said. "We have other business with Diego."

"Have we met?" Michael asked. "There's something about you."

"Levi's a bartender at Forbidden," Estrada said. "Levi, this is Michael Stryker, the manager of Pegasus."

"Ah, right. Pegasus is a fabulous club."

"So, you've been there?" Estrada asked.

"Once. I plan to return. I just don't get many nights off." Levi put down the pencil and ran his hands through his hair, then interlaced his fingers and leaned back. "I tried a few of your blood clots and the rest of the night was a blur. Your bartenders are chemists."

"Ah. That would be Michael," Estrada said. He regularly spiked the blood clots with ecstasy.

Michael extended his hand with the palm pointed down, as if it should be kissed. "Call me Mandragora."

Levi grasped the proffered fingers and squeezed. "Mandragora. You're a legend at Forbidden."

Michael pulled his lips to the right in an honest grin. "Come by the club again. I'll show you how I make the blood clots."

Estrada was amazed at the change in Michael. After last night's stupor, he'd arisen cocky and refreshed. Leastways, Mandragora had arisen.

Levi exuded a charm that lightened Estrada's mood and he was suddenly jealous. He'd been enjoying his time with Levi and wasn't in the mood to share this sexy stranger. Not with Michael. Not with anyone.

"Forbidden has its own allure. I hear you have *semi-private* rooms." Michael smiled at his own joke, then swaggered over to the bar and popped the cork on a bottle of wine. "Anyone?"

Dubh shook his head.

Estrada glanced at Levi who raised his eyebrows. "No thanks, amigo. We've been—"

TO RENDER A RAVEN

"Slumming," Michael said, glancing at the empty beer bottles stacked along the floor. "I see."

When Michael turned and sauntered out onto the back deck, Estrada followed. Michael sipped his wine and lit a smoke. It was unusually warm. Balmy even. The weather changed like Michael's moods.

"Feeling better?" Estrada asked.

Michael stared out at the sea and nodded. "I'm going for a swim."

"Now?"

"Yes. I rather like the Pacific at night. It's peaceful and oddly comforting." Michael poured another glass of wine and drank it all in one smooth swallow. "Care to join me? Perhaps, bring your friend?"

"No, I . . . " Estrada touched his shoulder. "Just be careful, amigo. There are monsters out there."

Michael sunk into his touch, turned, and buried his face in Estrada's neck. When he took a deep breath, Estrada felt his lips quiver against his skin.

"And you, compadre," Michael murmured. "There are monsters right here."

PARADISE

Michael swam through the sea, arms grasping and pulling, chin cresting the waves. The frigid saltwater heightened his hunger. He felt stronger than ever. Buoyed by his confrontation with Carvello. His timidity trumped by cockiness. That bastard pedophile would never mock or molest him again. If he had the chance, Michael would make sure Carvello never hurt another soul.

Glancing at the beach directly ahead, he spied the two yellow kayaks, he'd seen from the aft deck of the yacht. His vision was keener. His hunger instinctual. The kayaks lay on the sandy edge of the forest, and just beyond them sat the turquoise tent. It wasn't an official camping spot, just a place they'd found and claimed. Humans were such easy prey, especially out here on the coast. A bear was expected, but a man with teeth like razors? Michael would satisfy his hunger for blood and Estrada would stay safe one more night. A man will do anything for love.

Rising out of the sea, Michael felt the chill wind whip his naked body. He crept to the tent and knelt near the screened window. To capture the sea breeze, they'd left it open to the night. He heard them before he saw them. A young couple, all sporty and athletic, they were rocking the tent. Enjoy your last fuck, he thought, and watched.

When the man finished, he rolled over and began to snore. The woman—really she was just a girl—lay awake and rigid. Even in shadow, Michael could tell she was a beauty. A frustrated beauty. The prick had done nothing but ride her and had left her unsatisfied. Michael watched her breasts rise and fall with each breath. Could she sense danger lurking on the other side of this silky fabric?

One of these two must die tonight, so Estrada could continue his quest and rescue Lucy. Which one would it be? Beauty or the beast?

Michael eased away from the tent and hunkered down in the shelter of some spindly shrubs. Clouds covered the slight strip of moon and bathed the island in darkness. And then a burst of light. Someone had emerged from the tent and was walking toward him. A flashlight beam skittered across the ground.

It was the girl. Dressed in a long white T-shirt and likely nothing else, her long dark hair braided like a rope and hanging over her breast. She squatted within arm's reach, lifted the T-shirt and pissed.

Smelling the scent of love, Michael grew aroused. Felt his heart thump in his chest. Her blood calling his. He imagined covering her pretty pink mouth with his hand—the swollen mouth just pressed in kisses—and muffling her cries. Lying on top of her, his teeth sinking into her neck. Pushing inside as he drank. Slowly. With precision. Giving the girl what the man had not.

His body screamed YES, but his mind said NO. Mandragora has never raped a woman and he will not start now. You can control this compulsion. Tasting is one thing. You drink the blood to satiate your desire for Estrada. You drink the blood for love of him. Not for lust. And not to rape and murder.

The girl stood, smoothed down her shirt and tiptoed back to the tent in her bare feet. When she opened the zipper and crawled back inside the tent, Michael heard muffled voices. And then the man emerged.

Sitting in the darkness, as still as a tree, Michael appraised his quarry. The naked man was tall and strong, much heavier than that last kayaker by the lighthouse. Then, all it had taken was a rock to the back of the head. He'd dragged him into the bushes, drank at his leisure, and left him unconscious.

But this man was seasoned. Ripped. A gorilla with a shaved head. Upper body and arms sculpted from the constant pull of the paddle.

Michael's fingers curled around a heavy driftwood slab on the ground beside him. Focused on pissing, the man didn't hear the footsteps behind him. The crack of the wood resounded like a hockey stick against a puck. The bald gorilla wobbled but didn't fall. So, Michael hit him again. And again. And, at last, the body dropped.

Had the girl heard? Michael glanced at the tent but all remained dark. Kneeling, he laid his ear against the man's chest and listened to the frantic beating heart. His gaze followed the pulsing blood upwards from heart to brain. The man was squared-jawed, low-browed, and unappealing—apish—his beard ragged, his forehead marred by acne scars. Unable to control his ugliness, he'd built his body. Michael glanced down at the rippling abdominal muscles, the flaccid genitals, the hairy bowed legs that were less developed than the torso.

A vein throbbed in the man's upper thigh. Christophe used to offer him that vein, so the cuts couldn't be seen by the camera when he was modeling. It ran the length of the leg on the inside. Turning the flesh with his right hand, Michael used his sharp teeth to puncture and invade. Holding his left palm over the man's heart, he measured as he sipped, intent on stopping before death. There was a way to live like this—to feed and not to kill. With his hunger satiated, Michael left. The ape man would recover and no one would ever know what happened.

Floating on his back in the sea, Michael relaxed. The saltwater cleansed his body of matted blood and his long hair swirled like seaweed. Soon, he would lay back against Estrada's warm chest. He'd do anything for Estrada. Anything for love.

<hr>

The crash of thunder woke Estrada. His head throbbed, his gut churned, and rain streamed over his face. For a second, he lay dazed, trying to remember what had happened.

Ah yes. Levi and tequila.

When Estrada had passed out on the sunpad, Levi had been there, stretched out beside him, face up to the somber stratus clouds. The two men had played pass the glass with a two-six of tequila and partied all night. Estrada loved how talk of nothing could be talk of something. Things you hate. Things you love. Favorites and firsts.

But now Levi was gone.

The man had asked for nothing and that was a welcome relief. It hadn't gotten sexual, but it could have. One of the things Levi said he loved was a quick trip to Mexico because of the beaches and the men with their dark flashing eyes and casual approach to sex. They'd laughed about that—Estrada being Mexican and fitting Levi's description. Estrada had forgotten how good it felt to do nothing but drink with a stranger with no last name and no agenda.

Now fully awake, Estrada crept into the saloon, dried himself with a kitchen towel, and glanced around. Dubh was there, curled into a ball and soughing in his sleep. But where was Levi? Estrada checked the time. Five a.m. If not for the bleak gray sky that crowded down around them, dawn was imminent. Perhaps, Levi was in the head.

Estrada guzzled a bottle of water, stripped off his wet jeans and T-shirt, and stretched out on the sofa. Hangovers, especially tequila hangovers, could suck the life out of you. The last time he'd pulled a stunt like this, he'd been cured by a wise man in the woods and a feast of barbecued salmon. He could do with a hangover cure right now. He'd need his wits about him.

Today was the day. Today they would find Le Chateau de Vampire. Today he would rescue Lucy and take Diego down.

Estrada was just drifting off when he heard a strange sound—the slap of water—and it sent a surge of adrenalin through his veins. Rising on one elbow, he peered out at the back deck.

Naked and dripping and smoking a cigarette, Michael hovered in the doorway.

Curious, but relieved, Estrada rose and padded out to see him. It had been hours since Michael said he was going for a swim. Had he been gone all this time?

"Are you just getting back?" Estrada asked. He didn't want to sound like he was keeping tabs—that was something he hated in a relationship. But he was curious and concerned.

Michael nodded. "Come to bed, compadre. I'm chilled to the bone." Chattering teeth shook the whisper. "Come, warm me." Cool lips covered Estrada's as Michael's pelvis pressed him against the wall.

The next time Estrada awoke his head lay on Michael's chest. He shifted to his side, leaned over and touched his lover's slowly beating heart. None of this is your fault, he thought. You are who you are, and I love you no matter what.

"I love you too," Michael said aloud. He shifted to his side and their foreheads touched.

"What?" Estrada asked.

"I thought I heard you say—"

"I did, but not out loud. Can you hear my thoughts?"

Michael smiled. "It would seem so."

Both men laughed softly.

"I always hoped that would happen with us," Michael said. "I know you have a telepathic thing with Sensara."

"We practiced it. This is different. It's happened all on its own."

"I do love you, compadre." He ran a finger down Estrada's stubbly cheek. "And in a world gone mad, I'd choose you."

Estrada's lips sought his lover's in a lingering kiss.

"Would you choose me?" Michael asked.

Estrada's lips brushed Michael's neck and nipples, then traveled down his salty naked belly.

But Michael caught him and stopped him. "A blow job is not an answer."

"Choose you over what, amigo?" Estrada asked, rising to his knees. "Sensara and Lucy? Are you asking me to choose between you and them?"

"Of course not. Lucy is your daughter."

Michael joined Estrada on his knees and kissed him with a passion he'd not felt in years.

"If you can't answer, it's okay. I'll just take the blow job," Michael said, grinning.

"You know I love you," Estrada said, shoving Michael back on the bed.

"If I had only one breath left, I would give it to you," Michael answered.

"I wouldn't take your last breath." Estrada slapped his cheek playfully. "I can't imagine a world without you in it."

The lodge was built of hand-hewn posts and horizontal logs. Ocher-stained cedar, and trimmed in white and emerald green, it resembled something from another century. Worn steps led to a verandah where baskets of tumbling summer blossoms hung from beams. In tall letters above the door, PARADISE had been carved from wood and painted white.

Estrada stood staring from the aft deck. It was just after two p.m. and rain continued to pour in frigid torrents. The clouds were so low they hung on the lip of the sea. A canary yellow float plane landed as Carvello brought the *Ragnarök* into the dock. The bastard had finally emerged from his captain's quarters. His upper lip was swollen, scabbed, and raw. His attitude snarly.

Several boats were moored along the bleached cedar docks. Estrada pushed the damp hair back from his face and glanced around, hoping to catch sight of Levi among the milling fishermen in their flashy ball caps and rain gear. Perhaps this wasn't even the lodge where Levi worked. He hadn't said a name, and there must be a half dozen lodges scattered throughout these islands.

Still Estrada searched. Levi's disappearance bewildered him. He had no idea why Levi had left without a word. Even more perplexing was how. Levi's boat, with its broken propeller, was still tied to the back of the *Ragnarök*. Dylan planned to leave it here, tied to the dock. He was tired of towing it.

Estrada thought of the ravens and wondered if Levi had somehow been lifted from the bow as they slept. For a moment, he couldn't swallow past the sour lump in his throat, and his heart heaved for his new friend. But surely a raven couldn't carry a full-grown man. A salmon perhaps, even a baby seal. But a man? That was impossible. Ravens, like all birds, had hollow bones engineered for flying, not lifting. Could Levi have swum to shore? Michael had gone swimming last night. It wasn't far to West Cracroft Island and the water was at its warmest. But, if so, why? They'd already offered to take him back to the lodge.

The other possibility—the one Estrada chose to believe—was that Levi wasn't human. Cernunnos had promised to guide them to Lucy. If Levi was a spirit sent by Cernunnos, he'd done his work. Dubh and Carvello had used his hand-drawn map to maneuver the maze of islands through the marine park, and in a couple of hours they'd be at Le Chateau de Vampire.

Estrada hopped off the yacht onto the bleached wooden dock, wrapped the stern line around the cleats and tied it off as Dylan had taught him. After tossing out the fenders to cushion the sides of the yacht against the dock, Dylan was up at the bow tying knots of his own. Estrada gave him the thumbs up sign.

Sensara and Daphne came out onto the aft deck together. Sensara had been ignoring him all day. She was pissed. Estrada knew he'd neglected her since the night of the coven, when they'd returned to find Michael's teeth sunk deep in Carvello's face. He hadn't had much choice. Michael was volatile. And then they'd found Levi.

"Why are we stopping here?" asked Daphne.

Several fishermen were unloading their catch, lining fish up on the damp dock for weighing and proofing. One boat had just returned and the youngest of them was cradling a forty-pound chinook salmon in his open palms and grinning for the camera. Another was hooking a massive halibut on a weigh scale. The monster fish likely weighed more than Sensara.

Estrada hopped back onto the aft deck. "Let's talk inside," he said, brushing past the women and heading into the saloon.

"Why? Why are we stopping?" asked Sensara. "Did your boyfriend leave without saying goodbye?"

"Actually, yeah, he did. But before he left, Levi told me a couple of things. This place we're going isn't safe for you, Sensara. Or you," he said, looking at Daphne. "I want you both to stay here." Estrada stood with his hands on his hips and spoke with authority.

"I am not—"

"Don't argue. It's not safe."

"Lucy is *my* daughter and I'm going." Feet planted firmly on the floor, Sensara braced herself, every muscle taut.

"What's not safe about this place?" asked Daphne.

"Besides the fact there are vampires?" Estrada didn't want to terrify the women, but sometimes Sensara was too stubborn for her own good. "Diego hates women," he said, at last.

"A misogynist vampire. Could this get any more cliché?"

"Listen to me, Sara. This bastard will use you against me. If you're there, it will just make things worse."

"Estrada's got a point," Daphne said. "Diego took Lucy to lure Estrada here. If he gets a chance, he'll take you too."

"Listen to Daphne." Dubh had suddenly appeared. "Any decent villain will use love for leverage. It might be cliché, but it's effective. He'll torture you."

"And then he'll kill you both. Apparently, he uses women for fodder." Estrada hated to be so blunt, but he couldn't risk leading them into something so perilous.

Sensara's face blanched. "But if Lucy's there, I should be too."

"Sara, listen to me. Ruby Carvello was murdered, and Nora Barnes is still missing. Nigel got off easy with a concussion and two broken legs." Estrada placed his hands lightly on her shoulders. "Diego has an S&M chamber. It's like the Spanish fucking Inquisition in there. Michael's seen it. Even Levi said, you'll get eaten alive in this place."

"But, Lucy."

"Lucy's safe. Remember what Cernunnos said. She's loved and she's blessed. I'll find her and bring her back. I promise. Just trust me."

"I don't know."

Estrada touched her cheek. "Sara. If he tortures me, I can take it. But if he tortures you, I'll do whatever he wants. Do you understand?"

"I think we should stay here," Daphne said.

"How long?" Sensara had finally acquiesced.

Estrada shrugged. "I can't answer that. We're hoping to be there in an hour or two, so we can catch them while they're still at rest."

"*If* they rest," muttered Dubh.

"Do you even have a plan?" asked Sensara.

Estrada raised his eyebrows. No, he didn't have a fucking plan. They had scant information about Diego's lair or how the vampires lived. All they could do was get in undetected, find Lucy, and get her out. Kill as many vampires as possible using whatever they had. Guns. Knives. Fire. Magic.

"Like Dubh said, we're hoping they rest during the day and we can catch them unaware. Michael's been there and has an idea of the layout of the place. We have our magic and the blessings of the gods. And we can all fight. Fight for Lucy. We'll get in and out as quick as we can."

One of the fishermen whistled and flung a pail full of fish heads into the sea. Three eagles spiraled from the treetops and danced across the water with outstretched wings. Scooping up the fish heads in their talons, they flew off in opposite directions to feast.

And that's when Estrada saw the ravens.

He couldn't be sure it was the same terror he'd seen in the backyard on Hawk's Claw Lane. For one thing, there were twice as many. They clamored around the bare skeleton of an apple tree like something out of a Poe poem. Someone must have planted an orchard here at one time. Now, there was nothing but blackened branches and heckling birds.

"Alright." Sensara said. She too was staring at the ravens.

"Are those—?" asked Daphne.

"I don't know," Estrada said. "Let's get you both inside the lodge where it's safe."

Zion ruffled his feathers and gurgled his dismay. *Paradise.* This piece-of-shit lodge was no paradise. What Diego had happening on a good night, now *that* was paradise. A lineup of hipsters all eager for a shot at immortality. *Choose me. I want to stay young and beautiful forever. I never want to change.* Except, it didn't work that way. Those boys might keep their sculpted cheekbones and smooth brows, but aging had more to do with the mind than the body. Zion should know. He'd been Diego's henchman for a hundred and fifty years.

"The rain never stops in this fucking place." Zion's irritation erupted in a series of harsh chortles and croaks.

"It's a rainforest." Eliseo sat perfectly at ease, his claws hooked into a crooked branch in the slick wet apple tree.

These two had hunted together for centuries, both as ravens and vampires. Eli was clever and Zion indestructible. Zion knew this was the way Father regarded them and resented it.

"We could live anywhere. Why couldn't Father pick a place a little warmer and drier to build his fucking castle?"

"You know why, Zion. This is where Salvador was swept into the sea. El Padrino could never leave his son alone to rot in the ocean."

Zion scraped his head with a claw. Salvador died more than three centuries ago. Surely, the kid's bones had been picked clean by fishes and crusted with coral by now. He let out another irate squawk. Motherfucking rain. At times like this, he tried to conjure the sun of his torrid African home.

"Besides, the Native people here revere El Padrino. He is the Thunderbird of their legends. That's why we're not allowed to hunt them."

Zion cocked his head with interest. This was news. Eli knew more than anyone, except Father.

"When El Padrino first came here, he showed them his true nature. Then, he treated with their chiefs, hosted a potlatch and gave everyone gifts. He offered his protection and agreed to kill only the European explorers who threatened their territory. Their spirits were pleased by his generosity."

The villages had always been taboo, but Zion had never known why. It was just one of Father's rules. While the native people sickened and died and were removed from their land, the white folks never stopped coming. Sailors, whalers, explorers, loggers, gold-diggers, fishers, settlers, hunters, whores, and tourists were all fair game. Zion drank his fill and never bothered to question Father's rule.

Glancing at Eli, Zion cocked his head toward the back of the lodge. The heroes had dropped off their women and disembarked. It was time.

When Eliseo sprung from the rotting tree and flew around the back of the lodge, Zion followed. It was easy enough to find the women. The blinds were high and most rooms empty. The fishermen were off doing what they paid the big bucks to do—yank fish the size of toddlers out of the ocean.

Three floors up, Zion alighted on the window frame, cocked a marbled eye, and stared inside. The priestess was pacing. Her girlfriend in the bathroom washing up. The window was only cracked a sliver, but Zion could smell the soap. Lavender. He didn't care for women, never had, but this Daphne reminded him of someone he knew a long time ago. It was a distant image, like all his memories of West Africa. Perhaps an aunt or a cousin. Daphne's coffee-colored skin was a few shades lighter than his own, but her people had once lived there. She wore a black Mohawk and bleached the tips platinum. Zion liked her style and felt, in another place and time, they might have been friends. Now, he had no friends. Only brothers. And Father.

Tap tap tap. Zion banged his beak against the glass and waited for the scream. It came. Long and shrill like the wail of a she-wolf caught in a trap.

The priestess ran to the window to lock it, but Eliseo shifted and balanced on the outside ledge, jammed a fingernail in the crack, and pried it up. He was small and wiry, but centuries of blood had given Eli super strength. Sliding his palms underneath, he pressed upwards and the window came right off the frame.

Zion chuckled as Eli shoved it through the opening and dived in after it. The glass shattered on the plank floor. What a clown.

Daphne ran screaming from the bathroom to protect her priestess.

Zion flew in the opening and flitted around the terrified women who screamed louder and batted at him with pillows—another reason he didn't care for women.

Alighting on the plank floor beside Eliseo, Zion transformed. He was tall and muscular, like Diego's magician, naked and dripping from the rain, feeling cocky and pumped up and full of himself. Raising his upper lip like an angry bear, he snarled.

With bulging eyes and trembling lips, the women clutched each other.

"It's . . . it's the middle of the day," Daphne stammered. "How are you . . . ?"

Zion was shocked they could speak. Most victims never uttered anything except *please no*.

"Ah, you thought we'd be sleeping in our coffins?" Curling up the right side of his lip, Eliseo grinned. "Stories are just stories. The veiled sun does not harm us."

"Especially through our feathers. In fact, some ravens crave the sun." Zion winked at Eli.

"You were at Lucy's birthday party," Sensara said. "In the trees."

"In the trees. In her bedroom. In *your* bedroom," Eli said.

Zion leered. "We know *all* your secrets."

"Where's Lucy? Where's my baby?" wailed the priestess.

This business with the baby was getting boring. A week cooped up on *La Sangria* with a whiny child and a tasty wet nurse he'd been forbidden to touch, and Leopold pretending like he hadn't been turned and wasn't a fucking vampire. It was all too much for Zion.

"Don Diego requests your presence at Le Chateau de Vampire," Eliseo said, and made a mocking bow.

The women stood back to back.

"We're not going anywhere," the priestess said.

Daphne chanted words Zion had never heard before.

He stepped back, chuckling. "Incantations? Is that the best you got, Little Sister?"

The priestess raised her hands, calling power from the ethers, her palms glowing as if she'd conjured the sun. Focusing her lightning force on Zion, she aimed for his heart.

He felt it hit, like a mass of cattle prods, and flew backwards against the wall. Knocked the wind from his lungs and caught his ear on the window ledge. *Motherfucker*. That pissed him off.

Then Daphne leapt across the room, grabbed a shard of broken glass and jammed it in his neck.

Zion caught her wrist and squeezed until she dropped the glass, then flung her across the bed. His blood drizzled down his chest. Zion shook his head. "That was stupid, Little Sister."

Now the priestess was chanting. Eli rushed her, caught those venomous hands and twisted her wrists to turn her palms down.

Screaming and squirming, she tried to break his grip. Eli smirked. "I'll break you, priestess, bone by bone by bone."

"I don't care *what* you do to me," she said, jutting out her chin. "I've cursed you, and you won't last the night."

"You *should* care," crooned Eli, and grasping her little finger he snapped it back like a pencil.

Screaming, the priestess curled forward clutching her busted finger, and Daphne took up the chant.

"How many bones are in your baby's body, priestess? Two, three hundred? You will come quietly, or I promise to break each one." He licked his lips. "Before I bleed her."

Sensara's face contorted in agony and she wept. Resigned to her fate, she cradled her broken finger and stared at her feet.

Eliseo turned to Daphne. "Shut up, witch, and you need not be harmed. We only want the priestess."

"Fuck you," Daphne said, and continued to chant, faster and higher and louder.

"Let's fly." Zion was getting bored. In a blink, he pounced and had Sensara writhing in the air. Applying pressure to her windpipe with his thumb, Zion watched her fight for breath. Within seconds, she flopped into his arms.

Zion nuzzled her neck. This was the one Michael Stryker hated. Perhaps, he'd pierce a vein and have a taste. Better still, he could share her with Stryker, and then they could taste each other. His pupils flared. That thought made him hard.

Daphne screamed a throaty ear-splitting scream when she saw his erection, and Eliseo clapped his hand over her open mouth so hard she bounced backwards.

"Easy, Little Sister. This ain't for you." Zion heard boots thumping down the hall. Men were coming and he was in no mood for carnage.

"I told you we weren't here to harm you. But now . . . " Striking the side of Daphne's neck with the heel of his right hand, Eliseo smashed the vagus nerve below her ear, cutting off the oxygen to her brain.

Little Sister's eyes rolled back in her head and down she went. Humans were so fucking feeble.

"This was too easy, Eli."

"Bind her." Eli gestured to the priestess with his chin.

Men were banging at the door. Shouting. Jiggling the doorknob.

Moving with accelerated speed, Zion wrapped the wet rope around Sensara's hands and feet and tied it off. Then, he transformed, snapped his beak a few times and danced on his toes. He felt at home in his raven guise. Who wouldn't want the power to fly? He caught the ropes binding Sensara's wrists in his talons and lifted her easily. Eliseo followed, catching her bound ankles and raising her from the floor.

Then, through the open window and into the rain they flew carrying the priestess, her long dark hair streaming in the wind.

INNIS IFRINN

Magus Dubh's flesh broke out in goosebumps when the *Ragnarök* pierced the fleece of fog, and Diego's island appeared like the mythical island of Hy-Brasil. He remembered the story his Aunt Jackie used to tell him as a wean. A mysterious circular island off the west coast of Ireland, the *Beautiful Island*, or Hy-Brasil as it was known in Old Irish, became visible only once every seven years. If a ship was in the right place at the right time, the mist lifted to reveal the island to a fortunate few. Some cartographers had mapped it, and some explorers claimed to have seen it. But no one had brought back proof of its existence. And so, the island remained shrouded in Celtic myth. Like Diego's island, Hy-Brasil was said to be peopled by rich immortals and existed in a liminal world between the shadowy borders of the real and the fantastical.

Relieved Carvello was piloting the yacht, Dubh slipped on a plastic poncho, that fell almost to the ground, and went out on the bow to join Estrada. The shaman had been standing out in the relentless rain for the past hour, wrapped in a long black hooded trench coat, his back to the helm. Dubh wondered what he had on his mind. Lucy, no doubt. But there was also Sensara, who he'd left behind at the Paradise Lodge, and Michael, who slept below, and now, Levi, who'd vanished without a word.

Standing together at the edge of the bow, the two men surveyed Diego's island. At first, it was nothing but a mass of evergreens, shrouded by rippling mist, not much different than other islands they'd passed on their journey. But then, the yacht rounded a point.

The docking area to the southwest was jammed with boats, most wearing American tags. Dubh wondered if the people who cavorted in Diego's S&M fantasy hell did so freely, or if the vampire had conjured some compulsion to lure them in. A magnetic polarity akin to the Bermuda Triangle. How convenient would it be to have a never-ending food supply fueled by man's desire for sex and violence? Surely, a vampire who could transform himself into a dragon had abilities they'd yet to encounter. Though fascinated, Dubh trembled. What hellish deeds was Diego capable of perpetrating on the world?

"Does this island have a name?" asked Dubh.

"None that I've heard," Estrada said.

"*Innis Ifrinn.*"

"Innish Iverinn?" repeated Estrada, raising his eyebrow.

"Aye. *Innis Ifrinn.* The island where sinners go."

Estrada sucked back a breath as if he'd been punched in the gut, and Dubh felt guilty for making such an insensitive remark. The man's child was being held captive on this bloody island for fuck sake. He should have known better.

"Let's find a back door," Estrada said, and waved Carvello away from the dock.

They wended their way around the northwest side of the island through Knight Inlet, a jagged treeline etched in varying shades of gray and capped by cloud. A Pacific postcard. Picturesque, but perilous. Estrada paced the small bow, bounced on his toes, clenched and unclenched his fists. Quietly frantic. His mind focused on one thought now. *Find Lucy.* The only thing that diverted Estrada's attention was Dylan's arrival in his green and blue plaid kilt. Like Estrada, Dylan had pulled the hood of his navy windbreaker up over his head to shut out the rain.

"I knew you'd packed it," Estrada said, pointing to his kilt.

"Aye." Dylan looked as solemn as a Sunday priest. "For Lucy. I'd do anything for her, and you." The lad blushed at his confession, and then his skin blanched pasty gray. "Twice you've pulled me from the sea," he said, though there was no need to explain the brotherly bond between them.

Estrada punched him in the arm with a loose fist. "Let's not go for three."

Jaw muscles clenched, the lad stood stiffly at attention—an anxious soldier awaiting orders. Dylan was a scholar, not a warrior. Still, he was loyal. A brave heart who'd follow Estrada anywhere. To have such mates was a testament to the shaman's intrinsic goodness.

Sensing Dylan's trepidation, Estrada threw an arm around his shoulder. "We all need a drink. Let's go inside."

Estrada set five shot glasses on a tray and filled each to the brim with Irish whiskey.

"Gather round, lads." Dubh herded them around the helm.

Estrada. Dylan. Carvello. Dubh. Even Michael had appeared. Leaning against the counter in his usual lean black attire, he looked wasted. They each took a glass, raised it to the mission, and swallowed it down. Carvello snorted. Dylan coughed. And their sniggers broke the tension.

"We should prepare," Dubh said. "If we're lucky, these lads will be asleep. If we're not, we're walking into no man's land. What do we have for weaponry?"

Carvello slipped his pearl-handled revolver out of the holster beneath his ivory vest and admired the gloss. "Might not kill the bloodsucker, but it will certainly slow him down."

Dylan shrugged, dewy-eyed from the whiskey. "I don't—"

"Don't worry, man. I've got you covered." Estrada slipped off his trench coat to reveal a black leather jacket Dubh had never seen before. With a flourish, the shaman brushed his hands through the outside pockets and launched two fireballs into the air.

Dubh smiled and poured another round of whiskey shots. Perhaps, he was going to see Estrada's magic show after all.

"Jesus Christ. Don't burn the fucking yacht down," yelled Carvello. "I have to return this baby to Bjorn."

Estrada caught each of the fireballs as they descended, then clapped his hands together and they vanished.

"*Sláinte*," Dubh said, hoisting a shot to Estrada. "We can take this fucker. I feel it in my bones."

Estrada nodded and downed his second shot. Opening his leather jacket, he revealed an arsenal of knives.

"Estrada is an expert in the impalement arts," Michael said. "I should know. I'm usually the target."

"Now, there's a show I'd pay to see," Dubh said. "Estrada the Impaler."

The energy around the helm shifted as the men geared up. Dubh thought of all the rebel-rousing speeches his Scottish countrymen had made before racing, shrieking into battle. Pulling a thick cedar branch, the size of a baseball bat, from under the couch, Dubh held it beside him like a walking stick. He'd found it on the beach at Hardwicke Island the night of their coven ritual and spent hours carving and enchanting it under the moon. Just this morning, he'd completed his spellcasting and polished it with olive oil. A silver halo surrounded the staff like a full moon.

"Shaman." Dubh tossed the staff to Estrada.

The magician caught it and hefted it in his hand. "I can't wait to see what this can do." He winked at Dubh. "It's time. Find us a place to anchor, Victor. We'll take the tender and surprise these fuckers while they're sleeping in their coffins."

Once on the shore, Estrada hoisted Dubh on his back like a bairn and loped through the forest. The faintest of game trails led to Diego's lair and the shaman was on it, tracking with some inner sense that defied all reason. The others followed. Dylan keeping abreast. Michael, with a sudden burst of bravado, threatening to overtake the young Scotsman. Carvello lagging, tripping, and cursing. A man of glitz and city, the toes of his soft white leather loafers seemed to catch on every gnarled root or upraised rock.

Estrada stopped dead when he spied Diego's palace through a swathe of trees. "Jesus," he said, swinging Dubh down to the ground.

Like the Alhambra palace, pink light cut through the pale mist to reveal carved stone columns and Moorish arches. Dubh had always wanted to go to southern Spain to see the red castle and now this miniature version flickered before him. For a moment, it took his breath away. And then Michael Stryker brought it back.

"This is nothing. Wait till we get inside." Breath quickened and cheeks flushed, Michael was spiking.

The faint sound of techno-beats rustled the cedars. Was it just the adrenalin rush of return and confrontation? Or was the darkness Michael possessed now summoned by its maker?

Estrada noticed Michael's ardor and glanced at Dubh. When they'd talked briefly before docking at the Paradise Lodge, Dubh had confessed his suspicions. He'd wanted to leave Michael there with the women. Estrada refused. *I know he's not himself*, Estrada had said. *I'm not blind. I saw what he did to Carvello. But I trust Michael with my life. He may be sick. He may even be turning. But he won't turn on me.*

But what about *them*?

Dubh raised his brows and hoped Estrada understood. Would Michael sell them out to save himself and his lover? The man was a wild card, and if Diego held any sway over him, this is when he'd use it. Dubh was keeping a close watch on Michael Stryker and if he needed to be taken out, he'd do it. Pressing his lips tightly together, Estrada nodded once. The two men understood each other.

Dylan beckoned. He'd discovered a dusty wooden door in the stone. Lifting the iron latch, he pulled. "It could be a trap." Rusty hinges squealed and the door gave way.

"It could," Estrada said. "But what choice do we have?"

Assaulted by the reek of mold and rot and something long past life, Dubh sat back on his heels and wrinkled his nose. "Shite. It's boggin' in here, man."

"Aye," Dylan said. "Some palace. I thought a vampire might court luxury."

"We're not there yet," Michael said.

One staircase ran down into a grotto for storing wine—the dust as thick as a man's thumbnail. Another ran up into a neglected kitchen. When a rat skittered and disappeared into the darkness, they all flinched. The walls were cobwebbed, the grimy stone floor littered with rodent droppings.

Estrada raised a finger and up they went.

No sunlight had penetrated the greasy glass windows in decades, perhaps centuries. They followed on each other's heels, ever wary, flinching at the slightest sound, feeling their way through the rank grunge.

Dubh heard the drip and smelled the blood before he saw them. Three naked women. Hanging by their ankles, upside down from hooks, their blood draining into a golden trough.

Dylan wretched and slung a fist across his mouth, tried to contain his horror, and couldn't.

"Jesus Christ," Carvello said.

"Help me cut them down." Estrada opened his jacket and passed Carvello a knife. The two men sawed through the damp rope and the others caught the bodies as they fell.

"We should take them home," Estrada said.

If we make it home, thought Dubh. "You were right about Diego's misogynist streak."

"Fodder," Michael mumbled.

Dubh could see Michael's body trembling, his eyes shining wide with desire. Wringing his hands, Michael circled the trough of warm blood like an alcoholic in a bar, casting quick glances at Estrada, who held one of the women in his arms.

"Lay them here," Dylan said, swiping his arm across a dusty table. "Up off the floor." He ripped a curtain from one of the windows and covered the bodies as Carvello and Estrada set them down.

"In nomine Patris et Filii et Spiritus Sancti," Carvello said, crossing himself with the sincerity of a good Catholic.

They all stood silent; each man immersed in his own thoughts.

"Lucy," Estrada said.

Dubh knew what he was thinking. *If they could do this to a woman what would they do to a child?* "She's loved and she's blessed," he said. "Remember what Cernunnos said."

Estrada swallowed and set his jaw, and they walked on.

A door on the other side of the kitchen led into a hall. The thick cold set Dubh's teeth chattering. Clutching his wooden staff close to his chest, the druid mouthed incantations to the gods. *Deliver us from evil.*

They wandered through a stone tunnel and into an open patio where rain fell in waves onto marble tiles. Raising his face to the stratus sky, Dubh felt its fresh kiss on his tongue. After the rank scene they'd just encountered, it was a godsend.

"In there," Michael whispered, glancing through the lobed Moorish arches into a central courtyard that danced with pink light.

"Why is it unguarded?" Estrada said suspiciously.

"The guards are on the other side by the S&M gallery. No one comes this way."

And just how do you know that? thought Dubh.

Estrada pushed open the mahogany double doors and they stepped through. The deep scarlet walls were tiled, like the floor, in flamboyant waves of terracotta, ivory, and sapphire. Three tall pine trees grew from the earth, their tops reaching toward a glass coffered ceiling. All was quiet, though bodies swayed in woven hammocks from the branches, or lazed in piles on Persian rugs and red-gold damask pillows. An arm or leg dangled. Vampires passing the day, and not a coffin to be seen.

Let's kill them as they sleep, thought Dubh, raising his staff.

But Estrada touched a finger to his lips to signal silence and ventured into the nest. The others followed. The furniture, brightly patterned couches and chaises, pillows and ottomans, was scattered around tropical plants in a horse-shoe shape. Honeyed candles cast an eerie glow against the carmine walls. The room reeked of wax and wine, foul flesh, and something indefinable.

At the open end stood Diego's throne. An ornate masterpiece, the wooden chair was gilded in gold and upholstered in moldering vermillion silk and velvet. This must be where the vampire held court like some medieval king. In the center of the room, a steaming spring bubbled from the core of the island and bathed the room in an ethereal mist.

Dubh watched Estrada reach inside his leather jacket and extract a silver knife. Carvello clutched his pearl-handled revolver in his hand. The seconds ticked by and no one moved. What are we waiting for? thought Dubh, lifting his staff again.

"At last."

Dubh's heart jumped. For this voice, as lush as Spanish velvet, could only belong to Diego. From behind the throne, two lean pale hands, parted a set of dark drapes, and the vampire emerged. Dressed in a bishop's robe, Diego stood smiling, a silver crucifix dangling from a chain around his neck.

Dubh thought of garlic and crosses, holy water and wooden stakes, sunlight and coffins. Was anything from legend true?

Diego wore the face of a Spanish nobleman, and he wore it well. Dark deep-set eyes and aquiline nose, a full mouth brushed by mustache and pointed beard. His long black hair was swept back from his forehead by a widow's peak and caught by a band at the back of his neck. To Dubh's surprise, he was terrifyingly handsome.

Diego's smile widened and he showed his teeth. "Welcome to Le Chateau de Vampire," he crooned. "We've been expecting you."

Estrada felt enchanted, as if he'd suddenly been transported back to the Underworld or dropped too much of Michael's Ecstasy. Shadows shifted in numinous waves of heightened color. Slow motion. Vampires fell from the fringes and dangled from hammocks suspended in mid-air. They were surrounded.

Grasping a knife from his jacket pocket, Estrada aimed for Diego's forehead and let it fly. Take out the kingpin and maybe the rest will fall. But, Diego dodged, leaving nothing but lightning traces in his wake. So, Estrada pulled another. This time, he shifted his aim at the last second. The knife pierced the forehead of an amazed vampire to Diego's left. The creature's face contorted, and it dropped. As it hit the floor, its pale flesh withered and cracked like an autumn leaf.

"Yes!" He'd found one way to destroy them. Flinging knives, one after the other, he aimed for the brain and cut them down as they closed in. Seven. Ten. Thirteen lay withered on the ground. But still more came.

Dubh swung his magicked staff, but before he could do anything else, a dreadlocked vampire vaulted over the couch and ripped it from his hands. An orange sarong was tied around his waist, but the rest of him was bare and his dark flesh glistened as if it had been oiled. Crashing to the floor, the steely creature broke Dubh's staff in two with one thump of a bare foot.

Estrada saw the teardrop tattoos beneath the eyes at the same time as Carvello. They'd both heard Nigel's description of the killers, so there was no mistaking his identity.

"*You.* You murdered my Ruby," Victor Carvello said, and fired. Once. Twice. Three times in rapid succession.

The bullets blasted flesh and bone. Black blood oozed from craters along with ivory splinters. The creature stumbled backwards and hit the floor.

Then, with a new surge of fury, the vampires closed in.

In his victory, Carvello lunged forward to sneer at this monster who murdered his only daughter.

Inside, Estrada cheered the man's triumph. An eye for an eye.

And then, the vampire sprung up, grinning and blood-spattered. "You gotta do better than that, Mafioso. I can't die. I already dead." In slow motion, the monster grabbed Carvello's hand, turned the gun so the barrel pointed down, and pulled the trigger.

Carvello screamed as the bullet pierced his white leather loafer and blasted a hole through his foot.

Bending Carvello's fingers back until they broke, the creature extracted the revolver. Then, pointing it at Estrada, he grinned. "Time for a little sport, Father?" he said to Diego.

Everything stopped and Estrada took a deep breath. No knife was faster than a bullet.

Diego smiled. "Drop your weapons or Zion will shoot you and your friends."

Estrada glanced around the room. Carvello was on the floor crying and cursing and clutching his bleeding foot. Michael, Dylan, and Dubh had been grappled by vampires.

"There are at least two bullets left. Who will it be?"

Estrada's mind was racing. They were trapped and there was no way out. Perhaps a bullet was kinder than what they'd seen in the back kitchen. How long had those women suffered?

"Very well." Diego pointed at Dylan. "That one. I never did develop a taste for Scots."

"No. Wait."

"Drop your weapons," Zion said. "Now."

Estrada saw the truth as he locked eyes with the vampire. This couldn't be it. Estrada didn't give a shit about his own life. But Lucy. What would happen to Lucy?

Carvello's wailing was unbearable.

Estrada broke Zion's gaze and glared at Diego. What did this monster want from him? Why go to such elaborate lengths to exact revenge? It made no sense.

Diego cocked his head and glared back as if reading Estrada's mind. Then, he nodded to Zion.

The dreadlocked vampire took three long strides and set the muzzle of the pistol against Dylan's temple.

Estrada slipped off his jacket and it fell with a clatter.

Smirking, Zion sauntered back and kicked it aside with his bare foot.

"My baby. Please. I need to see my baby."

Diego sat on his throne, leaned back, and crossed his legs. The sadist was enjoying himself. "Come Estrada. Come, kneel before me."

"Never," Estrada said, and spit.

Diego smirked. "Stubborn and proud. Such attractive traits in an adversary. Eliseo, bring The Wheel."

Estrada watched as a boy—with an angel's face and devil's eyes—pushed an iron contraption into the center of the room on squealing metal wheels. The boy, Eliseo, couldn't have been more than thirteen when Diego took him. A raven-haired cherub.

The circular device the boy commanded was taller than a man and fitted with chains and shackles. Three ugly gargoyles stood guard at its base. Estrada knew this was for him. It was the kind of medieval torture device that would go over big in his magic act at Pegasus. Of course, there, he'd know all its hidden workings. Already, he was examining the contraption with an eye to escape.

It was now or never. Estrada took a deep breath, focused on Diego, and hurled two enormous fireballs from his hands. Surprised by their ferocity, he stepped back.

Diego winced as the flames skirted the flesh of his left hand. Two vampires beside him caught the flames and fell writhing on the floor. Estrada scanned the flickering candles in niches along the carmine walls.

"Enough," Diego said. "My sons prefer sport to theatrics."

Zion and Eliseo grappled Estrada and forced him against The Wheel. Surprised by their physical strength, he struggled, but to no avail. After closing the shackles around his wrists and ankles, they stood back looking smug.

"Sport, sport, sport," the vampires chanted.

Diego turned to Michael. "Mandragora." He pronounced the name as if it were some princely title, then sniffed and scratched his beard. "Since you brought Estrada to me, I will give you one last chance to save yourself. Can you prove you are worthy?"

A cold rush cut through Estrada's gut. Gasping, he shot a glance at Dubh, and then looked back at Michael. Had his lover betrayed him?

"I didn't bring you Estrada." Michael's eyes narrowed.

"Of course you did." Diego gestured to Estrada, who stood chained to The Wheel with his arms and legs splayed like Vitruvian man. "*There* he stands and here *you* stand."

Blanching, Michael stared at Estrada and stuttered, "Compadre, I . . . I didn't."

Two vampires pushed the iron wheel containing Estrada to the side, while others dragged Michael and Carvello into the center of the room. Carvello, who'd slipped off his shoe, left blood smears on the mosaic tiles. Moaning and crying, he fell to the floor, clutching his foot with his one good hand. The other, his gun hand, was swollen and misshapen, the fingers busted.

"I am told, Mandragora, this man molested you when you were a child. That he sold you for sex and stole your innocence."

Michael hung his head and refused to speak, as Diego's words hovered in the air.

Peter fucking Pan. Catatonia. Now it all made sense. Even the bite. Closing his eyes, Estrada sighed. Why had Michael never shared the secret of Carvello? Was he so ashamed? Amidst the darkness surrounding his lover, Estrada could suddenly see scarlet waves of anger. Michael's blood was boiling beneath his waxy exterior.

"Last chance, Mandragora. Vampire is the ultimate gift. You have tasted its power. Kill this scum you hate, and it's yours."

"No!" screamed Estrada, struggling to free himself from the shackles. "Don't do it." If Michael became a vampire, it would be the end of them. And the end of Michael. He'd be lost forever.

Michael stared at his lover, every muscle in his pale face taut, his red-rimmed eyes shimmering with tears.

"Don't be like them," Estrada pleaded, his eyes burning.

"But I *am* like them." Michael's pitiful stare ripped through Estrada's heart. "Forgive me, compadre." And then he lunged.

Taken unaware, Carvello careened backward. Michael's teeth were everywhere, biting and ripping. Carvello was screaming and trying to fight him off. Diego was sneering, and the vampires cheering. "Sport! Sport! Sport!"

In the bloody cacophony, Estrada felt bile rising in his gut. Clenching his fists, he racked at the shackles. Made the metal slick with his blood. Had to get free. Had to stop this butchery. Why the fuck hadn't he listened to Dubh and left Michael back at the lodge?

Then, suddenly Carvello shoved Michael and tried to stand. But with one wounded foot, he couldn't balance. When Michael came at him again, he threw a few punches, caught Michael in the jaw, and even managed, wobbling on his decent leg, to raise the other knee into Michael's crotch. But it wasn't enough. Despite his plasticity, Carvello was an old man, and Michael was stronger and faster than ever before. Like a terrier, Michael sunk his teeth into Carvello's neck, tore into it, and spit out a wad of flesh.

The image triggered a memory in Estrada's mind—the snake in the Underworld. The snake created from Dubh's staff. Diego had ripped its heart out and left a hole in the wood. But where was Dubh's staff now?

Estrada glanced at Dubh, then scanned the room. Lying in two pieces a few strides away, the staff glowed with its own internal charge. If one of them could get to it, they might turn this thing around. But how? Dubh and Dylan were bound hand and foot and flanked by vampires. Estrada closed his eyes and tried to will the wooden sticks to jump into his hands. In his mind, he saw it happen, but when he opened his eyes, the glowing sticks hadn't moved. He couldn't concentrate in all the chaos. The ecstatic creatures were cheering. What had happened?

Victor Carvello was sprawled on the tiles, his white Versace shirt splattered with blood. Michael was curled across the body—his face buried in Victor's neck.

This was no romantic love bite like the movies portrayed. This was cold-blooded murder, raw and graphic and nauseating. Michael had murdered Carvello with nothing but his hands and teeth. He lifted his head and hissed, and Victor's blood spilled from his open mouth.

He's a vampire and there's nothing I can do to save him. So much adrenalin pounded through Estrada's veins, his legs felt weak. Only the shackles that bound his wrists and rattled against the wheel, kept him upright. As much as he hated to admit it, Michael now belonged to Diego. Was there no redemption from this rendering?

"Perhaps, you will prove useful after all, Mandragora," Diego said, impressed by Michael's willingness to kill on cue. "Zion. Go to him. Tend to him and make him your own."

The dreadlocked vampire smiled triumphantly, swaggered over, and lifted Michael off the body. This was the bastard who murdered Ruby Carvello. Who broke Nigel's legs. The creature with the black teardrop tattoos. Surely, Michael remembered this, and would resist.

But no. Zion slipped an arm around Michael's shoulder and helped him walk to one of the couches. Michael's blood-streaked face was contorted, whether in grief or pain or shock, Estrada couldn't tell. Settling beside him, the creature cuddled close. The comforting boyfriend. The assassin.

"Silence," Diego said, and the room went dead. "Clean this up. We must not frighten the child."

The child. Lucy. Estrada's heart pounded as his hands and wrists wrestled with the bloody shackles that bound him to the wheel. If this motherfucker had harmed Lucy, he'd kill him with his last breath.

Vampires dragged Carvello's corpse to the center of the room and tossed it down a crater beside the hot spring. Estrada listened for a sound, the final thud, but heard nothing. The crater was a bottomless pit. And then, a sound like raking leaves on the sidewalk, as vampires dragged the parched bodies of their brothers along the tiles and flung them into the pit as well. A vampire with a shaved and tattooed head filled a wooden bucket with water from the hot spring and flung it across the blood-stained tiles.

Diego nodded. "Eliseo, bring the child."

When Lucy appeared, Estrada gasped. Sensara was there too, clutching his baby against her chest, one hand bound tightly with a rag. How did Diego get her? But it didn't matter now. They were all here together. His family. This was where it would end.

Lucy's legs were wrapped around Sensara's waist, and her sweet face lay against her mother's breast. She was wearing a pink onesie, splashed with hearts and teddies. Her hair was caught up in pigtails and tied with two pink bows. She looked remarkably unharmed and oblivious to the madness surrounding her.

"Lucita." Tears dripped from Estrada's eyes, and he tasted their salt on his tongue. He wanted to hold her, to hold them both. Hug them, and never let them go.

Lucy looked up and grinned. "Dada." She scrunched up her nose, perhaps wondering why her father was chained to The Wheel. "Ah?"

Estrada took a deep breath to steady himself. He couldn't fall apart now. He must find a way out. This was his family and he'd do whatever it took to save them. He glanced at Sensara, needed their combined strength. The muscles in her face were soft—the tension replaced by mother's love—though tears dripped down her cheeks.

Sensara stared back at him, then her gaze fell on the shackles that bound his wrist to the wheel. He heard her voice in his head. *Use your magic, Estrada.*

Magic, yes. He'd done this many times at Pegasus. Diego had shackled him to The Wheel but didn't know he was an escape artist. In his mind, Estrada imagined his bones softening, the joints thinning, the muscles melting like warm wax. And, as he released one long slow breath, his slick wrists slipped in the shackles. He glanced at Sensara and blinked.

Behind her stood Nora Barnes in a long, dirty, white nightgown stained with blood. Had they fed from her? Nora's face was gaunt. Her eyes ringed by sleeplessness. And beside her was—

"Levi?" The name slipped from Estrada's lips as his brain tried to comprehend. Was Levi not sent by Cernunnos? Was he Diego's spy? "You're one of *them*?" Estrada's mind was spinning. How did he not know?

Estrada remembered Michael's midnight swim. *There are monsters right here.* Did Michael know Levi was one of them? Surely one vampire could sense another. Had Michael betrayed him too? Bile rose in Estrada's throat and he fought to push it down.

"Ah, of course," Diego said. "You two are acquainted."

Levi stared at the ground—couldn't look Estrada in the eye.

"Leopold Blosch is my youngest son. A fledgling. Less than a month in our family."

"How could you?" Estrada remembered a night of tequila and talk, of stories and secrets. Flirtation. Possibilities.

"Do not blame Leopold for honoring his father. My island can be difficult to find and I needed to ensure your arrival." Diego leaned back in his chair looking smug. "But now, it is time. Eliseo, bring the child to me."

"No!" Sensara screamed. Accosted by two vampires, she was forced to give up Lucy to the boy, Eliseo.

"Don't be frightened, *hermanita*," Eliseo said, playing with Lucy's pigtail.

"She is *not* your baby sister," Estrada said.

"Lucita and I grew close this week. I fed her and played with her."

"Don't call her that!" Only Estrada could call his baby Lucita.

"But we are *familia* since I took her from her pretty pink bedroom."

Eliseo's sly grin enraged Estrada. "You are *not* her family!"

Estrada's anger and Sensara's frantic screams scared Lucy, and she began to cry.

"Silence the woman," Diego said.

One of the vampires threw an arm around Sensara's neck and squeezed until she passed out. Then he dropped her on the floor.

"Please, let me see my baby," Estrada said.

"Bring the child to me," repeated Diego, and Eliseo obliged. Rising, the vampire took Lucy in his arms. When she stared at Diego, her lips jiggled, but she stopped crying. Then, she touched his mustache where it curled at the corner of his mouth.

Lucy was not afraid. But Estrada thought he would piss himself. All the vampire needed to do was turn his head. Open his jaw. Lucy's tiny throat would fit in his mouth. Estrada thought again of the snake and glanced at Dubh's glowing staff.

Diego walked toward Estrada holding Lucy in his arms. Stopping a breath away, he stared into Estrada's eyes.

Lucy reached for her father and touched his chest. "Dada."

"Lucita," Estrada said, his eyes burning. *"Lucita es bonita.* The most beautiful girl in the world." He bit his lip to stop his heart from breaking. The last thing Lucy saw could not be her father's pain.

"We are the same, you and I." Lifting his left hand, Diego stroked Estrada's cheek. "I knew it the first time I saw you with Lucita. The night she was born. Such fatherly love."

"What? You were—"

"Watching, yes. From the trees. I saw you catch her in your hands. I saw the joy on your face. I have felt such joy."

Estrada's lip trembled. He wanted to throttle this demon that held the thing he loved most in the world in the palm of his hand.

"Like the dwarf," Diego said, glancing at Magus Dubh, "I am El Padrino."

The Godfather. "You are *not* Lucy's godfather. You will never be—" Turning his face, the vampire kissed Lucy's cheek, and Estrada's breath caught.

"I have watched over you and Lucita since the night of her birth. Every night, when she has been with you, I, or my sons, have been there too."

"You've been stalking us." Estrada's gut flipped.

"I've been waiting. At first, I wanted only to avenge Christophe's death, but then I came to admire you, Estrada. To respect you. We are the same, you and I. Fathers who love our children. Lucita is your Niño de Sangre."

Niño de Sangre. *Blood Child.* That much was true.

"You will not abandon her. Nor will I ever abandon *my* children."

Estrada thought about the father who abandoned him when he was twelve years old. About his sister, who died the same night. About his mother, who moved to Mexico with his other sister, and abandoned him to his bastard uncle.

Michael's words echoed in his head. *You always leave me.* Estrada's throat tightened. He'd learned to leave the people he loved because in the beginning, they'd all left him.

"You understand," Diego said. "We are both good fathers. We are the same."

"We are *not* the same," Estrada said, the words sliding from his clenched jaw.

Diego laughed, so stereotypically sinister it seemed forced. Then, he lowered his voice to a whisper. "This is my offer, and I make it only once." He paused, and Estrada wondered what devious drama the vampire had concocted now. "If you join me willingly, I will see to it Lucy and her mother are returned home safe and unharmed."

"Join you? As one of your *sons?*" Estrada said this with contempt, but Diego did not react.

"To become El Salvador is an honor. I could take you myself, right here and now." He stroked the pulsing artery in Estrada's neck with one pale fingertip. "But I prefer acquiescence."

Estrada glanced around the room. Sensara was reviving. Dylan and Dubh were still bound, and the vampires were lounging on couches. Without the lure of blood lust, they'd lost interest. Leopold, who sat beside Nora Barnes, caught Estrada's eye and shook his head ever so slightly.

"You want me to submit," Estrada said.

"I want you to join me. I offer you the ultimate gift. Immortality. Riches. Power. What more could a man ask for?"

Freedom to live as a man and not a monster? "And if I refuse?"

Diego shrugged. "Refuse, and they will all die, starting with Lucita."

Magus Dubh couldn't believe his eyes. Diego was holding Lucy and whispering to Estrada. He couldn't hear what was being said, but he knew Estrada's hands could easily slip through the shackles in that iron wheel. Dubh had been watching the magician work his magic for the last few minutes. Estrada's bones and flesh had shrunk and reshaped in such a way, were he only to pull, he would be free. And once he was free, they could all be free. Leastways, they'd have a fighting chance.

"Do you give your word?" Estrada asked, loud enough for Dubh to hear.

The vampire nodded. "I am Diego. A man of honor. I trust you are too."

A deal had been struck, even though Diego was no man and there was no honor among vampires. Any creature who lived off the life force of another was a thief and killer, not a man of honor. Surely, Estrada knew this, and didn't trust this parasite?

Diego walked smugly across the floor and handed the bairn to Nora Barnes, who sat on the couch beside Leopold. How betrayed Estrada must feel, thought Dubh. First Michael, and now this Leopold character who said his name was Levi, who said he would help them.

"Eliseo," the vampire said. "Estrada has agreed to join us."

Join us? A cold chill raged through Dubh's body. If they lost Estrada ... If he became a vampire, they were all dead. Why would he agree to a thing like that? The stakes must have been too high to refuse.

Dubh closed his eyes and sent a silent prayer to Cernunnos, to Cerridwen, to all the gods and goddesses. *Help us, you motherfuckers. No rhymes or riddles. Just fucking help us.*

He tried to remember the coven ritual, all the things Cernunnos had said. *The ravens could be dispatched as ravens.* That was one thing. He remembered Estrada burned the raven feather in the fire and cast a spell. But none of the vampires had shifted into birds. What else? *Accept what is offered*. Cernunnos was clear on that. Did Diego make Estrada an offer he couldn't refuse? Is that why he'd agreed to this ludicrous joining?

"You have been with me since the beginning, Eliseo. As my oldest son, I give you this honor."

"Oh, El Padrino. Gracias." Falling to his knees, he kissed the gold rings on the vampire's outstretched hand.

Dubh glanced at Dylan, who stood bound to a pillar beside him, and mouthed the words "we're fucked." He'd been working at the ropes around his wrists, but all he'd done was rub his skin raw. All the vampires were focused on Diego and Estrada, except for Zion, who'd disappeared with Michael right after Carvello's murder.

Dylan gestured with his eyes to the broken staff and then to the hot spring and crater beside it.

"Aye," Dubh whispered. The symbols he'd carved in the moonlight were glowing silver. Closing his eyes, he concentrated on the elemental forces.

Earth. Fire. Wind and Water.
Deliver us from evil. Deliver us from evil.

He chanted this over and over in his mind.

When Dubh opened his eyes again, he gasped. Eliseo was standing chest to chest and thigh to thigh with Estrada against The Wheel. Like a mirrored Vitruvian man, his arms and legs were outstretched. His palms covered Estrada's palms. And his teeth were sunk deep in Estrada's neck. Dubh could see the boy's throat ripple as he swallowed the shaman's blood.

Estrada's eyes were closed. His head lolled to one side. He was dying.

"No!" Dubh screamed. Focusing all his power on one piece of the glowing staff, it jumped from the floor into his hand.

In the same instant, Leopold sprung from the couch and swept up Estrada's leather jacket full of knives. Extracting one, he charged and jammed it into the back of Eliseo's head. The blade slid right through the boy's skull and emerged bloody between his eyes. The vampire crumpled and fell to the floor.

Emitting a ghastly screech, Diego leapt from his throne.

But Estrada did not wake up.

Leopold dashed across the room to Dubh and slashed the ropes binding his wrists and ankles. Then, he moved on to Dylan.

Dubh grabbed the other staff and held the two sticks like six guns. His hands shook with the power rife in each. Just as Diego was about to pounce on Leopold, Dubh released two fiery blasts.

The vampire screeched again when the back of his bishop's robe exploded into flame. Writhing and screaming, he ran.

Leopold cut Dylan lose with two swipes of the knife and then hustled back to Estrada.

"Just pull his hands free," Dubh yelled. Pointing his twin staffs, he sent streams of fire flying at every vampire he saw. Many were shifting into ravens now. The stench of scorched feathers and burned bird was nauseating. But they were winning.

Leopold slipped on Estrada's leather jacket with its arsenal of knives. Grasping the shaman's right hand, he stooped and pulled him over his shoulder in a fireman's carry. "Follow me," he yelled.

"Take Estrada and the women and go," Dylan said. "We'll cover you."

Nora had Lucy in her arms. Sensara clutched Nora's arm, and the two women followed Leopold out the door.

"Come with me," Dylan said to Dubh. At the hot spring, Dylan turned. "This crater goes deep into the island. With focused power, we can spark an earthquake."

"You want to blow the fucking island up?" asked Dubh, incredulous. This might be the craziest thing he'd heard yet.

"Aye. Destroy the nest. This coastline is a seismic catastrophe waiting to happen."

Dubh handed Dylan one of the twin staffs and the two men angled them into the crater. Dubh began to chant aloud and Dylan chimed in.

"Earth. Fire. Wind and Water.
Deliver us from evil. Deliver us from evil."

The power grew. At the lip of the crater, rock began to break free and fall. There was a slight rocking and then a rush of wind nearly knocked Dubh off his feet.

Glancing up, he saw the pterosaur turn for another attack. *"Fucking Diego!* Where'd *he* come from?"

Dylan flung his staff into the crater. "Let's move."

Dubh clutched his staff and ran. There was no way he was going to toss it down that hole—not with a pterosaur on his arse.

Dylan was right about the earthquake. As they ran through the palace, the world dissolved into chaos. People panicked. Running, falling, screaming, they launched themselves through doors and windows as the ground heaved beneath their feet.

Suddenly, they were outside and Dubh was trailing Dylan down a dirt path toward the docks.

"Here," yelled Leopold. He stood in a small craft beside Nora Barnes. Sensara and Lucy were huddled beside Estrada's inert body. Dylan grabbed Dubh like a child and flung him into the boat, then hopped in himself. Nora released the bowline, and Leopold cranked it up as the palace exploded with smoke and flame.

Dubh clutched his staff to his chest. *And now the sky is flecked with ravens' wings. Deliver us from fucking evil.*

BLOOD FOR BLOOD

Zion's secret place could only be found by slipping through a narrow limestone crevasse in the basement below Le Chateau and negotiating a series of caves. He wasn't sure how he was going to entice Stryker to do that. He didn't have much to offer, but himself and a whole lot of booze.

The caves themselves were outside the palace proper and no one knew of their existence. Not even Eli. Zion had discovered them by accident decades ago, and it had taken him years to decorate his subterranean grotto with pilfered goods from the palace. A spectacular hot spring bubbled up from the ground and formed a natural oasis. It was his comfort and sanity when chaos affected the nest. And it was hot. Africa hot.

One wall had been painted in petroglyphs centuries ago. Zion imagined some shaman crawling inside on his belly with a skin-full of paint in his hand. Imagined him sitting for days, naked and starving, hoping for a vision. In the end, the shaman had painted an antlered deer and a raven in red ocher. It was the raven who spoke to Zion some days, when he came here alone to rest. It was the raven who told him to bring Stryker here for The Turning.

Stryker was easier to manage than he expected. He wandered along behind Zion like a zombie. Since his brutal attack on Carvello, the man had been mute. Stupefied. Perhaps, he was in shock. Zion remembered how he'd felt after ripping the life from McClintock. Ecstatic, but also numb. When you hate someone that much, and then kill them with your bare hands, it can take a while to recover.

He settled Stryker into a nest of wolf skins they'd brought back from one of their sojourns in Alaska, then lit all the niched candles. Finally, he opened a bottle of whiskey and took a long haul. He passed the bottle to Stryker.

"You can relax here, man. No one knows about this place."

Stryker guzzled the whiskey. "Estrada," he said, eventually.

It was the first word he'd spoken, and it pissed the big man off. "I'll get him, and bring him here," Zion said. It was necessary bullshit.

"Why help us?"

Zion shrugged. Stryker was in shock if he thought Zion was helping them. "You don't think a vampire can have a conscience?" He scratched his itchy dreads. "Just stay here. I'll be back before you can finish that bottle, and I'll bring your man."

When Zion got back to the throne room, Eli was draining the magician. It was quite the spectacle. The magician's head lolling sideways, eyelids fluttering, the blood drizzling down his pale neck, while Eli stretched across him on The Wheel, acting like it was his first fuck, and wishing it was.

Of course, *he'd* been given the honor. Father's fucking favorite. Diego wanted Estrada as his companion, so he'd let Eli drain him for show, but *he'd* do The Turning in private. Once Father got Estrada alone in his chamber, he'd drizzle his blood into the magician's mouth and take him. Father had been watching Estrada for months and craved him like Zion craved Stryker. Zion hoped it would happen soon. Once Diego made Estrada his bitch, the magician would no longer be any threat to Zion, and he could do what he wanted with Stryker.

And then, Leopold Blosch did an unbelievable thing.

Vampire is not a race. It's a condition spread by a virus. A misunderstood condition. People don't walk around saying "I am Flu," though it too is spread by a virus. They say, "I have the flu." But over the course of time, Vampire had become an identity with a distinct set of physical and cultural attributes—like the ability to shift into flying creatures. It also had moral codes, the most important one being—never kill a brother.

Zion, now realized, he'd neglected to mention this to Leopold Blosch when he sired him. Which meant he was partially responsible for what happened next—the chef's fatal attack on Eliseo, the liberation of Estrada and his accomplices, and their escape from Le Chateau.

When the chef thrust that knife through Eli's skull, Zion shifted, and flew up into a tree to observe the chaos and plan his next move. Then, that fucking dwarf picked up the staff he'd busted in two, and Zion knew shit was about to escalate. Squawking furiously, Zion rocketed from the throne room, and flew through the tunnels, down to the basement. He wasn't about to lose Stryker now. He'd waited too long.

Returning to the grotto, Zion found his captive sprawled on his back with the near-empty whiskey bottle still in his fist. Three-quarters-drunk and docile as a lamb, Stryker was reciting fragments of poetry.

Zion shifted back into his manly form and lay down naked beside Stryker in the wolf skins. They were safe for the moment and Stryker was ripe for the picking. When the island rocked beneath them, Zion flinched. Had that fucking dwarf managed to trigger an earthquake? But the movement was brief, and then subsided. Zion had felt worse on this coast. Stryker didn't even notice. Zion hoped he wasn't going catatonic again. If Stryker did that, he'd be no fun at all, and Zion might just have to finish him.

Dubh shivered when he heard the priestess choke. Sensara was a tough woman, and despite everything she'd endured, including the kidnapping of her child, Dubh had never seen her fall apart.

Leopold had piloted them in the vampires' smaller craft, back to the *Ragnarök*. Now, in the aftermath of the disaster, they huddled together in the saloon. Survivors. Sensara, Estrada, Leopold, Nora, and the wee bairn. Out on the bow, Dylan was weighing anchor, while Dubh perched at the helm, hand on the throttle. Once Dylan signaled the anchor was secure, Dubh was ready to rip. He wanted to be far away from these murderous creatures.

Two white sectional couches surrounded a large coffee table in the saloon of the *Ragnarök* where Leopold had placed Estrada. From the helm, Dubh could see Sensara when he turned slightly. Sitting at the end of the longest couch, she cradled Estrada's head in her lap.

Back at the Paradise Lodge, the kid they called Eliseo had bent the little finger of her left hand sideways and busted it. Diego must have wanted her for insurance. Or perhaps just spite. Fortunately, the fractured bone had not punctured the skin. Dylan, who'd suffered several fractures and sprains as a footballer, had done his best to bring down the swelling and stabilize it. He'd just applied a small splint and taped it to her ring finger, then dosed her up on ibuprofen. Sensara said she was fine. Now, her right hand lay on Estrada's forehead, and her left palm, with its bandaged finger upon his heart.

Reiki and love, thought Dubh. Sensara's trying to heal her man with Reiki and love. Dubh looked a moment longer, then turned away. Watching something so intimate made him feel like a voyeur.

"He's dying," Sensara whispered. "Don't let him die, Cernunnos." As she pleaded with the god, her voice rose in level and pitch. "You said you'd help us. You care about him. Please *do* something. Estrada can't die."

Cernunnos did care and he *had* helped them, thought Dubh. He'd sent the Spunkie to light the path to Lucy. They'd rescued her from the vampires and that was all he'd promised. The horned god clearly said he couldn't interfere in the destiny of man. Though surely, dying here like this couldn't be the shaman's destiny.

Eliseo had drained Estrada of far too much blood. If Leopold hadn't betrayed Diego by acting when he did, the shaman would be dead. Or turned by Diego, which was a fate worse than death. Fuck, Dubh thought. Without Leopold Blosch, we'd all be dead by now. Fodder for the vampires. When Dubh asked Leopold why he betrayed Diego, he'd looked incredulous. *You saw them. Wouldn't you?*

"We have to *do* something," Sensara screamed.

Dubh startled and turned at her upraised cry. She'd clutched Estrada all the way back to the yacht, refusing to let him go, and her face was blotched with tears.

"We can't just let him die."

"You're right, Lady. As soon as we get clear of this fucking island." He glanced up through the massive skylight above their heads. Behind the blanket of mist, smoke and fire tarnished the sky. Ravens circled and careened, still caught in the chaos of their exploding nest. Ravens, who were vampires. He knew they were coming. It was only a matter of time. And now they had Michael to help them—Michael who had first-hand knowledge of the yacht and everyone aboard.

"We're witches for fuck sake!" Sensara cried, her frustration peaking. When she surveyed the room, Dubh knew what she was thinking. Hollystone Coven, *her* coven, had been torn apart by the vampire. Dylan was out on the bow—the only one left. Daphne was still missing. And Estrada . . .

Across the way, on the white loveseat, sat Leopold and Nora Barnes. Nora had nursed Lucy until the swaddled bairn fell asleep in her arms. Lucy is loved and blessed, thought Dubh. Cernunnos had been right about that. Nora Barnes cuddled the wee bairn like she was her own. Leopold had found the poor woman a pair of sweatpants and a hoodie on *La Sangria* before they changed boats. It was the yacht the vampires had used for the kidnappings, and he was well acquainted with it.

"I can save him," said Leopold, suddenly.

They all glanced up.

"If Estrada consumes my blood, he'll live. It's how Diego—"

"No! You stay away from him," Sensara hissed. "Or, I'll—"

"You don't understand. He can *live*," Leopold said, unfazed by Sensara's threat. "Keep his memories . . . even his humanity."

After what he'd witnessed at Diego's lair, Dubh doubted that.

"Estrada would rather die than become a vampire." Sensara's dark eyes blazed.

"I thought at first I'd become like them, but I didn't."

"You *are* like them. You're one of them!" Sensara shrieked. "Are you trying to say you haven't tasted blood?"

Leopold hung his head.

"I knew it. Why are you even here?"

"Leopold saved Estrada's life," Dubh said. "If he hadn't killed that bastard who was draining him . . . If he hadn't cut us loose and carried Estrada out of there, we'd all be dead now."

Sensara raised her head and shot Dubh an acid glance, then backed off and brought her forehead to rest against her man's.

"Leopold, you've given me an idea," Dubh said suddenly. "I don't know *why* I didn't think of it before."

Dylan stepped inside the galley. "All secure on deck. We're ready to roll."

"Aye. Good. Come take the helm."

Dubh leapt off the seat and faced Sensara. "Leopold is bang-on about one thing. Estrada needs blood."

"So?" Sensara bit her bottom lip.

"So, we give him blood. *My* blood."

"*Your* blood?"

"Aye. Estrada needs *my* blood. And before you say no, we've done this before, Estrada and me. Twice in Scotland we saved each other's lives by exchanging blood."

"Alright big man!" Dylan said. "You're as brilliant as you are blue." He raised his palm for Dubh to strike. "Leopold and I can pilot this craft. Off you go and do your magic."

Sensara brightened. "But how?"

Dubh thought of the last time they'd exchanged blood. Estrada was in hospital under a police guard. He'd been shot and beaten and just come out of surgery. There'd been no time for an I.V. Estrada needed Dubh's fey blood, so he could mend and catch the bastard who put him there. So, Dubh had simply nicked his wrist and let Estrada drink. They'd even joked about it. *Like a vampire?* Dubh had said when Estrada suggested it. At the time, neither of them believed in the existence of such creatures.

Leopold moved to the helm and sat down beside Dylan.

Dubh glanced again through the skylight at the chaotic sky and its circling ravens. "Keep a lookout," Dubh said to Leopold. "And get us as far away from here as you can."

Dylan looked up. "What about Daphne? Do you think she's—"

"She's still at the lodge," Leopold said. "They didn't kill her. I heard them talking back at the . . . " He gestured to the island.

"Right. Straight to Paradise."

Estrada's black leather jacket with its arsenal of knives lay on the arm of the white couch where Leopold had left it. After washing his hands at the bar sink, Dubh extracted one and examined the gleaming silver blade. It was a stage knife, blade-heavy for throwing from the handle, the steel sharpened to a razor point. Fucking deadly. Dubh thought of the vampires Estrada had taken down back at Diego's lair. Like popping balloons at a fair.

"Once Estrada comes around and starts to feast, you may need to stop him," Dubh said to Sensara. "My fey blood will give him a buzz, you see."

"You've really done this before?"

Dubh nodded. "Aye, Lady. You can trust me. The first time, we used an I.V. Estrada gave me his blood and saved my life. The next time, I cut a vein and he drank from me. Your man didn't have time to fuck about, you see." He held out his blue-tattooed wrist. "I still have the scar."

They both stared at the pale line against the tattoos.

"May as well use the same vein," Dubh said.

"Thank you, Magus. For this and everything else." She glanced at Lucy. "We couldn't have got her back without you."

"Don't thank me yet, Lady." Dubh needed Estrada back in the game. He'd been thinking about Michael Stryker. He'd been correct in his suspicions. Michael was one of them—a vampire. He'd killed Victor Carvello with his hands and teeth. Then, in all the confusion, he'd vanished with the dreadlocked demon—the bastard who murdered Ruby Carvello and broke Nigel's legs. Dubh didn't know how or when they'd come, but he knew they would. Neither Michael Stryker nor Diego was finished with them yet.

⇒≈⇐

Estrada floated through a vast expanse of indigo space, speckled with stars. There was no gravity, no pain. He floated weightless. Completely free. Completely at ease. Alone, and yet, not alone. For intrinsically, he knew each star held the soul of someone he'd once loved. And he'd lived many lives and loved many souls. They drifted around him, pulsing together in one celestial breath.

Estrada was returning to his home star to be reborn. Once there, some of these glittering stars would conjoin with his, in a dance to determine the destiny of his next incarnation.

The stars, at first shimmering diamonds, eclipsed with color. Sapphire, violet, incarnadine. Slipping inside the kaleidoscopic shapes, he smelled aromas. Almonds, berries, sea salt, pine, and copper. The scents collected on his tongue, rolled around his taste buds, and conjured emotions, memories, and tableaus.

Sensara. Her belly taut as a balloon, the skin transparent. Lucy, curled head to knee, her feet pushing against the edge of Sensara's belly. Spinning like a seal and swimming head-first through the bloody sea and into his hands. Her small slick head thick with black hair. She opened her eyes and stared at him. Lucy Lugh. Born of a Star. The blood, so raw and visceral, he could taste it for days. Could taste it now.

Estrada licked his lips. Just thinking about it made it real. "Lucita," he muttered. "Niño de Sangre."

He swallowed and licked and swallowed again. It was hot and salty, coppery raw. Running through a mesh of veins and arteries like the sap in a tree. The Tree of Life. *Crann Bethadh*.

"Baha," he breathed.

"Estrada."

He heard a voice. Not his own. It caught at the edges of his consciousness and tugged.

"Estrada, can you hear me?"

The voice. Female. A whisper. Tugging and pulling. He felt the weight of it. Muscle and bone. Then, other sensations. Pain and hunger. The warm pressure of flesh against his lips. The metallic taste of blood. Raising a hand, he grasped, pressed, and swallowed.

"He's coming back."

From where? Estrada thought. His eyelids fluttering. Light seeping through.

"That's enough." A different voice. Male, serious, anxious.

"Let go now," said the woman. Grasping his hand, she pulled it back.

Estrada opened his eyes.

"Sara." Vague memories. Michael killing Carvello. Diego holding his baby. "Lucy!" he cried.

"She's here. She's safe. And so are you." Sensara was crying, tears streaming down her cheeks. Leaning over, she touched his chin with her fingers, wiped the blood from his lips and dried it with her hair.

"What are you—?"

"Blood," she said. "Dubh's blood. He saved your life. Brought you back to us."

Estrada felt the wee man's hand on his shoulder.

"Dubh, did you just—"

"Ach aye, but now I need a wee belt of scotch."

"Lucy. Where's Lucy?"

"Here," Nora Barnes said, and tucked his child against his chest.

Sensara beamed. "She's good. Blessed and loved, just like Cernunnos said."

"Lucy," he said, crushing her in his arms.

"The chef. He's taken your man." Zion delivered this news to Stryker with as much drama as he could muster. Though the palace was an inferno, the vampire felt safe in his grotto; at least, for the moment. Once things calmed down, and he'd done what he came here to do, they'd clear out too. Grasping the whiskey bottle, Zion took a swig, and settled back into the wolf skins beside Stryker.

"What'd you say?" asked Stryker, his words slurring. Inebriated, he was lounging in the nest like a man after sex Though they hadn't got quite that far yet. After digging around in his jacket pocket, Stryker pulled out his gunmetal case and lighter. He caught one of the cigarettes with his lips, and lit it with a lick of flame, then offered one to Zion.

It had been years since Zion felt the urge to smoke. "What the hell. Can't die of cancer. I already dead."

There was something incredibly sexy about Stryker, something Zion couldn't put a finger on. He'd waited a year for this moment. Waited and watched. Had wanted Stryker since that first taste. Wanted him now.

When Stryker flicked the lighter for him, Zion took a deep drag and exhaled. He felt suddenly lightheaded as myriad chemicals surged through his blood stream. Nicotine rush.

"The chef," Zion repeated, slowly. "Leopold Blosch. He's taken your man."

"You saw Estrada? He's alive?" Stryker's eyes flickered bright with hope. Of course, the last he'd seen of Estrada, the man had been chained to The Wheel, awaiting his fate.

"Alive?" Zion shrugged. "All I know is Eli drained him. And then, Leopold Blosch—*that* crazy motherfucker—he took out Eli."

Though he'd never cared for Eliseo, Zion had hunted with the boy for centuries, so the two knew each other intimately. The chef, though . . . What a dark horse he'd turned out to be. Shoved a knife right through Eli's fucking brain. Dusted him. Right in front of Father.

Zion didn't know it was possible for them to be destroyed like that. In a hundred and fifty years, he'd never seen a vampire die—not until the magician had pulled out his clutch of knives and started popping skulls.

"Drained him?" The soft underbelly of Stryker's cheek pulsed as he considered his lover's fate. "Then, he must be dead." His green eyes lost their spark.

Zion groaned and shrugged again. "Dead? Alive? What the fuck does it matter?"

"Or turned? Could he be—?"

"That depends on Leopold Blosch."

Fuckin' Chef. There was no telling what he'd do. The chef had a hard-on for Estrada. That much was evident the night he'd stayed aboard the *Ragnarök*. If he wanted the magician for himself, it would be easy enough to feed him his blood while the man was still unconscious. A few drops in the mouth was all it took to kindle the hunger. The Turning was simple. Deciding whether you wanted to turn the man, that was hard. Zion had made mistakes. Turned men who excited him, only to find himself bored in no time. Stryker, though. He seemed different. He might be the one.

"I just thought you should know. The chef took your man. They gone, and they ain't comin' back."

Stryker sighed. "Estrada is not *my* man." He said this with such utter dejection, for a second, Zion pitied him.

"Coulda fooled me. These raven eyes see through cracks."

Stryker swiped a tear from his cheek with the back of a fist, then crushed out his cigarette. "Estrada's not *anybody's* man," he said, with a hint of venom.

"Ah. He don't want no ring on his finger." Stryker had seen Estrada that night on the yacht with Leopold Blosch and was jealous.

Reaching over, Zion stroked the back of Stryker's hand slowly from his wrist to the tips of his fingers. "I ain't got no ring. Neither do you."

Turning the hand gently, Zion ran his thumb over the inside of Stryker's palm. He sensed the rush of blood through the man's body as he grew aroused. Stryker would soon forget the magician.

Raising the hand to his face, Zion ran his tongue across the palm, and watched Stryker's pupils grow round and black. "I remember the night you came here with that little French fuck."

"Christophe."

"Do you remember me, Mandragora?" He used Stryker's pet name to remind him of the mad bad man inside.

"How could I forget you? You bit me, here." He turned his head and touched the vein Zion had punctured that night a year ago.

"You liked it." Zion smiled wide to show his canines.

"I loved it."

"That little French fuck was jealous."

"Obsessed. It's his fault all of this is happening now."

"Forget him. Forget them all." We can paint the future in blood.

When Stryker licked his dry lips, Zion nicked the tip of his finger with a fang and placed it just in the center of that warm lower lip.

Stryker's jaw relaxed and opened slightly to take it in. His eyes shone again when he tasted Zion's blood.

"You will love Vampire, Mandragora. Do you mind if I call you that?"

"No, I like it." Stryker's breath quickened as the blood trickled through his veins. He suckled the finger, already wanting more. Zion knew exactly what he was feeling. Had felt it a million times.

"I can feed your hunger. Take you higher than your *erotigens*." Zion knew all about Mandragora's ecstasy trade at Pegasus. The orgies he was famous for directing. His hedonism.

Stryker's neck, so pale and exposed, drew Zion's gaze—the furiously beating carotid artery throbbing faster with the threat of danger. Though Vampire ran through his veins, Michael Stryker was still as human as he'd been a year ago when he first entered Le Chateau.

"I'm afraid to die." The words emerged in a breath so quiet, Zion could barely hear them, in a confession so intimate the vampire felt priestly.

"You will never die, Mandragora." Zion's lips brushed his ear. "Never grow old and feeble. Never be a slave to a decrepit body."

He continued to rub his bloody finger over Stryker's damp mouth as they talked. Enjoyed watching the pale tongue tap the trail of blood.

"Trust me. I know what it's like to be a slave, and then a free man."

"Were you . . . ?"

"Once, a long time ago."

"I'm sorry."

"Don't be. I ripped McClintock's throat out. Hate is a powerful weapon."

Stryker squeezed both eyes shut. "I killed Carvello."

Zion slapped his cheek. "You sure as fuck did. It was beautiful. I was proud of you."

Stryker opened his eyes. "Proud?"

"You ain't even turned yet, wild man. Right now, you a legend, but I can make you a myth."

Stryker blinked and furled his brow curiously.

"Eternal. Like your Lord Byron. *He* would have said *yes* to Vampire." Leaning over, Zion brushed the hair back from Stryker's brow. "I know all about you, Mandragora."

Reaching up, Stryker touched the teardrop tattoos beneath Zion's eyes. "Then you know you killed the woman who raised me." Sitting up suddenly, he turned his back on Zion. "Ruby was my mother, my sister, my friend."

"I'm sorry about Ruby Carvello. Father wanted us to leave a clear message, and I can't cross Father."

"Did *Father* tell you to break both of my grandfather's legs?"

"Sometimes, I get overzealous." Zion was suddenly irritable. Managing Stryker was starting to feel like work. He was tired and hungry, and that made him hornier than hell.

Then Stryker stood and stared down at Zion, something the vampire never could tolerate. "What do you want from me?"

Leaping to his feet, Zion grasped Stryker by the shoulders. "You don't know?"

Flipping him with one hand, Zion caught the back of Stryker's neck in his teeth and shoved his belly up against the rock wall, hard and fast. Stryker screamed, and Zion tasted blood. It was just a love bite, a little foreplay to whet his appetite.

As Zion released the pressure of his jaw, he felt Stryker sink against him. Then, the thin silk shirt ripped under the force of Zion's fists and Stryker's back felt warm against his bare chest. Zion continued to nuzzle his neck, moving ever closer to the artery, his fangs etching the pale flesh, his tongue catching the drops. Zion felt Stryker growing weaker—the human inside was dying to the pleasures of Vampire.

"Do you want this Mandragora? Say yes, and I will make you a myth."

"Yes. Yes. I want it. I want it all."

Piercing Stryker's carotid artery, Zion tasted the hot blood as it gushed into his mouth.

Stryker flinched with the force of the intrusion, then sank back against Zion's dancing body.

The vampire brought him almost to the point of death, then tore open his left wrist and wrapping his arm around Stryker's neck, held the spurting vein to the open mouth.

"Drink from me, Mandragora. Drink, and become a myth."

Stryker moaned as they fell into the wolf skins. There was no going back now.

TO RENDER A RAVEN

Estrada cuddled Lucy on Sensara's bed. With baby girl fingers, she tickled his belly and when he laughed and tried to get away, she giggled and cooed. His energy was still depleted, but his senses were ripe. Dubh's fey blood had that effect.

Sensara had just bathed Lucy and checked every inch of her tiny body for damage. Having proclaimed her daughter unharmed, she'd massaged coconut oil into Lucy's skin. He could smell its pungent sweetness. It was warm below deck and Lucy was now cavorting on the bed wearing just a diaper, her dark hair still damp and flipping up at the ends.

"I can't believe Eliseo actually packed a bag for Lucy when he abducted her." The muscles in Estrada's throat tightened when he said the boy's name. He'd never forget that name or the kid's dark eyes shining with pride and anticipation just before his teeth punctured his neck. It was no romantic interlude. The intense pain sent him into shock.

"*I* can't believe I didn't notice she was missing clothes." Sensara pulled a coral hoodie and leggings out of the plastic bag, and a tiny pair of frilly white socks. It was an outfit Estrada had picked out himself on a cruise to Hawaii last winter. A giant white pineapple ringed in hibiscus blossoms was splashed across the front.

"Come here." Grasping Sensara's hand, he pulled her down on the bed and kissed her sweetly. Then, he tucked Lucy in between them and kissed her too. When he tickled Lucy's toes, her giggles brought tears to his eyes. "We don't do this enough."

Truthfully, they'd never done it. There'd always been a void between them, an invisible boundary they were both too hesitant to cross.

Sensara stretched out on her side and cuddled Lucy against her breast. "I still have my milk," she said, pulling up her blouse. "Not as much as before, but it'll come back."

Thrilled to be offered the fountain of true happiness, Lucy attached herself to Sensara's nipple and burrowed into her belly. With her other hand, the babe played with her mother's hair.

Again, Estrada teared up. There had been too many intimate moments he'd missed and could never get back. Lying beside them, he propped his head up on his hand and watched. Madonna and child. His family.

"You look like I do after smoking a joint," he said, after a while. Waves of peace and love flowed from them to him.

Sensara sighed, was finally coming down from the chaos. "It's the oxytocin. They call it the love hormone."

"I gotta get me some of that Oxy. It's addictive, you know."

"It's oxytocin, not OxyContin, you ass. She flicked him with her finger. "And I'm sure you feel it all the time. It's released through nursing, but also through orgasm."

"Oh? You can get a natural high from sex?" he said, cheekily. "Who knew? Perhaps, we can explore that theory after Lucy goes to sleep." What he wanted more than anything was to remain sealed in this room with Sensara and Lucy for the next week. It would help him forget the nightmare of today.

"We're docking," Sensara said, shattering the dream.

He heard the engine slow as they maneuvered into the dock. Perhaps, they should spend the night in the lodge. It might be safer. Then again, it hadn't helped the women. Another mistake he'd made.

"I hope Leopold's right and they didn't hurt Daphne," Sensara said, glancing at her bandaged hand.

"Was he with them when they attacked you?"

Sensara shook her head.

"What do you remember?"

"Ravens at the window, and then men in our room—naked and dripping wet from the rain. That boy who . . . " She couldn't say the words, *bled you*. "He lifted the window right out of the frame. He was so strong. And he did this," she said, holding up her hand. "Zion, the one with the tattoos . . . He grabbed my throat and choked me until I passed out."

He'd closed her windpipe so the oxygen couldn't get to her brain. It was a simple technique Estrada had used himself on occasion. He'd also had it done to him and knew how frightening it felt to have no air and no power.

"Sorry Sara. That must have been terrifying."

She swallowed. "The next thing I knew, I woke up in a room with Nora and Lucy." Leaning down, she kissed the top of Lucy's head. "Leopold came and stayed with us. He and Nora are friends."

"Friends? What kind of friend abducts you?"

"Nora forgave him. She told me Diego turned Leopold against his will and was keeping him prisoner. Diego promised to let him go free if he found a nurse for Lucy. He also promised no one would be harmed."

A naïve vampire? Did Leopold *really* believe no one would be harmed? Perhaps. Diego was charming and persuasive. But Estrada still didn't like that Leopold had boarded the yacht pretending to be someone else. If he wanted help extricating himself from Diego's clutches, he should have told the truth right then. They could have used his expertise getting into the palace undetected. They might even have avoided the scene with Michael and Carvello.

"If you can find a way to save Leopold, please try," Sensara said.

"Save him? Why?"

"When you were critical . . . " Sensara touched his cheek. "Leopold offered to turn you into one of them. He said you could continue to live your life. Keep your memories. Your relationships. Even your humanity."

"Are you fucking kidding? You saw them. They cheered when Michael killed Carvello with his bare hands. And all those torture devices? I would rather die than become a vampire."

It was the first time, Estrada had uttered Michael's name since he'd witnessed the spectacle. The image of Michael biting and tearing at Carvello's flesh appeared whenever he closed his eyes. Goaded by Diego, some evil force had turned his friend into a fiend. Estrada had never imagined Michael capable of such an act. If he had, he would've heeded Dubh's advice and left him behind at the lodge. Not that it would have made much difference given what happened to Sensara and Daphne. Still, killer or not, Estrada had to rescue him. Michael had not betrayed him, like Leopold had. Michael was sick. And, Estrada couldn't leave his friend and lover of so many years living with those demons.

"I know. I wouldn't let Leopold turn you," Sensara said. "But he seems different. Kind. I like him, even though he flirted with you." She flicked Estrada's cheek playfully and he laughed. The flirting went both ways. That was the problem.

"I thought you didn't like him?"

"I'm not suggesting he join us, only that you try and help him if you get the chance. Remember, he saved your life, and ours."

Estrada lay awake in the dark, cuddling Sensara and Lucy, and trying to sort this colossal mess. A racing mind and punk body were conspiring against him. His head was aching. His gut churning sour acid into his mouth. He might have Lucy back, but Michael was still out there with Diego and his terror of ravens. Victor Carvello was dead—killed in cold blood—and though his body would never appear, the police would ask a million questions. If they survived that long. And to top it off, that lying vampire who'd played him for a fool was now aboard the yacht.

Estrada gently untangled himself from his sleeping beauties, scooped up his cell phone, and slipped out. It was just after ten p.m. Clattering dishes and muffled voices caught his attention. After popping into the head to freshen up, he climbed the stairs.

Rain still battered the skylight, but it was bright and cheerful in the saloon. Daphne had returned.

"Hey man. Did you have a good sleep?" Dylan asked. His arm was wrapped around Daphne's shoulder, something Estrada never expected to see.

Estrada nodded. They were obviously celebrating Daphne's return. He glanced at the grinning vampire, who leaned against the kitchen counter in their borrowed yacht and broke out in a sweat. *Save him? Forgive him?* Leopold Blosch had lied to him, tricked him, and betrayed him. He might have saved his life, but he'd also put them all in peril.

Daphne turned, and her face lit up. "Estrada! Join us. Leopold made us all vegan banana splits with coconut ice cream and hot cherry sauce." She had her hands full between bowl and spoon.

"Don't forget the chocolate liqueur." Dubh sat cross-legged against the end of the sofa. Dipping his finger in the chocolate, he licked it off like a kid.

Leopold leaned over the counter in the galley. "Can I make you one?" he asked, cheerily.

Estrada shook his head. "I just came up to see if Daphne was alright." He wasn't ready to banter with the vampire. Not yet.

Dropping her bowl and spoon with a clatter, Daphne leapt up and threw her arms around Estrada. "I missed you too, handsome. I wasn't sure I'd ever see you again."

When Estrada hugged her, he picked her up off the ground. "What happened, beautiful? Did they hurt you?" Though, Daphne appeared unscathed, there were hurts that couldn't be seen.

"Karate chop to the neck. Very Bruce Lee." She tilted her head to show him the bruise. "The most terrifying part was when he turned from a raven into a man. It happened like that." She snapped her fingers. "Suddenly, he was standing there. Teardrops tattooed on his cheeks and his dreads dripping. He was naked and I thought he was going to—"

Estrada narrowed his eyes. "Zion." The bastard who'd taken Michael. How he'd love to be alone in a room with that motherfucker.

"Hey, I got him. Stabbed him in the neck with a piece of glass," she said proudly, holding up her bandaged hand.

"Good on you. I always knew you were a wonder woman."

Daphne beamed, but Nora Barnes sat stiffly on the opposite couch all by herself. Though she'd showered and styled her short brown hair and was dressed in one of Daphne's long floral gowns, she looked forlorn. No doubt, she was missing Joe and Zachary. Sensara had just given him a talk on nursing mothers and the pain they experience when they stop. No doubt, Nora's breasts were full and sore, since Sensara had started nursing Lucy again. Nora was a hero in Estrada's eyes. The woman had nursed his daughter through hell.

He glanced again at Leopold and wondered if Nora had forgiven him as much as Sensara assumed. After all, he was the man who chose her for this role. To forgive that would take a saint.

Estrada nodded. "How are you, Nora? Did you talk to Joe?"

"No service," she said, holding up Daphne's cell phone, "but I'll keep trying."

Dubh held up an empty glass. "Since you're close, Leo, could you pour me another jigger to chase that delicious dessert? How about you, Estrada?"

"A double." Then glancing at Leopold, he muttered. "I'll get it."

Over at the wet bar, Estrada poured two tall glasses of amber whiskey. "Anyone else need a nightcap?"

Leopold sauntered over to the bar. "Sure."

Estrada poured another shot and pushed it along the counter.

"We've been nattering about sleeping arrangements," Dubh said, after a long sip of whiskey. "Since the king-sized bed in the Captain's Quarters is now free, someone should move in there." Dubh liked to get right to the point. "We thought perhaps you, Sensara, and Lucy would like that room. It's the largest and has a head. You could rig up a cot for the bairn."

"Thanks for the thought, Dubh, but they're already settled in for the night. I can talk to Sensara in the morning." Everything had changed on the yacht with Michael and Carvello gone, and Nora and Leopold now aboard.

"Best bleach the sheets. Not to speak ill of the bawbag, but Lord knows, it'll be mingin' down there." Dubh's gaze shifted to the front staircase beside the helm. The Captain's Quarters were directly below them in the bow, so the skipper had easy access to the cockpit.

"I'll take care of it," Leopold said, heading for the stairs.

"I'll help you," Estrada said, surprising himself.

"Make love, not war, lads," yelled Dubh. He'd drained his glass of whiskey and was holding the empty in the air again, hoping for the gods, or perhaps Daphne, to intervene.

Downstairs, Leopold discovered a closet masquerading as part of the wall. It was stocked with extra pillows and crisp sheets still in laundry wrap. The huge bed, which stood in the center of the bow-shaped room was a mess, the covers askew.

Estrada ripped off the quilts and flung them in a corner, along with the pillows. As Dubh had suggested, no amount of Prada could cover Carvello's reek. It was a stench beyond the physical that would require smudging with sage.

From under the sheet, Estrada pulled a glossy magazine. He leafed through. "Jesus, Victor. There's liberal and there's sick." Closing it, he flung it into a corner by the stairs.

"What'd you find?" asked Leopold.

"Proof of Carvello's depravity. Not that we needed proof."

"Diego doles out judgments and sentences like he's a king. But, no matter what Carvello did, he didn't deserve to die like that."

"Yeah, your vampire friends are maniacs in the truest sense of the word." Estrada thought again of Michael's bloody face wedged in Carvello's neck and shivered.

"They're *not* my friends," Leopold said. "You forget. A month ago, I was a man, just like you."

"You're right, and I owe you my thanks. I heard that you destroyed Eliseo and carried me out of there. Sensara says if it wasn't for you, I'd be . . . " Estrada shrugged. "I don't know what I'd be."

"You'd be Diego's property," Leopold said, ripping open one of the fitted sheets and flapping it in the air. "He keeps a harem." Leopold spread the sheet out on the bed and smoothed it with his hand. "The highlight of the night was going to be him feeding you his blood. Once he turned you, Diego would have owned you."

Estrada swayed backwards, caught himself, and leaned against the wall. When he agreed to Diego's ultimatum, he hadn't considered sexual enslavement.

"I'm sorry," Leopold said. "I thought you knew."

"Knew?"

"What he wanted from you."

"I thought he wanted to kill me. I thought it was payback for Michael's boyfriend—the kid who killed himself. Eye for an eye."

"It might have started out like that, but Diego liked what he saw."

"So, does someone own you?" Estrada stepped up, grasped the fitted sheet and pulled it over the corner, mirroring Leopold's actions on the other side of the bed. "You seem to have a mind of your own."

"No. Only Diego has that power and he didn't turn me."

Estrada cocked his head. "So, who turned you?"

"Zion. Diego gave me to Zion."

Like Michael, thought Estrada. Diego had given Michael to Zion too. If Leopold had escaped from Zion, perhaps Michael still had a chance.

"So, you and Zion are—"

"God no." Leopold grimaced. "But Diego knows Zion has a thing for blonds, so . . ."

"But you're not blond."

"Actually, I am. Surfer-boy platinum." He pulled his hair apart to show Estrada the silvery roots. "I cut and dyed my hair before I went out in the boat."

Estrada grasped the flat sheet that Leopold flapped in the air and helped him smooth it over top. "Right, the boat." He smoothed out the sheet, then stood back and scratched his fingernails through his hair. Leopold made him nervous. "So, why did you come? And why did you stay up all night drinking with me?"

"You really don't know?"

Estrada's eyes flashed. "I'd like to hear it from you."

Leopold tilted his head. "Fair enough. Like Diego said, he sent me to make sure you'd find your way to Le Chateau. But when I met you, I liked you."

"Just like that?"

"Just like that. I enjoyed getting drunk with you. I wanted to stay, but they had Nora and your baby. I couldn't risk it."

"So, when did you decide to change teams?"

"I was never on their team. I want them all dead. Just like you. Those fuckers took my life. Kept me prisoner. I figured you were my best way out. And like I said, I like you." When Leopold leaned forward, he stopped working the sheet and played with his fingers.

"Surfer-boy platinum, eh?" Estrada smiled. "Why the disguise? We've never met before."

"No, but I was afraid Nigel recognized me that night in his room, since I recognized him."

"You did?" Nigel *had* mentioned a blond. That much was true. He'd said that the man reminded him of Michael with his long, straight, blond hair. Looking at Leopold, Estrada could see there was an uncanny resemblance. "So, is that why you used a different name?"

Leopold shrugged. "Vancouver's a small place in the trendy food and entertainment business. Joe and Nora Barnes brought Nigel and Ruby to Ecos a few times and introduced us. I didn't know where we were going that night and I tried not to hurt them when I realized who it was Zion was after."

Estrada decided to change the subject. There was no way to change what was in the past. "Ecos?"

"My vegetarian bistro. It's off Robson."

"So, you're *not* a bartender at Forbidden." The lies were piling up like the laundry. Estrada flung the quilts on the bed and fluffed up the pillows.

Leopold was jamming Carvello's loose clothing into one of the plastic bags. Estrada checked the ensuite, and when he discovered the blood-stained silk leopard robe hanging on a hook on the back of the door, he felt queazy. He'd forgotten that Michael had taken his chunk of flesh that night too. Whatever Carvello had done to Michael when he was a kid had lasting effects.

Leopold appeared beside him holding open the plastic bag. "I *was*, when I was in college."

"Was what?" Estrada balled up the robe and stuffed it in the bag, while Leopold bundled up the used towels.

"A bartender at Forbidden. That's how I got through."

For a moment, they both paused and looked into each other's eyes.

"I didn't lie to you because I wanted to, Estrada. And I really didn't know what Zion was going to do that night at Stryker's. We were just supposed to take Nora. Diego wanted a nursing mother to look after Lucy and I knew that Nora would take good care of her. She's a giver. And they were both supposed to go home free and unharmed."

And fucking terrified. "You're naïve."

"Did you believe Diego when he told you he'd let Lucy and Sensara go free if you joined him?"

Estrada answered with a loud sigh. He felt an urge to reach out and touch this man, this *vampire*. Hold him to his chest and weep. Diego had taken too much.

A splash of water slapped his wrist and brought him back to the moment. Leopold had turned on the faucet and was washing off bits of beard, shaving cream, and toothpaste splotches with one of the cleaning cloths from under the sink.

Estrada caught Leopold's reflection in the mirror and their eyes met again. Cedar-green, like no color he'd ever seen.

"You're pretty good at wiping counters." Estrada meant it as a joke, to lighten things up, but Leopold answered him with a serious face.

"I've lived alone a long time and, I'll admit, I'm slightly OCD about germs. You should see my kitchen at Ecos."

"So, no partner? No serious relationships?" Estrada couldn't remember if they'd talked relationships that night.

"No time. I wanted a bistro and that's all that mattered. Now I've got nothing."

"You can still run a restaurant, can't you?"

"A chef that can't eat his own food?"

"If you're good—which you must be if the Barnes used to come to your place—you'll know without having to eat it. And, you can always hire a taster."

Leopold's bottom lip turned out as he considered this. "That's actually not a bad idea."

Estrada smiled at him through the mirror. "Hey, I can see your reflection. Shouldn't you be invisible? Isn't that one of the tell-tale signs?"

"Ah, the old mirror trick. You know that none of those myths are true. The sunlight, the garlic, the crosses, the wooden stake through the heart."

"Yeah, you've tried it?"

Leopold punched him in the arm and it hurt. The one part of the myth that was true was their strength and speed. Estrada raked his fingernails through his hair as he continued to watch Leopold in the mirror.

"So, why Levi?"

"Hmmm?"

"Why did you call yourself Levi?"

"Oh." Leopold glanced down at his jeans and swung out his right hip to show the label. "Nothing symbolic, man. It was the best I could come up with on short notice."

Since they'd finished up in the bathroom, they wandered out into the bedroom again.

Estrada sat down on the edge of the bed. "How did you end up at Diego's lair?"

"I feel like I'm at a police interview," Leopold said, sitting down on the bottom step.

"You're a vampire and you're on our yacht. I need to know I can trust you."

"Fair enough. Lorne Wiseman, my friend and financial advisor, said that he'd discovered this marvelous investment opportunity. A private castle in the archipelago with all manner of entertainment. He wanted to invest and brought me there to see it." Leopold sniffed and rubbed his nose. "He invested alright."

"What happened to him?"

"Diego chose me and turned Lorne into fodder for the prisoners."

"Prisoners?"

"At Le Chateau there are many young men, some as young as sixteen. Diego is holding them prisoner. That's what he did to me. After they turn you by feeding you their blood, they chain you up and force you to drink until you're addicted."

Estrada thought of the three women they'd found hanging in the back kitchen. The S&M playpen was just a front to attract food to the island.

"But you're not addicted—"

"Of course I am. I just refuse to give in."

Leopold swayed, then hung his head in his pale hands. He looked wasted.

"When's the last time you ate?"

Leopold flashed his sad green eyes.

"Sorry," Estrada said. "I didn't mean to—"

"It's the thing I hate the most."

"But you have to eat."

"I know. Everything's gotta eat." Leopold scowled. "That's what Zion says."

Perhaps, Estrada was just being selfish and Sensara was right. The guy had lied about who he was, but he had his reasons. Being imprisoned by Diego would force anyone to lie. Or do worse.

"You saw how Dubh brought me back, right?" asked Estrada.

"Yes, it was a miracle. We all thought—"

"So, do you think that something in Dubh's faerie blood might help you?" Sensara had said he should try to save Leopold and after their talk, Estrada believed she was right. Leopold was as much a victim in this madness as everyone else. If there was the slightest chance, he had to try.

"I don't know enough about it."

But Estrada had already decided. "Drink from me. You need your strength to fight Diego when he comes, and who knows? It might render you human again. You said yourself it was a miracle."

"But you're so weak. Eliseo nearly killed you."

"I'm fine. Look." Estrada stretched out his neck.

Leopold stood and walked to the bed. He pushed back Estrada's hair and inspected the wound, then touched it with cool fingers. "Completely healed. It *is* a miracle." He wavered again.

"Faerie blood is fierce. Lie down beside me and . . . Just be gentle. When Eliseo bit me, I almost passed out from the shock."

"But I've never bitten anyone. What if I lose control? I don't want you to risk your life for me."

"I'll tell you what." Reaching down, Estrada pulled the knife from his boot. "If you lose control, I'll jam this through your fucking brain. Deal?"

Leopold swallowed hard. "Well, there's an offer I can't refuse." He stretched out on the bed beside Estrada.

For a moment, they both stared up at the ceiling in silence and neither man moved.

"Any chance I'll turn into a vampire from this?" Estrada said, at last.

"Only if I drain you to the point of death and feed you my blood."

"That's comforting."

Another silence ensued.

Finally, Leopold spoke. "Listen. The blood. It doesn't just fill the emptiness in your belly. It creates another kind of hunger."

"What do you mean?"

"The blood is a kind of aphrodisiac."

Estrada laughed. "Oh, I see. So, if I feel something hard against my thigh, I shouldn't be too concerned."

"I just thought you should know that—"

"It's not me that turns you on. It's the blood."

"Well, that's not true either." Leopold laughed.

"Look man. Don't worry. It's nothing I haven't felt before. You have my permission to get as hard as you like."

"You really think this faerie blood might be a cure for Vampire?"

"I don't know, but we have to try."

Leopold sighed. "Alright. Eliseo drank from your right side, so I'll take the left." Turning onto his side, Leopold leaned up on his elbow and stroked Estrada's neck from his earlobe to collar bone. "Thank you for this," he said, looking him in the eye. He tapped lightly on the artery with his fingertips, and then his lips touched the warm flesh of Estrada's neck. It began as a kiss, and then . . .

When he felt the puncture, Estrada gasped, and Leopold flinched. Reaching out with his right hand, Estrada grasped the vampire's head and pressed gently, holding his mouth in the crook of his neck. It felt electrifying and he didn't want it to end.

Closing his eyes, Estrada felt himself get aroused. And no, it wasn't the blood. It was something between them. Something he'd felt that night on the bow. As the vampire's gentle kiss lulled him into bliss, he turned to press against him.

"Oh my God." It was a woman's voice—Sensara—and it pulled Estrada back into the room so fast, he nearly passed out.

Leopold let go and Estrada's blood spurted down his chest.

"I can't believe you," she said.

"I'm just trying to help him, like you said. It's faerie blood to fight the virus."

"Except Dubh's the one with the faerie blood, and you're the one with the hard-on."

A VAMPIRE PRIMER

Zion felt another tremor shake the rock wall of his grotto. Their world was falling to pieces. The initial earthquake was minimal; at least, here below ground, beyond the foundations of the palace. But these aftershocks were growing in intensity. He paced around the cave, squatted, sat, then got up and paced some more.

While Stryker slept, Zion had transformed and flown around the palace to assess the situation. Above him, Father circled through the clouds with his remaining ravens. He must be devastated, thought Zion. This had been his home for two hundred years. Plus, he'd witnessed his favorite son killed by someone he trusted. What anguish would Father's broken heart unleash upon this world? Should Zion join him? As one of the originals, Diego would expect it. But no. Stryker was a gift and Father knew what was needed to complete The Turning.

For the moment, Stryker was unconscious, lying on his back like a corpse, eyes shut, palms up. Zion didn't understand why this trancelike state was an integral part of the process, but he'd never seen anyone avoid it. Father said to be Vampire, a man must die to his old life and be reborn. And Stryker truly did look dead. His skin, always pale, was now a pasty gray, his lips mauve.

Eli used to say the physical process was akin to a blood transfusion. First, the vampire siphoned off the old blood to nourish himself, and then he fed the fledgling with the Vampire virus. It was the virus that triggered The Turning.

Once, long ago, Eli had explained Vampire to Zion. A virus hid in the brain like a living tumor. It demanded nourishment and its favorite foods were the plasma and protein from hemoglobin. If the host didn't feed it, the virus fed off the host and made him weak—a point Zion had tried to make with Leopold. Everything's gotta eat. Especially the virus.

Once the process was complete, Stryker's skin would take on a healthy glow as vampire blood flooded his cells. His hair and nails would continue to grow, his cells to replicate. The only thing he wouldn't do was age. Diego had discovered the Fountain of Eternal Fucking Youth.

Stryker's transformation was complicated because Father had bitten him a year ago and injected him with some of his saliva. Since then, a small quantity of the virus had been percolating in his bloodstream. It wasn't enough to turn him, but it had affected him. The fatigue and brain fog, the food repulsion, and especially the hunger for blood, alcohol, and sex were all aspects of Vampire, he'd been experiencing. The pleasure-seeking virus loved sex because the increased blood flow sent nutrients racing through the system and it could feast. Once Stryker's initial hunger was satiated, if he continued to feed regularly, these symptoms would abate, and he'd feel powerful and strong. Except for the hunger—it never left.

Squatting beside Stryker, Zion laid his palm on the man's naked chest. Seeing no reaction, he shoved him a few times. "Wake up, Mandragora. We gotta move."

But still Stryker slept. The walls trembled again, and this time several shards of rock broke free and fell clattering to the ground. Zion leapt out of the way.

"Stryker! Wake the fuck up!"

When a large rock smashed his thumb, Stryker blinked and grimaced. He stuck his thumb in his mouth instinctually, then licked his lips and stared at Zion.

"I am fucking starving." Pulling back his upper lip with his bloody thumb, he touched the razor-sharp canines. While he slept, they'd grown to twice their size. His eyes shone wide in anticipation.

"You should be." The virus craved sustenance. Zion stood and walked around a corner of the cave. There, he found the bound woman. Grasping her by her long red hair, he dragged her back to Stryker. Her blue eyes bulged above her freckled nose. She wore a thin yellow summer dress and didn't look the type to be in a place like this. When her cries escaped through the hastily tied gag, he cuffed her across the head to end them.

Zion had found her hiding behind a couch in the S&M Gallery, where she'd been trampled by the hordes rushing to escape the fire. Her ankle was swollen, busted, and bruised. He flung her down on the wolf skins. "A gift."

Stryker needed no coaching. "More," he said, when he'd finished feeding. He was spiking on the blood.

"That's enough for now. We have to leave before the earthquake that Scotsman triggered takes down this whole fucking island."

"Earthquake?" Stryker stood, stretched his neck, and pumped his muscles.

"Yes. Earthquake. Fire. Our destruction. Thanks to *your* friends."

"What happened? Did they get away? Is Estrada—"

"Enough talk," Zion said, as another tremor sent rocks tumbling down around them. "You must learn how to transform into Raven. Then, we can fly to safety."

"You're going to teach me to fly?" Stryker looked like a kid who'd just found a gold nugget.

"Originally, only Father was given the power to transform. Thunderbird became his refuge. But, as his strength grew over the decades, he asked if his progeny could also share the gift of flight. It was decided Diego's children would be given the power to shift into ravens."

"Who? Who gave him this gift? Not God?"

"God?" Zion scoffed. "No, not God."

"An angel? A demon?"

Zion laughed. "All I know is, it was a great spirit from this land. Deals were struck. Since that time, Diego's children have inherited the gift of Raven during their Turning."

"So, I have it? I can turn into a raven?"

"Yes," Zion said. Stryker was driving him mad with his questions. They needed to get off the island before the whole thing came crashing down. "But you can only transform by creating the image of Raven inside your mind and focusing on it. So, shut up and listen."

Stryker sat up and closed his eyes.

"Think of Raven's inky feathers. The strong wings and leathered talons. The sharp curved beak that cracks shell and bone to dust. The eyes that see the tiniest movement from afar. The tufted feathers around Raven's face. Keep him in the front of your mind and think of nothing else. And then pour yourself into his body."

Zion flew up to a ledge along the rock wall and peered down at Stryker, who'd made the transformation amazingly well on his first try. Zion opened his beak and ruffled his wing feathers, then clapped his bill several times to get Stryker's attention. A few croaks and whispers, and the message was relayed. *Follow me. Do as I do.*

The dark narrow passageway continued underground, but along the top ridge was a hole in the limestone shelf, just big enough for a raven to squeeze through. This was one of the reasons Zion had chosen this refuge. With a secret exit, he could never be trapped.

From his perch on the ledge, Zion surveyed the landscape. The stench of burning feathers, fabric, and trees sickened him. Le Chateau de Vampire had been a good place—his home for well over a century. These vampires were his brothers. But soon the island would be gone. Sunk beneath the waves. Where would they live?

Zion had always wanted to see the world, to return to his home in Africa, but Father forbade it. He kept a close rein on his progeny. But now Zion was free and could fly wherever he desired. He even had a mate.

Pushing down with his strong thighs, Zion gathered his strength, lifted his wings and pushed off, using the force of his legs and feet to springboard into the air.

The two ravens swooped through the thermals. Then, Zion flew high, jack-knifed and dove straight down to show off for his new mate. Stryker soared and followed. He seemed happier than Zion had ever seen him. To be Vampire was to be free. Stryker had learned his first lesson. The freedom of flight was more liberating than sex or drugs could ever be.

Estrada sat on the edge of the bed and stared down at Leopold. After Sensara's intrusion, the vampire had fallen back on the bed and passed out. Estrada thought an infusion of blood would have empowered him, but it appeared to have had the opposite effect. Estrada shook him gently, trying to awaken him. No response. The vampire's eyes moved behind his closed lids as if he were dreaming. His chest rose and fell erratically. Estrada laid his cool palm against Leopold's cheek, then felt his forehead. He was burning up.

"I hope you're okay, man. I don't know how to help you." Dropping his head into his hands, Estrada ran his nails through his hair and scratched his scalp. Though, he could feel his own heart beating madly, he was freezing. Noticing smeared blood on his chest, he touched the wound Leopold had made in his neck. It was tender and bruised, but no fresh blood came away on his fingers.

Feeling suddenly weak, he fell back on the bed. Leopold's body was radiating heat, so he snuggled in beside him and dragged a quilt up over them both. He hadn't felt this light-headed when he'd given blood to Dubh in Scotland. The vampire must have drunk a considerable amount. He had no idea how much, but it could have been two or three cups. He'd seen so many stabbings as a kid in L.A., he knew losing eight cups of blood could kill you. Half of that required a transfusion. Perhaps, losing such a massive amount of blood to Eliseo, less than twenty-four hours earlier, had weakened his system. Had Sensara's intrusion been a blessing after all?

His heartbeat kicked up. Vibrating, he broke out in a cold sweat. Something was wrong.

Pulling his cell phone out of his jeans, Estrada called Dylan. It rang and rang, then went to message. "Listen man. I need your help down here."

He hung up, closed his eyes, and considered his options. He could try and drag himself upstairs, but he didn't think he could make it. He tried calling Dubh, but it rang and rang. Sensara was pissed at him again, and he couldn't deal with her right now. Daphne would help him, but she was likely with Sensara. He'd just have to wait it out. No doubt, he'd recover in a few minutes. But what about Leopold? Why was he unconscious?

Laying his head against the vampire's chest, Estrada listened to his heart beat. Heartbeat? How could a vampire have a heartbeat? The same way he had a reflection?

Feet thumped on the stairs. Then whispers.

"What the fuck?" Dubh was suddenly standing beside him. Dylan leaning over him.

"Hey. I just—"

"You fed Leopold." Dubh sighed.

"He needs sugar. I'll go get juice," Dylan said.

"Stealthy now, mate. Don't wake the burds." Turning to Estrada, he touched his forehead and then took his pulse. "Your blood pressure is as low as a nun's at vespers. You're in shock, man. What were you thinking, trying something like this without telling us?"

"I thought I'd be alright. I thought the fey blood might cure him. He was starving."

"So, you offered yourself up to the vampire." Dubh shook his head. "I love you, mate, but sometimes you're a fucking eejit."

Dylan returned with a bottle of orange juice and a handful of cookies. "Here man. Sit up and get this into you. It'll raise your blood sugar."

"And if it doesn't, I'll give you another shot of my blood," Dubh said.

"No. Save your blood for Leopold."

Dylan had gone around to the other side of the bed and was examining the vampire. "He's flushed. Look at his cheeks." He touched Leopold's forehead. "Christ, he's burning up."

"What if the blood's not compatible? Could he die?" Estrada asked.

"You're forgetting he's already dead," Dubh said.

Estrada shrugged. "Except, he's not. I heard his heartbeat."

"Did ye, aye?" Dubh said sarcastically. "You're right off yer head, you are."

"If you don't believe me . . ."

But Dubh was already leaning over Leopold with his ear to the vampire's chest. "Wheesht now. I'm listening to this fucker's heartbeat."

"Who's the idiot now?"

TO RENDER A RAVEN 223

"He's got more than a heartbeat," Dylan said. "Think about what happens when you have a virus and your immune system kicks in."

"You get a fever," Estrada said. "If you're human."

"Aye. Something in the fey blood has triggered Leopold's brain to create heat and produce T-cells to fight the virus. His body is attacking it."

"That's pure dead brilliant," Dubh said.

"Do you think the fey blood could make him human again?" Estrada asked.

Dubh blinked. "Dylan, can you find me a knife? Something clean?"

"What are you going to do?" Estrada asked.

"Top him up. If Leopold's reacting this strongly to diluted blood, let's see what happens when we give him the real thing."

"Wait. My boot. There's a knife."

"Estrada, you might have found a cure for Vampire."

Michael, Estrada thought, and memories flooded his mind. Sitting outside the Creel Café in Kitsilano in the rain, Michael smoking his James Bond cigarettes and drinking espresso. Swaggering around Club Pegasus in his black silk cape and red contacts playing the Byronic vampire. Standing on stage beside him, dressed in his neon skeleton suit, and then, lopping off his head with the stage guillotine. That memory always made him smile. All those nights in the dressing room at the club and later in Michael's flat—dark nights of coke and wine and smoke and sex and freedom. Nights before Diego, when intimacy and freedom conjoined and everything seemed possible.

In a world gone mad, I'd choose you, Michael had said. Surely, the world could be no madder than this? Estrada couldn't give up on Michael. Not yet.

Leaning over, he clutched Leopold's hand. If they could save *him* from Vampire, they could also save Michael. Life could return to the way it was before. There was nothing that couldn't be forgiven.

Dubh laid down, nicked a vein by his right knuckle, and held it against the vampire's lips. "There now. Suck on this."

The muscles in Leopold's throat rippled as the fey blood seeped into his mouth and slipped down his throat.

But Leopold Blosch did not wake up. Not that night, nor the next morning.

Dubh steered the *Ragnarök* out of the dock at the Paradise Lodge at six a.m. Having shared his faerie blood with Leopold, he was weak and weary. But Dylan sat beside him at the helm—another pair of hands and eyes, and a knowledge of the sea that seemed inherent. After days of rain and fog, an epic sun burst through the snow-dusted mountain peaks to the east lighting a cloudless azure sky. A dawn of hope.

Zion had told Daphne the veiled sun couldn't hurt vampires, but Dubh assumed a bright sun could. What was the sun if not fire? And fire, he knew, blistered and burned these fuckers of the night.

"So foul and fair a day I have not seen," Dubh muttered, and wondered why this fragment from the old Scottish play had suddenly popped into his mind.

And then Environment Canada posted a wind warning for later that afternoon. There could be no lally-gagging. Dubh planned to take the *Ragnarök* as far and as fast from Diego's lair as possible. Flee the Broughton Archipelago. Every instinct told him so.

At noon, Daphne and Nora set steaming bowls of Indian curried dahl and rice on the counter in the galley, along with a bowl of creamy cucumber and yogurt raita.

"You should anchor, Magus Dubh. Rest and eat," Daphne said.

"Aye. Smells brilliant it does, but there's no time. We've two or three hours at best before this weather hits. They've upgraded it to a gale warning."

Their heading was Blind Channel, just southeast of Sayward on the shore of West Thurlow Island, a sanctuary where they could gather supplies and fuel up the yacht. Dubh had been staring at nautical maps all morning. Just past the resort, there appeared to be a few secluded spots suitable for anchorage. He didn't want to be anywhere near innocents when Diego struck. And, he could feel Diego's rage growing along with the gale.

"We can take turns," Dylan said. "Take a break and refuel your brain, Skipper."

"Aye, you're right. We'll all need our wits and strength."

Neither Sensara nor Estrada had appeared all morning. She'd stayed in her room with Lucy, and he was watching over Leopold in the Captain's Quarters. The tension on board was as thick as the fog they'd encountered at Chatham Point.

"I'll take a bowl down to Estrada," Nora said.

The poor woman needs to check on Leopold, Dubh thought. Nora Barnes was an angel. Who else could forgive the man who'd arranged her abduction? Taken her from husband and child in the dead of night, and imprisoned her with vampires?

"Thank you," Daphne said. "I'll take some down to Sensara and Lucy."

"I'll do that, if you don't mind." Dubh wasn't sure what Sensara had witnessed, but it was enough to send her into hiding. Perhaps he could incite a little forgiveness himself. They were strong together, Sensara and Estrada, a unique pair, and he'd never seen parents who loved their bairn more. He hoped they could find a way through this.

Gripping the tray, Dubh walked downstairs. He expected to find Sensara enraged or grieving, and stood outside the door for a moment, listening.

All was quiet, and then Sensara spoke. "Come in, Magus Dubh."

He set the tray down on the floor in the hallway and pushed open the door. Lucy slept on the bed, a gentle curve of child, covered by a pale sheet. Dressed in a white gown, the priestess sat cross-legged on the floor, palms up, as if in meditation.

"Forgive me for intruding," Dubh said. "I thought you might like some lunch."

"You thought you might come and defend your man," she said, a slight smile pulling up one corner of her mouth.

"Aye. Well, I . . . " He lifted one shoulder in a shrug.

"There's no need. I'm not concerned with Estrada's philandering." She paused to take a deep breath. "But I am concerned with his survival."

Dubh stared dumbly. Her voice had deepened, her eyes widened. Sensara had transformed from being the bairn's mother into a Wiccan High Priestess. He'd seen her like this that night on the island. Entranced. Magicked. As fey as Galadriel. He resisted the impulse to fall on his knees.

"Come in. Sit."

He picked up the tray and set it on a side table, then shut the door and sat on the floor in front of her.

"What do you know, Lady?"

"The creature, Diego, is no ordinary vampire."

"Ordinary vampire. Now, that's an oxymoron." Dubh sniggered, but she did not react. "What is he then?" he said, pushing down his smile with a fist.

"Winged dragon. Sea monster. Fanged demon. No mortal weapon can destroy it."

"Then what?"

"Magic."

"A spell? An incantation?"

"Energy," she said, rubbing her palms together. "Energy can melt a city, rocket a spacecraft into orbit, transform a life. Energy is the Creator and Destroyer."

Christ. She's spouting philosophy when what we need is a fucking plan. "Forgive me, Lady, but what did you see?"

"Fire. Water. Earth and Air. All the elements collide."

"And in the end?"

"I cannot see the outcome. But the creature comes tonight by moonlight."

She'd told him nothing he didn't already know, but Dubh was strengthened by her transformation. They would need her magic and her leadership when the time came. Sensara was the glue that held Hollystone Coven together. To know she was focused and in control of her emotions buoyed his spirit.

By two o'clock, the wind threatened thirty knots, whistled and groaned, and the sea heaped up and foamed like a charging herd of white horses. The gale was imminent.

"We need to tie up at the resort and wait this out," Dylan said, gesturing to the docks at Blind Channel. "She's coming on too fast."

"Aye, that she is." Dubh hated to risk the lives of other innocent people, but they had innocents on board themselves. If the storm died down before dark, he'd weigh anchor and tie up further down the channel.

Daphne and Nora assisted in the docking. It was a miracle they made it in and tied her up to the creaking dock. This wind has an energy all its own, Dubh thought, as he watched Dylan help the women fight their way up the path to the resort. At least, they could rest safely inside and get a bite to eat. Sensara had once again become a mother. Arms wrapped around her bairn, she pressed Lucy tightly to her breasts.

Glancing up at the bending evergreens against the wall of gray, Dubh searched the shifting sky. Finally, he sighed, feeling safe for the moment. He hadn't seen a raven in hours and even that fucking dragon couldn't outmaneuver a gale.

The *Ragnarök* bucked and bashed against the bumpers as he walked gingerly downstairs holding the handrail.

Estrada sat on a chair beside the bed, bathing Leopold's cheek with a cool cloth.

"I brought more ice," Dubh said, passing the bowl to Estrada. "Is he still—"

"He's burning up," Estrada said, and slid an ice cube across the fevered lips. "But I feel like the fever's a good thing. Once he spoke."

"Delirious?"

"Perfectly lucid."

"What did he say?"

"We're going to make it home."

"Did he now?"

"I believe him," Estrada said. "I have to."

"Aye." Once you lost faith, you were doomed. "Well, we're tied up at a resort and everyone is safely inside. You should lie down and get some sleep. I can watch him for a while."

Estrada shook his head. "You're the one who's been driving the boat all day through rough seas. I've had plenty of chances to close my eyes."

"True enough." Dubh was exhausted. Crawling up on the huge bed, he laid down on the other side of Leopold and crossed his hands behind his head. "I had a word with Sensara," he said, closing his eyes.

"She thinks we were having sex," Estrada said. "We weren't. Though I suppose, if she hadn't come in, we might have. At any rate, we weren't."

Methinks thou doth protest too much. "When I said make love, not war, I was speaking metaphorically," Dubh teased.

"It was the blood. Leopold said it's an aphrodisiac."

"Which blood? Human blood? Fey blood? Vampire blood?"

"All three, I suppose. He warned me he'd get aroused before he drank, and then, when he sank his teeth into my neck . . . " Estrada sighed.

"A virus is an intelligent life form. It seeks human blood on which to feed, and it needs to move through the bloodstream to live and reproduce. What better means than to sexually stimulate its host?"

"I wanted him," Estrada confessed, glancing at Leopold. "And I want him still. Blood or no blood. But I can control myself. Wanting him and having him are two different things." He cleared his throat and swallowed. "God, I've been thinking about this for hours, Dubh, and I can't decide. What's more important—freedom or family?"

Dubh opened his eyes. "A question unique to the man asking it." He stared through the shadows.

Estrada raised his shoulders and shook his head. "But why must I choose? Why can't I have both? How can making love to one person harm another?"

"If it helps," Dubh said, "Sensara said she wasn't bothered by it."

"She's lying."

"There are as many kinds of relationships as there are people. It's the trust between people that counts."

"She doesn't trust me."

"In some ways, I think she *does* trust you. I mean, she trusts you with Lucy, and she trusts your magic, your power, and your ability to protect them."

"That's true. But it's not enough." Leaning over, Estrada touched Leopold's hair with his fingertips. "She wants—"

"What do *you* want, man?"

Estrada sighed. "When I was a kid, I wanted a family."

"As most weans do."

"I *had* a family once, a great one. Then, my sister was killed, my father disappeared, and my mother fell apart. She gave me to my uncle and moved home to Mexico with my other sister. I lost them all. Since then, I've been searching for ways to be happy."

"And sex makes you happy."

"Well, yeah. Doesn't it make *you* happy?" Estrada said cheekily.

"Aye. If it's good." But happy was not the right word. When you factored in hormones and libido and the power surge attained by fulfilling your desire, sex was a complex affair.

Estrada snorted. "Sensara gets so jealous. Michael used to call her Ms. Hetero Monogamy."

"Monogamy is a social-moral-religious construct created by patriarchs to keep bastard sons from inheriting their father's wealth," Dubh said.

"I see."

"And it's most often applied with a double standard. I think, Sensara is just afraid of losing you. The Michaels and Leopolds of the world are a threat to her security. Let's face it. Who can resist a sexy man with a hard cock?"

They both glanced at Leopold and laughed.

"Tell me something. How would you feel if Sensara brought home a sexy man?"

Estrada cleared his throat but didn't answer.

"Perhaps, if Sensara felt assured you'd always be there for her and Lucy, and you didn't flaunt your liaisons, she'd allow you your freedom. She'd come to accept you for who you are."

"And who's that?"

"A man who loves fiercely, but also freely. History abounds with men like us," Dubh said. "And women. Though I think they've learned the hard way how to be discrete and keep their secrets."

"But, how can I ever make Sensara feel assured? Just when I think we're getting somewhere—"

"Most women find that a ring . . . "

Estrada's eyes narrowed. "Marriage?"

"That circular band is a potent symbol of security."

"Do you think she'd say yes?"

"I can't answer for the Lady. But, clearly, you want a family, and when I see you together, that's what I see."

"They *are* my family, but so is Michael, and—"

"Then, why not marriage? You're about to do battle with a fucking vampire. If you can survive this, you can survive anything."

THE CURE

By early evening the wind diminished to ten knots. Under a monochrome sky, the crew of the *Ragnarök* reluctantly left the security of the resort and ventured out into the blind channel.

One small light burned in the Captain's Quarters where Estrada sat on the floor in the shadows with his back to the wall, listening.

Leopold lay comatose, his pale skin simmering. How long had it been? Almost twenty-four hours? A murmur or a moan, some simple sound to signal his awakening was all Estrada needed. But apart from the purr of the propeller and the rhythmic slap of sea against bow, there was nothing but silence, and the unceasing drone of his own voice in his head. The voice said he'd made a horrible mistake by feeding the vampire his blood. Leopold had saved them all. He was a hero. He'd betrayed Diego and killed Eliseo. He'd carried Estrada out of that hellhole on his back and taken them to a boat, so they could escape Diego's lair. Without Leopold, they would not have saved Lucy. They would not have survived.

Leopold had found a way to live with the virus and in his haste to save him, Estrada may have destroyed him. Now, he was afraid to leave him. What if Leopold woke up feverish, frightened, and alone? Worse yet, what if he didn't wake up? Could Estrada travel again into the Underworld and retrieve the fractured pieces of Leopold's soul like he'd done for Michael?

The sound of the engine died and Estrada heard a splash as the anchor broke the surface of the water. Fumbling in the darkness, he grasped his cell phone and flicked it on. 10:17. *Fuck*. He needed a drink. A double tequila to quell his conscience.

Muffled voices in the hallway. Female. The women were going to bed.

Sighing, Estrada glanced at Leopold. Sensara was avoiding him, and with good reason. She'd caught the two men in bed and there was no denying the intimacy of what she'd witnessed. Leopold was a sexy man. Another one. Dubh's question echoed in his mind. *How would you feel if Sensara brought home a sexy man?*

Estrada had wanted to say, *Fine. We're not exclusive. We're not even in a relationship. Sensara's free to do whatever she pleases. I'd be fine with it.* But that was a lie.

When he closed his eyes, Estrada could conjure the memory of Sensara dancing at Pegasus—her body poured into a black snakeskin corset unlaced to her belly, her long black hair threaded with blonde braids. Teetering in thigh-high leopard boots with stiletto heels, she'd crushed against that dark knight, and when she'd left with him, Estrada had followed them into the alley and attacked the man. Sure, the guy might have been the witch-killer and Sensara had unknowingly ingested Ecstasy, but there was more to it. Seeing her with that man tore a hole in his heart. He remembered his rage. Knuckles pummeling the slick face. The spit and the blood. How the pain in his bones eased the pain in his heart.

He was not fine with it.

And then, last Summer Solstice, when she'd jumped the bonfire with Yasu instead of him, Estrada had been so enraged, he'd run naked from the beach. And Yasu wasn't even a sexy man. He was just a man. A man holding hands with Sensara. A man she might love. Estrada told himself at the time, he was angry because Yasu might take his place as high priest in the coven. And it was true. But it wasn't the whole truth. As much as he wanted his freedom, Estrada wanted Sensara all to himself.

Fuck. The Double Standard. He was a world-class asshole. Why did she even put up with him? He'd been sleeping with Michael this whole trip, making love to him on the other side of *her* wall. When he wasn't making love to her. No wonder she resented Michael. No wonder she'd cursed him. And though she'd tried to lift the curse, where was Michael now? With hands and teeth, he'd killed Carvello and then disappeared with that murdering bastard Zion. If that wasn't cursed, nothing was.

Estrada's fingers twitched. He needed tequila. His mouth watered as he imagined the hard salt and sour lime. He'd been down in the bow of this boat for close to twenty-four hours. He crawled on his knees to the edge of the bed, leaned over and held Leopold's warm hand. Beneath the fever, the vampire appeared to be sleeping peacefully. "Listen, man. I need a drink, but I won't be far."

The hair on the back of Estrada's neck stood up. Releasing Leopold, his hands clenched tightly into fists as he turned his head. Sensara stood at the bottom of the stairs, clutching the silver pentacle that hung from a leather strip around her neck. She appeared angelic, in her white-hooded robe, except for the dark rings beneath her eyes and the stooped shoulders. Dropping his head, Estrada stared down at the floor.

Sensara took a deep breath, then cleared her throat. "We need you upstairs."

Estrada waited until she turned and mounted the stairs before he stood. Then, he berated himself. He should have said something.

Upstairs, Estrada walked into a coven. Every surface in the saloon flickered with candle flame. They'd turned the large coffee table between the L-shaped leather couches into an altar and it was now adorned with ritual tools. Dressed in their robes, Daphne, Dubh, and Dylan waited. Estrada glanced down at his jeans, then noticed his black leather jacket and ritual robe folded over the corner of the couch.

"Thank you." He pulled on the knife-studded jacket and tugged the robe over his head.

Sensara came and stood before him. She adjusted the robe, ran her fingers through his hair, and touched his cheek. "You are my High Priest and I need you. Here and Now."

"I don't know why you need me at all," Estrada said, feeling tears burn his eyes. "I'm a colossal fucking ass."

"You have your moments," she said, staring into his eyes. "But this can't be one of them. *This* is bigger than both of us. Are you with me?"

Leaning forward, he caught her soft dark hair in his fingers. "Yes," he said, his voice cracking. "Sara, I'm sorry."

"I know," she whispered. Then, she turned away from him and addressed the coven. "Well, this will be a first. I'm not even sure which direction is east."

"The bow of the boat is pointed east," Dylan said. "I can hold that quadrant."

"Thank you. I'll begin there and cast the circle clockwise."

Dubh perched on the back of the long white couch, and Daphne stood behind the loveseat.

"South is beside the kitchen sink," Dylan said, winking at Estrada.

He nodded and took his place in the circle.

Standing in the center beside the altar, Sensara took a deep breath and held her wand high in the air.

Following the glow from her crystal wand, Estrada stared up through the enormous skylight above them. A waning crescent moon in a star-spattered sky. There was not one cloud. Perhaps the afternoon wind had whipped them all away. The calm ocean barely rippled. He breathed in the silence. And then Sensara began.

Moving her wand and pivoting in a wide arc to take in the whole of the yacht, she cast the circle.

> *"I conjure this circle as sacred space*
> *I conjure containment within this place*
> *Thrice do I conjure the Sacred Divine*
> *Powerful goodness and mystery mine*
> *From East to West, and from South to North*
> *I cast this circle and call magic forth."*

Then, kneeling at the altar, she struck a match to light the smudge pot. The scent of dried sage filled the space as she fanned it with a feather. Picking up the pot, she spread the smoke around her aura. First above her head, and then to her forehead, mouth, throat, heart, belly, and finally to the earth. She moved around the circle fanning the smoke, as each of them caught it in their hands and bathed themselves in its essence.

When she finished, Sensara tapped her wand against each of the items on the altar as she spoke. A pale conch shell brimming with seawater. A red clay dish heaped with pink Himalayan salt. An eagle feather gifted to Daphne long ago by a friend. A honeyed candle burning straight and tall.

"I ask the gods of the sea, and of the air, of earth, and of fire, to strengthen and empower us as we join forces against the evil that comes. We cannot fight this creature alone. We ask your aid in this endeavor. Join us in our quest for justice. Join us in destroying this demon who tortures and murders for his own profit and amusement."

Daphne picked up her frame drum and set a slow beat. Sensara held her left hand across her heart and raised her wand in the air with her right. She began to chant the names, invoking the gods and goddesses of war and justice with each breath. "Kali, Krishna, Athena, Poseidon, Isis, Osiris, Odin, Morrigan." After each invocation, the witches repeated the name of the god or goddess. "Throughout time and space, in many cultures, you have aided our ancestors. We ask that you bless us here, today." Her breath quickened with the beat of the drum. She sang the first four, took a breath, and then sang the second four. And it became a kind of rolling round as the witches picked up the rhythm.

Estrada felt his heartbeat quicken with the frenzied beating of the drum and the breathing and the chanting. The energy built to a crescendo and then ended on a drum crash. Everything went quiet. He felt the blood rush through his body. And then, after a deep exhale, he blinked. The candle wicks sputtered in stubby liquid pools. How long had they been chanting? No one moved.

"We must hold the force. Do not break the circle."

But how long can we hold it? And why? What has she seen? His eyes opened wide as Sensara held her hand in front of her heart and the crystal glowed.

"The gods have imbued us with their power. Hold your palms together and feel it. You must know the force you wield."

Estrada rubbed his hands together, feeling the staccato charge of a live wire. Like Sensara, his hands glowed. When he pulled one of the knives from his jacket, lightning streaked across the blade. He dropped it with a clatter when the metal seared his fingers. "*Fuck!*"

Sensara smiled. "You hold the power. It does not hold you."

"You'll never convince Estrada to join us." As Zion shook his dreads and rolled his eyes like an annoying older brother, Michael swallowed hard to contain his angst. The bastard was always so sure of himself.

"He loves me," Michael said He couldn't conceive of immortality without Estrada. Closing his eyes, he imagined Estrada's face. Those dark slightly turned-up eyes lined in kohl, the deep shadows beneath his cheekbones, those heart-shaped lips. Michael wanted to kiss him and hold him and never be apart from him again.

Zion cleared his throat and spat. "Love," he scoffed.

The two vampires were sheltering in a thick pine grove. They sat naked on the earth, facing each other, with their spines against two thin trees. Clothing was an unnecessary encumbrance for men who could transform into birds. They were waiting for the winds to calm, so they could fly again. Once they'd taken on their raven form, they would hunt for the *Ragnarök*. They were close. Tonight, they would overtake the yacht.

The power Michael derived from Vampire surpassed cocaine and heightened his emotions. He loved it, but felt lonelier than he'd ever felt in his life. He missed Estrada and needed him. Plus, he'd been assigned his first task as one of Diego's henchmen. Tonight, Michael must convince Estrada to join them and the only way he knew to do that was through love.

"He may have loved you once," Zion said. "Before he saw you murder a man with your hands and teeth."

Michael's face fell. He hadn't wanted to kill Carvello. That was Diego's doing. It was kill or be killed.

"Estrada knows I had no choice. He'll forgive me, and when he feels the power of Vampire, he'll understand that killing is necessary for our survival."

"But first, he must feel the power. And he'll never agree."

There were times, such as this, when Michael hated this creature who'd taken him and turned him—this monster who'd killed Ruby and broken his grandfather's legs. The rest of the time, he drifted between disgust and desire. Michael knew he was already addicted, in thrall to this bastard with the blood who made him feel so incredibly high. And it incensed him.

Picking up a jagged rock, Michael hurled it at Zion's face with such force it gouged a hole in the tree behind him.

Laughing, the vampire picked up the rock and flung it back.

Its sharp edge gouged Michael's shoulder with the force of a bullet, and blood trickled down his pale breast. "You motherfucker!" he spat.

"I like your fury, Mandragora, but your aim is shit."

"Yours is no better."

Smirking, Zion picked up a smooth flat stone and twirled it between his fingers, teasing. "I could take your eye out with this."

Michael believed him. "But, you wouldn't."

"Perhaps not right now." Zion bit hard into his own wrist like it was an apple and held out the punctured flesh. "Come Mandragora," he said, with a beckoning finger. "After, I will tell you how you can convince your lover to join us."

Climbing to his knees, Michael took Zion's bloodied arm in his mouth. The warm coppery fluid raced through his body. He wanted more. Leaning forward, he punctured the vampire's neck and drank. It was better than a long line of coke. When Zion cradled him against his chest, Michael felt oddly safe and comforted though his body buzzed.

When Zion spoke, his breathy voice tickled Michael's ear. "Your problem is easily solved."

"How?"

"The woman and the child. Without them, Estrada is yours, or I should say, ours."

"Meaning?"

"We kill them."

"Kill them?"

"Don't worry. Estrada will never know who did it."

Kill them? Kill Lucy? A month ago, he and Estrada had taken her to Kits Beach late one afternoon during a heat wave. Michael had watched Lucy dig in the sand with her tiny fingers. Her face lit up when she found a clam shell, and then later they'd discovered a dying jellyfish and Lucy had wanted to bring it home. She cried when they left it behind on the beach and the look on her face almost broke his heart. Though he'd been fucked up much of the year, he knew one thing. Lucy was the closest thing he'd ever have to a child of his own. He was her Uncle Michael and he wasn't about to let this maniac kill her.

Michael's head spun with fragments of remembered conversation.

In a world gone mad, I'd choose you, compadre. Would you choose me?

Choose you over what, amigo? Sensara and Lucy? Are you asking me to choose between you and them?

Yes, thought Michael. Yes, I am. And for Lucy's sake, you must choose me. Because I don't know if I can stop this monster from killing your family.

"Where's Lucy? Is she safe?" Estrada asked Sensara. Despite, or perhaps, because of, the electrifying power coursing through his hands, he felt a sudden sense of foreboding.

"Of course she's safe," said Sensara, as if she'd never leave their daughter somewhere unsafe. "She's downstairs in our room with Nora."

"I need to see her," he said, pulling off his black robe. He dropped it on the couch and skipped down the back stairs two at a time, then stopped abruptly at the door of the stateroom. After tapping lightly, he walked in.

Nora's surprised face softened into a grin. "Shhhh," she whispered, touching a finger to her lips. "She just fell asleep." Noticing her bare breast, she covered herself with a blanket, but not before he admired the large rosy nipple beside his baby's pursed lips.

Estrada took a slow breath and touched his heart. There was something in this most motherly of acts that soothed his spirit. Nora needed to keep her milk flowing for Zachary, so she and Sensara were taking turns nursing Lucy. Despite the circumstances, Lucy seemed content.

"Do you mind, Nora? I just need to see her."

"Not at all." Nora eased away from Lucy, then stood and smoothed out her clothes. "I won't be far," she said, and slipped into the bathroom.

Estrada laid down on the bed and pulled Lucy onto his chest. The sweetly sour scent of mother's milk wafted from the tiny O between her puckered lips. They were heart-shaped, like his own, and as pink as ripe watermelon. Her chubby cheek sank into his heart. And when he touched her silky black hair with his giant hand, it covered her whole head. She was so perfect... so beautiful. He ran his hand down her back, all the way to her feet, touching each tiny bare toe as a piggy rhyme rolled through his mind.

"You're safe, Lucita," he whispered. "Daddy will never let anyone hurt you ever again."

He saw the silver charm bracelet dangling from her wrist, and rubbed each charm between his fingers, incanting their powers. The magic is with us tonight, he thought. We have the power of the gods, of the sun, and the moon.

"And I am the wolf," he whispered aloud. "But not the big *bad* wolf, who attacked little pigs in their homes or followed a young girl and gobbled her up along with her grandmother. I am the big *good* wolf." He thought of how wolves live and hunt in packs. About how much he loved *his* pack.

It had grown this past year, with the addition of Lucy and Dubh. It had also been diminished by the loss of Michael. Estrada had been trying not to think about what had happened to him, but desperately wanted him back. Years of love beat between them, years that could not be erased or forgotten.

Estrada still felt like an asshole for flaunting his relationship with Michael in front of Sensara, because he knew how much it bothered her. But it didn't make it any less real. The two men were friends, brothers, lovers, mates who'd shared everything. He realized that over the past year, since Michael's illness, they'd stopped seeing other people and had been living together as a couple. Now, he'd lost a piece of himself.

Estrada would die for Michael, just as he would die for Sensara or Lucy or anyone in his fractured family. And he would kill.

He hoped Michael had not died for him. If he was imprisoned by the vampires, as Estrada feared, he must find a way to free him.

The door opened, interrupting his thoughts. He stared at Sensara's pale face, her trembling lips and wild eyes.

"There are ravens circling," she said.

Estrada's muscles tightened around Lucy and he took a deep breath. This was it. Kill or be killed. He kissed his baby's soft cheek.

Nora slipped by and scooped up Lucy. "Don't worry. I'll keep her safe."

Feeling the familiar breast, Lucy snuggled against Nora and dropped her head, unaware of the threat hovering over their heads.

Estrada reached inside his leather jacket and pulled out a knife. "Keep this close, Nora. If one of them gets down here, aim for the brain. That's the only way to kill these motherfuckers."

Nora's jaw clenched as she gestured with her eyes to the bedside table.

Estrada set the knife down, then turned, and kissed Lucy again on the top of the head. *"Te amo, Lucita."* Strange, but not *so* strange, his Spanish resurfaced around her. Lucy looked almost identical to his baby sister, Maria, who'd been gone for eighteen years. Even made the same faces. Sometimes, he wondered if Maria had been reborn to him in his precious Lucita.

Lucy's thick dark eyelashes fluttered in response. He thought of butterfly kisses and bit his lip.

Stopping on the other side of the door, he closed his eyes and imagined impregnable steel walls enclosing the room where Lucy and Nora hid.

Sensara followed him up the stairs. At the top, the first thing Estrada saw were two enormous ravens perched on the stern deck.

"Shit!" Sensara grasped his arm.

Dubh, Dylan, and Daphne stood in a semi-circle staring at the ravens. Then, the smaller of the two birds croaked and everyone held their breath. The larger bird clapped its beak together several times, then alighted from the deck and careened off into the darkness.

In a flurry, so fast Estrada's eyes couldn't comprehend, the remaining raven transformed and Michael was suddenly standing before them. Naked and pale as a porcelain statue, he grinned—his green eyes searching, imploring.

"Michael!" Estrada charged toward him.

"No!" screamed Sensara. "That's not Michael."

"Of course it is." Estrada felt nothing sinister emanating from his lover. Those bastards may have infected Michael with the virus, but Leopold had convinced him that a man didn't lose his humanity just because he was a vampire. Being infected with the virus only meant Michael was sick, not evil. And sick people needed to be healed and loved, not destroyed or abandoned or feared.

Throwing his arms around his lover, Estrada crushed him to his chest.

"Ah, that's the welcome I was hoping for," said Michael, nuzzling Estrada's neck. "I've missed you, compadre."

But Sensara was suddenly there, her hands like cattle prods, sending jolts of electricity through Estrada's arms and shoulders as she tried to pry them apart.

"What the fuck?"

"He's a vampire, and he's nuzzling your neck," Sensara said. She looked at Estrada like he was crazy. "*And* he's not alone." She gestured to the enormous raven that had just flown around the yacht and landed on the railing.

"Back off," yelled Michael to the raven. "I need time."

"Time for what?" asked Sensara.

Ignoring her, Michael squeezed Estrada's shoulder, and drew closer.

Sensara crossed her arms over her chest and glared.

But Estrada was more concerned with the large raven. Its eyes were black and threatening, its beak and claws quick and deadly. The creature let out a terrifying squawk, ruffled its feathers, and flew off into the darkness. "Who's that?"

"Zion."

Estrada's eyes widened as he leaned back. "The fucker who murdered Ruby?"

"Yes, I know. I haven't forgotten. But Zion won't hurt *you*. He turned me, and—"

"You mean, he infected you." The more Estrada thought of vampire as a virus, the easier it was to accept. And though Leopold had not awoken, Estrada still hoped for a cure.

"Can we talk? *Alone?*" Michael glanced at the nervous audience who hovered in the doorway.

Estrada stared into Michael's mossy eyes. He looked young again, the way he looked when they first met. Years of partying purged. The lines around his thirty-something eyes, as he called them, were gone, the pale skin, plump and unblemished. He looked like he'd been airbrushed to a sexy twenty-two. His cheekbones cut ridges that darkened the hollows beneath. His honey-blond hair hung thick and straight to well below his shoulders. Reaching out, Estrada touched it and exhaled. Michael's hair had grown at least three inches.

Estrada glanced down. Michael's hair was not *all* that had grown. Every muscle in his lover's wiry body was plump, hard, and defined.

Michael smiled as if he could read Estrada's thoughts. Eyes gleeful and glittering, he caught his palm behind Estrada's neck and pulled his face forward.

When their lips touched, Estrada felt his body soften in multiple ways.

"Come," whispered Michael, dancing Estrada out onto the stern deck, "and I'll explain everything."

When he turned to close the door behind them, Estrada caught the look on Sensara's face.

"I'm sorry, but it's Michael," Estrada said. Michael, who'd been turned into a vampire, but had returned to him. Surely, she could feel how his heart pounded with joy.

Turning her eyes away, Sensara swallowed hard.

"You accepted Leopold, and he's a vampire. Why can't you accept Michael? He won't hurt us."

"Never," Michael said softly. His pale hand brushed his heart as if he had taken an oath. "I'm here to help you."

Sensara scoffed and turned her back on them. "I'm going to see our daughter," she said, laying on the guilt as she walked away.

For the moment, Estrada didn't care. In Michael, he saw hope. Regeneration. Knowledge about Diego they might use to take the bastard down. And above all, love. His pack mate had returned, and he was not about to let him go.

Once they were alone on the back deck, Estrada took Michael's jaw in his hand and ran his thumb down the hollow in his cheek. When he squeezed, Michael furled back his lips and opened his mouth.

"Touch them," he said, eyes glittering.

Against his flushed tongue, Michael's teeth appeared hard and white, almost unreal. Estrada ran his finger down a razored canine. "Tell me what it's like."

"I can do better than that." Leaning forward, Michael made a tiny slice, no bigger than a papercut, in his own wrist, and a drop of blood beaded on the pale flesh. "It won't turn you into a vampire. And remember, just a lick, man, or you'll be spun."

Estrada knew this was not the time to indulge. He needed to keep his wits about him. Diego was coming and he had his family to protect. But it was like staring down a long line of coke just before dawn and knowing this one little taste could give you a crazy fucking edge—the confidence and courage to face anything.

Lowering his mouth, Estrada lapped up Michael's blood. Then, clutching the extended wrist, he held it to his lips and sucked. Closing his eyes, he savored its every nuance. It was his first taste of vampire blood, and was, like all firsts, his best.

"I wish we were *really* alone," Michael said. "I've missed you so much."

"Me too," growled Estrada, as his lips moved against Michael's wrist. Running his hands over Michael's perfect body, he kissed him until he knew he must either stop or make love. "Jesus," he said, pulling away in a rush of breath.

"Yes. Vampire is a religious fucking experience."

"It feels—"

"Like snorting blow when you're peaking on ecstasy?"

"Yeah . . . yeah."

Michael held Estrada's jaw and kissed him slowly again and again. "I adore you," he said, between long delicious kisses. "Come with me, compadre. It can be like this forever."

"But I can't, man. Lucy. I have to look after Lucy and Sensara and the others."

Michael glanced away, then laid his chin in the hollow of Estrada's collarbone. They stood silently for a moment wrapped in the sounds of the sea and the sensations of vampire blood coursing through their veins. "I came back here tonight for you," Michael said, at last. "I chose *you*, compadre."

"Michael, I'm sorry," he said. And he was. Sorry that love wasn't all a man needed. The Beatles got it wrong. "I wish we could fix this. I wish we could—"

"We can. Listen to me. If you join us . . . If you become a vampire . . . Diego will let them go. Sensara can take Lucy home, and you can visit them whenever you want, just like you always have. You can still play with your witchy friends and be a magician. We can both work at Pegasus. It will be just the same as it's always been except, I'll be a *real* vampire. And so will you. We can feel like this forever. Can you imagine what your act will be like when you can't die? When every injury heals instantly?"

Estrada's head was spinning. How many CEOs and rock stars and surgeons and politicians were vampires? An old boys' club born and reborn, vaping on the virus, lining their pockets with blood and covering each other's indiscretions.

"We can be together forever. Young and virile and potent and powerful."

When Michael licked the open cut on his wrist and kissed him again, blood surged through Estrada's body, like a hormonal torrent. Vampire blood was the most intoxicating substance he'd ever encountered.

"Jesus. You make it sound so perfect."

"It can be. Come with me now. If I'm the one who turns you, Diego will have no hold on you. We can travel the world together. Be free."

When Michael's teeth grazed his neck, Estrada closed his eyes and reveled in the sensations flooding his soul. Catching Michael's face in his hands, he pulled him so close their foreheads touched.

"We'll make love like we've never done before, compadre." Dropping to his knees, Michael took Estrada's hands and kissed them, then stared into his eyes. "I promise to love you forever, to never forsake you, to give you everything you've ever wanted. Just say yes."

"NO!"

Estrada turned at the sound of this new, but familiar, voice. "Leopold?"

The vampire stood in the doorway, half in and half out. Behind him, Estrada could see Dylan and Daphne watching. Each of them holding a knife.

"He's lying," Leopold said. "Diego will never let you go. He'll own you, like he owns them all. Like he owns Michael. Like he owned me."

Estrada looked at Leopold. There was something different about him. Even in the shadows, Estrada could see color streaking his cheeks. His energy had changed too.

"The fever. Is it gone?"

"Yes," Leopold said. "I'm cured. You did it."

"What?" Estrada couldn't believe what he was hearing. Stepping away from Michael, he turned to Leopold and touched his forehead. "Your skin is cool," he said. "Are you really—"

A flurry of indigo feathers cut Estrada's sentence short as Zion landed on the deck and instantly transformed.

"Leopold Blosch," the vampire roared.

"What do you want, Zion?" Leopold asked.

"You Chef. I want you."

"Why? Why do you care about me? I'm nothing to you."

"Oh Chef. You're wrong there. You killed Father's favorite, so there's a bounty on your head. Human or vampire, you goin' down."

THUNDERBIRD

Estrada leapt in front of Leopold as Zion pounced. With no time to seize a weapon, he simply held his tingling hands up and prayed the power the coven had invoked in ritual would be enough to thwart the vampire. A surging current flew from his palms and hit the creature at chest level.

Pulling his broad shoulders forward to protect his heart, Zion recoiled, grimacing as if struck by lightning.

Seconds later, a blast of fire with the force of a blowtorch shot past Estrada and sent Zion reeling sideways. The big man covered his face and screeched, as his long dreads went up in flames. The acrid scent of scorched hair and flesh filled Estrada's senses, as Zion vaulted over the side of the yacht.

Turning, Estrada found Dubh holding the broken staff firmly with both hands. Raising it high in the air like a victory flag, he shouted, "Score!"

Estrada released the breath he'd been holding in a quick exhale, turned to Leopold and grasped his shoulder. "Are you alright, man?"

"I'm . . . Yes, I'm just . . . I feel so . . . " His forehead lolled against Estrada's shoulder as his body crumpled. Estrada caught him just as he hit the floor.

"He's half-starved," Dubh said. "Get some protein into him, man. Real protein. None of that vegan shite."

Estrada scooped up Leopold in his arms and was halfway through the door into the saloon when the charred raven burst back through the surface of the sea. The yacht shifted and a spray of water cascaded over the railing. Battering with beak and wings, the vampire knocked Dubh over and then grasped Estrada by the shoulders. He could feel the razored edge of its talons, even through the leather.

Estrada hurled Leopold into Dylan's open arms and Daphne slammed the door. As he pivoted, Estrada broke free from the bird's clutches and drew a knife from his leather jacket.

"Get behind me," he yelled to Michael.

But Michael just stood staring as the screeching bird flew in circles above their heads.

"Michael! I can't lose you!"

Estrada's desperate cry brought tears to Michael's eyes. "Nor I you. Come with us. That's what he wants. Come now."

"Who? Zion?"

Michael nodded. "If you don't join us, he'll kill—"

"Michael, you don't have to be a vampire." Reaching out, Estrada grasped Michael's hand and pulled him against his chest. "We found a cure."

"You don't understand," Michael said, shaking his head.

Zion suddenly shifted and stood on the roof above their heads. "No. We must make him understand." When the vampire leapt onto the back deck, his weight sent the boat rocking.

Estrada braced himself and clutched Michael tighter. "I won't let him take you."

"Ah magician. I've already taken him." He sniffed and rubbed his nose with the back of his hand. "Many times."

"Why? Why would I come with you?" Estrada asked.

"Because you love him." Zion's dark eyes glowed.

"I can love him here without you and your horde of vampires."

"Oh magician, you thick. Mandragora might *want* you, but he *needs* me. He *needs* my blood."

Estrada stared at Michael. Had his lover become addicted to vampire blood so fast? Or had a year of the virus created this dependence? Leopold wasn't drinking the vampire blood or any blood for that matter. That's why his body was starved for nutrients. But Michael? Estrada shook his head. Michael was not Leopold. Michael craved a high. Any high. And vampire blood was the ultimate high. Michael had been feeding off Zion.

"He won't need *your* blood after he's had *mine*."

Estrada turned at the sound of Dubh's voice. He'd forgotten he was out there with them on the deck. Dubh stood beside him, jaw set, eyes glaring, fingers curled around the carved staff.

"Let's ask *him*." Zion's hard eyes drilled into Estrada's and he felt the sway the creature flaunted. Bracing himself and conjuring his own wall of power, Estrada sent it back. "What do you want, Mandragora? To be weak like the chef? Or young and strong and high forever?"

Michael's lip trembled. "Come with us, compadre. I beg you."

A crash of thunder overhead, and they all stared up at the clear star-studded sky.

They glanced at one another bewildered, and Estrada clutched Michael tighter. "I'm not going and neither are you. We can fight them."

Another crash, and then another, louder and more intense, hurting their ears, sounding more like cannon fire than a storm.

Dubh grimaced. "Thunder?"

"That ain't thunder," Zion said, smirking. "That's the thunderbird."

"Get inside," Estrada said to Dubh. "Michael, come with me. We can fix this." Scooping Michael up in his arms, he started toward the door.

"No," Michael said and with a strength Estrada had never felt before, he broke free and leapt to the ground.

Zion laughed. "Last chance, magician. No one has ever fought Don Diego and won. Father's eyes flash lightning and when he beats his wings, he shakes the world."

This was something greater than the bird Estrada encountered in the Underworld—a creature, not of science, but of legend.

"Mandragora, forget that feeble fucking witch and come to me." Zion said this with such authority, Estrada thought the vampire must have power over him.

Michael glanced sideways at Zion, and then stared into Estrada's eyes. That telepathic crack they'd discovered earlier opened wide and suddenly Estrada knew exactly what his lover was thinking. He shivered as he felt Michael's cool fingers creep inside his leather jacket.

Swallowing his fear, Estrada sent one thought back to Michael. *I love you.*

Turning to face the vampire, Michael cleared his throat and spat on Zion's bare foot. "You're worse than Carvello, you motherfucker. You murdered my Ruby." The thunder clapped and lightning lit the sky as Michael sprang and thrust the knife into Zion's forehead. "Did you think I'd let that go? Did you think I'd let you kill Lucy too?"

The surprised vampire fell backwards with the force of the blow—eyes wide, mouth yawning in a great dark O. The air turned fetid with his final breath, and then his body imploded, crashing to the deck like a sack of dry leaves.

"He wanted to kill Lucy?"

Michael was vibrating. "He can't hurt her now."

Estrada glanced up at the clear starlit sky, now ravaged by raven's wings, and grasped Michael's hand. "No, but Diego can. We gotta go, man. Now."

Another crash of thunder, this time directly overhead, and lightning illuminated the broken leathered shell that had once been Zion.

Michael saw the first of the ravens as Estrada yanked him in the door and slammed it behind them. Swooping and screeching, the creatures converged on the yacht and congregated around Zion's parched, lifeless body. Killing that murdering bastard was the one good thing he'd ever done. By biding his time, he'd made it back to Estrada and cleared his conscience. Regardless of what happened now, at least Ruby was avenged, and Lucy safe from that murdering bastard.

Glancing around the saloon, Michael saw the frightened, angry faces of the others. They had every right to hate him. His dalliance with Christophe. His decision to run from Diego's palace and steal a yacht. His mistaken confession to Diego of his love for Estrada. Everything had brought them to this moment. If he'd only kept his mouth shut and let Diego kill him on that island, none of this would have happened.

Sensara tossed him a towel. "Cover yourself," she said, as if he was a misbehaving child. "Better yet, go get dressed."

Michael glanced down at his naked body and felt his face flush. He'd never cared what anyone thought before. Why was he ashamed now? He tied the towel around his thin hips and refused to look at her.

The bolts of lightning Diego shot from his eyes pierced the tinted skylight above their heads and lit up the saloon in eerie flashes. Gritting his teeth with the next clap of thunder, Michael clutched Estrada's arm and glanced up. Diego circled above them. He was gaging his attack.

"It *will* work," Dylan said, pushing past them. Dubh followed him, shaking his head.

"What?" Estrada asked.

"We can net those bloody ravens if we're quick," Dylan said. "I saw a fishing net."

"You're crazy," Sensara said. "We can't open the door, let alone go out there."

Michael stared outside. Ravens flew or perched all over the couch and table on the stern deck. There must have been fifteen or twenty of them. The cacophony of squawks and screeches made the hair stand up all along his arms.

"We have to do something. We can't just stand here and wait for them to attack en masse." Dylan pounded his clenched fists together, an action that pumped up his biceps. In his green plaid kilt, he looked like a Celtic warrior.

"Dylan's right," Daphne said. "If we each take an end, we can fling it over top of them. We won't get them all, but . . . "

"The rest of the bastards, we can burn." Dubh twirled his staff.

"Where's the net?" Estrada said. "I'll get the other end."

"No!" Michael didn't want to lose him now.

"Stay here, amigo, and keep out of the way."

Michael felt useless. More than useless. All of this was his fault and now he was expected to do nothing. "But I'm strong. Have you forgotten?" Baring his teeth, he hissed. "I'm Vampire. I can fight them."

"Not all of them."

"Enough of them."

Dylan hauled a massive nylon fishing net out of a bin near the back door. Twisted and crumpled, it looked like it had never been used.

Estrada and Dylan were pulling it apart when the first of the ravens crashed against the back window and it cracked. Michael jumped back and bumped into Daphne.

"Jesus," Estrada said. "If they all start—"

A tremendous thunderclap, a flash of light, and then a deafening crash of glass as Diego shattered the skylight above their heads. Michael lurched and covered his head as broken shards rained down. Sensara, who was standing closest, screamed and jumped past the debris.

Diego hovered in the space between, golden eyes lighting up the sky. His long, leathered talons clawed the air in the galley while his massive wingbeats thundered overhead.

You have destroyed my sons. You have burned my home. You have taken everything I love. Now, I will destroy your world.

Michael stared at Diego, then glanced around. The creature's beak hadn't moved. Had Michael heard his thoughts?

Turning, Dubh aimed his staff at Diego's thighs. Fire shot from the end of the carved wood and the creature flailed and screamed as flames scorched his flesh.

Sensara and Daphne stood together shooting power from their hands. The stench of scorched bird was nauseating. Still, Diego screeched and howled, and Michael covered his ears with his hands. *Destroy the world? Could Diego do that?*

With a sudden whoosh of wind, the bird vaulted upwards leaving a trail of flame in its wake.

"We have to do it *now*," Estrada said, grabbing an end of the net from Dylan. "If they get inside, we're fucked."

Michael watched as Dylan opened the back door. Then they were both outside hurling a net over a crowd of ravens, grappling it down onto the deck, and fighting back the ones they'd missed. Blood dripped down Dylan's bare legs where the ravens pecked at him through the netting. Estrada too was bloody. Cut deep across the back of his neck, his T-shirt shredded and streaked in scarlet.

Dubh came rushing out, shooting fire from his staff. Dylan grabbed a boat hook and beat at the birds inside the net. Over and over, he swung and bashed. The screeching. And the blood. And the stench. Michael bent over, gagging. When he glanced up again, Estrada and Dylan were hauling the bloodied net of birds over the side of the yacht and heaving it into the sea. Dubh was laughing, still shooting fire from his staff. The three of them were caught in some violent frenzy, smiling and snarling. They came inside punching each other's arms.

Diego had risen from the broken skylight and disappeared. Sensara and Daphne stood at the front window looking out over the bow.

"He dove into the sea and hasn't surfaced," Daphne said.

"He won't," Sensara said. "He's a coward and he's lost his minions."

But Michael knew he'd never let this go.

Turning to Daphne, the priestess hugged her. "I'm going downstairs to check on Lucy."

Pushing past Michael, Estrada went to the sink and washed his hands, then slipped off his jacket, leaned over, and splashed water over the gash in his neck.

"Bastard got you good," Dylan said.

"It's just a scratch."

"Aye, and nothing a dose of fey blood can't cure." Dubh was perched on the couch, still clutching his staff.

"We got those motherfuckers," Estrada said. His skin was slick with sweat, his eyes wide and wet.

"Aye, we did," Dylan said, grinning.

For a moment, they all paused in a victory breath.

Then, Leopold appeared at the top of the stairs clutching a first aid kit. "Sensara said, you're hurt." Taking a white kitchen towel, he dabbed at Estrada's wound. "That's deep man. Needs antibiotics and sutures."

"Nah. Just a dose of my blood," Dubh said.

"Or mine." Leopold raised a corner of his lip in a sly grin. Taking a knife from the galley, he approached Estrada, who grinned back.

Michael felt his vampire blood boil. Leopold was one of them now, his body coursing with Dubh's fey blood. He scowled. During his time away with Zion, everything had changed. What could he do for Estrada now that no one else could do?

"You should patent this shit, Dubh," Estrada said, grimacing as Leopold cut his palm and drizzled blood into the wound.

Suddenly, a spray of saltwater soaked them all. The thunderbird had risen from the sea. Thrusting its muscular legs through the broken skylight, talons reaching and grasping, it attacked. They all jumped back, but as Estrada turned, the creature caught him by the shoulders. Blood spurted from Estrada's chest and he screamed.

Michael knew that feeling—the squeezing and breaking of bone and flesh. Clutching Estrada, Diego began hauling him up through the broken skylight. His feet were off the floor. In another second, he'd be gone.

Michael vaulted. Leaping up, he clung to Estrada's back, and pulled at the curled talons embedded beneath his clavicle. Though his hands were flayed by the vampire's claws, still Michael pulled. He heard Estrada's bones break. And then they were both free and falling.

But suddenly, the claws were in Michael's chest, piercing his heart. Blood streamed down. He heard Estrada hit the floor. Saw him dragged away. And then he was in the sky, being buffeted by the night wind as the creature carried him up and up. Finally, as if in sudden recognition of the mistake it had made, the thunderbird somersaulted and careened down.

When Michael's body hit the surface of the sea face first, it felt like he'd fallen several stories onto concrete. Pain surged as the bird dragged him along the surface of the waves—gasping, broken-faced, drowning. And then he was under and saltwater filled his lungs.

<hr />

"Diego doesn't get to fucking win!" Sweeping his hand across the galley counter, Estrada sent shards of glass flying to the floor. He pounded it with his fist. "Bloody Michael! Why did he do that?" Estrada couldn't believe what he'd just seen. Michael. Wrenched from the boat. Dangled in the air. Dragged across the water. Drowned.

"He did it to save your life, man."

"Aye. Dylan's right. Diego was after you." Dubh had cut his wrist and was feeding Estrada his blood, while Leopold painted his injured shoulders. Both his collar bones were broken. Blood drizzled down his chest in twin streams where Diego's talons had pierced the muscles like meat hooks. The pain was excruciating. But worse was Michael's sacrifice.

"We can't just sit here and wait for that fucker to come and pick us off one by one. We hunt him down. Now. I want him. I want his fucking head on a stick!"

"You're thinking like a man." This, from Sensara, in a belittling tone.

"I *am* a man," he shot back.

"No. You're more than that."

Estrada rolled his eyes. His lover was dead. Had given his life for him. He wanted to feel it like a man. Needed to.

"You make a good point, Lady," Dubh said.

"Estrada, you are the High Priest of Hollystone Coven. We conjured the gods here tonight. We have power. We need only believe it." Again, her voice had taken on the lilt of the goddess.

But it was hard to believe they could fight a legend and win. Even with magic.

"His sons have abandoned him, and he's alone. His nest destroyed." Dubh said. "That must be devastating for a vampire who fathered an army."

Estrada nodded. "He'll rebuild and come after us. We need to destroy him *now* before he goes on another bloody rampage."

"Yes," Leopold said. "One thing I know about Diego is that he loved his sons and hated being alone. He always had an entourage."

Estrada scowled. "So, where the fuck is he?"

Michael awoke. His throat and lungs ached from ingesting saltwater, and he was so drowsy he could barely open his eyes. When he did, he understood why. Diego had sharpened branches and driven them through his palms. He was staked out on a sand beach and the vampire was sprawled across his thighs. Diego had pierced his femoral artery and was feeding from him—using his blood to heal the burns inflicted by Dubh and the women.

Diego looked up lazily. "I finally found a use for you."

"Kill me," Michael said.

"When I am ready. When I have *him* and can begin again."

Three in the morning. The witching hour. They sprawled along the white couches in the galley—Dylan, Daphne, and Dubh—curling and leaning against each other on the couch opposite Estrada. They were all here—exhausted survivors—except Sensara, who'd gone downstairs to snuggle Lucy. Estrada wanted to be down there too. With *them*. His family. But he had to stand guard. Diego was close. He could feel it in his aching bones.

Leopold laid on his back with his head on the opposite end of Estrada's couch. He snored softly—a symptom of his reclaimed humanity. They were both tall men and their long legs tangled in the middle, a mess of sharp knees, bare feet, and jeans. Leopold had been rendered a raven against his will, like Michael, and so many others. Like the bulging net of ravens, they'd tossed into the sea.

Estrada glanced up at the broken skylight and shivered. A cold draft filtered through the space as the wind picked up. He pulled his leather jacket tighter, fingered the knives embedded in the lining, and then crossed his arms over his chest. Closing his eyes, he listened for sounds of Diego's approach. But there was nothing but lapping waves against the hull, and silence ringing in his ears.

Michael, too, was out there, silent in the sea. A willing sacrifice, he'd pulled Estrada from Diego's clutches only to be beaten and drowned for his betrayal. The image of his lover being towed beneath the waves reappeared at intervals and spawned an aching in Estrada's chest. Tears drizzled down his cheeks and he swallowed to relax his tight throat.

What would have happened if he'd gone with Michael and Zion? Would Michael still be alive? Could they have lived happily ever after, the way Michael described it? Could Estrada really have had it all—

family, lover, freedom, eternal youth, immortality? Then that scene in the lair erupted in his mind—Michael, all teeth and claws, ripping through Carvello's neck. The answer was no. Vampire was no Romance.

Shaking the image free, he imagined Michael swaggering through Pegasus in his long black cape, the way he used to do. Just over a year ago, Michael reveled in his own fantastical life. He was the notorious Mandragora. The high and joyful, confident and sexy, Lord Byron of Vancouver. Estrada breathed deeply into the image and conjured others. Nights together when all that mattered was feeling good. The muscles in Estrada's face tensed again as he choked back tears. *Michael. You can't be gone. How can I never see you again?*

Exhausted by pain and grief, Estrada dozed until a strange thumping noise woke him, and he startled. Rubbing his eyes open, he blinked. Gasped. A pale face was plastered up against the tinted window in the bow. *Michael.* Their eyes met and Michael smiled.

Leaping up, Estrada rushed out the door. Careening around the bow, he set the boat rocking with his heavy, careless steps. Sliding, he crashed to his knees and fell on top of Michael's broken body. It could be a trap, but even if it was, he couldn't stop himself. Not now. Not with Michael beneath him once again.

Scooping him up in his arms, Estrada kissed his lips and their foreheads touched. "You're alive. I thought you were gone forever."

"Compadre, I love you so much."

"And I love you. Everything will be alright now. We'll cure you and—"

Michael shook his head fiercely. "Hide. He's coming." Staring past Estrada's face, he gasped. "Fuck! Don't let him take you."

Estrada turned his head, following Michael's gaze. Behind him, the creature emerged from the shadows, eyes flashing lightning. No sound. No warning thunder. Just that god-awful glare. Wings outstretched, it floated in the thermals churning above them. Estrada clutched Michael tighter and held his breath.

And then it dove. Caught his leather jacket in its talons and yanked. But, weighted with knives and hanging undone, Estrada's arms slipped from the silk-lined sleeves, and it came off. Knives slid from their custom pockets and clattered to the fiberglass bow. Angrily, the vampire dropped it and swung around for another round, this time his wings thundering rage.

Grasping the jacket, Estrada flung it over Michael's naked body. Then, he picked up a knife. Rolled it in his palm. Hefted the weight. Readied himself to spring.

The creature swooped in low and landed on the bow.

"Don't let him take you," Michael cried, clutching his arm with both hands and holding him firm. His strength had multiplied. "He wants you for his consort. You'll never be free."

"I have to destroy him. It's the only way."

The creature screeched its fury and clapped its beak together several times. Where were the others? Surely, they could hear this earsplitting racket.

Estrada tried to pull free from Michael's grip. He needed to fight this thing. To drive it from the earth.

And then the thunderbird struck. One second it was hovering in the air above them, and the next, its talons scraped Estrada's shoulders. Then Michael shoved him with such force, he keeled sideways. The enraged bird turned on Michael and drove its beak into his forehead, pounding like a jackhammer.

Estrada slashed at the creature with his knife, trying to penetrate its armor and puncture its brain. Reaching out, Michael clutched Estrada's thigh and clung to him. Blood everywhere. Flecks of brain and flesh. Then Michael's grip loosened and his hand fell limp.

Estrada turned. A wail escaped his open mouth as he raised the knife and slammed the bird in the back of the head. The knife pierced bone and brain, sliding through to the hilt. Yanking it free, Estrada struck again. And again. And again, in a wild fury of blows.

Diego shifted and fell on top of Michael, his naked body aflame. Blazing like a pile of dry leaves.

Estrada swiveled. The others stood behind him, projecting power at this creature who had taken so much. He turned back to the vampire. And then he saw it. A small blue tattooed leg jutting out from beneath Diego.

Crashing down heavily to his knees on the sunpad, Estrada pulled Magus Dubh free of the smoldering corpse. "Jesus, Dubh. How did *you* get here?"

Dubh was unconscious, his skin as charred as the carved staff that lay beside him.

"He was determined to stop Diego." Leopold reached out. "Here. Let me take him."

"Don't let him die," Estrada said, suddenly remembering Dubh's dance with Death at Pegasus.

"After he saved my life?" Leopold shook his head. "Not a chance."

Estrada dragged Michael's limp body away from Diego's carcass.

Slipping in beside him, Sensara held Michael's wrist. "He's gone."

"No. He can't be." Below the bloody injury, Michael's face still held its youth and beauty. But, even as Estrada set his cheek against Michael's frail, gore-spattered face and breathed in the familiar scent, he knew she was right. Why had his body not dehydrated like the others? Perhaps, because he'd just been turned, he would escape this last indignity. Perhaps, if Estrada could just get some fey blood into him, he might turn the process around and save his life.

Spying a knife beside him in the chaos, Estrada picked it up and sliced into his palm. Holding the bloody slash to Michael's mauve lips, he sobbed. "Drink it. Please amigo." How many times could he lose his lover?

"Sensara's right, mate. He's gone." Dylan thumped his shoulder and crashed down beside Estrada on the bow as the boat shifted in the rising winds. "Let me bind your hand," he said, taking a white hanky from his pocket.

Estrada held out his bloody hand. Michael was gone and no amount of faerie blood could resurrect the dead.

"Look!" Sensara pointed to the roiling waters beside the boat.

Estrada glanced up when he heard her voice.

"The super pod. They're back." All around the boat, Pacific white-sided dolphins and pods of orcas were leaping and breaching, the ocean roiling. "They know Diego's been destroyed. They're celebrating."

"Celebrating?" Estrada said. Had Diego's evil infiltrated the sea? He thought of the ravens they'd cast overboard. Was it possible that destroying Diego had destroyed them all?

"Cetaceans are sensitive," Daphne said. "They feel things we can't."

"Did you see that?" Sensara asked, as an enormous whale breached just off the starboard bow.

"Humpback. She's gone under the boat." They felt her passing beneath them and then she leapt into the air on the port side and sea spray soaked them all. Screaming, they reached out to hold each other.

Estrada broke. Fractured from feelings so intense, they couldn't be voiced.

"You saved us," Sensara said, wiping the tears from Estrada's cheeks. "We can go home now."

Daphne brought a blanket and handed it to him. "Wrap Michael tightly and bring him inside. We'll hold a vigil and send him off with love."

Daphne lit candles and incense in the consecrated space, while Dylan and Estrada laid Michael out on the coffee table that spanned the length of the long white couch.

Sensara boiled water and perfumed it with Frankincense. "This will clear any negativity and bring him peace."

Estrada took the bowl of fragrant water, inhaled its essence, and washed the salt and gore and blood from Michael's face and body with a clean white cloth. Daphne gave him one of her rainbow scarves to bind the deep wounds in Michael's forehead.

"I wish we had his black cape," Estrada said. "He should be wearing his black cape."

"Let him wear white for once," Daphne said, handing him a white sheet. "Michael is a hero. It's only right."

HOME

Dubh sat at the helm and glanced around the *Ragnarök* at the shattered skylight, the blood-stained bow, and the battered stern deck. "I'll be gobsmacked if this vessel makes it to Vancouver," he said, and wrinkled his nose in disgust. "It's boggin', man. Rank-rotten. And if the weather turns again, we're fucked."

"We're fucked *now*," Dylan said, nibbling his nails. "Two dead? What are we going to tell the police? That vampires are real? That they can transform into giant fucking ravens?"

Dubh snorted and shook his head. He'd arisen before dawn, fully healed and hopeful. After his second dance with Death he'd been badly burned, but now there wasn't even a scar visible against his blue tattoos. His elation lasted until he took a good look around the yacht at the chaos Diego had left in his wake. Dylan rarely swore, so Dubh knew he was petrified. He was also correct. They'd survived vampires, but they might not survive the polis.

"Ach, aye. We'll need magic or miracle to navigate this shite," he said, glancing at Michael's corpse, which laid stretched out on the coffee table. Estrada lay beside it on the white leather couch, eyes closed, softly breathing, his palm on Michael's chest. He'd been there all night. Refused to leave his lover's side.

"You know, I've been thinking," Dylan said.

"Look out, world." The last time Dylan had a thought, they'd spawned a minor earthquake and blown up Diego's lair.

Dylan narrowed his eyes, streaked red and ringed by dark bags, and ignored Dubh's sarcasm. "We all saw Diego drag Michael down into the sea." He spoke softly so as not to awaken Estrada.

"Aye."

"And the bastard kept him down there."

"Aye?"

"We never saw Michael come back up."

"What's your point, mate?"

"Just an observation. Michael was submerged for who knows how long, but he didn't drown."

Dubh scratched the coarse beard on his chin. He remembered that Zion jumped overboard and stayed under for several minutes after being set aflame. "Well, they *are* dead," he said, at last. Vampires burnt and blistered, but water didn't seem to faze them.

"Thomas Huxley said that birds evolved from reptiles and I agree with that theory. They share many traits, and some reptiles can stay underwater for long periods of time."

"Where you going with this?" He imagined Dylan sitting in a library, nose stuck deep in a tome.

"Those ravens . . . the ones we tossed into the sea—"

"Ach, Jesus. You best shut-up right now."

Dylan ignored him. "Those ravens are trapped in that net down there, and they're alive."

"Maybe. Maybe not. They might have been destroyed with Diego." Dubh shook his head. "Even so, you call that living?"

"I know they're vampires, but—"

"Keep nattering like that, mate, and you'll go daft. Right off yer head."

They both glanced out the window at the churning ocean where dolphins still cavorted in the waves. Dubh pictured the battered bundle of wet birds below and goose bumps erupted on his skin.

"You know I'm right," Dylan said, after a while.

"They're better off in the sea than at Innis Ifrinn."

"Aye, but—"

"Wheesht," Dubh said, in a warning tone as Leopold appeared carrying a tray of steaming coffees. Taking a cup, he cradled it in both hands.

"I heard you say that you're worried about the damage to the yacht. We could put in at the resort and get a water taxi," Leopold said. "There's an airport in Campbell River—"

"No," Estrada said.

The three men turned at the sound of his voice.

Sitting up, Estrada rubbed his eyes. "We can't risk it. If the RCMP get wind of this, they'll seize Michael's body. Coroner? Autopsy? I won't do that to him." Standing up, he accepted a cup of coffee from Leopold. "Plus, they'll seize the boat, and we don't even know the owner. It'll look like we stole it."

"Insurance and registration papers are here," Dubh said, touching a drawer beneath the console. "The name's not Bjorn."

"Shocker," Estrada said sarcastically.

"Carvello's responsible for the craft. Security at the marina can corroborate that." Dubh sniffed. Already, his mind was churning with possible explanations to feed the polis.

Estrada sipped his coffee. "We should clean it up," he said, glancing at the blood on the deck, "and fix what we can."

"The main damage is to the skylight," Dylan said.

They all stared up at the open frame edged in broken bits. They'd already swept up the debris. Diego was fierce. It took force to shatter plexiglass.

"Aye," Dubh said. "In the meantime, if anyone asks, we can say that a branch broke through during that gale."

"There are cleaners in the galley. And bleach," Leopold said.

"Good. What about the hole? Is there anything we can use to cover it?"

"There might be a tarp. I'll search the hatches," Dylan said.

"We still need a credible story. We can't avoid the cops completely." Estrada took another long sip of his coffee. "They know about Lucy's abduction and Ruby's murder. They'll ask where we've been, and how we got Lucy and Nora back. And they'll want to know what happened to Michael and Carvello."

"Revenge for a drug deal gone wrong," Dubh said, spinning out his thoughts. "Keep it simple. Carvello was mob. Michael's a dealer. Even your man Nigel must have his shady side. The polis will already have them on their radar. It won't take much convincing."

"True," Estrada said. "But, why take Lucy?"

"To get you out in the islands, so they could fuck with you. And they did." Dubh gestured to the mess of the yacht. "Once they got their pound of flesh, they let the others go."

Estrada bit his bottom lip. "It's a place to start. If we leave now, and don't stop, can we make Vancouver by tomorrow morning?"

"Ach, that's cutting it close. A day, maybe two, if we run full tilt and the weather holds. The northwesterlies might just blow us home."

Estrada glanced at Michael's body and sighed.

Dubh wrinkled his nose and sniffed. A grimace crept over poor Michael's face. Rigor. He didn't much fancy having tea with a corpse. "Perhaps you could stow your mate below deck before he—" Dubh paused to clear his throat. "Stiffens much more?" Michael's body would grow fully rigid and stay that way for several hours as the muscles contracted. But, by the time they arrived, the process should have reversed and the muscles become flaccid again. In the wee hours, they could move his body off the yacht and skedaddle, no one the wiser.

"Right. We don't want anyone to see him and start asking questions." Estrada stood, and slipped his arms beneath Michael's back and legs. Bending his knees, he lifted. "He can stay in our old room," he said, through a slight groan. Dylan threw down the tarp he'd retrieved and ran over to assist. A body's not heavier after death, only awkward to carry and maneuver, especially down a flight of stairs.

"Best put him on ice. He was a good man, your mate. And you're a good man for tending him. I only hope I have someone to watch over me when my time comes." Soon Dubh would be flying back to Glasgow and already, he was feeling lonely. He'd miss these mates.

"You're officially a Hollystone witch now," Estrada said, looking back over his shoulder. "So, you'll have us all, whether you want us or not."

Estrada called Nigel Stryker just hours before they arrived and asked him to arrange transportation. The driver would need the twelve-passenger van they used to shuttle special guests to and from the club. Two of Nigel's most trusted sentinels should meet them at three a.m. They must avoid all major marinas with twenty-four-hour security as they didn't want to be seen. Nigel knew of a small, out-of-the-way docking facility where they could leave the yacht and disappear discretely.

When asked about their current condition, Estrada told Nigel they were fine. They'd rescued Lucy and Nora Barnes and just wanted to come home without being accosted by police or journalists. Daphne had been texting with Raine, who said that the stories had been in the paper as unrelated news items. But, once the press knew that Lucy and Nora had been found, the real vampires would descend. Estrada didn't tell Nigel about Michael. He couldn't. Not over the phone.

The black van was crowded. The mood somber. Leopold had said his goodbyes at the dock after they'd exchanged phone numbers and promises to keep in touch. He'd been missing for over a month and was anxious to see what had become of Ecos in his absence.

For the others, the music of arrival was dampened by Michael's death. The sentinels, Dell and JJ, watched as Estrada and Dylan carried Michael's body to the van and belted him into one of the seats. They were professionals who knew better than to ask questions. With its dark tinted windows and macabre cargo, it felt like they were being driven in a hearse.

Estrada had tied a black scarf around Michael's head to conceal the injury inflicted by Diego. Since Michael had packed no clothing, Estrada dressed him in his own clothes—his favorite black jeans and T-shirt. The contrast against his pearly skin was striking, even in the shadows.

Estrada had kept himself busy, tending to Michael's body, watching for hazards, weather, and the Coast Guard, as the others took turns piloting the *Ragnarök*. But now, he was trapped in the silent van with nothing but his own voices.

Michael's head lolled against his shoulder. Estrada zipped up his leather jacket and closed his eyes. He tried to meditate, but always the image of Michael swaggering through the club in his black silk cape appeared. Those were good times. Carefree times. They'd made magic together, got deliciously stoned, and engaged in outrageous sex with anyone they chose. Michael loved drama, so they dressed in costume and lived like rock stars. But now, the red contacts and fake fangs only seemed childish and ironic. Michael had been turned into a vampire, and then been murdered by one.

Estrada chewed his lower lip and pressed his arms tighter against his aching chest. Something was gone. Something besides his friend and lover. Tears dripped slowly and silently down his cheeks as they cruised the sleepy Vancouver streets. This was the end of an era. He couldn't imagine walking into Pegasus without Michael. He couldn't imagine walking into Pegasus ever again.

Dell dropped Nora Barnes off first. They all sat and watched, tearful as Joe opened the door and took his wife in his arms. She'd called him as soon as they got cell service, to let him know she was safe, and again every day after. In many ways, Nora had saved Lucy's life by keeping her quiet and comforted while evil hovered around them. She knew that if Lucy cried and made a fuss, bad things would happen. The woman was intelligent and strong, and there was no way, Estrada could ever repay her. Swallowing the lump in his throat, he watched as the door closed behind them. Nora Barnes had not looked back.

When Dell pulled into the Stryker's driveway, Magus Dubh hopped out first. He refused to leave Estrada's side until he walked into the airport. Releasing Michael from the seatbelt, Estrada took his lover in his arms.

Standing at the doorway of the Stryker home, he watched Dell back up the black van, and turn onto the street. They would continue driving east with Dylan, Daphne, Sensara and Lucy, and see them safely home. Feeling sad and impotent, Estrada watched the van carry Sensara away. With his arms full of Michael, he couldn't even wave.

Not quite two years ago, he'd watched something similar. That night, Sensara had disappeared in a taxi after Michael's prick of a brother informed her of Estrada's misalliance with a killer. That night, also, they'd conceived Lucy. But her departure in the taxi signaled the end of them. They'd rekindled something the last couple of weeks under the shared strain of losing their daughter, but now, Sensara was leaving again, taking their daughter home. They hadn't talked much the last few days. Had not made love since the night of Michael's intrusion, and Estrada wondered if they were finished for good.

He took a deep breath. Felt alone. Empty. But perhaps that was fitting. His penance for his selfishness. He'd wanted them both and now might end up with neither.

When the door opened, Nigel sat staring from a motorized wheelchair. He looked his usual impeccable self in a burgundy dressing gown over white silk pajamas but had aged since they left. His hair was brighter silver, his hazel eyes, damp and bloodshot.

"I knew," he said, staring up at Michael's body. "When you called, I just knew."

"I'm sorry, sir." Estrada stepped inside carrying Michael in his arms, tears rolling down his cheeks. Dubh stepped up beside him. The soft purring of Nigel's motorized wheeled chair seemed comforting as he led them through the silent house and into his sanctuary.

The wood-paneled den was richly furnished in overstuffed brown leather, the walls adorned with abstract paintings and shelves lined with books. It was Nigel's favorite room, as well as Estrada's. Cool, despite the August heat. Familiar scents permeated the air. Leather and wood polish. Coffee. The almond lotion Nigel rubbed on his hands. The smoky scent of aged Scotch. Cherry Cavendish—a pipe tobacco blend imported from England that Nigel kept on his huge wooden desk in a decorative tin. The handmade Briar pipe Michael had bought his grandfather for Christmas, the year they read *The Lord of the Rings* out loud to each other. It was the closest thing to a Gandalf pipe that Michael could find, and Nigel smoked it happily while sitting in his leather armchair. The room was a repository of memories as wonderfully important things had occurred here. It was here that Michael first suggested that Estrada perform his magic show at Club Pegasus.

"There," Nigel said, gesturing to the billiard table at the end of the room near the shuttered windows. Dubh unfolded a quilted throw from the overstuffed sofa and spread it out on the felted surface, so Estrada could finally set Michael's body down. It was an English billiard table, seven feet in length, and Michael fit with only inches to spare.

Estrada crossed his arms over his chest and rubbed them gently. Now that his hands were free, he didn't know what to do with them. Words caught in his throat, and he feared that once he began to talk, they'd escape in a torrent of tears. He glanced at Michael, lying on the quilt like he'd just passed out after a night of cavorting, and then looked away. Estrada could wait forever and Michael would not wake up. This time it really was the end.

Nigel opened the crystal decanter he always kept full on the mahogany sideboard and poured each of them a tall glass of Scotch. "Tell me how it happened. Was it Carvello?"

The mention of Carvello triggered images from Le Chateau. The jeering vampires. Michael's terrifying face. Carvello's expensive white shirt spattered with blood.

"No. Carvello's dead. He was killed on the island when we went to get Lucy. We couldn't bring back his body."

"Victor could be an ass, but he was once my friend. He was Michael's godfather and my father-in-law, I suppose." Raising his glass, he said, "cheers" and took a long drink.

Carvello was also a killer and a pedophile. But that was something Nigel didn't need to know. That had been Michael's story and it died with him. It would only hurt Nigel to know what his friend had done to his grandson.

"Victor helped rescue Lucy and Nora. He got us to Diego's island and taught me something of navigation." Dubh, too, raised his glass to the man. "Sláinte Victor."

"Thank God they're safe." Leaning over the table, Nigel laid his palm on Michael's hand. "Tell me about my boy. Did he suffer?"

"No." Estrada answered quickly, determined not to cause Nigel anymore pain. "It was fast."

"How did it happen?"

"The vampire. After we rescued Lucy and Nora, we escaped by boat. He followed us."

"Ach, aye. He was ragin' cause we blew up his island," Dubh said. "Turned himself into a thunderbird and—"

"Came after me," Estrada said.

"A thunderbird? First vampires and now thunderbirds?"

"Aye, and ravens that attacked in a horde."

"A terror." Estrada shivered. "But Michael saved me." There was no need to explain everything that happened out there on the boat. "He shoved me out of the way and Diego took him instead."

"Did he?" One corner of Nigel's lip turned up for the first time since they'd entered the house.

"Yes, sir. Michael died a hero." Estrada felt hot tears graze his cheeks again. "Twice he risked his life to pull me from the vampire's clutches."

Raising his glass, Estrada gulped the whiskey. His burning throat reminded him of what must be done.

"Before the police seize his body, sir, we should cremate him. In case there's evidence of the vampire. We don't want them asking questions we can't answer." Subjecting Michael to an autopsy would only reveal the unexplainable—tainted blood, the virus, whatever lurked in the wound. Burial wouldn't suffice. Michael's body could be exhumed.

"Aye," Dubh said, "and the sooner the better."

"Yes, I suppose that's wise. I have a friend."

Nigel always had a friend. "And, we'll need a Death Certificate. Someone to say that Michael was stabbed and bled to death. We've decided to call this a drug deal gone wrong."

"Well, that's something the police will believe, especially since Victor's involved." Nigel pulled his cell phone out of his dressing gown pocket. But, after glancing at the time, he tucked it back away. "It's four a.m. We should give him another hour." Grasping the whiskey decanter, he refilled their glasses.

Estrada clutched the full glass and gulped. The whiskey was making him drunk, but the waiting was making him crazy. Nora Barnes had been abducted and Ruby Carvello murdered right outside. What if the police still had eyes on the Stryker home?

"Perhaps, it's not expedient to wait," Dubh said, voicing Estrada's concern.

When the door opened suddenly, all three men flinched and turned.

Mrs. Stryker stalked into the den in a silver housecoat that matched her pixie cut. She crossed her arms over her chest. "I thought I heard voices," she said, in her very English accent.

Estrada could never remember a time she'd walked into Nigel's sanctum before. It was something of a Gentlemen Only Club. Was this in response to Ruby's murder?

She sized them up soberly and then caught sight of Michael's corpse. There was no time for lies or softening the blow. Michael was clearly dead. Not asleep. Not passed out. Though the muscles in his face had relaxed, his bloated flesh emitted an ivory sheen that turned his lips purple.

"Oh, my lord. Michael," she said, making the sign of the cross. "What happened?"

All three men stood still and none spoke. What was the correct answer to that question?

"There was an accident," Estrada said, at last. "Michael fell and hit his head. We couldn't save him, so we brought him home."

Leaning over the billiard table, she brushed Michael's hair with her fingertips. "Poor sweet boy. You were my angel. The sweetest little boy ever born. I only hope you're with the angels now and not in . . . " She caught herself mid-thought. Beatrice Stryker was a God-fearing Christian, but she feared the devil more.

She stared at Estrada. "I always liked you, Sandolino, but I know you're lying. Perhaps to save Michael's reputation. Perhaps to save your own."

Then, turning on Nigel, she raised her hand and struck him hard across the face with her open palm. Estrada wondered if she'd ever done that before, or if that slap held years of angst. He couldn't fault her for it. Nigel's mistress had been found murdered on her doorstep. Her grandson was dead. The woman's life would never be the same again. "This is your doing. You let him do whatever he wanted. You sent him off with thugs. You killed my boy before he even had a chance to grow up."

Nigel shook his head. "Sit down, Bea, before you—"

"Michael was all I had left of James. You knew that, and still you turned him into a criminal. He emulated you." She pounded Nigel's chest with her fists, her voice shrill and breaking with each word. "Murderer. I will never forgive you." Then, gasping, she ran from the room.

"Will she call the polis?" Dubh asked.

"No. She'll take her pills. It's just the shock."

"All the same. Best call your mate."

"Dubh's right, sir. The last thing we want is for the police to seize Michael's body. It's a suspicious death and if they do an autopsy there are things we can't explain."

Nigel pulled out his cell phone. "Did I tell you my friend is the coroner?"

Estrada swayed, and then collapsed into one of the leather armchairs. Too much stress. Too much scotch. Too much sorrow.

Estrada and Dubh went with Nigel in his caddy to see Michael off at the crematorium. There were no flowers, no musical overtures, no eulogies. Estrada had said all he needed to say many times over, and Nigel was too heartbroken to speak. Beatrice Stryker had swathed him in guilt he might never shake.

Afterwards, Dubh caught a cab to the airport, and Estrada and Nigel drove back to the house. Estrada said goodbye to Nigel, then climbed the stairs to Michael's flat.

After lighting all the candles in the bathroom, he smoked a fat joint, and soaked in Michael's Jacuzzi until his swollen eyelids closed and he feared he would pass out. After blowing out the candles, he turned off his phone, and climbed into Michael's bed. Caressed by silken sheets and memories, Estrada fell into a deep sleep for the next three days. And he was not alone.

You are woven into the fiber of my being, amigo. Every breath. Every word. Every touch and caress. I can mold and stitch you from this alone. Free to love and bound in spirit, I choose you.

Estrada closed the snaps on Lucy's new turquoise onesie and scooped her up for a hug. *Daddy's Best Girl* was printed in gold lettering across the front. Pulling her close, he gave her a big butterfly kiss on the cheek. Giggling, she grabbed his nose.

"Hey!" He grabbed *her* nose and pretended to pull it off. "I've got your nose, Lucita," he teased. When he showed her his closed fist, her face crinkled.

"Bah," she ordered, with a fearsome pout.

"It's okay. I've got it right here."

Her eyes narrowed as she stared at what she believed was her nose between his fingers. "Bah," she said again, and her lips jiggled.

"Okay. I'll put it back," he said, pushing her button of a nose before she began to cry. "There you go. Good as new." He tickled her neck. Then touched the inside of her ear and pretended to pull something out. "What's this?" He opened his hand. "What did Daddy find in your ear?" It was a golden sun pendant on a fine gold chain.

"Suh!" she said, brightening when she saw it.

"Let's put it on." After setting her down in her crib, he opened the clasp and placed the necklace gently around her chubby neck.

Picking her up again he stood in front of the mirrored dresser so she could see herself. "*Hermosa. Lucita es hermosa.* Beautiful."

"Dada Dada," she jabbered, and scraped his stubbly chin with her fingertips.

Sensara walked into Lucy's bedroom looking beautiful herself. She'd just changed into a sleek red dress that fell to her ankles. Her long hair fell in silky tresses around her face and silver crescent moons dangled from her ears.

"What's this?" she asked.

"Daddy went shopping today."

"I see. That's a beautiful charm and a cute onesie. But, if Lucy is Daddy's best girl, what does that make me?"

"I've got that covered. But first, let's put our baby to bed."

Sensara checked to make sure the window was locked, then glanced at the charm bracelet around Lucy's wrist. She hadn't taken it off since the night they'd reunited on the island. Standing together beside the crib they gazed down at Lucy. Daphne had made her a nature mobile of suns, moons, stars, ladybugs and leaves. Sensara turned the dial and the music box began to play a lullaby. Lucy blinked heavily as soon as the tinkling tune began.

"Come on," Sensara said. "She'll be asleep before it ends."

Estrada followed Sensara down the stairs and out onto the back deck. Raine had decorated it in twinkling faerie lights for their arrival home and bought a fire pit. She was so happy to see Daphne, she'd booked off work and whisked her away to a friend's cabin in Whistler.

"It's a glorious night," Sensara said, glancing up the tree at Lucy's bedroom window.

"She's fine." Estrada hoped this nightmare would eventually fade and they could return to something normal.

"I know."

The sound of Remy shoving open the french doors made them both jump. It would take time before they could relax. Wiggling, and wagging his tail, the black Lab brushed against Estrada's leg as he tried to open a bottle of Shiraz.

"Can you stay tonight?" Sensara asked suddenly. "We're not ready to be alone, even with this fine black dog to protect us."

"I thought you'd never ask." Estrada handed her a glass of wine.

They touched their glasses together and drank. Then, setting down his glass, he caught her face between his palms. "I love you, Sara."

"I know you do." When she kissed him, it was soft and affectionate, and he wondered if this was how kisses changed over time.

"Sit down," he said, gesturing to the swing. "We need to talk."

"That sounds ominous."

He raised his eyebrows and grinned. "One of Nigel's friends owns a nightclub in Los Angeles. He's offered me a gig there."

"Oh. What about Pegasus?"

"I can't go back there. Not now."

"But L.A.? Have you been back there since your family—"

"No, and I won't go now unless . . . "

"Unless?"

Slipping his hand into the front pocket of his jeans, he slid down to his knees. When he opened his hand, the ring glittered against the faerie lights. "Unless you come with me. You and Lucy. Marry me. We can be a family. Make a fresh start." Taking her hand, he slipped the ring on her finger. The silver band was twisted like a snake and set with a black diamond. He'd never seen anything that reminded him so much of Sensara. Staring into her eyes, he held his breath.

"Es, I . . . I wasn't expecting . . ."

"We love each other, Sara, and we both love Lucy. She is more important to me than anything in the world."

"I know."

"And, I know I've been an ass. I've been thoughtless and insensitive and unfair to you. But I can change."

"I can't ask you to change."

"Sara, we could have died out there. We could have lost her." His voice quavered at the thought of losing Lucy. He never wanted to feel that way again. He wanted to be with her every minute of every day.

"You're grieving and you're scared. This is not the time to do something rash."

"Rash?" That made his proposal seem thoughtless and impulsive, and it wasn't. He'd thought long and hard about what Dubh had said about marriage. Sure, he wanted his freedom, but he needed his family.

"Estrada. You've just lost your partner—the man you've been living with for the past year. I know you loved him, and I can't imagine what you must be going through."

Estrada hung his head and covered his face. He was trying to forget. And then a strange thought—if Michael had lived, would he be proposing to Sensara or slipping a ring on *his* finger? Was Michael truly the love of his life?

Sensara put her arms around Estrada's neck and hugged him. "I will wear your beautiful ring," she whispered in his ear. "And I'm not saying no."

"But you're not saying yes."

"What did Cernunnos tell you to do? Accept what is offered. You should go to L.A. You have unfinished business there."

Unfinished business. A father that vanished. And something else . . . Something he'd tried for years to forget.

"We'll come and visit. But . . . "

"But?"

"I can't marry you. Not now."

Estrada's lip trembled. Even sitting beside Sensara on the swing, he felt alone. Like a part of him had been left out there on the coast. "I won't go without you and Lucy. I've missed too much of her life already."

"Will you ask me again in three years?"

"Three years? Why three?"

"Three is a magical number. You know that."

Of course. Whatever energy a witch put out returned three times. The Wiccan Rule of Three was one of their most important tenets.

"And what will your answer be when I ask again in three years?"

"I cannot foresee the future," she said, quite seriously. "I'm not that kind of psychic. But I love you and I'll wear your ring. Is that enough for now?"

"Three years." Sweeping Sensara up in his arms, he held her.

No one could see into the future, but the shadows of the past were falling away like distant raven's wings.

SERIES CHARACTERS

The Witches of Hollystone Coven (British Columbia, Canada):
- Sensara Narado: High Priestess. Therapist and psychic, Sensara created the coven, makes and enforces the rules.
- Sandolino Estrada: High Priest. Estrada is a free-spirited magician who performs weekly at Club Pegasus in Vancouver when he's not performing at other venues, or out solving crimes.
- Lucy Estrada: Sensara and Estrada's daughter named after the Celtic Sun God, Lugh as she was born on August 1, Lughnasadh
- Dylan McBride: a Canadian archaeology student, raised by his grandfather in Tarbert, Scotland, Dylan travels the world playing bagpipes with the university pipe band.
- Daphne Sky: a landscaper gardener and earth mother
- Raine Carrera: a journalist for an alternative press who recently joined the coven. Raine and Daphne are partners.
- Dr. Sylvia Black: a Welsh university professor who publishes books on Celtic Studies. When Dylan arrived from Scotland, Sylvia adopted him and introduced him to the witches of Hollystone Coven.
- Jeremy Jones: an exceptional costume designer who specializes in medieval clothing, ritual tools, and paraphernalia. He sells through his online shop, Regalia. Jones is banished in To Charm a Killer.
- Maggie Taylor: Canadian girl who joins the coven in To Charm a Killer and later moves to Ireland

Other Characters:
- Nigel Stryker: entrepreneur and owner of the Club Pegasus in Vancouver, Canada

- Michael Stryker/Mandragora: Hedonistic manager of Club Pegasus, Michael is Estrada's best friend and lover. He believes himself to be the reincarnation of Lord Byron and likes to play vampire.
- Magus Dubh: the blue tattooed half-fey dwarf who is the proprietor of The Blue Door, an antiquities shop in Glasgow
- Sorcha O'Hallorhan: a rather unconventional Irish archaeologist. Cernunnos says her name as Sow-r-ka.
- Primrose: the sweet Irish witch who becomes a faerie. She is one of the loves of Estrada's life and one of my favorites.
- Leopold Blosch: chef and owner of Ecos, a vegetarian bistro in Vancouver
- Zion: vampire from Africa
- Eliseo: vampire from Peru, the original Salvador
- Don Diego: Father of the Vampires, Diego can transform into a thunderbird
- Cernunnos: the ancient Celtic fertility god
- The Oak King: an ancient Druidic god discussed by Robert Graves in *The White Goddess*

ACKNOWLEDGEMENTS

A book needs people to cheer its conception, nurture it as it grows, offer advice before its birth, and support it as it leaves home to find its way in the world. I am blessed to have such people who support my books and my journey, and I thank you. Without readers where would writers be?

When I started writing *To Charm a Killer* years ago, I had no plan, and no idea it would morph into a series. When I finished writing one, another called. My muses are loud and insistent. If you're curious where the characters are heading, subscribe to my seasonal newsletter.

But, for the moment, let me express my gratitude to the following people.

Language is always tricky. Special thanks to my old friend Carmen Lishman for help with Lucy's one-year-old baby talk. Carmen is not only a gifted Speech Language Pathologist, she's a mom. When I wanted to know how Lucy would talk, I thought of her.

And on the other end of the spectrum, I must thank Kenny Turner for his delightfully witty emails detailing the Glasgow slang of Magus Dubh.

I didn't experience firsthand the sea journey my eccentric crew undertook but spent time around Johnstone Strait when I worked as a relief lighthouse keeper in 2013-2014. There I saw the superpod of Pacific white-sided dolphins, humpbacks, orcas, and island vistas too beautiful for words. Using Google Earth, I was able to plot a basic route from Vancouver to the Broughton Archipelago, but I needed Ivan Dubinsky from Scarlett Point Lighthouse to answer some of my nautical questions. Ivan also kept me inspired with his gorgeous raven photographs.

And, I must thank my singing sisters at Sacred Web for their continuing support, particularly Mary and Enneke for reading a finished draft and providing honest, detailed feedback—all of which I used. Thanks also to Joanie and Michelle, who gave the ARC once last glance.

My author-friend Sionnach Wintergreen, who is always a huge support, also beta-read this book and provided candid commentary. Thank you, Sionnach!

Many thanks to Yasaman Mohandesi who created the original tattoos for this series. Each tattoo is worn by a character in the story. The raven on this cover is one Estrada gets on his right bicep at the close of this story to remind him how he blew the ravens apart with the force of his right arm, and how close he came to losing his daughter. You can read more about it in book four. If you get this tattoo, please send me a photograph. I'd love to see it. See Yasaman's work at www.behance.net/yassi_artdesign and on Instagram @ym_blackrose_art.

Big thanks to my editor, author Eileen Cook. Your candid sidebars make me laugh, Eileen, but also open my eyes to the not-so-obvious.

I'm grateful to the gregarious gang at *The Creative Academy* who are the most supportive and inspiring group of writers I've ever encountered.

And as always, love to Tara, who hears it all.

Now, it's up to you, dear reader, to raise *To Render a Raven* to new heights as it soars into the world.

Blessings and all good wishes,
Wendy

ABOUT THE AUTHOR

W. L. Hawkin writes "edgy urban fantasy with a twist of murder" among other things. Her Hollystone Mysteries Series features a coven of witches who solve murders using ritual magic and a little help from the gods. Wendy is also a teacher, blogger, book reviewer, Indie publisher, and poet, with a background in Indigenous Studies and English literature. Myth, magic, and meandering in the paranormal realms are her faerie food. She lives in the Pacific Northwest where she wanders the woodlands with her beautiful yellow lab in search of stories. Although she's an introvert, in each book, Wendy's characters go on a journey where she's traveled herself.

ONE LAST THING . . .

Did you enjoy this book? Reviews keep books and authors alive. Please take a moment to leave a few words with your favorite retailer and/or at Goodreads or Bookbub. The Hollystone Witches, and I, thank you.

Are you curious to know more about the Hollystone Witches? Come by bluehavenpress.com and subscribe to my seasonal newsletter for more myth, magic, and meandering.

Find and follow me on:
Instagram @wlhawkin
Twitter @ladyhawke1003
Facebook @wlhawkin and
Pinterest @W.L. Hawkin
Bookbub @w.l.hawkin

Blessings and all good wishes.
Wendy

CPSIA information can be obtained
at www.ICGtesting.com
Printed in the USA
BVHW070732070421
604376BV00001B/72

9 780995 018464